THE
SILENT
VICTIM

Published by Bookouture in 2019

An imprint of Storyfire Ltd.
Carmelite House
50 Victoria Embankment
London EC4Y 0DZ

www.bookouture.com

ISBN: 978-1-83888-094-1
eBook ISBN: 978-1-83888-169-6

DANA PERRY

THE
SILENT
VICTIM

bookouture

PROLOGUE

Then

On the night that changed my life forever, I remember thinking about chocolate marshmallow ice cream.

I'd bought a pint of it – my all-time, ultimate, off-the-charts, favorite treat – and it was waiting for me at home.

That's why I was walking through Central Park that night. I'd attended a concert with a group of other people, but left early by myself. There was a big wait for cabs or any car to get out of there, so I decided it would be quicker to just walk through the park to the 79th Transverse Road and then out the Fifth Avenue entrance to my East Side apartment. I really wanted to open up that damn chocolate marshmallow ice cream carton.

I never worried anything bad would happen to me. Not back then.

No, everything seemed perfect in my life before that night I went into Central Park.

I was young.

I was pretty.

I was successful.

I had absolutely no hint of the dark days ahead of me until it was too late.

CHAPTER 1

Now

The first bulletin came on the seven o'clock morning news while I was doing sit-ups in front of the TV.

It said there'd been a shocking murder in Central Park. The body of a young woman had been found in a wooded area near the Park Grille Restaurant on the west side of the park. The victim had not yet been identified. Authorities said she had been killed sometime the night before, but no one knew anything else about her, why she was in the park or the exact cause of death.

I had a decision to make. Should I stop doing sit-ups and call the city desk right away? Or wait until they called me? I knew that if I stopped my sit-ups, I'd feel guilty all morning. Besides, the office knew where to find me.

Sure enough, some fifteen minutes later, my phone was ringing when I came out of the shower. It was Danny Knowlton, the assistant city desk editor at the *New York Tribune*, the newspaper where I work as a crime reporter.

"Listen, Jessie, there's just been a killing—" Knowlton began.

"I'm way ahead of you. I saw the news bulletin on TV."

"Well, we've got more details now. This sounds like it's going to be a big story."

The victim had been identified as Margaret Kincaid, who worked as a campaign aide on the re-election committee of U.S. Senator Frank Lansdale. Margaret Kincaid was twenty-nine years old and lived downtown in the SoHo area of Manhattan. She'd only been in New York City for a few months – she was originally from Santa Barbara, California.

"If you get a cab right away, you can be at the crime scene in ten minutes," Knowlton said.

"What's the big hurry?" I asked, working a comb through my wet hair.

"The big hurry is I'd like to beat the other papers in town on this story."

"Margaret Kincaid's not going anywhere. I mean, she's not going to jump up and walk away or anything."

"But all the other reporters will get there first—"

"That's not what I do, Danny."

"What exactly is it you do again?"

Knowlton knew the answer to that, of course. I didn't use the police as the primary source for my crime stories. I preferred to write about crime from the perspective of the victim. *Why did it happen to them? Who were they? What were the consequences and the repercussions of the crime?* That was my specialty. I'd made a living doing that.

I glanced over at a picture of myself hanging on the wall of my apartment – a framed cover of *New York Magazine*. The headline said: "STOP THE PRESSES – CENTRAL PARK VICTIM JESSIE TUCKER IS FAMOUS!" There was a picture of me standing next to a *New York Tribune* delivery truck, looking very much like a modern-day version of Lois Lane.

"Haven't you heard?" I laughed to Danny Knowlton. "I'm a legend."

I got dressed then. I put on a pair of Calvin Klein blue jeans, a pink silk Christian Dior blouse, flat Italian sandals and a funky cowgirl-style belt with a big buckle that I'd bought on Bleecker Street in Greenwich Village a few weeks before. I put some sunscreen on my face and pulled my wavy, dark hair into a simple ponytail. Then I checked myself out in a mirror. *Not too bad for thirty-six*, I told myself. Yep, all the sit-ups had really paid off.

Of course, I really had no choice in the matter. Those were the doctors' orders. Even all these years later the daily exercises had to be done, no matter what. But the looking good part that came with it – well, that was a nice bonus too.

I still walked with a slight limp from the injuries I suffered that night.

Every once in a while, I even had to use a cane – but never out in public where people could see me. And then there were the minor aches and pains that the doctors said would never completely go away. But, all in all, I was in pretty good shape. The scars on my body were very faint now.

But what about the scars you can't see? The ones inside you?

The doctors can't do anything about them.

I thought about Margaret Kincaid lying dead there in Central Park. A woman in the wrong place at the wrong time on a hot summer night. And now she was dead.

Nope, it was no surprise that the *Tribune* had assigned me the story.

I was the ideal reporter for it.

I was perfect.

CHAPTER 2

The Margaret Kincaid murder was a slam-dunk, open-and-shut case, according to the cops.

She had left her job at the New York City campaign office of Senator Frank Lansdale at 5:31 p.m. on the night she died. She made two stops. The first one was at a print shop on Madison Avenue where she picked up a package. The second was to the Park Grille, a trendy new restaurant on the west side of Central Park, near 86th Street, where she was meeting Jonathan Lansdale for dinner. Jonathan Lansdale was the senator's son and also his campaign manager.

They had been dating for a few months – pretty much the entire time she'd been working for his father. Jonathan Lansdale told police afterward that Margaret had seemed upset by something during dinner, but she wouldn't say what it was. Finally, while they were having coffee and dessert, he asked her again what was bothering her. Instead of telling him, she began to cry and ran toward the women's room. She never came back.

A parking lot attendant on duty outside remembered seeing a distressed woman come out the front door of the restaurant at about that time. She had her cell phone out and was talking to someone, he said. Then she began striding quickly across the parking lot toward the park itself.

The attendant called out after her to see if she wanted him to call a cab. But she waved him off. She disappeared into the trees, apparently headed toward an exit from the park. She never made it.

Lansdale, her dinner companion, waited at the table for a long time hoping she'd come back. When she didn't, he called her apartment in Soho to see if she was there. She wasn't, but he kept calling her phone every five minutes or so for much of the night – increasingly desperate to find out what had happened to her.

At 3:30 a.m., Lansdale – confused, worried and unsure of what to do next – called the police. Of course, she was long dead by then. But his reporting of her as a missing person was one of the reasons the police were able to identify her so quickly.

A passerby spotted the body a little after 5:00 a.m., when the sun was just starting to come up. The police at the scene reported that Margaret Kincaid had been bludgeoned to death with a rock. The bloody rock was found on the ground a few feet away from the body.

Her death was not instantaneous, according to the medical examiner's office. Their theory was that the first blow had struck her on the left temple, just above the eye – and stunned her enough to prevent her from fighting back. But she was probably still conscious. There were several other blows from the rock, and much of her face was crushed in. She took a few minutes to die, the ME's report said.

Her skirt was pushed up and had been ripped, but there was no further evidence of sexual assault. It wasn't clear why – maybe her attacker heard someone coming and needed to get away in a hurry.

But he took her purse, a pearl ring, a pair of earrings – and her cell phone was missing too. Investigators also found three cigarette butts at the crime scene, which they figured the killer had smoked while he waited there for a likely victim.

Sometime the next day, police – acting on a tip – raided the hotel room of a man named Joseph Enrico, who was staying at a cheap flophouse called The Stanton on Amsterdam Avenue. They said his fingerprints matched fingerprints found on the bloody rock. They also found Margaret Kincaid's purse, earrings and ring in his room. When they attempted to handcuff him, he pulled a gun from his pocket and opened fire. The police shot back, killing him instantly. Enrico had a rap sheet dating back twenty years for burglary, forgery and auto theft.

I put all this in my story for the *Tribune*. There was a picture of Margaret Kincaid that ran with it. We'd gotten the picture from the Lansdale campaign office, and it showed her standing next to her desk there. She was blonde, beautiful and looked full of life. That haunting last image made her violent and senseless murder seem even more tragic.

The death of Margaret Kincaid was like too many New York City crime stories – just an innocent person in the wrong place at the wrong time.

If Margaret Kincaid hadn't left her boyfriend and run out of that restaurant, she'd be alive today.

Or if she'd turned around in the parking lot and waited for a taxicab.

Or if the path of a career criminal like Joseph Enrico hadn't crossed hers at exactly that moment…

We all make a hundred decisions like that every day without ever suffering any real consequences from any of them.

And then one day there are consequences. But by then it's too late.

A lot of my stories are very complicated. They take days from the time of the crime until the arrest and eventually the trial. Or, they go unsolved without anyone ever knowing all the answers.

But this one wasn't like that.

Margaret Kincaid was murdered, the obvious perpetrator shot to death during the arrest and the case cleared off the books – all in less than twenty-four hours.

It was easy.

Maybe too easy.

I had some problems with it.

First, what was Margaret Kincaid so upset about in the hours before her death? The woman had jumped up in the middle of a restaurant, burst into tears and ran outside alone into the woods. Didn't that mean something? Of course, it could just be a coincidence. But I wondered how extensively the police had questioned Jonathan Lansdale. Lansdale was the last person with her, which normally would have made him a prime suspect. But he was immediately cleared. Of course, he was the son of a U.S. senator. And there was no evidence linking him to the crime. Besides, he was still sitting inside the restaurant waiting for her to come back when she disappeared from sight.

Second, who did she talk to on her cell phone outside the restaurant? Was she calling for a taxi to take her somewhere? Probably not, because the parking lot attendant offered to get her one, but she waved him away. Whoever was on the other end of that phone – assuming she actually reached someone – was the last person to talk to Margaret Kincaid. So who was that, and why hadn't he or she come forward with their story yet?

Third, why didn't she accept the offer of a taxi? It certainly was better than walking all the way out of the park to wherever she was headed. What if she had been trying to get away from Jonathan Lansdale? He could have come out of the restaurant at any moment and caught up with her. But, if she'd just gotten in a cab, she'd have been long gone.

Fourth, Joseph Enrico seemed to be an odd person to have committed this murder. It didn't seem to be his style. None of his previous crimes – burglary, forgery or auto theft – included random street attacks like this. That wasn't his MO. So why did Enrico stand there in the woods with a rock in his hand waiting for someone like Margaret Kincaid to walk past? Also, it turned out Enrico didn't smoke. So where did the three cigarette butts at the crime scene come from? The cops decided they'd probably been left there earlier by someone who had nothing to do with the murder.

Of course, none of this meant anything if you accepted the obvious conclusion the way the police did: that Joseph Enrico killed Margaret Kincaid in a simple case of robbery, attempted sexual assault and murder just because she happened to be there on that particular night.

Because then all the rest of it – the crying scene in the restaurant, the cell phone call, the refused taxicab – was clearly irrelevant to the way she had died.

That's how cops solve most of their cases. They focus on a likely suspect – the person they believe did it. Then they accumulate evidence that could back up this version of how it happened. The police don't particularly care about any evidence they happen to run across which takes them in a different direction. That only complicates things. Not that there is really anything wrong with this approach. Most of the time it works.

On the other hand, if you started out with the hypothesis that maybe Joseph Enrico *didn't* commit the murder, then all these other questions become very important to the case again.

The crying. The taxicab. The phone call. The lack of any apparent motive for a career criminal like Joseph Enrico to kill Margaret Kincaid. And what about the shootout at the end that killed Enrico? Why did he pull a gun when they came to arrest him? He must have known that he was signing his own death warrant. Enrico had been to jail plenty of times. He knew the score. He'd never done anything like that before.

None of this bothered the cops.

Or the District Attorney's office.

Or any of the people covering the story for the other newspapers and TV stations and news websites in town.

But it bothered me.

CHAPTER 3

I sat now in the city room of the *Tribune*, nursing a chipped mug of black coffee and reading an old news story about myself that I'd called up online.

A chill ran down my spine, and I shuddered. I was supposed to be working on the Margaret Kincaid murder story, but the discovery of Margaret Kincaid's body in the park had sure brought back a lot of the old memories.

Terrifying memories. The nightmarish ones that I kept telling myself I'd finally put behind me after twelve long years. Except I knew, deep down inside, that I really hadn't done that at all. All it took was an event like this – an attack on another woman in the park just like happened to me – to bring back the rising nausea all over again.

And when I'd googled for articles on Central Park crimes to find out how many others there had been over the years, I came across this piece about myself:

MIRACLE ON 77th STREET

By Ellen Robbins
Tribune Reporter

Jessie Tucker lies in a bed in Rm. 321 of Lenox Hill Hospital on East 77th Street, just a short distance away from

Central Park where she was found beaten and near death months ago. She has suffered two broken legs, a broken hip, a cracked fibula, massive internal injuries, severe damage to her head which left her in a coma for weeks and cuts and lacerations that will take months of plastic and reconstructive surgery to repair. She can only be out of bed for 10 to 15 minutes at a time. Even then, she is confined to a wheelchair. Doctors say it will be a long time before she can learn to walk again – and they're not offering any guarantees she'll ever have a normal life going forward.

But Jessie Tucker knows she's lucky.

She is still alive.

"I'm just taking it one day at a time," she told the *Tribune* yesterday in an exclusive interview – the first she has given since she was brutally beaten and left for dead. "But I'm going to be OK. Tell everyone that. I'm going to make it all the way back."

It was four months ago that an early morning dog walker found Jessie's bruised and battered body lying behind some trees about 100 yards into the park, near 79th Street and Fifth. She was unconscious and had gone into shock. She was near death.

Central Park has long been known as one of the city's most notorious spots for crime. There was the Central Park jogger in the 80s, when a young woman was attacked while running in the park. The preppie murder of a pretty young Upper East Side woman that became a tabloid sensation. And so many other murders, assaults and rapes that have occurred there over the years.

But crime has gone down dramatically in the city in the last decade – and what happened to Jessie Tucker is a shocking reminder to New Yorkers of those bad old days.

For several days after the attack, Jessie lay in a coma –
and doctors said there was no more anyone could do for
her except pray for a miracle.

And we all did.

The miracle, when it happened, came slowly. One
day she opened her eyes. Then she moved a finger. After
that, her whole hand. And, finally, she began saying her
first words.

"I never wanted to become a poster girl for sympathy
and pity," she says now from her hospital room on East
77th Street, where she looks out at a bustling Manhattan
street and dreams of one day being out there walking
around like all the other people again.

"But I guess everything happens for a reason. I know
my life will never be exactly the same as it was before. I
also know though that I'll be a stronger person because I
was able to survive all this.

"And I'll never forget the outpouring of kindness from
so many people I don't even know."

She looked around at all the cards and flowers and
gifts that adorned the room.

"They say New Yorkers are hard-hearted and cynical.
But it isn't true. I still can't believe the way everyone in
this city has opened up their hearts to me."

One of her goals is to testify against the man arrested
for the attack against her. His trial is set for early spring,
and Jessie vows she'll walk into that courtroom to tell
her story.

Everyone who knows Jessie believes she can do it.

"She's a fighter," said Dr. Janet Spitz, who has been
by her side every step of the way in her battle to recover
from her devastating injuries. "I've never seen a patient
so determined to get well. She's come so far. I know she'll

walk again. Hell, I think someday she will be the same woman she always was."

"She won't be alone," promised Gary Bettig, a lawyer whom Jessie had been dating for several months before the attack. They recently got engaged and plan to be married in the spring. "I'll be there for her. She's going to need a lot of love and support. That's what I'm going to give her."

And her bosses at Wiley, Farrior and Mueller say her job as an advertising account executive will be waiting for her there whenever she's ready to come back.

"We were proud of Jessie before this terrible thing happened," said Robert Wiley, senior partner of the firm. "But now we're just bursting with pride and joy that she's come so far. She's a very special person. There will always be a place for her at Wiley, Farrior and Mueller."

There were two pictures with the article. One was a profile of me sitting in a wheelchair and looking out the hospital window. It was taken from the side, and the angle of the shot hid the bruises and injuries I still had when the interview was done. The other was a file picture the *Tribune* had gotten from Wiley, Farrior and Mueller. I looked at that picture now. The woman in the picture was young, self-confident, unafraid of anything.

But, like I said, that was a long time ago.

Now, well… I wasn't sure I even knew that person anymore.

When I got home later, I was still thinking about that article.

I poured myself a glass of wine, relaxed on the couch in my living room and tried to lose myself in a movie I was watching on Netflix.

But I couldn't get those memories from out of my mind.

A lot has changed since the article was written.

Robert Wiley, the senior partner at the advertising firm I worked for then, got himself indicted several years later for embezzlement and misappropriation of company funds. He left the firm in disgrace.

Gary Bettig is gone too. Not long after his touching words of love and devotion in the article about us, Bettig stopped coming to see me in the hospital. He said it was just too depressing, and he wanted to date other women. "I want to have sex with my girlfriend, I can't be with a cripple," is what he told me the last time I saw him. I heard he eventually got married to someone else, had a couple of kids and was practicing tax law somewhere in the city.

And then there was the tragedy of Dr. Spitz. Kind, gentle, compassionate Dr. Janet Spitz. A truly wonderful woman. I never would have survived without her. One day she left Lenox Hill Hospital and walked to a fast food restaurant a block away to grab a sandwich for lunch. A man with a gun tried to hold up the place while she was there. No one knows exactly what happened, but shots were fired – and Janet Spitz was hit in the heart. She was gone by the time the ambulance got there and the killer was never caught. I used to dream that I would be the one to avenge Dr. Spitz's murder, but I never got anywhere with that. In the end, there were never any real answers for what happened. Just another senseless death in a city too often filled with senseless crime.

As for me, I never went back to the Madison Avenue advertising job. The experience I'd endured really had changed me. Suddenly I didn't want to spend my life working on slogans and ad campaigns anymore. I wanted to do something more meaningful. I became friends with Ellen Robbins – the newspaper reporter who'd done the interview with me – and it was Ellen who suggested that I try writing for the *Tribune* about other victims of violent crime.

Now I was the crime specialist for the *Tribune*.

Around the time of my attack, I had been written up in *People*, *USA Today* and a lot of other major publications – and even now

I have a crime blog with hundreds of thousands of followers, although I write less and less on it these days. Someone had even put out a quickie book about me that made the *New York Times* bestseller list, followed by a made-for-TV movie called: *Miracle in Central Park: The Jessie Tucker Story*.

Yep, I'd made it a long way back. Just like Dr. Spitz had predicted in that newspaper article twelve years ago.

She was wrong about one thing though.

When she said that one day I would again be the same woman I always was… I knew I'd never be the same again.

CHAPTER 4

The newsroom of a big city newspaper – especially when you're working on a good story – is the most exciting place in the world.

Reporters pounding away on their keyboards. Editors screaming. Telephones ringing. People racing around the room frantically as their deadline approaches.

At the *Tribune*, the newsroom is a football field-sized space in a building on Sixth Avenue near Rockefeller Center, with huge, plate-glass windows overlooking Radio City Music Hall on one side and Times Square on the other.

The old newsrooms from movies with typewriters and wire machines spewing out copy are long gone now. The *Tribune* newsroom looks more like an insurance office – carpeted floors, modular furniture and computer terminals where reporters write their stories and store all their copy. There are also a half-dozen big flat-screen TVs on the walls alongside the desks so reporters and editors know what is going on everywhere in the news. And, of course, everyone is constantly checking their phones for texts and updates.

Even after all these years, the excitement of walking into a newsroom is still there for me.

I felt it now as I went to talk to Danny Knowlton, the assistant city editor. "I've been thinking… I want to keep covering the Margaret Kincaid story," I said to Danny.

"I thought the story was over."

"Not for me it isn't."

Danny smiled. I think he had expected this.

"I noticed what you wrote about it for us wasn't exactly objective, Jessie." Danny pushed his glasses up his nose and raised his eyebrows.

"It wasn't meant to be."

In the article I'd submitted the day before I'd included all my questions and reservations about the results of the investigation into Margaret Kincaid's death.

"The police are calling it a closed case."

"So? Let's reopen it. Or at least look a little deeper into the facts of what happened to Margaret Kincaid."

"How do you do plan to do that?"

"Just some basic investigative reporting, Danny. Talk to people in Senator Lansdale's office about her. Talk to the senator's son who was dating her. Talk to other people who knew her. Retrace all of her steps on the night she died. Even if we don't find out anything new, it's a great angle for the *Tribune*. 'Former Central Park Crime Victim reports on new Central Park Murder Victim'. Everyone will be talking about me and the story. Which means they'll be talking about the *Tribune*." I leaned up against his desk, fingers drumming on the wood as I spoke.

I could tell Danny liked the idea. And why not? It was the perfect story for an ambitious young newspaper editor to milk for as long as possible. And no question about it, Danny Knowlton was definitely an ambitious young newspaper editor. Me, I had slightly mixed feelings about it, despite it being my own suggestion. I had no desire to be back in the limelight… but, if that's what I had to do to stay on this story, I was willing to make the sacrifice.

The city editor of the paper, Danny's boss, was a man named Norman Isaacs. Everyone figured Danny would take over Isaacs' job soon. It was just a matter of when.

Isaacs was close to sixty-five years old, and retirement was just around the corner. He didn't ever want to rock the boat and do anything to jeopardize that retirement. No problems, no hassles, no messes – even if it meant no good stories either. "I want to work a clean shift today," he often announced in the morning as he sat down at the city desk. Everyone nodded and agreed with the sentiment, but behind his back they made fun of him. No-Guts Norman, they called him. He wasn't really a bad guy. Somewhere along the line he'd just lost the fire in his belly.

The truth of the matter was that Isaacs – even before his retirement began to loom as a real possibility – had always been a cautious, play-by-the-rules kind of editor. He had reprimanded my friend Ellen more than a decade ago for putting on a hospital worker's clothes to sneak up to my room and get that exclusive interview with me. A year or so later, just before Ellen left the paper, she posed as an EMS technician to get a deathbed interview with a dying mob boss. This time she didn't tell Isaacs how she did it. The story won a New York Press Club Award, and Isaacs gave a speech at the dinner where it was presented to her. He talked about how journalists should do good, honest reporting and not stoop to sensationalistic methods to get the job done. He cited Ellen's story as an example of this. As far as anyone knew, Isaacs never suspected a thing.

Norman Isaacs was simply not an aggressive or chance-taking editor. He always moved very slowly and thoughtfully. Even in these days of instant news on your phone, viral videos and trending Twitter topics, he prided himself on cautious, serious journalism. Not always jumping in right away to gain the competitive edge.

But every reporter has the competitive juices flowing inside them.

And that certainly included me.

So, on most of my stories, I always tried to deal with Danny Knowlton instead of Isaacs.

Oh, I'd heard some not so nice things about Danny along the way. People said he would belittle and backstab Norman Isaacs whenever he got the chance, openly salivating for the moment Isaacs decided to take his gold watch or whatever and retire from the *Tribune*. Which was understandable on Danny's part, I guess. But still not a cool thing to do.

There was also a rumor about a reporter who had been fired the year before for making a mistake that got the paper sued. The thing was, the reporter insisted he never made the mistake. That Danny Knowlton had changed his copy to make the crucial facts wrong. Danny just kept pointing the finger of blame at the reporter though, and the higher-ups at the paper all believed him. There were still people who felt Danny set up the reporter as a fall guy to cover his own mistake.

"I would never trust Danny Knowlton," a veteran staffer at the *Tribune* told me once. "He loves you when you're breaking big stories for him and making him look good as an editor. But God help you if you stop producing those big stories. He'll turn on you in a heartbeat. Don't get me wrong: I think Danny Knowlton is a really good editor. But as a human being… well, I'm just not sure."

Before I left his desk that day, Danny asked me if I thought I'd find it difficult to continue covering a Central Park murder story like this after my own near-death experience there.

"I can't even begin to imagine what you went through," he said, shaking his head. "And I think it's just incredible the way you pulled your life together after something so terrible. I really like and respect you for that, Jessie. Everyone here does. But it's got to be tough to live with the memory of something like that inside of you. So when a story comes along like this that triggers those memories again… well, I just want to make sure you know what you're getting into."

I wasn't sure if he really cared. In fact, I was pretty sure he didn't – he had assigned me to the story in the first place, after all – but he clearly felt this was the correct thing to say to me in this situation.

Either way, it didn't really matter.

I smiled warmly and gave him the answer he wanted to hear.

"That was a long time ago, Danny. What happened to me is in the past now. I hardly even think about it anymore."

CHAPTER 5

Jonathan Lansdale, the senator's son and campaign manager, said he still couldn't believe she was dead.

"Margaret was sitting there, right where you're sitting, the other day and she was so full of life." He shook his head sadly. "She was so beautiful, so talented, so dedicated. And now she's gone."

Lansdale and I were sitting in his office at the Lansdale campaign headquarters on Lexington Avenue. Lansdale was about thirty, with glasses and short, curly brown hair. He looked more like a computer geek than a political campaign manager. He spoke softly too, almost in a monotone. I had seen his father on television, and Senator Lansdale was a colorful, charismatic man who delivered speeches in a loud booming voice. Definitely not a case of like father, like son.

I nodded solemnly. Interviewing friends and relatives of murder victims was one of the toughest parts of my job. I'd never gotten used to it.

"I know this is a hard time for you," I said, "but there are a few questions I'd like to ask."

"I understand. You're just doing your job, Ms. Tucker."

I looked down at some of the things I'd jotted down in my notebook before coming there.

"How did Margaret Kincaid come to work for you?"

"She just showed up one day and volunteered her services."

"Did that seem unusual?"

"Not at all. We have many volunteers here. People who come because they want to be a part of the vision that my father, Senator

Frank Lansdale, has for this country – creating a brand-new American dream—"

He was slipping into campaign oratory now. He seemed very comfortable talking about this. More comfortable than talking about the dead woman.

"Tell me about the kind of work Margaret did here," I said.

"Well, she started as a volunteer. She did secretarial work, filing, correspondence and various other administrative assistant duties. She was hard-working, bright and everyone loved her. We put her on staff as a paid campaign aide after a short time. Of course, that doesn't happen for most of our volunteers, but Margaret was a very special woman."

"What kind of money do you make as a campaign aide?"

"Not much. Working on a political campaign isn't a place to get rich, Ms. Tucker. It's more like a basic stipend to live on rather than a salary."

"So how did Margaret pay her bills?"

"What do you mean?"

"Like her apartment, for instance. Have you seen it?"

"Well, no… I mean, I—"

"It's in a really nice neighborhood in SoHo. The place must have cost her a lot in rent. Where did she get that kind of money?"

"What are you trying to say?"

"That maybe she had some other source of income besides what you paid her for the campaign job. I don't know what that could be or if she ever even told anyone about it. And it probably has no connection at all to her murder. But it bothers me. Little things like that drive me crazy."

He shifted uncomfortably in his chair, so I changed tack and got him to tell me about that last night at the restaurant.

"Margaret was already upset when she got there," he said. "So I knew it wasn't anything I had done. But she just kept getting worse. First, she didn't like the table they sat us at. She was complaining loudly about it. I wanted to make her happy, so I got them to move us to another table. That didn't help though. She jumped up again right away and said she desperately needed a cigarette. It seemed a little rude, to be honest – did she have to go right then? She went outside to smoke for several minutes, then came back to the table. But she was still jumpy, jittery and seemed upset. I kept asking her what was wrong, but she wouldn't say. Finally, after we'd eaten, she got up, said she was going to the ladies' room and never came back."

"Was your relationship with Margaret serious?" I asked Lansdale, turning to a new page in my notebook.

"We'd been seeing each other for a while."

"That doesn't exactly answer the question."

"I thought Margaret was one of the most incredible women I'd ever met."

"I mean, do you think you might have even gotten married or something, if this hadn't happened?"

"I guess we'll never know now," Lansdale said sadly.

I asked if I could meet with his father, Senator Lansdale.

"He's in Washington this month, but he's coming back for the memorial service. I'm sure he'll be happy to talk with you then."

As I left Lansdale's campaign office, I noticed a woman standing outside on the street smoking a cigarette. I recognized her as the secretary at the front desk who let me in to see Jonathan Lansdale. I knew from experience that secretaries sometimes told you more than their bosses. I walked over to her.

"Thanks for helping set up the interview, Ms… I'm sorry, I didn't get your name."

"Betty. Betty Whalen."

The woman shook my hand. "It's a real shame about Meg," she said.

"Meg?"

She took a drag on her cigarette. "That's what everyone called her – Meg. She preferred it – said Margaret sounded like an old lady's name. It's all so sad."

"Did you know her pretty well?"

"Yeah, we spent a lot of time together here."

"You mean at the campaign office?"

"Actually, I meant out here on the sidewalk. Meg was a big smoker, just like me. So we were always out here together, puffing away."

I remembered Jonathan Lansdale telling me about the scene at the restaurant when she jumped up from the table, said she desperately ran outside for a smoke. I mentioned that to Betty Whalen.

"That's Meg." She smiled. "She had the habit really bad – wanted a smoke every ten minutes. Everyone knew that. We smoked the same brand – Marlboro Reds – and she sometimes bummed cigarettes off of me when she ran out. Totally dependent." She threw her own cigarette down on the sidewalk and ground it out with the heel of her shoe. "But I'm hardly one to talk, I guess."

"What about her and Jonathan Lansdale? Did they seem serious about each other?"

"I don't pay attention to people's personal business in the office," she said quickly.

"How about the senator? Did he know her well?"

"Oh, sure. This is a very small office. Everyone knew everyone. And Meg was playing a big part in the senator's re-election campaign. When I saw him yesterday, he looked totally devastated, he was really shocked by her murder."

"Where did you see him? In Washington?"

"No, here."

"The senator's been in New York since the murder?"

"Yes. He's in town now. Why?"

"No reason."

*

Turning away from Betty, I took out my cell phone, dialed the number for City Hall and asked for Libby St. John. Libby St. John was the mayor's top aide. Twelve years ago, Libby's boss – Mayor Jack Hanrahan – had been elected to his first term in office amidst a wave of public outrage over the attack on me. Hanrahan campaigned for more police in the park, tougher crime laws and he visited me in the hospital regularly until election day. We had met once before in a professional capacity, but I never really knew him as a person until he started visiting me in the hospital. Sure, I realized that Hanrahan was using my story to help him get elected and, at first, I was suspicious of his sincerity because of that. But eventually I decided that Jack Hanrahan was really an honest and kind man. Afterward, we'd remained friends. Me and Libby St. John – who was Hanrahan's most trusted aide – stayed close too. Libby and the mayor had even pulled some strings to help me with stories when I first started at the *Tribune*.

Libby was a walking encyclopedia of knowledge about New York City. She could tell you everything from the number of subway stations in the Bronx to what the City Council president liked for breakfast. I frequently pumped her for information for stories.

"Tell me what you know about Senator Frank Lansdale," I said now, when Libby came on the line.

"Heads up the Senate Commerce Committee, which means he gets to decide who brings what into this country – which is a pretty powerful assignment. He's put bills through Congress on drug enforcement reform, school decentralization and various budget-cutting measures. Been in the Senate for two terms, he's up for re-election again this fall. Probably going to win. Hell of a record before that. He was a big war hero – won a medal for bravery in the first Iraq war back in '91. Then he became a successful businessman. Started up his own construction company and got rich doing that. He's a big man in the community too – helps kids go to day camp, works with the homeless, finds jobs for people. Some well-known charity named Lansdale as their 'Man of the Year' last spring. He's been married to the same woman all his life, he's got two daughters in college – plus his son, Jonathan."

"He sounds like a great American," I said.

"Whatever."

"Anything bad about him?"

"Just some rumors. There was some talk about some campaign financing irregularities a few years ago, but it never went anywhere. And then there's the usual stuff you hear about politicians and womanizing. A few years ago, some intern in his office was supposedly going to do a tell-all interview about having a romance with him. Claimed he'd used taxpayer money to wine and dine her at some of the most expensive places in Washington and New York City. But she backed off at the last minute. The story never became public. I've heard some other dirt too, but the bottom line is he's never been caught."

"So, what you're saying is Lansdale's no worse than any other politician?"

"Except for Mayor Hanrahan."

"Okay, except for Mayor Hanrahan."

"Yeah, something like that."

I still didn't know what was going on, but I sure didn't like Jonathan Lansdale's story.

For one thing, he kept calling the dead woman Margaret. But, according to Betty Whalen, everyone who knew her well called her Meg – because she didn't *like* being called Margaret. So why didn't Lansdale say Meg when he was talking about his dead girlfriend?

Also, he'd admitted that he'd never seen her apartment. If they were having a relationship, wouldn't he have been there at some point? Of course, maybe they always used his place, but it seemed a bit strange.

Then there was Lansdale's account of what happened at the Park Grille Restaurant. According to Whalen, all of the dead woman's friends knew she couldn't go ten minutes without a cigarette. So why was Jonathan Lansdale so annoyed when she went outside for a smoke? Didn't it come up every time they went to dinner?

Finally, Lansdale had told me that his father had been in Washington all month, but his secretary said she had seen the senator here, and he looked very upset about the death. One of them – Jonathan Lansdale or the secretary – was lying.

Individually, none of these things meant very much. There were always unanswered questions, loose ends, things that didn't add up right in any story. I knew that. And I was being very careful about jumping to any conclusions. But the loose ends were *really* starting to add up in this case.

Nothing about Margaret Kincaid was turning out to be what it seemed.

So maybe her murder hadn't happened the way it seemed either.

CHAPTER 6

Ellen Robbins – my best friend and the reporter who'd written the original story about me in the hospital for the *Tribune* – and I were working out next to each other on a pair of exercise bikes at the gym.

I'd been going to this gym several times a week pretty much ever since I got released from the hospital after my attack. It was my home away from home. In fact, sometimes I felt like I spent more time in the gym than I did in my apartment.

The gym was located on the fifth floor of a big building on Park Avenue South, near Union Square, which was not far from where I lived. The fact that it was on the fifth floor meant there was no glass window facing the street where people could look in on you exercising, which I always hated.

The main area when you walked in consisted of a large workout space filled with free weights, dumbbells, barbells and other equipment like that. I had spent much of my time there in the early years, when I was trying to strengthen my body as I went through the long, painful recovery process from all my injuries.

Now, my favorite area was the cardio/exercise room with rowing machines, stationary exercise bikes and treadmills. There was even a TV in there so I could watch the news while I was working out in the morning before heading to work at the *Tribune*.

There was also a huge – nearly Olympic-sized – swimming pool on the floor above the main gym. Swimming is supposed to be the best exercise there is, and I had swum many, many laps in that pool over the years.

I used to tell myself that I spent so much time in the gym because I needed it to recover physically from all the damage that had been done to my body. But, at some point, I realized that I didn't just need the place to cure my physical wounds – it helped me to deal with the emotional ones too.

For some reason, working out furiously had helped me exorcise the demons from that horrible night in the park better than anything else in my life had. And so I did it religiously.

Ellen was less enthusiastic and I often had to drag her along with me, but it was worth it because I liked the company. "I don't want to become a fanatic about it," she always said. "Someone like you."

Ellen was a high-profile book and movie agent now, having given up newspapers soon after her big story about the mob boss. She always admitted that she was more of a promoter than a reporter.

Me, on the other hand, well, I had quickly fallen in love with the newspaper life and left Madison Avenue for good to become a crime reporter. We'd become best friends – and sometimes marveled about how both of our lives had been changed so dramatically by my near-death experience.

"I really need this workout," I said to Ellen, pedaling away furiously on the exercise bike. "I've been so tense the last few days. Maybe it's this new Central Park case, and some of the memories it brings back. But this is good. Throwing myself into exercise makes me feel so much better. Don't you feel better?"

Ellen shook her head sadly and slowed down.

"What?"

"Who's your best friend?" she asked.

"You."

"Who made you a national hero?"

"You."

"So, listen to me now when I give you some advice. This is not the only exercise you need. You need something a bit more… well, exciting."

"What are you talking about?"

"Sex."

"Oh, that."

"How long has it been anyway?"

That was a tough question. One I wasn't really sure I had the answer for anymore. I hadn't been in a serious relationship since I'd been attacked in the park.

Back then, I'd had what I thought was a pretty healthy sex life. I was engaged to Gary Bettig, we were going to be married soon and we made passionate love all the time. It all seemed so easy. Maybe that was the problem. It was too easy. Until I wound up in a coma and spent months rehabilitating in a hospital – and everything changed. I cried for a long time after Gary Bettig walked out on me. Eventually the tears went away, but not the emptiness. I've tried going on dates since, but it's never worked out very well. At some point, I guess I just gave up on having a healthy romantic relationship. I recovered from most of my physical wounds in the park that night, but the ones deep inside of me were harder to deal with. I wasn't sure I ever could.

"It's been a long time," is all I said to Ellen, pushing back my hair and pedaling harder.

"So, go screw someone."

"Why are you so concerned about my love life?"

"I just think you work too hard."

"I like my work."

"You're all work and no play," Ellen said, and then, inspiration striking her – "what you need is a good lay!"

I laughed. Ellen always made me laugh. I sometimes think that saved my life back when I was in the hospital. She'd gone quickly from reporter covering the story to my friend. She brought me scrumptious takeout food – things like bagels with cream cheese, cold cuts and barbecued chicken wings – as a relief from the boring hospital food. And, most importantly, she was funny. Her jokes made me feel better and that life was somehow worth living again, even when I was at my lowest point. Like with Jack Hanrahan, I was suspicious in the beginning that she was just out for her own gain – to get a big exclusive story by interviewing me. Probably she was, but it didn't matter because Ellen always made me feel better back then. And she was still doing that.

But there are other people in my life just like Ellen – people who became my friends when I desperately needed a friend.

Like I said earlier, Mayor Jack Hanrahan is one of them. He was running for his first term as mayor when I was beaten and left for dead that night in the park, but he made time in his busy schedule to come visit me at the hospital constantly while I was recovering. Look, I'm a realist. I know that being identified with me was good for him politically. He got elected mayor that year in part because of the outrage of New Yorkers over the senseless crime that had happened to me. But no one, not even a consummate politician like Hanrahan, could fake the kind of sincerity he'd shown.

His wife Christine, a former TV reporter who he'd met on the campaign trail a few years earlier, accompanied him on many of his visits to see me, and we became friends too. She and Hanrahan promised they'd invite me to have dinner with them at Gracie Mansion once I was out of the hospital. That had seemed like a long time away to me then. But it became one of my goals. Just like walking or leaving the hospital and being able to go outside on the street or living in my own apartment again. I would lie in bed or sit in my wheelchair and dream about that dinner at Gracie Mansion. I made it too. Four months later, I sat at the table with the mayor and his wife and they toasted my incredible recovery. I've been back numerous times since then over the years.

And along with Jack Hanrahan, there's always been Libby St. John. I've turned to her so many times for help, just like I did when I wanted to find out more about Senator Lansdale.

Libby goes everywhere with the mayor, and a lot of people – including Hanrahan himself – believe she is the reason behind his political success. Libby is brilliant, unbelievably politically savvy, ruthless when she's dealing with the mayor's enemies and totally obsessed with her job. She works like eighteen hours a day, seven days a week – she's always on call.

No one knows if she has any kind of personal life outside the job. I asked her about that once. "No, I don't have a husband or boyfriend," she said. "And I'm not gay, if that's what you were wondering. I just don't have time for that kind of thing, no matter how weird people think I am. Okay, I'm weird. But I know what I want my life to be, and that's what I'm doing. My life is this job and protecting the mayor." Me, I love spending time with Libby. She's so full of energy and drive and optimism that it always makes me feel better about myself too.

There's even a police officer on the NYPD – Steve Fredericks – who been a big part of my life. Fredericks had been the lead detective investigating my case, but afterwards he became a friend as well.

During those long months in the hospital when I was having a tough day or feeling sorry for myself, Detective Fredericks would drop by to check in. I looked forward to his visits as the highlight of my day. Looking back on it now, I suppose I'd fallen in love with Steve Fredericks. Not really in love, of course – I knew he had a wife and two small children at home. But I needed him for a selfish reason of my own. I so desperately wanted answers about what happened to me in the park that night – *who did this to me and why?* Steve Fredericks was the one who got that information and kept me abreast on every step of the case.

I depended on them all back then, and I still do. The people around you make a big difference when you have no actual family to depend on.

My father died when I was just a baby… or so I thought for a long time. You see, my mother always spoke about my father in glowing terms – this wonderful man who was taken away from us too soon. Turns out it was all a lie. My father wasn't taken from us; he just left of his own accord right after I was born. Abandoned my mother and me before I ever got to know who he even was. When I found out, years later, I was furious at my mother for not telling me the truth. I deserved to know the damn truth about my own father. Once I became a reporter, I thought about trying to track him down and get some answers. But I never have. I guess I'm not sure I want to know.

My mother never really recovered from his leaving and being forced to raise a child on her own. It changed her life irrevocably. She was always critical of me and whatever I did, almost like she blamed me for everything that had gone wrong in her life. For instance, when I finally came out of the coma in the hospital, the first words my mother said to me were; "Why did you do something so stupid as going into that park alone?" No, we did not have a very good relationship, my mother and I. When she died a few years ago, we had barely spoken for a long time.

That's why I had been so excited about marrying Gary Bettig. He was going to be the beginning of the family I never had. Except he'd abandoned me when I needed him most, just like my father had done to my mother. That's why what Gary Bettig did hurt me so much. I wasn't just losing a boyfriend or a fiancé. It was my father – the father I had never even known – abandoning me all over again.

But it was funny how a tragedy like mine could bring so many good things and so many good people into my life.

Ellen. Jack Hanrahan and his wife. Libby St. John. Steve Fredericks… These people are my family now.

And each day I wrap this safe little world of mine – and all the people in it – around me tightly like a security blanket to keep the bad memories away. Sometimes it works.

CHAPTER 7

The print shop Margaret Kincaid visited on the last night of her life was on Madison Avenue, near 45th Street, several blocks away from Senator Lansdale's campaign office. I wasn't even sure why I was there. But the dead woman had come here that last night. Maybe it meant something.

I pushed open the door and walked in. There was a crunching sound under my feet. I looked down and saw several pieces of ground glass on the floor. A window next to the door had a gaping hole in it. Someone had cleaned up most of the mess, but they hadn't gotten everything.

"Sorry about that," a young guy behind the counter said.

"No problem."

"I thought we picked it all up this morning. That sucker really shattered."

"What happened?"

"Oh, somebody broke in here. Tried to get into the cash register. Fortunately, we always put all the money away before we leave. But they got a couple of our expensive computers in the back. Walked right out of here with them. Can you believe it? Well, I guess that's New York City for you." He shrugged. "So, what can I do for you?"

I told him who I was and why I was there. He said his name was Dan Hanks, and he was the assistant manager.

"Yeah, I remember the woman," he said. "I waited on her. I realized it when I saw her picture on the TV news. I called the cops – I guess that's how they knew she was here. I just thought someone ought to know. They came out and questioned me for a few minutes about it. But I couldn't tell them anything. Her coming in here had nothing to do with what happened later. Christ, what a shame though, huh? That girl was a total babe."

"What did she say to you?"

"Nothing much. She just picked up some printing job. I found it and handed the box over to her. Then she paid and left. End of story."

I told him about the scene she'd put on at the Park Grille Restaurant a short time afterward.

"Did she seem upset while she was here?"

"No."

"Nervous?"

"Nope."

"Angry?"

Hanks shook his head.

"Sorry, but the police asked me all these same questions. I couldn't help them either. What is it you're looking for exactly?"

"I'm not sure. I'll know when I find it."

"A clue everyone else has missed, huh?"

"Something like that." I smiled.

I asked him about the print job the woman had picked up. He didn't remember what it was.

"Was it for the senator's office?"

"I have no idea."

"How much did she pay?"

"I really don't remember that either."

"What about a credit card receipt?"

"She paid in cash."

"Isn't that unusual?"

"What do you mean?"

"Well, assuming she was doing it for Senator Lansdale's office, why pay for it out of her own pocket? You would have thought she would have billed it to the senator somehow, right?"

"Beats me. Look, we've got a lot of customers here. I only remember waiting on her because she was so beautiful, you know what I'm saying?"

I nodded. That made sense. I asked him a few more questions, but he wasn't able to tell me anything that helped. Probably because there wasn't anything to tell. Just like the cops decided. We all do a hundred mundane things in a day. Most of them have no significance. I had hoped there might be something here that did matter. Obviously, there wasn't. The woman had stopped at the store before she died. A few hours later, she was attacked in Central Park. One thing had nothing to do with the other.

I thanked Hanks for taking the time to talk to me.

"And good luck with your burglary," I said, looking down at the glass on the floor. "I hope you get your computers back."

"The cops think they'll catch the guys that did this. They got clear-cut shots of the burglars on the security camera. They think they'll be able to identify them from mugshots."

"You've got a security camera?"

"Sure." He pointed to a camera hanging from the ceiling above us. "Put it in after the last break-in we had here. It runs twenty-four hours a day."

"Was that camera running when Margaret Kincaid came in here?" I asked.

"Yes, I guess so…"

"How long do you keep the video?"

"Oh, maybe a week or two."

"So you might still have video from that day?"

"Yeah," he said slowly, "I guess we would."

*

There was a lot to wade through on the video. Hanks and I fast-forwarded through hours of comings and goings. There was no time log, so we had to watch customer after customer in the store until the video finally got to Margaret Kincaid.

It was a shock to see her on the screen. I'd seen her picture, of course. But this was different. It was positively eerie. There she was – beautiful and still looking full of life – walking in the front door of the store.

She was wearing the same outfit she had worn when she was attacked in the park. It was a pink suit – even though you couldn't really see the pink clearly on the grainy video. That matched the police account of what happened that night. They said she'd never gone home after work – just another fact that I could now confirm.

On the video, Margaret Kincaid moved toward the counter.

There were two people ahead of her. Hanks waited on them. I watched in morbid fascination as the doomed woman fidgeted in line waiting her turn. At one point, she took out her cell phone, fiddled with it and looked at herself in the reflection on the screen. Probably checking herself out for her date with Jonathan Lansdale. The kind of thing everyone does every day without thinking. The difference here was this was the last day this woman would ever do it. In a few hours, the way she looked wouldn't matter. She would be dead.

I watched her intently to see if there was any sign of the agitated state everyone said she was in at the restaurant, but she seemed fine. Whatever upset her must have happened later, when she was on her way to the restaurant.

Now it was her turn to be waited on. She handed Hanks a slip for the material she'd had printed. He walked over to one of the shelves, found her stuff and passed it to her. It was a medium-sized cardboard box. She paid him in cash, just like he'd said. Then Hanks turned away to go to the back of the store for something. The Kincaid woman started to leave.

That's when it happened.

Suddenly, everything changed. Margaret Kincaid's expression became agitated, angry, almost hysterical. She was gesturing at someone outside the camera's range of vision – apparently on the other side of the door, but not actually inside the store yet.

Finally, the person came in and the camera picked him up. A man. A big man dressed in a suit. At first, that was all I could see because he had his back to the camera. Margaret Kincaid's face was clearly visible though. She really looked upset. And the man who'd just come into the store seemed to be the cause of it all.

"Turn around," I said out loud to the figure on the film. "Turn the hell around."

Finally, he did.

"I never saw any of this," Hanks was saying.

"That's because you were in the back."

"Hey!" Hanks yelled as the man's face came into focus on the screen. "That guy looks familiar."

"Yeah, he does," I said.

Very familiar.

"I've seen his picture in the paper and on TV," Hanks said. "It's that Lansdale guy."

That's who it was, all right.

Not Jonathan Lansdale.

This was his father.

Senator Frank Lansdale.

CHAPTER 8

No one at the Park Grille Restaurant wanted to talk about the murder. The Park Grille was already a popular, four-star place, and the people there weren't looking for any publicity. Especially the kind of publicity that came from a grisly murder case.

The manager of the Park Grille said he didn't know anything about what happened that night.

So did the maître d'.

And the bartender was downright hostile when I sat down at the bar and tried to ask him some questions about the murder.

"Look, I know you've been nosing around here, trying to get people to talk to you about what happened to that woman," he said. "But I don't know nothing. Not a thing, got that? Now do you want something to drink or are you just taking up space on that bar stool?"

I walked outside and talked to the parking lot attendant.

He was the same one who had been on duty the night of the murder. He was a lot friendlier than the people inside. Maybe they'd forgotten to tell him he was supposed to treat reporters like the plague. He told me again the story about how the dead woman had come out of the restaurant, talking on her cell phone and ignored his offer to get her a taxicab to walk into the park.

"How did you happen to notice her?"

"Are you kidding? That lady was a real fox."

"So you were checking her out—"

"I kept my eye on her the whole time."

"I understand she was quite upset that night."

"Sure was."

"And she was on her cell phone?"

"Yes, she was talking to someone. I'm surprised the phone even worked though."

"What do you mean?"

"She was so mad she threw it on the ground. I thought it might have broken. But apparently it didn't because she was still using it."

"So, she was really that emotional when she came out of the restaurant?"

"She didn't throw the cell phone leaving the restaurant. It was on her way in. She was talking to somebody on it then. I guess she didn't like what they had to say."

I tried to figure out what this new information might mean. I had absolutely no idea.

"I thought she might need a ride home. I asked her if she wanted me to call a cab or car service. But she just started walking into the park."

He pointed toward the clump of trees where her body had been found the next morning – and said that's where she had been headed.

I took the same path through the trees that the dead woman had on that last night. I wasn't exactly sure why. Maybe I just wanted to put myself in Margaret Kincaid's footsteps for a few minutes. Except for the grace of God, I could have wound up like she did. There were no miracles for poor Margaret. No dinners at Gracie Mansion. No TV-movies of the week. She was dead, she'd be buried and then she'd be forgotten about – just like the hundreds of other people who are murdered in New York City every year.

When I got to the spot where the murder had happened, I stood there for a long time, wondering what it was like for her. Wondering what she had thought about in those last few minutes of life. I remembered how my first reaction as a crime victim had been disbelief at what was happening to me. Mercifully, I had lost consciousness soon after that. I hoped that was what happened to Margaret Kincaid. The ME's report speculated that she had still been alive after the first few blows of the rock, but maybe the report was wrong.

I was just about to leave when I saw it. A flash of red and white. It was partially buried in the dirt. Probably from all the people walking around here the day after the murder. I dug it out. An empty pack of Marlboro Reds.

The cops probably did a pretty thorough search of the area, but they always missed something. This wouldn't have meant much to them anyway. Most of the stuff at a crime scene didn't. Except I knew something the cops didn't know. The cops said that Joseph Enrico didn't smoke, so they believed the cigarette butts they found in the area probably had nothing to do with the murder.

But Margaret Kincaid did smoke.

And she smoked Marlboro Reds.

She was the one who had smoked the cigarettes!

Right from the beginning, this was supposed to have been an open-and-shut case. Joseph Enrico had murdered the woman in a totally random attack in the park, then he'd been shot to death in a shootout with cops. No loose ends. End of story. Only now it wasn't.

I still had a lot of questions, but there was one thing I was now sure about from all these new facts I'd uncovered.

One inescapable conclusion.

This was no random murder.

Margaret Kincaid had waited for her killer.

CHAPTER 9

"I think I've got a really big story," I said to Norman Isaacs, the city editor of the *Tribune*. We were in his big corner office – I had headed him off on his way to lunch. My arms were full of notes and I was already on my third coffee of the day.

"What's the story?" Isaacs asked.

"Who killed Margaret Kincaid."

"Joseph Enrico."

"What if he didn't do it?"

"The police say he did."

"Exactly."

Isaacs looked confused. "So?"

I groaned. "That's the story, Norman."

I really hated taking this story to Isaacs. I badly wanted to keep working with Danny Knowlton, like I usually did, but this story was too big for just an assistant city editor, even one as ambitious as Danny. It was going to have to go to Isaacs one way or another and I figured it was best if I was the one who made the pitch to him personally.

I laid it all out for him. First, the police account of how the murder had happened. Then the things I'd found out from my digging during the past few days. I didn't give any opinions, I didn't editorialize – I just stuck to the facts.

"Are you telling me that you think Senator Lansdale had something to do with this?" he asked incredulously when I was finished.

"I'm saying there are big holes in the cops' case against Enrico. I'm saying that the senator had an ugly argument with the woman just before she was murdered. I'm saying that his son lied about where Lansdale was the night of the murder. Nothing about the police version of this story makes any sense." I suddenly became aware that I had raised my voice and the people outside the office were starting to stare.

Isaacs crossed his arms. "Jessie, there is no way I believe that Senator Lansdale walked out into those woods and killed that girl."

"I didn't say that he did."

"Well, what exactly are you saying?"

"I'm just saying that I think Senator Lansdale knows more than he's telling us. I think that he was involved." I shifted from foot to foot, impatient to stop having this conversation and get back to my desk.

"Involved how?" Isaacs eyebrows shot up.

"My guess is the senator was having an affair with her."

"I thought it was the son who was dating her."

"That's the story they put out."

"But you think they're lying?"

"Yeah. Look, it just doesn't make sense. The son didn't know about her smoking, that she liked people to call her Meg instead of Margaret – and he'd never even been to her apartment. That doesn't sound like a passionate love affair to me. So what was going on here? I think he was covering up for someone else who *was* having a romance with her. Now who would he do that for? There's only one answer. His father."

Isaacs shook his head like he wasn't buying any of it. "He's a United States senator, for God's sake, Jessie!"

"Hey, U.S. senators are human beings just like anyone else. They screw around with women who aren't their wives, they fight with them, maybe they even murder them in a fit of rage. It happens."

"When?"

"Huh?"

"When has a U.S. senator ever murdered a woman?"

"Well, I can't think of one right now…"

"Exactly."

"But there's a first time for everything."

I had known Isaacs was going to be a tough sell, but here I was anyway, talking about what every instinct in my body told me was a blockbuster story to a man who just wanted it to go away.

"There're a lot of holes in your theory that Enrico wasn't really the murderer," Isaacs said.

"Like?"

"Enrico's fingerprints were on the rock found at the crime scene. The rock used to kill Margaret Kincaid. How do you explain that, Jessie?"

"I don't know."

"If Enrico was innocent, why did he pull a gun and try to shoot it out with the cops who came to arrest him? That's the act of a guilty man."

"I don't know that either."

"And what about the dead woman's belongings they found in Enrico's hotel room? How do you explain that?"

"Don't know," I repeated.

"What *do* you know?"

I leaned back against a rusty steel filing cabinet that looked older than Isaacs himself and sighed. "Look, let's just imagine Lansdale was having a romance with her. And that – from the looks of their argument on the video at the print shop – the romance had gone sour. Maybe he got tired of her. Maybe he was worried about the potential political fallout. Maybe he felt guilty about what he was doing to his wife and family. So, he breaks it off. But she doesn't take this well. Maybe she threatens to tell people about it. A woman scorned and all that. So he meets her outside the restaurant – after his son has dinner with her there – and he kills her.

"But now he's got a big problem. This is a high-profile murder in Central Park. The press will go crazy with the story, unless there's a quick arrest. So there's a quick arrest. An ex-con who's gunned down before he can even be questioned. End of story. Everybody's happy about this. The cops, the public, the press – and, most of all, Senator Frank Lansdale.

"Think about it, Norman. How did the cops find Enrico? How did his fingerprints get on the rock that killed Margaret Kincaid? Why did he open fire on the police? The cops said they had to shoot him in self-defense, but what if it wasn't like that at all? What if they executed Enrico and then planted a gun on him and made it look like he'd shot first? More importantly, who has the power to pull something like that off? Railroad an innocent man, plant phony evidence, manipulate the police? Someone very important, that's who. Someone very powerful. Someone like a United States senator."

Isaacs stood there without saying anything for a long time.

"I'm worried about you, Jessie," he said finally.

I realized what he was saying.

"You think I'm reliving my own story all over again, don't you?" I said, raising my voice again. "That my judgment has been impaired because I went through something very similar. That I can't see the facts objectively."

"When Danny assigned you to cover this murder, I told him I didn't think it was a good idea. But he insisted he wanted you on it. And, like a lot of other things around here these days, I let Danny have his way. But now I think we might have opened up some kind of Pandora's box of emotions that you've kept bottled up inside you for a long, long time. So maybe it would be best if you worked on something else until—"

I couldn't let him take me off the story.

I put my hand on his arm and smiled. "Norman, you're right. I'm sorry if I sounded a bit crazy there before. I just got carried away. Of course, I don't *really* think Senator Lansdale had anything to do with this murder. I'm sure there's a simple answer to all these questions. I just want to find out what that is. Okay?"

I looked at him earnestly. Trying my best to convince him I was a dedicated reporter, not some paranoid lunatic who saw conspiracy theories everywhere. I was responsible. I was sensible. I was logical. I had no personal agenda in this other than writing a good story.

"This is just another story," Isaacs told me.

"I know."

"It has nothing to do with what happened to you."

"I know that too."

Isaacs nodded a little sadly. He still didn't seem convinced, but I knew that he trusted me. I'd worked with him for a long time, and I'd never done anything really irresponsible.

"Look, I'll make a deal with you, Jessie. You get the rest of the week to work on this case. See what you come up with. If there's no story by then, we move on. Okay?"

"Okay," I said.

Isaacs looked relieved. I understood that. And I appreciated his concern for me. "The person who did that terrible thing to you, he's long gone now," Isaacs said, as I turned to leave his office. "The system worked. Justice was done. He can't hurt you any more, Jessie."

He didn't have to tell me.

I knew that.

But I still thought about it every day.

CHAPTER 10

My trial had been front-page news for weeks.

Several days after the attack on me, police had arrested a nineteen-year-old named Darryl Jackson and charged him with committing the horrifying crime.

The break in the case came when Detective Steve Fredericks had arrested Jackson for the robbery of a bodega on Avenue C on the Lower East Side of Manhattan. The kid had walked into the place, pulled a gun out of his pocket and announced a stickup. But then it all went wrong for him. The owner was an ex-transit cop who kept a loaded shotgun behind the counter. He pretended to reach for the drawer of the cash register, went for the shotgun instead and came up blasting. The first shot hit Jackson in the shoulder, the second took away part of his ear. By the time Fredericks arrived, he was screaming in pain, pleading for a doctor and claiming that his rights had been violated.

Fredericks didn't care about any of that. What he cared about was an iPod he found in the kid's jacket pocket. The iPod still contained the name of the original owner. Jessie Tucker. Fredericks had seen a memo on the missing iPod – taken from me during the attack – before he started his tour of duty that day. Suddenly this was not just a simple bodega robbery – it was a clue to the most high-profile crime of the year in New York City.

When police searched Jackson's home at a housing project on the Lower East Side near Delancey Street, they found my wallet, credit cards, some jewelry and other possessions of mine stashed under his mattress. Faced with the evidence against him, Jackson confessed to the crime. He said he had sexually assaulted other women in the park too – but this time it just got out of hand.

A few days later, Jackson tried to recant his confession. He had a lawyer now – a high-profile, public defender activist – who had attached himself to the case. He said that the confession had been coerced out of Jackson and that he had been deprived of his right to talk to a lawyer. He talked about the rush to judgment in the Central Park jogger attack of 1989, when five young African-American men were sent to jail for the crime – but later exonerated. And, of course, he pleaded Jackson not guilty at his arraignment.

The trial was ten months later.

My goal was to testify against Darryl Jackson at the trial. From the very beginning, almost as soon as I regained consciousness, I thought about that constantly. It became more important to me than anything else. An aim. A challenge. A first step toward reclaiming my life.

Everyone told me I didn't have to appear. The police and the District Attorney's office said they had enough evidence to convict him without my testimony. The judge in the case had allowed Jackson's original video confession to be admitted as evidence. They also had my iPod found on him, plus my belongings he hid at his house. It looked open and shut.

But I knew this was something I had to do.

When I first woke up, I had trouble remembering exactly what had happened that night in the park. And the memories – when they did begin to return – were fleeting and troubling. The shock. The pain. And then details I learned later about what happened to me when a beautiful summer night in the city I loved suddenly turned into terror.

Detective Fredericks had helped me. He sat with me day after day – patiently going over everything that had happened, comforting me, helping me to remember the events of that night.

Eventually, my memory began to come back. I remembered seeing Jackson in the park just before I was attacked, and now all I had to do was get healthy enough to testify against him at the trial. I could have just filed a deposition or affidavit with the court naming him as the one who did it, but that wasn't good enough. I wanted to look him in the eye. I wanted him to pay for what he had done to me. I wanted to make sure he never did it to any other woman ever again.

The scene in the courtroom was one of high drama. The case became a national sensation. When I leaned forward in the witness box and pointed to Darryl Jackson at the defense table as my attacker, it was picked up by CNN, *60 Minutes* and run on newscasts by every TV station around the country. The jury took less than an hour to deliberate. There was nothing to deliberate about. Jackson was as guilty as any defendant had ever been in the history of the American justice system.

After that, the media blitz had really started.

There was a cover story in *People*. Appearances on *Oprah* and *Dr. Phil*. A true crime book about the case. A TV-movie.

I became America's most famous victim.

I'd never given up.

I'd fought back.

I'd won.

As the years went by, I followed the life of Darryl Jackson in prison as closely as I used to follow market sales and advertising trends when I worked on Madison Avenue. Jackson had received a long sentence, but there was always the possibility of parole. Or an overturned verdict. Or a successful appeal.

I had sometimes woken up in the middle of the night – sweating and gasping for breath – after having a nightmare that he'd gotten out of jail. The nightmares had gotten fewer as the years went by, but they'd never gone away. Not completely.

The good thing was that, these days, there was no possibility of that ever happening.

Jackson was stabbed to death during a jailhouse brawl at Attica State Prison in upstate New York. Paramedics worked on him for forty minutes in the prison courtyard, trying to keep him alive, but they couldn't do it. I was glad. I always thought those paramedics should have gotten a medal for not saving him.

Darryl Jackson was gone.

He had suffered a horrible death.

And now I wanted him to rot in hell for eternity.

I don't know if that makes me a bad person or not, but that is the goddamn truth.

CHAPTER 11

There is a moment in every big story when a newspaper reporter suddenly realizes the magnitude of what he or she is dealing with. Most of the time, even big stories start out looking like small or routine ones. But then somewhere along the line something happens to change that. A significant turning point in the investigation. A major breakthrough. A sudden intuitive understanding by the reporter that this story is different to the hundreds of other stories a newspaper carries each day. This one is something special.

Sometimes reporters go through their entire careers without ever encountering a story like that.

You have to be very good to pull it off.

Or very lucky.

I was a bit of both on this story.

Several days after the murder of Margaret Kincaid, a man came to see me in the *New York Tribune* newsroom.

He was carrying a copy of the front-page article I'd written about the killing that first day.

"My name is Logan Kincaid," he said.

I picked up on the last name right away.

"Husband?"

"No, her brother."

"I'm sorry."

Kincaid shrugged. He was in his early thirties, maybe a year or two older than the dead woman. He was dressed casually – khaki pants, a brown plaid shirt with the collar open – and had dark wavy hair that was pushed back from his face. I glanced down at his left hand to see if he was wearing a wedding ring. He wasn't.

He tossed the copy of my article on the desk in front of me. The headline above it said:

TRAGEDY IN CENTRAL PARK

Political Aide Slain During Brutal Robbery

Below the headline was the picture of Margaret Kincaid that the *Tribune* had gotten from the Lansdale campaign office. She smiled up at us, unaware of her grisly fate.

"Did you write this article?" Kincaid asked.

"That's my byline."

"Where did you get your facts?"

I raised my eyebrows. "From the police. The senator's office. A few other sources here and there. Why?"

"And nobody questioned any of this stuff they told you?"

"No…" I said slowly.

"Then why did you write this?"

He pointed to a section of the article that read:

Despite the swift conclusion to the case, there are still some unanswered questions.

Why did Margaret Kincaid make that walk through the woods of Central Park? Why did she refuse the offer of a taxicab? Who did she call outside the restaurant? What was she so upset about in the hours before she died? And why did Joseph Enrico get in a final shootout with cops that he must have known he had no chance of surviving?

The police say they will probably never know the answers to those questions now.

And neither will we.

But they will continue to haunt us for a long time, just as the senseless murder of Margaret Kincaid haunts all New Yorkers…

"How come you said that?" Kincaid asked.

I shrugged. "I wasn't satisfied with some of the answers I was getting."

"Everybody else was. None of the other articles or newscasts brought up any questions like the ones you asked."

"Well, I'm not everybody else."

His mouth twitched. "That's why I came to see you."

He laid another newspaper clipping with a picture down on the desk. It was a picture of another woman. She was blonde too, and about the same age as Margaret Kincaid. She had two blonde-haired children in her arms, who looked to be only a few years old.

"Who is this?" I asked.

"My sister."

"Okay…" So Logan Kincaid had another sister. I still didn't understand what he was saying.

He pointed down at the woman in the picture. "She's dead," he said.

"You've had two sisters who died so young?"

"No, I only had one sister."

I looked down at the newspaper page again. I realized it was actually an ad. One of those ads that warn about the dangers of drunk driving. There were several other pictures on the page too. All of them had been fatal victims of drunk drivers. Underneath the picture that he had shown me first the caption said: "Margaret Kincaid, along with her two young children." It said she had died two years ago.

"My sister, Margaret Kincaid," he said. "She had two kids, she was twenty-nine years old – and she did live in Santa Barbara, California, like your article said. That was about the only thing that was right. You see, she and her two children were killed in that car crash. So she didn't die in the park a few days ago. She's already been dead for a long time.

"The driver of the car that killed her fled the scene," Kincaid continued, staring intently at me. "It turned out that the car was stolen, and the person behind the wheel at the time of the accident has never been identified. Witnesses said he'd been weaving all over the road and they speculated he was drunk.

"I've tried private investigators, cops, the works – but they never got anywhere. I'm hoping this murder could be a lead… did the dead woman use my sister's name for some reason? Did she know something about her death? Or did she just pick out a dead woman of about the same age and physical characteristics because she needed to assume a new identity?

"I thought maybe you could help me find out the answers. What do you think?"

I drummed my fingers against my desk. "Is it possible there might have been two Margaret Kincaids from Santa Barbara?" I asked him.

"Both twenty-nine years old?"

"Not very likely, huh?

"Just to be sure, I did check. There's no record of any other Margaret Kincaid living in the Santa Barbara area. This woman they found dead must have stolen my sister's identity for some reason."

I sat there, looking down at the picture of Margaret Kincaid. The real Margaret Kincaid.

If this woman had been dead for two years, then who was the body in the park?

CHAPTER 12

Her name was Cheryl Lee Barrett.

I found that out from Detective Lieutenant Thomas Aguirre, the homicide cop in charge of the Central Park murder investigation. I had a bad feeling about Aguirre as soon as I met him. Three-piece suit, expensive silk tie, oiled hair. The kind of guy who just lived to get assigned a high-profile murder and see his face on every front page and TV news show in town. I've worked with a lot of cops, and I generally get along pretty well with most of them, but I was pretty sure I wasn't going to like Aguirre.

Aguirre didn't want to give me the information about the identity of the victim. He wanted to announce it at a press conference in front of TV cameras. But he was in a tough spot. I had broken the story in the *Tribune* about the real Margaret Kincaid. And I'd done Aguirre a favor by telling him about the story first so he wouldn't be blindsided – and so he could tell the police brass about the ID mix-up before they read about it in the newspaper.

Now it was payback time.

Aguirre agreed to give me the Cheryl Lee Barrett story exclusively, but there were some conditions. One, his name had to be mentioned in at least one of the first three paragraphs of the article. Two, a picture of him would run with the story. Three, there would be at least six individual quotes clearly attributed to him and identifying him – in a highly positive way – as the lead investigator on the case.

"Are you sure you don't want to divide up the film rights now too, just in case it gets made into a movie?" I asked after we finished working all of this out in Aguirre's office in the squad room of the Central Park police precinct.

Aguirre's partner – a plainclothes detective named Phil Erskine who was typing a report on a computer at the next desk – snorted loudly.

"What's so funny?" Aguirre snapped.

"She is."

Aguirre frowned. "Hey, partner, I'm just trying to make sure both of us come out of this looking good."

"Us? Gee, I must have missed the part where you mentioned my name."

Aguirre grumbled something unintelligible and strode out of the office towards the coffee pot in the main squad room.

"As you've probably noticed, the lieutenant is a great believer in self-promotion," Erskine told me. "He never met a TV camera he didn't like. The word is he's got a big future in this department. He's a real up-and-comer. He's definitely on the fast track."

"Wow, I thought he seemed like the shy, retiring type," I replied.

Erskine grinned. He looked to be about fifty, he was balding and carried about twenty pounds too much weight, most of it in his stomach. He seemed tired when he talked. Erskine wasn't an up-and-comer in the department. He wasn't on the fast track to anywhere, except maybe retirement.

"Me, I never cared much for that PR stuff," Erskine said. "I've been on the force for a long time. I always figured that if I did my job well, that was all that mattered. The rest of it – promotions, awards, etc. – would all take care of itself."

"That sounds reasonable to me."

"You think so? Well, the lieutenant there is fifteen years younger than me – and they're already talking about making him a captain. So who's the smart one?"

Aguirre came back carrying two cups of coffee. He handed one of them to me. The coffee looked terrible and tasted even worse, but drinking coffee was part of the cop–reporter mating ritual. I had spent hours and hours drinking bad coffee in precinct houses all over the city. Because when a cop offers you a cup of coffee, it's a kind of peace offering. A bonding thing. It means he's taking you into his confidence, letting you into the inner circle, accepting you into the cop world. At least for a little while. So I sipped slowly on the coffee and listened as Aguirre talked about everything he'd found out.

"Okay, her name is Cheryl Lee Barrett," Aguirre said, occasionally looking down at a file on his desk as he talked. "She's from Kettering, Ohio – a little town outside of Dayton. Lived in Chicago for a while. Then L.A., Santa Barbara and a few other places in Southern California. She came to New York about five months ago. Don't you want to know how we found all this out?"

"How?"

"Fingerprints. No reason to check them the first time. I mean the senator's kid and a lot of other people in Lansdale's office told us who she was. Or at least who they thought she was. Once we knew that wasn't true, the rest of it was easy. We ran the fingerprints through the whole network – and suddenly we got all sorts of hits. I mean, we were able to track this Barrett broad all across the country. Of course, the girl's fingerprints would have only turned up as a match in the computer base if they were already there for something else. In other words, she had to have—"

"A criminal record," I said.

"Bingo! You are a smart girl, Tucker. Yeah, Cheryl Lee Barrett had a criminal record." He began reading from the file in front of him. "Loitering and resisting arrest, Dayton, Ohio. Unlawful solicitation for a sex act, Chicago. Prostitution and solicitation charges, Los Angeles…" He looked up. "Well, anyway, you get the idea."

"My God, she was a hooker!"

"There's more," Aguirre said with a big smile.

He was enjoying this. Giving it out slowly, piece by piece. But he had information I didn't have – and needed for my story. The only way I was going to find it out was to sit quietly and let him play out his entire little routine.

"Okay, we got another match on the fingerprints from another police department database. At first, we figured it was just going to be one more prostitution bust. But this one is serious stuff. A murder. California authorities were definitely looking for our girl. It seems someone murdered her pimp, stole his money – and she hasn't been heard from since. There's been a warrant out for her arrest as a suspect in the killing since January."

"Where in California did this murder take place?"

"Santa Barbara."

The same place that Margaret Kincaid died in a traffic accident two years ago. Maybe she'd seen the picture of the Kincaid woman in the newspaper ad and decided she looked enough like her to use her identity when she came to New York.

"But how would she have got hold of Margaret Kincaid's ID? And she must have needed an ID to work for a U.S. senator…"

Aguirre rolled his eyes dramatically. "Do you have any idea how easy it is to get a phony ID these days? Especially a driver's license? Identity theft is everywhere. Maybe the real Margaret Kincaid's ID was stolen, or maybe it was just copied and Cheryl bought a fake off the black market."

"Okay."

"There's still something wrong with this scenario though."

"What?" I was getting tired of playing this game with Aguirre, but didn't want him to stop talking.

"The money."

"You mean the money she stole in the murder. How much was it?"

"That's just it," he said. "It was hardly anything. A couple hundred or so. Then, a few weeks later, she turns up in New York City and gets a job first as a volunteer – then as a full-time staffer – in the campaign office of Senator Frank Lansdale, who's running for re-election this year. She rents a fancy apartment in Manhattan, starts wearing the latest designer clothes to the office and flashes all sorts of expensive jewelry.

"And what was she even doing working in Senator Lansdale's office?" he continued. "I mean, here she is dating the senator's son. She's suddenly got all this money. Where did she get it all and what the hell was she doing here anyway?

"Of course," Aguirre shrugged, "none of this has anything to do with her murder. We know who did it. No problem there. Joseph Enrico was a career criminal who was looking for a quick score and she just happened to be the victim. It didn't matter to him whether she was Margaret Kincaid or Cheryl Lee Barrett. So all of this is irrelevant in the end. We're just jerking ourselves off here. Right?"

"You're right," I agreed.

"It all adds up to absolutely nothing."

"Nothing at all," I said.

CHAPTER 13

My apartment was in Gramercy Park, on a quiet little street called Irving Place, which was just six blocks long from the park south to 14th Street. Not nearly as much traffic or people on the street as in the rest of the city – sometimes it seemed like my own little oasis in the heart of Manhattan.

I was on the top floor of a brownstone, which gave me a view of the Empire State Building in the distance and Gramercy Park itself from my living room window. I'd got lucky finding this apartment after I'd moved out of my old Upper East Side place near the park – too many bad memories. I'd looked around at a few other locations, but the minute I saw this apartment – and the area around it – I knew it was where I wanted to live.

It was technically a one-bedroom, but there was also an alcove big enough for me to use as my home office. The alcove was supposed to be a dining area, and the previous tenants had eaten off a big table there. But because I wasn't the dinner party type, I had replaced that with a desk, computer table and filing cabinets to keep all of my papers. There was a full kitchen too, which was unusual for a Manhattan apartment.

Both the living room and the bedroom were filled with books. I'd had shelves built for them soon after I moved in. I loved having all these books so close to me, and I also loved the feeling it gave the apartment. Books are great for that. I also had two big flat-screen TVs – one in the living room and another in the bedroom – that I could use to follow the news when I was working out at home.

It was comfortable, not that far from my office at Rockefeller Center and I guess I just enjoyed the solace of being there alone.

Like I was now, doing my morning exercises on the equipment I had in the bedroom. My morning routine was always the same.

I got up early – anywhere from 5:30 to 6:30 a.m. – and did at least one hour of exercise before I went to work. I warmed up with twenty minutes or so of pedaling on the stationary bike in front of the TV. Watching the morning news made the repetitive boredom of the exercise more bearable. After that, it was sit-ups followed by pushups.

On Mondays, Wednesdays and Fridays I went to the gym. As I said, I liked all the cardio activities I could do there on treadmills and bikes and the rest, but I also still loved the intensity of doing heavy sets on the leg press and the leg curl machines in the weight room. I'd gained considerable strength in my lower body and enjoyed the sensation of being able to push myself to the limit. This gave me a sense of control that I often didn't feel in other aspects of my life.

I swam on Tuesdays and Thursdays, doing laps that sometimes left me so exhausted that I was ready to go back to bed rather than begin a long day of work at the *Tribune*.

It was all worth it to me.

Because I knew the exercise was what had helped me get my life back after the terrible thing that had happened.

I still remember waking up in that hospital bed and the long, grueling struggle I went through to learn how to walk again. Hell, it wasn't just that I couldn't walk after all the injuries – physical and emotional – that I'd suffered. I couldn't even take a single step.

"Jessie, you need to force yourself to get out of that bed and try to walk again," Dr. Spitz told me at some point during my recovery.

"I can't," I said.

"One step, you only have to take one step, okay?"

"I'll fall."

"If you do, I'll catch you.'

I did fall the first time. And Dr. Spitz did catch me. I started crying then. I didn't want to do this. It hurt too much. I wanted to go back to bed and sleep forever.

But Dr. Spitz made me try again the next day. I fell then too. And the day after that. And the fourth day. Then, on the fifth day, I somehow managed to take an entire step without any help from her. It seemed like the most momentous achievement of my life.

"That first step is the toughest, Jessie," Dr. Spitz told me encouragingly. "They get easier after that."

Sure enough, pretty soon I was walking again. A little wobbly and uncertain of myself, but still walking. It was an arduous and frustrating struggle for me to get through all of the physical rehabilitation I needed. More than once, I burst into tears when things didn't go well. It wasn't only because of the physical pain. It was the emotional pain I was going through too. I was so sad and lonely and filled with self-pity about my life and – even more importantly – about my future.

I couldn't stop thinking about Gary Bettig. How he'd abandoned me in my time of need, just like my father had abandoned my mother and me. I used to lie in my bed at the hospital and fantasize various scenarios involving Gary Bettig. In some of them, I would murder him – or at least hurt him very badly – to make him pay for what he'd done. Other times, I imagined he came back to me pleading for forgiveness and telling me how much he loved me and couldn't live without me. I was never sure which fantasy was the most satisfying. But I desperately needed some kind of closure, and I never got it. Just like my mother had never gotten closure with my dad.

My mother was no help when Gary dumped me either. You have to understand something about my mother. After my father left her, she became totally focused on – okay, obsessed with – turning me into the perfect daughter. Which wasn't a good thing for a girl growing up. If I got six As on my report card, she wanted to know why I didn't get 7 As. When I finished runner-up as a silver medal winner in the county swimming competition, she told me I should have swam faster and won the gold medal. The head of the school debating team took me to my senior prom, but my mother said I should have held out for the student class president to ask me.

I always wondered why she'd become so consumed with the idea of perfection in me. I had always wanted to think it was because she wanted to make me into a better person. But I finally realized it was all about her – not about me at all. She had been devastated when my father left her. And so, she somehow rationalized, if she couldn't be a perfect wife, she could still be a perfect mother – which meant I had to be perfect too. Weird, huh? If she were still alive, maybe we could go on *Dr. Phil* or something and talk it out. But it's too late for that.

Which is why, I guess, she couldn't handle my being battered and bruised and broken in that hospital bed. She wanted her daughter to be perfect. And I wasn't perfect anymore.

I've always wondered if Dr. Spitz showed me so much compassion and support because she had some sort of deeper understanding of the hellish ordeal I'd lived through… But in any case, Dr. Janet Spitz was a wonderful doctor and – even more importantly – a wonderful human being.

"You got a second chance, Jessie," Dr. Spitz had told me early on in my rehab when I complained about the exercising. "Not too many people get a second chance like you did. So enjoy it, savor it, live every day to the fullest. You never know how long it's going to last."

And that's what I did.

I wondered if Dr. Spitz had followed her own advice. If she'd enjoyed her last day of life before being gunned down in that McDonald's robbery. I hoped so. I'd long ago stopped wondering how a good, decent caring person like Dr. Janet Spitz – who'd helped so many people – could die so senselessly like that.

I'd seen a lot of people die in my job as a reporter who shouldn't have died.

But it always hurt the most when it was someone you knew – and really cared about – like Dr. Spitz.

Life is unfair, someone once said. Sometimes the good do die young.

But I was still alive.

That was the important thing to remember now.

CHAPTER 14

The memorial service for Cheryl Lee Barrett was held at a funeral home on Lexington Avenue.

Jonathan Lansdale had made the arrangements in the first few days after the murder, before he knew the truth about her double life and secret past as a prostitute and accused murderer. Once the truth did come out, after my story ran, he decided to go ahead with the service anyway. He delivered the eulogy for the woman who he said was his girlfriend. He said her murder – no matter who she really had been in another life – was a terrible tragedy. He said we shouldn't be too quick to judge her harshly because we still didn't know the truth about her. He said we all had good and bad in us, and that he believed she was basically a good person. He said a lot of other things too, but I wasn't really paying attention. I was more interested in watching the people who had turned out to pay their last respects.

Senator Lansdale was there, sitting in the front row with his wife and two college-aged daughters. Mrs. Lansdale was on the far side of fifty, but she looked pretty good. She had platinum-blonde hair and a still-firm body that looked as if she spent a lot of time in the gym or maybe under the plastic surgeon's knife. I'd seen pictures of her before. She was very active in social events and church activities – even teaching Bible classes – while the senator was in Washington. The daughters were attractive, too. All in all, it looked like the perfect All-American family. Except for Jonathan, who still looked a bit geeky to me.

Mayor Hanrahan was there too, sitting next to his wife Christine and Libby St. John and an entourage of several other aides. I smiled to myself when I saw him. Hanrahan went to every major funeral in New York City. Cops, crime victims, even a few gangland hits. He'd told me once that he had probably gone to more than a thousand funerals during his years as mayor. "And it was almost a thousand-and-one," he said. "Because I would have gone to yours. Thank God I didn't have to." I told him I was pretty glad about that too.

All the people who were there were ones who knew the dead woman as Margaret Kincaid. There was no one from Cheryl Lee Barrett's past. No relatives, no friends, no johns from her working-girl days. I heard that the only living relative that she had was a mother back in Kettering, Ohio. The mother had been notified by police of her death, but Lieutenant Aguirre said she told him she was too busy to get involved in the funeral. It must have been a beautiful mother–daughter relationship, Aguirre had snorted as he related the conversation.

There was one person at the funeral who was a surprise. Logan Kincaid. He was sitting about ten rows back, behind Hanrahan and Lansdale, listening intently to the proceedings. Kincaid was more dressed up this time. He was wearing a dark, pinstriped sports jacket, charcoal slacks and an open-collared white shirt. He looked good. But the woman who had called herself Margaret Kincaid wasn't really his sister. She was just an imposter. So what was he doing here?

Maybe I should ask him.

But my first priority was Senator Lansdale. I waited until the service was over, then positioned myself by the door so that he would have to pass by me on the way out of the funeral home. I hoped I could get him away from his family. I needed his full attention.

"Senator!" I yelled out when he got close to the door. "How are you?"

He looked over in my direction. At first, I didn't think he recognized me, but he smiled anyway and gave a big wave. Always the consummate politician.

"It's Jessie Tucker," I said. "From the *New York Tribune*. I interviewed you once a few years ago?"

"Jessie, of course!" He was smiling even more broadly now. "Great to see you! You look terrific!"

I made my way through the crowd to get closer to him. I limped deliberately as I did so. Lansdale noticed the limp and grimaced in sympathy. That was good. I wanted him to feel sorry for me. I needed every advantage I could find.

"My condolences, Senator," I said, nodding toward the casket. "I realize this must have been very difficult for you and your son."

"A terrible shock. Two shocks really. First the murder. Then all these things about her past." He shook his head sadly. "I guess you never can really be sure about some people…"

"Did you know her well?" I asked.

"I just know she was a very loyal campaign aide. And, of course, I know that my son was quite fond of her. But other than that… No, I guess I didn't know her much at all."

Lansdale was still smiling. Distractedly, he looked around at the other people leaving and searched for familiar faces, working the room all the time.

"Did you ever spend much time alone with her?"

"No." He seemed startled by the question. "Not really."

"So your relationship was always just about business?"

"Of course."

"Then why did the two of you have an argument just a few hours before she was murdered?"

"I don't know what you're talking about," he said.

He wasn't smiling anymore.

"You were seen having a loud fight with her at a printing shop on the same night that she died."

"That's not true."

"I saw the video, Senator."

"Video? You saw the video?"

"Yes, I saw the video."

"But how…"

He looked visibly distressed now.

"I don't know about any video," he said quickly then.

There was a whirlwind of activity happening around us. Jonathan Lansdale grabbed his father by the arm and began pushing him out the door. His wife and his two daughters hurried after him, looks of confusion on their faces. A bodyguard suddenly stepped in front of me and stopped me from following. Lansdale and his family jumped into a waiting limousine without looking back. The door of the limousine slammed shut. Then the car peeled away from the curb and sped down the street.

"What was that all about?" Jack Hanrahan asked.

I turned around and saw the mayor standing behind me. He'd been watching the whole thing. He had a bemused expression on his face. I remembered hearing somewhere there was no love lost between him and Senator Lansdale even though they belonged to the same party.

"It's called being a nosy reporter," I said.

"You do that very well."

"I've had a lot of practice." I laughed.

"Do you know something about the death of this girl that the rest of us don't know?" Hanrahan asked.

"Not yet."

"Well, tell me if you do."

"You'll be the first to know, Mr. Mayor."

Libby St. John was there now too.

"That was some scene there, Jessie," she said.

"I don't like Senator Landsale," I said.

"No one does." Hanrahan laughed.

"So why does he keep getting elected?"

The mayor smiled at the question. "Oh, on the surface, Lansdale seems like a good guy – Gulf War hero, successful businessman, dedicated, God-fearing family man. The voters love him. Me, I don't like him very much either."

"How come?"

"Let's say I have my reasons."

"Such as?"

"Like I said, sometimes you have to scratch under the surface to find out the truth about a person."

I wanted to ask him more about that, but Mrs. Hanrahan joined us at that point.

"Jessie Tucker, it seems like ages since you've been over to Gracie Mansion for dinner," Christine Hanrahan said. "We used to see you all the time. Now you hardly ever stop by. How long has it been, anyway?"

"Too long," I admitted.

"Did Jack tell you? We now have a weekend place up in Westchester County that we really love." She winked. "You have to come up and visit us there too."

"I'll try to do that very soon."

After saying goodbye to the Hanrahans, I spotted Logan Kincaid loitering on the sidewalk outside the funeral home. I walked over to him.

"Would you like to get some coffee?" I asked him.

"Love to."

"Good, because I want to talk to you about something."

"What?"

"Your sister."

"You found out something new about my sister?"

"That's what I want to talk to you about."

CHAPTER 15

"What do you know about my sister's death?" Kincaid asked.

"Only what you told me."

We were sitting in a coffee shop on Lexington across the street from the funeral home.

"I'm trying to find out some answers about who killed the woman who was using your dead sister's name. Finding out more about your sister might give me a lead on how to do that. I don't know whether you can help me or not, but I want to find out. Maybe we can help each other. Anyway, I thought it was worth a try."

"In other words," Kincaid asked, taking a sip of his coffee, "you're just grasping at straws?"

"Something like that."

"Me too," he said.

Then he started telling me more about his sister and her death.

"The thing is," Kincaid said slowly, "I really hoped this thing with the dead woman in the park using my sister's name was going to be some kind of breakthrough. I've been consumed by this thing for two years. My sister was a radiant, fun-loving, wonderful person. When she died, it was like a piece of me died too. I couldn't bring her back. But I could track down whoever did this terrible thing to her and bring them to justice.

"Only I never got anywhere. I believed in the cops at first. I kept thinking during those first few weeks after it happened that they'd get a tip or a clue or some sort of break in the case. But after a while – with nothing happening at all in the case – I pretty much gave up on them. They gave up too, I think. Oh, they kept telling me the file was still open. But there were new crimes, new cases – and no one seemed to give a whole lot of priority to just one more drunk driving case.

"I hired some private investigators next. I hoped that if I was paying someone, maybe they'd be more motivated than a regular cop. I tried a few of them, but they all came up with nothing too. They took my money though. A lot of my money. Eventually I decided I'd be better off spending the money myself. So I started looking on my own.

"I'm an architect and I had a job with a big architectural firm in Southern California at the time. I had some vacation time coming, so I took that first. After that, I took a temporary leave of absence. Eventually all of my time ran out, and most of my money. I lost my job, my savings, even my wife – and I still have nothing to show for it."

"Your wife?" I asked.

I tried to make the question sound casual.

"Yes, she left me – told me I was obsessed. Maybe she was right. I just couldn't live with the thought that this creep was still out there and getting away with taking away the life of a beautiful person like my sister Margaret."

"I'm sorry about your marriage," I said.

"Things happen."

A waitress came by and asked us if we wanted refills of our coffee. I quickly said yes.

"You were my last hope," Kincaid said, after the waitress had left. "When I found out about the dead woman here in New York – and I realized she'd taken my sister's name – I hoped there might be some connection to her death. That's why I came to you the other day. But if there is, I can't find it. Cheryl Lee Barrett was on the run, she needed a new identity and so she took my sister's. End of story. Now I'm right back where I started. With nothing."

"Why did you go to her funeral?"

"I don't know." He shrugged. "It just seemed like something I needed to do. To give it all a sense of closure."

"Then what are you going to do now?"

"Keep looking for my sister's killer."

I took a deep breath. "Look, maybe your ex-wife was right. Maybe you need to forget about what happened to your sister and put it behind you. Maybe it's time to just get on with your life."

"Is that what you would do?"

"Yes."

"I don't believe you." Kincaid smiled across the table. "After we talked the other day, I read up on you. I was curious. You were kind of famous there for a while, weren't you?"

"There are better ways of becoming famous than nearly dying," I said.

"But you didn't die. You survived."

"Yeah, I survived."

"And they caught the person who did this to you right away?"

"That's right."

"What if they hadn't caught him? Would you have been all right with that? Would you have been able to get on with the rest of your life? Would you have been able to just walk away from it – the way you want me to?"

"No," I said, "I wouldn't. I would never have rested until he was behind bars. No matter how long it took."

"Exactly."

He asked me some questions then about my attack. I answered them openly. More openly than I did with most people who suddenly realized who I was. I wasn't sure why. I'd only met him before the one time in the *Tribune* office. But I liked him.

Finally he asked me the question that was the toughest part for me to talk about.

"Did he… did he… do things to you?"

"You mean sexually?"

"Yes."

"Sort of."

He didn't understand.

"The thing is," I said, suddenly visualizing waking up in the park all over again, "I don't remember a lot of what happened. I remember he ripped my skirt while he was hitting me – and then I lost consciousness. They told me later that there was no physical evidence of rape. I don't know why he stopped."

"Just like the woman who was using my sister's name."

"Yeah, kind of weird, huh? I figure that whoever killed Cheryl Lee Barrett didn't have time to finish, so to speak. But what about me? Did someone come along that night too before he was finished with me? I used to think about that all the time. Sitting there in that hospital bed, going over it and over it again a million times in my mind. Why did he do it? If it wasn't for sex, what was it? I was only carrying a small amount of money and my jewelry was hardly worth anything. And if it was for sex, why didn't he finish the job? I never did find out the answer."

"I guess something like that leaves a lot of psychological damage for a long time."

"You might say that."

"But you're OK now?"

I wasn't sure how to answer that. Did I tell him that it took me five years before I was able to work up the courage to go out on a date with a man? Even longer before I could think about having sex again. And that even now – twelve years later – I still had not had a boyfriend since that terrible night in the park. Did I tell him about the nightmares? The way I sometimes woke up in bed screaming and gasping for breath? The fear that was a constant companion to me now whenever I was alone in the dark? Probably not a good idea.

"I'm fine."

My cell phone rang. I took it out and looked at who was calling. Norman Isaacs. I didn't want to answer it, but knew I had to. I had a pretty good idea what his call was about.

"What the hell did you think you were doing at the funeral, Jessie?" he yelled at me once I was on the line. "Harassing the senator? I just heard about it."

"All I did was ask him some questions, Norman."

"I thought we agreed you weren't going to pursue this whole crazy Lansdale angle of yours anymore."

"You told me I had until the end of the week to come up with a story. Lansdale is part of the Cheryl Lee Barrett case. I'm trying to get some answers."

"Yeah, well, I'm thinking now maybe that wasn't such a good idea for me to allow you to keep working on it at all."

"C'mon, Norman—"

"You better make damn sure you stay away from Senator Lansdale from now on!"

He hung up on me then.

"Problem?" Kincaid asked me.

"My boss. He thinks I've become obsessed with this story."

"Sounds like my ex-wife."

"I know why I'm so interested in this," I told him. "Besides the fact that it's a good story, I really feel myself relating to Cheryl Lee Barrett because what happened to her in that park was so similar to what happened to me. Except she died, and I lived. No question about it, that has played a big part in this for me. But what about you? I don't understand why you would care at all about Cheryl Lee Barrett. Enough to come here and go to her funeral."

"I'm not sure. I guess I really thought that the stolen identity thing had to be more than coincidence, and that maybe I could get some answers for my case by helping you on this one. I didn't get any answers on my sister. But here I am still spending time with you. Maybe I just enjoy spending time with you."

He smiled when he said that, and pushed back his hair. I smiled back. I wasn't exactly sure what was going on here, but I liked it.

I was still a bit shook up from my phone call with Isaacs – I knew I was on my own now. I had so many things going through my head – Cheryl Lee Barrett, Senator Lansdale, Enrico… I felt like I might explode if I didn't talk to someone about this case.

"What are you thinking about?" Kincaid asked, stirring his coffee.

"I'm glad you asked."

There was something bothering me. Something that Senator Lansdale had said. It had been nagging at me ever since our confrontation at the funeral service, but I couldn't quite put my finger on it. Now I remembered what it was. I told Kincaid some of the things I'd found out about Lansdale and the dead woman. Then I repeated what Lansdale had said when I told him I'd seen him and the dead woman on the video at the print shop.

"He seemed surprised," I said. "Not that there was a video. But that I'd seen it. Then he must have realized what he was saying because he denied knowing anything about a video. What I didn't realize at the time was that he must have been talking about a *different* video."

"There're two videos?"

"There has to be. Lansdale wouldn't know about some security video at a printing store. No, he must have been referring to another video. One that I don't know about."

"What do you think is on it?"

"I don't know, but I have a pretty good hunch…"

"Sex?"

"That would be my bet."

"So where is this video?"

I had been thinking about that too.

"Maybe in Cheryl Lee Barrett's stuff. At her apartment. They probably haven't had time to clear it out yet."

"Wouldn't the police have already searched there?"

"Not necessarily. The cops already found the guy they say killed her – Joseph Enrico – within hours of the murder. And now he's dead. There's no reason for them to be looking for clues or evidence or anything like that. This is an open and shut case, remember? The file is closed."

I was getting really excited now as I talked about it. I felt that surge of adrenaline I always got at key moments on a big story. Sure, it was a long shot. But it felt good to me. It felt right. I was just going to roll the dice and see what happened.

"So how do you get inside the apartment?" Kincaid wanted to know.

"Ask the landlord."

"And you figure he'll just open up the dead woman's apartment to a reporter?"

"No," I smiled at him, "to her brother."

CHAPTER 16

The landlord turned out to be easy.

No, he told us, no one had come to claim Margaret Kincaid's belongings. He said he'd heard about her murder on television, but that was really all he knew about what happened to her. He said he had been trying to decide what to do about the apartment and her things inside. The rent was paid up until the end of the month, but he was anxious to rent it to a new tenant as soon as possible.

I realized as he talked – referring to the dead woman as Margaret Kincaid – that he hadn't heard any of the new revelations about her identity and secret past life as a prostitute named Cheryl Lee Barrett.

Which was good.

Of course, the landlord probably would have let us inside anyway – he was that anxious to do something about it all – but it was a piece of cake when he found out that Kincaid was the dead woman's "brother".

"I'm very sorry for your loss."

"Thank you," Kincaid said, playing his part perfectly. "It's been a terrible shock."

"If there's anything I can to do help you—"

"Well, I'd like to see my sister's apartment," Kincaid said. "To get a look at the place where she lived."

"I understand," the landlord said sympathetically.

"Some of the things she kept there were very important to her. I want to have them as a memory of her. It's all I have left of Margaret now."

*

The apartment was a spacious one-bedroom, with a full kitchen, a den area off the living room and a nice view of Lower Manhattan. I thought again about how a young woman who had just started working as a Senate campaign aide a few months earlier had been able to afford something like this. I wondered if Senator Lansdale was paying the bills. There might even be some evidence of that here.

We started in the living room, which was really a mess; Cheryl Lee Barrett apparently had not been much of a housekeeper. Clothes, books and makeup were strewn around. The books were about fitness, diet and pop psychology. Nothing about politics or current events, even though she'd gone to work for a U.S. senator. There were some DVDs next to the TV, but nothing of interest. Nothing that looked like a sex video.

The den area didn't tell us much either, at first. There was a laptop on her desk. I figured that was my best bet to find the video I was looking for. Especially after I opened it and found I was able to view her files without a password. But there was no video I could find there either. Damn. Maybe she'd hid it somewhere in case anyone did what I was doing now… but where?

In one of the drawers of the desk, I found receipts for her rent. It was always paid in cash, so it didn't give any clue about where the money came from. Neither did anything else in a checkbook or the bills I found. The bills were for very expensive items – designer clothes, fancy jewelry, a reservation for a cruise to the Caribbean in the fall that she would never take now. I still wasn't sure where Cheryl Lee's money came from, but the woman sure knew how to spend it.

At one point, while we were searching the apartment, my hand touched Logan's as we were reaching for the same thing. It was only for a few seconds. But he looked at me – and I looked back at him. It was a nice moment. I couldn't help but hope that we'd have more nice moments like that – I didn't know him very well, but I was glad we were working together on this.

We were almost finished in the den when I stumbled across the picture. It was stuck in a drawer of the desk. It looked worn and very old. Cheryl Lee wasn't in the picture. There were two men, both wearing army uniforms. One of them was an officer, the other an enlisted man. They were shaking hands and posing for the camera. There was an army truck parked in the desert behind them. One of the men in the picture seemed very familiar, but I couldn't quite place him.

There was an inscription on the back of the picture that read:

Dear Cheryl,
I love you very much. I can't wait to see you. You may not understand this now, but someday you will.
Love,
Dad

I stared at the picture for a very long time. Then I picked it up and put it in my pocket. I wasn't sure exactly what it meant, but I had a feeling it was important.

In the bedroom, there were lots of clothes. Expensive evening gowns, dresses, sweaters and pants suits. Hundreds of pairs of shoes. And plenty of jewelry. But nothing that would explain why Cheryl Lee Barrett – who called herself Margaret Kincaid – had wound up dead one night in Central Park.

The kitchen didn't provide any clues either. The refrigerator was filled with diet soda, mineral water, yogurt and lots of cottage cheese. Cheryl Lee Barrett seemed to be the kind of woman who was constantly on a diet. *Maybe she had to be*, I thought. You probably didn't get someone to pay for your apartment and buy you clothes and fancy jewelry if you didn't take care of yourself.

Being a kept woman looked like a tough job – the lifestyle was good, but you had to pay a pretty stiff price for it.

I was still convinced a video had to be here somewhere. So Logan and I started all over again. Back through the living room, the den and finally the bedroom. That's when I found it. I was admiring some of the jewelry inside a dresser drawer when I picked up a heart-shaped locket. But this wasn't jewelry at all – it wasn't attached to a chain or anything. I realized then what it really was: a memory stick, which Cheryl Lee Barrett had hidden amongst the jewelry.

I plugged it into the computer, clicked on the file it contained and then looked at what came up on the screen.

A video of Cheryl Lee Barrett.

With Frank Lansdale.

CHAPTER 17

This was the second time in the past few days that I had watched a video of Cheryl Lee Barrett and Frank Lansdale.

The first time, at the print shop, had been an accident – a lucky break that the argument between the two of them had happened to be partially captured by the store's security camera.

This time the video was no accident.

It was shot in a hotel room, probably using a hidden camera. The results weren't exactly Spielberg material. It was, in fact, a very bad porn film. It was ragged, and sometimes out of focus, but it was good enough to see what was going on.

"You think I should make some buttered popcorn while we watch this?" Ellen asked.

We were at her desk in her office with the door closed.

"Be serious," I told her. "I'm not doing this for cheap thrills. This is my job."

"It's a dirty job," Ellen sighed as she looked at what was happening on the screen, "but somebody's gotta do it."

The video had started with just the empty hotel room. That lasted for maybe thirty seconds or so. Then a figure walked into the room. Cheryl Lee Barrett.

She really was a beautiful woman, I thought to myself as she walked over to the bed and sat down on it. In the first video, made by the security camera at the print shop, she had been dressed very modestly for her job as a campaign aide. Now she was dressed for the job she was doing now. A tight, very short leather miniskirt, a sexy, low-cut blouse that showed off her ample cleavage and towering high heels. She fidgeted as she sat on the bed, waiting, looking toward the camera once or twice. Probably wondering if it was working properly.

Finally, after a few minutes of this, there was a knock on the door. Cheryl stood up and went to answer it.

"Okay, here we go," Ellen said, rubbing her hands together in anticipation. "Lights, camera, action."

A man walked into the room.

"Frank Lansdale," I said when I saw his face.

"Who did you think it was going to be – Brad Pitt?" Ellen asked.

I ignored her and concentrated on the action.

Cheryl threw her arms around Lansdale as soon as he came into the room. They kissed. Then his hands began exploring various parts of her body. Her breasts. Her buttocks. Finally, he slid his hand up her miniskirt and began pushing her toward the bed.

"Hasn't this guy ever heard of foreplay?" Ellen asked.

"Maybe he's very busy."

"Oh yeah, he's a U.S. senator, isn't he? Probably has to rush back to Washington after this to spend millions of our tax dollars on a nuclear missile system or something. Of course, he looks more interested in launching a missile between Cheryl's legs right now, huh?"

"Shut up, Ellen!" I hissed at her.

They were really going at it on the screen now. Lansdale had pushed her onto the bed. She rolled over on her back and spread her legs seductively – almost daring the senator to take her. He didn't need any urging. They rolled around on the bed, and pretty soon her clothes began coming off. The blouse first. Then the miniskirt. Finally, her stockings and bra and panties. Lansdale stood up and hurriedly took off his clothes too. When he did that, I could see that Frank Lansdale had a very large erection.

"Wow," Ellen said, when she saw that, "he's sure got my vote."

"You don't feel this is just a little bit gross? The man's married, for God's sake! And he's twice her age!"

"He's just following in the footsteps of some of our greatest politicians. John F. Kennedy. Bill Clinton, Donald Trump…" Ellen looked over again at the screen where Lansdale had jumped back into bed on top of Cheryl. "Yep, I'd say our boy here is definitely White House material."

The action was getting serious now. He was inside her, pumping rhythmically as she cried out in passion. Was Cheryl acting? Or was she really into it? Whatever it was, she was very good. But then she'd been a hooker for most of her life. She'd had lots of practice.

It lasted for a while. When it was over, Lansdale very quickly put his clothes back on. He leaned over and kissed her on the cheek. Then he was gone. Cheryl Lee Barrett was still naked on the bed.

"Wham, bam, thank you, ma'am," Ellen said. "He's not much on cuddling or sweet talk afterward, is he? I'm surprised he didn't leave money on the table next to the bed."

"I'm not sure they have that arrangement," I said.

"So, what did Cheryl get out of this besides a quick roll in the hay with a United States senator?"

"How about an apartment? Lots of nice clothes? Expensive jewelry? I think we just saw what Cheryl Lee Barrett's real job was with the Lansdale campaign."

There were three more videos. All of them similar to the first one. The couple would meet – sometimes in a hotel room, once at Cheryl's apartment – and get it on. It wasn't clear who had set up the camera – either Cheryl herself or an accomplice she was working with. But it was obvious she knew what was going on. The question was why.

"Blackmail?" Ellen asked. "That seems to be the most likely scenario to me. She shakes him down by threatening to go to his wife or the press with these tapes. It kind of ruins that clean, wholesome family image of his, don't you think?"

"Maybe," I said. "Or else it was insurance. Something Cheryl wanted to protect herself in case she got into trouble and needed some kind of edge. Something to deal with."

"Protection against what?"

"Maybe the murder charge she was running from, or something else we don't know about yet."

"What are you going to do with the tapes?" Ellen asked.

I shrugged. "I'm not sure yet."

"Did you watch these with this Logan Kincaid guy? I mean he was in the dead woman's apartment with you when you found them."

"No, we wanted to get out of there as fast as possible so we wouldn't get caught."

"Too bad. It might have given him some good ideas for the two of you…"

I sighed.

"Just back off, huh, Ellen? This is my life we're talking about here, not yours. Let me live it my own way."

Before I left, I showed Ellen the picture – with the inscription that said "Love, Dad" on it – that I'd taken from Cheryl Lee Barrett's desk.

"It took me a little while, but I finally figured out who that one is," I said, pointing to the army officer in the picture. "It's Frank Lansdale. A younger Frank Lansdale."

"You think Frank Lansdale might have been her father?" Ellen asked. "Now that's heavy."

I shook my head no. "Actually, that was the first thing that crossed my mind too. But I think her father was probably the other guy. The second man in the picture. He's got blond hair just like her, there's even a pretty strong facial resemblance when you look at him closely. The uniform he's wearing, the desert terrain that's in the background – I'm pretty sure this was taken in Iraq. This guy looks like he probably was about the same age as Cheryl when she died. Yeah, I'd say it's her father."

"Let me get this straight," Ellen said, putting her elbows on the table and swinging her legs. "This woman's father served with Frank Lansdale in the Gulf War when she was a baby. All this time later, she travels across the country to come and work for him. She has an affair with him and she secretly makes sex videos – either by herself or with an accomplice – of the whole thing. Either, you say, for blackmail or some kind of protection. Then she winds up dead. What in the hell is going on here anyway?"

"That's what I need to find out," I told her.

CHAPTER 18

That night, I had a nightmare.

I'd gone to bed excited about a lot of things – the big story I was working on, my brief moments of flirtation (or whatever it was) with Logan Kincaid and all the other things that had happened over the past few days.

Those were the kinds of things I wanted to dream about.

But instead I wound up having another dream about what happened to me that long-ago night in Central Park.

The nightmares came less frequently now. Sometimes I went weeks – or even months – without having one. But they never went away completely. It was like a scar that wouldn't heal. The doctors who had fixed me up told me everything was going to be fine, but those doctors only knew about the wounds they could see with their eyes or their medical instruments. They didn't know about what was inside of me.

And the truth is that I wasn't fine.

The dreams actually first started while I was still in a coma, hovering between life and death in the hospital during those few weeks after the attack. But back then I had trouble distinguishing between dreams and reality. I didn't even know who I was. Or why I was there. The dreams were my world, the hospital seemed to be a fantasy.

Later, I realized they were only terrible nightmares, but that didn't help me to deal with them. I became an insomniac, staying up late into the night because I was afraid to go to sleep. I sometimes watched TV or read into the early morning hours. I would do anything to avoid closing my eyes and coming face to face with my demons one more time. Of course, I told the doctors about the dreams. But they never had any solution. Just the usual clichés about how time heals all wounds.

Time had helped.

Like I said, the dreams became fewer as the years went by. The intensity of them seemed to diminish too. Sometimes I realized – even while I was still asleep – that I was only having a dream. That this wasn't really happening. That I would wake up in a few minutes and be in my own bedroom. But the fear was still there. The fear that it was happening all over again. And the fear that it somehow wasn't over yet.

Sure, the man who did this to me was sent to jail and now was dead. But I never really felt it was totally resolved for me. The memories of that night – and all the questions I still had about it – continued to haunt me even now, although I knew there was no logical reason for me to feel that way.

The dream itself was always pretty much the same.

I was back in the park, and someone was chasing me. No matter how hard I tried, I couldn't seem to get away. My feet felt like cement, my legs like molasses. It was as if every part of my body was moving in slow motion.

Over the years, the images in the dream had become a bit clearer. Like a camera that's out of focus and then begins to adjust the picture. I saw myself running. The trees and grass of the park around me. And the lights of the traffic from a city street, which beckoned tantalizingly in the distance.

Like a life raft to a drowning swimmer. If I could only make it in time…

But I never did. Not in the dream. And not that night in the park when it was happening for real.

Instead, I felt strong hands grab me and pull me down to the ground.

All I remembered after that was the pain.

And the shock.

And finally the darkness.

I had never seen the face of Darryl Jackson – the man who attacked me – in my dreams. This was always a faceless kind of terror. Not that it really mattered, of course. The man who had done this to me was dead. So the fact that I could never see his face in the dream didn't mean anything. I'd seen him in court at the trial and in the park that evening before it happened. That had been enough. Anyway, it was just a dream. Nothing more.

Except there was something different about my dreams now.

I could hear and see things in the dreams I hadn't seen before. More details.

I also hear some of the vile things Darryl Jackson screamed at me while he was doing it – calling me "whore" and "bitch" and "tramp".

And I even see that Darryl Jackson is wearing something on his head. A baseball cap. A New York Yankees baseball cap.

Dr. Spitz used to say that she believed I had buried some of the memories of that night into my deep subconscious in order to avoid the shock of having to deal with the actual reality of it. She predicted that as more time passed, all the memories from the night of the attack would eventually come back to me.

I hope she was wrong about that. Some things are better left untouched.

CHAPTER 19

There were a lot of stories and information about Frank Lansdale online.

He'd been a senator for a long time, and a successful business-man before that. I found hundreds of items about his business and political dealings. Election runs. Campaign financing. Bills he'd sponsored in the Senate. Political speeches that he'd made. There was no way I could read through everything. But that wasn't what I was looking for anyway.

I added the sub-topic of Iraq to my search, and I got sixty-five hits on the screen. Some of them were just brief mentions of his military record in stories about other subjects. But a dozen or so – a few from a long time ago and some from more current profiles about his life – gave more details about the time he spent in the army.

Lansdale fought in Iraq during the first Gulf War in 1991. He had graduated from Syracuse University the year before, where he'd been commissioned as a second lieutenant in the ROTC program. He was assigned to a unit in the 101st Airborne Division, which was part of Desert Storm – the American and allied military action against Saddam Hussein. It wasn't a very long war – the massive U.S. superiority in technology and military might overran Saddam's troops in just a few weeks.

But there was still room for individual heroics. Brave soldiers who rose to the occasion to do great things that could never be forgotten.

Frank Lansdale was one of those men.

One of the articles in the *Times* talked about how he won a Silver Star for heroism. The headline read:

PROFILE IN COURAGE

By a young lieutenant during Desert Storm

During World War II, John F. Kennedy etched a memorable profile in courage when his boat – *PT 109* – sank in the Pacific. He somehow was able to save the lives of members of his crew after a long ordeal on an island with the Japanese enemy all around him. That amazing feat of heroism eventually carried JFK all the way to the White House.

Frank Lansdale – who has political ambitions these days too – displayed his own "Profile in Courage" as a young military man during the Gulf War against Iraq.

Lt. Frank Lansdale was in charge of a convoy that was ambushed by a huge Iraqi force in the desert near a place called Medina Ridge that was still being controlled by Saddam Hussein's government. The enemy was all around them before they knew what had happened. Many of the members of Lansdale's squad were killed within the first few minutes of battle. But, despite suffering these heavy casualties and facing overwhelming odds, he was able to escape the ambush and lead a group of survivors through a torturous trek on foot across the desert until they were able to reach an American base camp.

Military observers called it an amazing feat of heroism and leadership by the young lieutenant.

"These soldiers are alive today because of what Lt. Lansdale did," said the commander of the American Forces then in Iraq as he honored Lansdale at a ceremony later. "Great men do great things in times of war. There were many American heroes in World Wars I and II, Korea and Vietnam, but we have heroes here in this war too. Lt. Frank Lansdale is a hero. America is very proud of him."

It was an impressive war record. Certainly not the record of a man who years later would murder a woman he was having an affair with and then frame an ex-convict for the killing. Or was it? Nobody was perfect. Not even war heroes and U.S. senators.

I skimmed through the rest of the items I found online.

There were stories about him leaving the army, then starting his own construction business which made him a multi-millionaire. Many of the apartment and office buildings in New York City had been built by the Lansdale Construction Company.

Later, he ran for Congress and was elected. After serving a few terms in the House of Representatives, he won a hotly contested three-way primary race for the Senate and then a narrow victory in the fall election. He was re-elected again six years later, and now he was running for a third term. The voters seemed to like him anyway; he'd never lost an election.

The closest he'd come to leaving office was this past year when there had been a lot of speculation that Jack Hanrahan would run against him. Hanrahan was a popular mayor. But the law only allowed him to serve three terms – he'd be out of office soon. A lot of people thought he could have beaten Lansdale in a head-to-head battle.

But, several months before the election, Hanrahan announced he had no interest in a Senate seat. Lansdale now was expected to win easily against his opponent in the fall. Some people were saying he could even be a future candidate for the White House.

Reading about it now, I suddenly wondered why Hanrahan had pulled out of the Senate race. Libby St. John hadn't mentioned that during our phone conversation about Lansdale, and the mayor had certainly expressed a dislike for Lansdale at the funeral. I made a note to myself to ask Libby or the mayor more about the Senate decision as soon as I could.

I went through more stories about Lansdale. All of them made interesting reading, but none of them told me anything new about the murder of Cheryl Lee Barrett. Until I found another one on Lansdale's Iraqi war exploits. It told the story of his heroism in the desert again, but this time the article also listed the other soldiers who survived the ordeal with him. Their names were Jack Olsen, Fred Sutter, Scott Barrett and Joseph Enrico.

I stared at the last two names in amazement.

Was Scott Barrett Cheryl Lee's father – the soldier I'd seen with Lansdale in the picture I'd found at the dead woman's apartment?

And Joseph Enrico was the same name as the man who was gunned down by cops after the murder.

It all seemed too incredible to just be a coincidence.

I picked up the phone and called the Veterans Administration offices in Washington, D.C. They have a database there that holds the records of all U.S. servicemen. I'd used it several times before on stories. I told the public relations officer on the other end what I wanted. When he came back with the information, it was pretty much the way I figured it would be.

"The Joseph Enrico you asked about – the one with the later criminal record you described – did serve in Iraq with Lt. Lansdale's unit during Desert Storm," the person on the other end told me.

"And yes, in answer to your other question, there was a Scott Barrett in that unit too. His personnel files say he was from Dayton, Ohio, and he had a wife named Dorothy and a baby daughter listed as Cheryl Lee. Barrett died in action later – after the incident Lansdale won his Silver star for. Does that help you any?"

I thanked him and said that it sure did.

"Oh, there's one more thing here you might be interested in—"

*

I googled the names of Scott Barrett and Joseph Enrico after I got off the phone. There was nothing on Barrett, but that didn't surprise me – I'd just found out he'd been dead since 1991. I didn't expect to find much on Enrico either. He was a small-time criminal and – until the murder in the park and the subsequent shootout with police at the hotel – there really wasn't much about his life that was newsworthy. The media accounts of his death and involvement in the murder over the past few days were there on the computer screen. I had already read most of them. But there was one I hadn't. A long article from the previous Sunday's edition of a small local paper, the *News-Telegram*. I called it up and began to read:

VICTIM OF IRAQ

The Story of One Soldier Whose War Never Ended
By Andrea Gelman

A long time ago, a teenager named Joseph Enrico scored the winning touchdown for Pacific High in the biggest game of the year, with neighboring Santa Rosa. The score was tied 7–7, with only seconds left to play. Enrico faded back to pass, saw that all his teammates were covered and so zigzagged all by himself through the enemy defenders for 57 yards into the end zone. There are people who were there that afternoon and still talk about his memorable run.

This week, Joseph Enrico was killed in a shootout with police in a seedy New York City hotel. They had come to arrest Enrico – who had been in and out of jail most of his life – for the murder of a young woman in Central Park.

What went wrong? How did a one-time high school football hero turn into a tragedy?

People at home who knew Enrico said he'd never been the same since coming back from the first Gulf War nearly three decades ago.

He returned from Iraq and was discharged from the army in the early 90s.

From then until his death he was arrested a total of 17 times – on charges ranging from bookmaking to fraud to drug dealing – and spent most of his life behind bars. He never held a job for more than three months. He had no wife, no family, no known friends of any kind.

"It's like he left a big part of himself back in that war," said one man who knew him in high school. "He was never the same person when he came back."

The strange thing is that no one ever knew what had happened to Enrico during that long-ago war that made him like he was.

People say he never talked about it. If you asked him about Iraq and his time in the army, they'd say, he would just shrug and tell you it was pretty bad for him. Never anything more.

Except for on one occasion.

Jack Billings, who went to high school with Enrico and played with him on the football team, later became a local police officer.

Billings yesterday recalled for the *News-Telegram* the day he arrested Joseph Enrico on a drunk driving charge – and Enrico told him the story about what happened to him in Iraq during Desert Storm.

"He was out on a night patrol that got ambushed," Billings said. "Most of the men in his unit died. It was terrible. But Joey and a few others survived. He said they spent days wandering through the desert before being rescued.

"They kept him in the hospital for a while and eventually discharged him as recovered. But he wasn't. He was never right again."

Billings has a theory about why his old high school classmate chose to shoot it out with the police when they came to arrest him – knowing he must have been writing his own death warrant.

"I think Joey figured he should have died a long time ago back there in that desert in Iraq," Billings said. "That's what drove him nuts. He didn't belong here. In his mind, he belonged back there with his dead platoon. So when he pulled out that gun with the cops – in effect, killing himself right then and there – well, I think he was just sort of putting things in order."

The article jumped to another page. There were several pictures of Enrico that ran with it.

One was Joseph Enrico scoring a touchdown in his high school football uniform and another of him at the high school prom with a pretty date on his arm. There was also a police mugshot from one of the times he had been arrested in his hometown of Santa Barbara.

Santa Barbara.

Joseph Enrico was from Santa Barbara.

Cheryl Lee Barrett had lived in Santa Barbara before she came to New York City as Margaret Kincaid.

The real Margaret Kincaid lived in Santa Barbara too.

Just on a hunch, I punched the name of Senator Frank Lansdale into the computer again, this time cross-referencing it with the town of Santa Barbara. I got one hit. An article from the *News-Telegram* from the previous year. It said that Senator Frank Lansdale of New York had spoken at a nationwide party fundraiser in Santa

Barbara. The date was just a few weeks before Cheryl Lee Barrett left town and later turned up in New York City.

I sat there for a long time trying to make sense of it all.

Frank Lansdale, Joseph Enrico and Scott Barrett – Cheryl Lee's father – had all served in the same army unit in Iraq.

Lansdale had gone on to fame and fortune after, while Enrico's life had been irrevocably damaged by the war and Barrett never made it home.

Now, all these years later, Barrett's daughter had gone to work for Lansdale's Senate campaign, seduced him, made secret videos of their lovemaking – and then been found murdered in what police said was just a random attack.

Except the alleged murderer, Joseph Enrico, had come to New York from Santa Barbara, just like Cheryl Lee Barrett; he'd served in the army with her father and with Lansdale; and Cheryl Lee had apparently been waiting to meet someone – maybe Lansdale or Enrico – in the park just before she was killed.

That sure added up to a lot of coincidences.

CHAPTER 20

A big story is like a jigsaw puzzle. You put the pieces together the best you can, and then you see what's missing. The trick is not to concentrate too much on the pieces that fit. It's the ones that don't fit that you need to worry about. Because they are the solution to the puzzle.

One piece that didn't fit in the Cheryl Lee Barrett puzzle was Jonathan Lansdale, the senator's son.

The official story was that he was the dead woman's boyfriend. They had been involved in a secret romance. Then she was murdered. Jonathan Lansdale said he was devastated at her loss.

Except now I knew it was the father, Senator Frank Lansdale, who had been sleeping with Cheryl Lee.

Of course, the son could have been in on it – a father and son combo. Guys always talked about mother and daughter action – but a woman might be sleeping with both the father and the son too. Except I didn't think so. I had a feeling – call it women's intuition or whatever you want – that there was something else going on in Jonathan Lansdale's sex life.

I knew I had to tread carefully here though. Yes, Isaacs had said I could continue working on the story – but he'd also warned me to stay away from Senator Lansdale. I assumed that warning covered Lansdale's son too. Isaacs could take me off the story at any moment if I kept pushing too hard on the Lansdale angle.

I wished, not for the first time, that Isaacs was a more aggressive editor. But I knew someone who was.

I called Danny Knowlton and told him – without getting into all the details – that I was on the trail of some explosive new information linking Lansdale to Joseph Enrico and the Cheryl Lee Barrett murder story.

"Wow, that sounds like it might be really great!" Knowlton said. "What are you going to do next?"

"I want to go back to his son, Jonathan, again."

"Go for it!" he said, and I could hear the excitement in his voice. He clearly hadn't spoken to Isaacs about me yet. "Let me know what he says. You and me, Jessie – we'll break this story wide open."

I felt a bit badly after I hung up about what I was doing. Playing Knowlton against Isaacs like that. But if this thing blew up in my face, I needed to be able to say I'd cleared what I was doing with an editor. I wasn't sure I could trust Danny Knowlton to stand up for me in a crunch situation, but at least I was covering myself as best I could.

Then I went looking for Jonathan Lansdale.

I found him at a bar in Greenwich Village, near Christopher Street. It was clearly a gay bar. Everyone inside except me was male. The men – many of them dressed in business suits and ties – were at the bar or little tables around it. Some of them held hands, and a few had their arms around each other.

One of those sitting at the bar was Jonathan Lansdale. He was with another man.

I sat down on a bar stool next to him.

"Hello, Jonathan," I said.

He whirled around. There was a look of astonishment on his face as he recognized who I was.

"What are you doing here?" Lansdale blurted out.

"I followed you after you left your father's campaign office."

The man with him was confused.

"Who is she?" he asked.

"She's a newspaper reporter," Lansdale said.

"Did you come here to out Jonathan?" the man asked me.

"Why would you think that?"

"Because you're a reporter and you've been tailing him."

I turned back to Jonathan Lansdale.

"Look, Jonathan, I don't care what you do in your personal life."

"What do you want then?"

"The truth."

"About what?"

"You. Your father. Margaret Kincaid, who later turned out to be Cheryl Lee Barrett. He was the one having the affair with her, wasn't he? You were just the cover story so no one – especially your mother – would ever find out what your father was doing? Am I right or am I right?"

It took a lot of prodding, but eventually – especially after I promised him I would keep his secret, and everything he said would be off the record – he told me everything. About him and Margaret Kincaid/Cheryl Lee Barrett. About how his father had come to him a few months ago with the plan for the two of them – Jonathan and Margaret – to carry on a public romance to divert any attention away from the real affair going on with the senator.

"Why would you do something like that?" I asked. "That's a pretty big thing for him to ask of you, even if he is your father. Why didn't you just tell him you wouldn't do it?"

That's when he told me about his troubled relationship with his father, and how he always desperately wanted to please him. "I never came through for him," Lansdale said sadly. "I knew I was always a disappointment. He's Frank Lansdale, war hero and charismatic senator. Me, I'm not like that. I know that's always bothered him. I tried hard to be the kind of son he wanted, but nothing ever seemed to make him happy. I am what I am. I thought maybe this would make us grow closer. I know that sounds crazy. But I really wanted to make him proud of me. I would do anything for that. Even if it involved helping him cheat on my mother. He's a very persuasive man, my father – as you've probably guessed. I've always done what he wanted me to, if I could. That's why I did this too."

"Does he know about your sexual preference?"

"We never talked about it. But I guess he suspected it. That's why this whole thing with Margaret – or Cheryl Lee or whatever her name really was – was so difficult. The longer the charade dragged on, the less respect he had for me. Like he thought I should have wanted to screw her like he did."

I still didn't understand why his being gay was such a big deal. "Who cares if you're gay?" I asked Lansdale. "Gay marriage is legal. Mainstream, even."

"Not in my family: *our son, the fag*. I knew that was what my parents thought of me. Oh, they didn't actually say it, but they didn't have to. I knew that was what they were thinking – especially my father. My relationship with my father – hell, my whole life – is all one big lie."

What a mess, I thought to myself. A psychiatrist would have a field day with the Lansdale family. But I wasn't here to solve their problems. I needed to find out about Cheryl Lee Barrett. I asked him more about her.

"She was nice. The funny thing is I really got to like her during the time we were putting on this fake romance for everyone to see. She knew I was gay, and we talked about that. I could see why my father was so smitten with her. If he was going to cheat on my mother with a girlfriend, I was glad it was her."

"What happened that last night at the Park Grille?" I asked.

"We were supposed to have dinner. That was for public exposure – to keep up the pretense that we were dating. Then my father would 'accidentally' run into us, and he'd join us for a while. Afterward, I'd go do my thing, and they'd go do theirs. That was the plan anyway. Only it never happened that way."

"Why?"

"She was too upset when she showed up. Christ, she was almost hyperventilating. I'd never seen her that way. She said she was quitting her job with the campaign. She said she was breaking off her relationship with my father. She said everything was different now."

"What was she was so upset about?"

"I don't know. I kept asking her that. But she just got more and more agitated.

"Once or twice she left the table. Finally, she stood up and stormed out of the restaurant for good. That was the last time I ever saw her."

"And you have no idea at all what was bothering her?"

Lansdale thought about it for a second.

"Well, there was one thing she talked about that night."

"What?"

"Iraq," he said.

"The war?"

He nodded.

"She kept talking about my father and the war in Iraq. Like I said, it didn't really make sense – but it was something about the Silver Star my father won over there. She said it wasn't his. She said it really belonged to her father. Then she said something really bizarre. She said… she said that my father had killed her father."

CHAPTER 21

"Are you telling me they gave this guy Lansdale a heroism medal for losing nearly his entire unit?" Logan asked.

"That's war," I told him. "Don't you remember the story about *PT-109* and John F. Kennedy? That made him a hero too. He got a medal for surviving the sinking of his ship in the Pacific during World War II. But there's a lot of people who say that the damn ship wouldn't have sunk in the first place if he hadn't screwed things up. He wound up being president. War's a strange business."

Logan Kincaid and I were sitting outside next to a big fountain on Sixth Avenue, across the street from Rockefeller Center and the Radio City Music Hall. He'd called me earlier to find out how the story was going. I was surprised that he was so interested in the results. When I told him what I'd been up to, he wanted to come to my office and hear all the details. The Cheryl Lee Barrett murder really had nothing to do with the death of his sister, but somewhere along the line he seemed to have begun to identify with the Barrett woman – probably because she had taken his sister's name. Maybe he felt he was somehow doing something for his dead sister by finding out who killed the other Margaret Kincaid. Or maybe, just maybe, it was like he had said and he simply wanted to spend time with me. I still wasn't sure, but I was glad to have a reason to keep in contact with him.

I didn't feel comfortable having him come up to the office though, since I was still doing a lot of things on the story without Norman Isaacs knowing much about them. I didn't want Isaacs to start asking more questions if he saw Logan. So we had agreed to meet here instead.

"How many men were in Lansdale's platoon?" Logan asked me now.

"Twenty-three."

"How many died?"

"Eighteen. Lansdale and four others were the only ones who made it out alive."

"So Cheryl Lee Barrett's father died in that desert. For some reason, she blames Lansdale – who was his commanding officer. We don't know how or why or anything more about what happened. But Lansdale must have done something – or at least she's convinced he did – that resulted in her father's death. She figures it out and all these years later comes to New York and tries to blackmail him with a sex video as revenge for her father's death. Only somebody kills her before she finishes the job. Makes sense, doesn't it?"

"Except for one thing," I said. "Scott Barrett – Cheryl Lee's father – didn't die in that massacre."

"He survived?"

"Yes, he and Enrico were two of the four people who made it out of the desert with Lansdale."

"And now Enrico's dead too."

"Yes," I said.

"Who were the other two survivors?"

"A corporal named Jack Olsen and a Private First Class Fred Sutter. I checked them out as best I could. Olsen died in 2002 in a plane crash. A private charter that was taking him on a business trip from Boston to a sales convention at some seacoast town in Maine. Only the plane never showed up. A search party found the wreckage in a remote wooded area of northern New Hampshire. Nothing suspicious about it – the FAA listed the probable cause as either engine failure or pilot error. Sutter seems to have vanished.

There was a work address for him at an auto parts plant in Pontiac, Michigan after his discharge. But when I checked, the personnel office said he'd only stayed on the job for a year or so. No record of him anywhere after that. At least I couldn't find any. But then, it's been a long time since the war. People move, they die, things happen to them."

"What happened to Cheryl Lee's father?" Logan asked.

"Scott Barrett died from injuries suffered in action in Iraq a few weeks later," I said, repeating the details I'd gotten from my call to Washington.

"So Barrett survives the massacre, but then dies in a random incident shortly afterward?"

"So it seems. At least that's the official version. There's one more thing. I found out when I was asking about this stuff that I wasn't the first person to do it. The person I talked to in Washington said someone else had asked them the same questions a few months ago. It was Cheryl Lee Barrett."

"She was investigating her father's death," Logan said.

"What about those videos we found in her apartment?" he wanted to know later, as we were buying coffee from a vendor on 50th Street. There're a lot of street vendors around that area, and it's one of my favorite places to hang out near our office. "Did you watch them?"

"All four of them."

"And?"

I gave him a blow-by-blow account – as non-X-rated as I could make it – of the trysts between Lansdale and Cheryl Lee Barrett on the videos.

"That's really pretty sensational stuff, Jessie. The senator and the hooker in a hotel room going at it like that. What are you going to do with the videos?"

I sipped my coffee. "I'm not sure."

"Did you show them to your boss at the *Tribune*?"

"Not yet."

"Why not?"

"I haven't told my boss a lot of things about what I'm doing on this story. I've been operating pretty much on my own. And, in any case, I'm really nervous about revealing I have these sex videos, because the first question he's going to ask is how I managed to obtain them."

"And that's a problem?"

"We stole the videos, remember?"

"What about the police?"

"Same problem. I'd have to explain to the police how I got them. The answer would be by breaking the law. Actually, I'm pretty sure we broke a bunch of laws that day by going into Cheryl Lee Barrett's apartment under false pretenses and taking her stuff."

"Well, sooner or later, you're going to make the videos public, right?"

"I guess. I just don't know yet how and when to do that."

It sure was nice spending time with Logan like this, but then it got even better. Before he left, he said: "Would you like to have dinner with me tonight?"

"Dinner?"

"It's the meal after breakfast and lunch." He grinned.

I hesitated before answering. "Maybe some other time," I finally said. "I'm kinda busy right now."

"When then?"

"Some night soon."

"I'll call you," Logan said.

CHAPTER 22

I still wasn't sure exactly what was going on with the Cheryl Lee Barrett murder and her father and Joseph Enrico and all the rest, but I was convinced Frank Lansdale had played a part in it. I needed to find out more about him. I knew one person who might have some answers.

I met Libby St. John – Mayor Hanrahan's top aide – for lunch the next day.

Lunch with Libby St. John turned out to consist of a hot dog and a soda on a park bench near City Hall.

"I was kind of thinking maybe we'd go to a restaurant," I said.

"I don't go to restaurants," Libby told me, looking down at her watch. "No time. As a matter of fact, I have to be at a meeting with the teachers' union at two o'clock. They're threatening to go on strike again. You've got twenty minutes with me. So what's this all about anyway?"

"Libby, don't you ever think about stopping for a minute and… well, smelling the roses or whatever?"

"Do you?"

"Not very often," I admitted.

"Hey, we both love our jobs," Libby said, taking a big bite out of her hot dog. "Nothing wrong with that."

I said I needed to find out more about Frank Lansdale.

"Why all the sudden interest in our esteemed senator?" Libby asked.

"I'm not satisfied with all the answers I've gotten about his dead campaign aide."

"You figure the senator was sleeping with her?" she asked casually.

I stared at her in amazement. "How did you know that?"

"Duh," she said. "That one's kind of a no-brainer, Jessie. First you covered the girl's murder. Then you had this scene at the funeral with the senator. And now you're asking me all these questions about him. I'm not stupid, you know. Do you think Lansdale had anything to do with her murder?"

"Tell me more about Lansdale," I said, deliberately not answering her question.

"Such as?"

"Anything. Sex, drugs – you tell me."

She laughed. "What the hell have you found out about Lansdale anyway?"

"Nothing. That's why I'm asking. C'mon, you told me on the phone the other day that there was a bit of a scandal a few years ago with him and some young intern. What was that all about?"

Libby took another giant bite out of her hot dog, nearly finishing it off. She threw the rest into a trash can, then gulped down some of the soda. She looked down at her watch again. I knew that Libby was trying to decide how much she wanted to tell me.

"The intern thing wasn't really much of anything," she said. "Her name was Lori Eichorn. The kid was just a Monica Lewinsky wannabe – a twenty-one-year-old with big breasts whose rich daddy got her a job with a U.S. senator. Her father was a big financial backer to Lansdale's political campaign funds. Anyway, she developed this crush on Lansdale and followed him around all the time like a lost dog. Then one day there's this office party, they both had a few drinks and, well, nature took over. Nothing really happened, just a lot of groping and kissing. But people saw it, someone told her father and he threw a fit. Threatened a lawsuit for sexual harassment and all sorts of stuff. The senator's people did some digging and found out that the girl had done the same thing at college with a couple of her professors – and she'd even had a messy affair with one of her father's business partners. Eventually everyone decided to drop the whole thing. End of story.

"The real scandal happened about ten years ago," she continued. "Not too many people have heard about that one. The senator's people did a good job of keeping it quiet. Lansdale fell in love – I'm talking serious love here – with a young woman named Alice Woodward. They carried on this hot and heavy secret affair for maybe six months or so. She was a big socialite around town – and they'd pretend to run into each other at parties, theater openings, stuff like that. Eventually Lansdale's wife found out about them though and threatened to divorce him. She said she'd make the divorce dirty enough so that he'd never even be able to get elected dogcatcher after it was over. Lansdale had a choice to make – and he took the easy way out. He broke it off with Alice. She was heartbroken. Two months later, they found her dead in her bedroom. The ME's office said she'd swallowed poison. A messy suicide."

"Jesus!"

"Mayor Hanrahan told me he talked to the senator about it once. He said they were both pretty drunk when somehow her name came up. The mayor told him he knew about the story and how that must have been really tough on him. He asked Lansdale if he ever felt guilty about the socialite's suicide. He said Lansdale told him: 'We do what we have to do. Sometimes when you're making an omelet, you have to break a few eggs.'"

"Nice guy," I said.

She shrugged. "He's a politician."

"And Lansdale's wife never left him?"

"No, they apparently made a deal. He'd never play around again, and she'd keep up the pretense of a happy marriage. It had to be a tough thing for him to agree to. He always liked the ladies. But I guess being a senator is more important to him than getting laid."

"You've never heard about him messing around with anyone else since then?"

"Nope. That's why I asked you about the Barrett woman. Do you figure his son was only pretending to be banging her to cover for his father, who was really the one having the affair with her?"

"It's just a theory," I said, not wanting to give away any more about what I knew to Libby than I had to.

There was one other thing I wanted to ask her.

"Why did Mayor Hanrahan decide not to run against Lansdale for the Senate?"

"Frank Lansdale is very popular. He has a lot of political clout."

"So does the mayor."

"Which makes it even more important not to waste it on a fight he might not win."

"Retreat and live to fight another day?"

"That's one way of looking at it."

"I remember Jack Hanrahan sitting at my bedside day by day when he should have been out campaigning. I remember him fighting to make sure the man who attacked me got convicted. He doesn't seem like someone who scares easily."

"It's not about being afraid, Jessie. It's about political realities."

Libby St. John rushed off to her two o'clock meeting, and I headed back to the *Tribune.* I sat down at my desk and googled the names of the two women that Libby had told me about.

The Alice Woodward suicide had been big news – Page One stories in every newspaper in town. I remembered it now, even though I hadn't worked on the story at the time. All the articles reported that Woodward had been depressed over personal problems, but no one explained what those problems were. Like Libby said, the senator's campaign people had done a good job of keeping a lid on the scandal.

The incident with the intern never got any coverage at all in the press. There were only a few brief mentions of the Eichorn girl. One in a group photo of the senator and his office staff. In another picture she was standing in the background at a press conference by the senator. I looked at Lori Eichorn's face in the picture. She was a cute brunette with a pixie haircut. She didn't look anything at all like Cheryl Lee Barrett, if that meant anything. Probably didn't. Lansdale's taste in women probably ran to all sizes and types. There was another article by a political columnist that said that one of Lansdale's big financial backers, Walter Eichorn, was feuding with him and would make no further contributions to his campaign. Everyone in the political world was speculating about what had happened to split up the two longtime allies. *How about feeling up the guy's daughter*, I thought. *That sure as hell might just do it.*

I sat there at my desk trying to figure out what to do next. I could track down Walter Eichorn and talk to him about Frank Lansdale and his daughter. Maybe talk to her too. But what would that accomplish? Not much probably. It just seemed like a messy incident at a party between a young, impressionable girl and a powerful man – unhappy in his marriage – who'd had too much to drink.

The affair with Alice Woodward seemed more significant, but that was ten years ago. By all accounts and appearances, he'd been well behaved since then. And for a good reason. His wife threatened to divorce him and torpedo his political career if he ever strayed again. Lansdale had a deal with his wife, Libby had said. He was afraid of her.

So what would have happened if Lansdale's wife had found out that he was having an affair with Cheryl Lee Barrett?

Would she have divorced him?

Would she have cleaned him out financially?

Would she have destroyed his political career – just like she threatened to do ten years earlier?

Most importantly, was all of this enough of a motive for the senator to murder Cheryl Lee Barrett?

It sure worked for me.

I had a big decision to make about what to do next.

Like Logan had said, sooner or later I was going to have to tell someone about the Cheryl Lee Barrett/Senator Lansdale sex videos.

But it was more than just the video.

I hadn't revealed to Danny Knowlton or Norman Isaacs, to the police or to anyone other than Logan all the other things I'd found out in recent days. The true nature of the relationship between Jonathan Lansdale and Cheryl Lee Barrett. The senator's sex scandals of the past and his promises to his wife that made him an inviting target for a sex blackmail shakedown – like Cheryl Lee Barrett had apparently been doing. And, most importantly of all, the Gulf War link between the senator and the dead woman's father and the man accused of killing her.

I was a reporter, and my job was to get stories in the paper. There sure was a story here, as far as I was concerned.

But I still didn't think that Isaacs would go for it. Even though none of this new information meant for certain that Lansdale had anything to do with the murder, it did prove he was cheating on his wife with the daughter of a man who'd once served with him in Iraq. I could hear Isaacs' words now if I told him about all this: "The *Tribune* is a prestigious newspaper that prides itself on not printing stories that are just about gossip and innuendo and scandal." I'd heard that speech a lot of times from him over the years.

I wasn't sure I could trust Danny Knowlton on this one either. I remembered the story about Danny hanging a reporter out to dry for something he didn't do, and I wondered if he would do the same to me if this blew up in his face – especially the stolen video I'd taken from Cheryl Lee Barrett's apartment.

Besides, I had found out from going through Lansdale's background that the senator had a lot of powerful friends. It would take a very strong editor to get that kind of a story in the paper once the senator got wind of what was happening. Norman Isaacs was not a strong editor. And Danny Knowlton was a guy who played office politics, and he might not want to upset Lansdale's friends at the paper either.

So I just kept doing what I'd been doing – at least for the time being.

First, I went into Isaacs' office and lied to him that I hadn't really found out much more. I said that I'd spend the last few days of the week tying up any loose threads on the Cheryl Lee Barrett story as we'd agreed, but then I'd move on to another story. He said that was a good idea.

"Just remember, Jessie, don't do anything to rile up Senator Lansdale again. He could make a lot of trouble for you. For all of us at the *Tribune*. I don't want to go down that road. I'm too old to go looking for another job."

Then I went back to Danny Knowlton and told him I was still working the hell out of the Cheryl Lee Barrett story – especially the Senator Lansdale angle. I told him a little bit about what I'd found out – not a lot, just enough to whet his appetite. And I certainly said nothing about the sex videos. But it was enough. I said I was pretty sure I'd be able to nail down a story very soon about Senator Lansdale and his relationship with the dead Cheryl Lee Barrett.

"That's great, Jessie," he said excitedly. "Let's just keep this between you and me for now. No need to bring in Isaacs yet. This is going to be our story when it breaks – you and me, right?"

"Absolutely, Danny," I said.

It was a dangerous game I was playing here – pitting Knowlton against Isaacs, with myself in the middle. Sooner or later, they were going to talk to each other about it all and figure out the truth about what I'd been doing.

But I'd worry about that when it happened.
Right now, all I cared about was this story.

I was still trying to figure out my next move when I took the subway from my apartment to work the next morning. On the ride downtown, I read a story about Senator Frank Lansdale in the *New York Times*. It said polls showed that Lansdale was ahead of his opponent for re-election by a huge 24-point margin. Even though the election was still several months away, the article said, it would take a miracle for Lansdale's opponent to win.

There was another story about Lansdale in that morning's *New York Times* too.

This one showed him dedicating a children's recreation center in the Bronx, posing with a group of kids. The article quoted him as saying that "there's nothing that brings me more satisfaction than being able to put a smile on a youngster's face."

I made a face as I read it.

I didn't like Frank Lansdale. Everything I'd found out so far indicated that he wasn't the type of man who should be a U.S. senator.

But I still wasn't exactly sure what to do about it. I needed something more.

Something to connect Senator Lansdale to Cheryl Lee Barrett's death.

So I finally decided to do what I always do when I come to a crossroads in a big news story.

I went looking for more information.

And the best place to get that was from the cops.

CHAPTER 23

I laid it all out for Aguirre and Erskine. Well, except for the part about the sex video I'd stolen from Cheryl Lee Barrett's apartment. That incident had to remain my secret for the time being.

Instead, I told the two homicide cops about Lansdale's long-ago military connection to Joseph Enrico; about the links to Cheryl Lee Barrett's father as well as Enrico from Iraq; and all the questions about how Cheryl Lee suddenly wound up in New York working for the senator's campaign and living the good life.

I talked about the argument in the print shop between Lansdale and Cheryl Lee just before she died.

And about my discovery that the supposed romance between Lansdale's son Jonathan and Cheryl Lee was not real.

"I believe it was our esteemed Senator Frank Lansdale who was actually having an affair with the dead woman."

"Do you have any proof of that?" Aguirre asked, putting his feet on his desk and leaning back in his chair.

I thought again about the videos of the senator and Cheryl Lee having sex. About my off-the-record interview with the senator's son Jonathan and all the other things I'd found out – but couldn't reveal to Aguirre and Erskine.

"Let's just say I have a pretty good reason to believe it's true," was all I said.

Aguirre shrugged.

"Even if it is, so what? What does any of this have to do with us?"

"I thought the information might help your investigation." I crossed my legs and fixed him with a stare.

"And how exactly would it do that?"

"Let me see," I answered, trying not to let too much sarcasm seep into my voice. "Well, here's an idea. Enrico and Cheryl Lee's father and Lansdale were all in the same unit in Iraq. Scott Barrett wound up dead, Enrico got all screwed up and Lansdale came home a hero. Then Enrico and Barrett's daughter somehow hooked up all these years later, and they decided this was unfair. Maybe they figured Lansdale owed them something. I think they came to New York with a plan for Cheryl Lee to first seduce Lansdale – and then shake him down for money as revenge. Only something went wrong somewhere along the way. Maybe Lansdale got tired of paying the rent on her fancy apartment, buying her all the fancy clothes and whatever else. Maybe Mrs. Lansdale was getting suspicious. Maybe he was worried about it coming out during the election. Maybe he found out she was just setting him up for sexual blackmail. Whatever, he definitely had a problem. So he murders Cheryl Lee, then sets up Enrico to take the fall for it. End of problem." I smiled at the two cops. "What do you think?"

But Aguirre just shook his head. He wasn't buying any of what I was telling. And I knew why.

If it was an open case, then all this information would certainly point to Frank Lansdale as a man with a possible motive for murder. But it wasn't an open case. They already had their man, Joseph Enrico, and the whole thing was wrapped up nice and neat. No cop – certainly not an ambitious one like Aguirre – was going to be willing to rock the boat by taking on a U.S. senator for no apparent reason.

"How did he know Enrico would shoot it out with the police?" Aguirre asked.

"Huh?"

"How could Lansdale be certain that Enrico was going to open fire when we came to arrest him – and then be shot dead? That's a big flaw in your theory. If Enrico's not dead, then he tells the story about Cheryl Lee and the senator as soon as he's arrested. He might go down for the murder, but Lansdale's secret is out, which is the motive you give him for killing the girl in the first place. It doesn't make sense, Tucker."

I nodded. I'd wondered about that too.

"It doesn't matter anyway," he shrugged, "because you've got a bigger problem. Enrico's fingerprints are all over the rock that was used to kill the girl. Plus, her purse and other stuff – things she had with her when she walked out of the restaurant that night – were found in Enrico's hotel room. How do you explain that?"

"Evidence isn't always what it seems, Lieutenant," I said.

"Forget it. I got an airtight case that says Enrico did it."

"But what if Lansdale—"

"He had nothing to do with the murder."

"How can you be sure?"

"Something new has come up. Something you don't know about yet."

"Like what?"

"We've got a witness."

The witness' name was Phyllis Lachman.

Lachman was a twenty-one-year-old Columbia University student who was roller blading through the park near the Park Grille on the night when Cheryl Lee Barrett was murdered. She was the daughter of a federal prosecutor in Washington, D.C. She was a straight-A student at Columbia. She was a member of Phi Beta Kappa. She was, as Aguirre said smugly, one helluva witness.

"Lachman saw someone come running out of the woods," Aguirre said. "Bloody hands, bloody shirt, blood all over a New York Yankees baseball cap he was wearing. She thought at first the man had been hurt and called out to ask if he needed help. But he didn't answer. Instead, he just ran away from her toward an exit from the park.

"She thought maybe she should call the police then. But she wasn't sure what to say. So, like a typical New Yorker, she just minded her own business and went home. By then, she'd pretty much forgotten all about the encounter in the park. Finally, after reading about the murder, she realized she needed to come forward and tell what she knew.

"She never really saw the guy's face, but remembers whoever it was she saw wearing the bloody Yankees baseball cap was short, not very tall at all."

"Enrico was short," Erskine pointed out. "It sure as hell wasn't Frank Lansdale. He's well over six foot tall."

"The thing is," Aguirre said, "there's no way that Enrico didn't do this killing. We've got fingerprints. We've got the stuff we found in his hotel room. And now we've got an eyewitness who saw someone fitting Enrico's physical description in the park too. So even if Senator Lansdale was having an affair with this broad, it's totally irrelevant to our case. And that's all I care about. I'm a homicide cop. Not the morality police. If the senator can't keep it in his pants, that's none of my business. Besides, it's not a good career move for a police lieutenant to go after a senator. I don't like the odds. You know what I mean, Tucker?"

I didn't say anything. I was barely listening to what he was saying. I was too much in shock from something the new witness, Phyllis Lachman, had said she saw the man in the park wearing on the night of the murder.

A New York Yankees baseball cap.

Just like the one I had begun seeing in my dreams.

The one I now remember Darryl Jackson wearing.

"Did you find a New York Yankees baseball cap with Enrico?" I finally managed to mumble.

"Nope," Erskine told me.

"He probably threw it away," Aguirre said.

CHAPTER 24

I had never gone back to the spot where I'd been attacked.

Oh, I'd been to the park lots of times, the most recent being the investigation of the Cheryl Lee Barrett murder. I'd driven through it on my way across town and even went biking there sometimes. But I'd never returned to the exact location. Not once in twelve years. Not even when the city wanted to hold a ceremony there to honor me for my bravery. I convinced Mayor Hanrahan to move the event to the steps of City Hall. I was never sure why I didn't want to go back there. What it was that I was so afraid of. Maybe because I still was never totally convinced – not really, deep inside me – that I had all the answers to what had happened to me that night. But it was a door to the past that I never wanted to open up again.

Until now.

Now the fact that the man who attacked Cheryl Lee Barrett in the park was wearing a New York Yankees baseball cap – just like I remembered my attacker wearing – had opened up that door of fear and doubt and terrifying nightmares all over again.

Sure, there were a lot of people who wore New York Yankee baseball caps in New York City – hundreds, maybe even thousands of people. The fact that two different men in the park, both linked to crimes twelve years apart, were wearing the same cap was not all that unlikely. But I still couldn't shake the feeling that it was something important. A clue.

The place where I'd been attacked was nowhere near where Cheryl Lee Barrett died. Her body was found near Central Park West and 86th Street. That's where the Park Grille Restaurant was.

I'd been much further south in the park, near the 79th Transverse Road leading out to Fifth Avenue on the East Side. I'd gone with a group of people from my ad agency office to a concert on the Great Lawn inside the park. I'd been to a lot of great concerts there in the past – Paul Simon, Diana Ross and others. But this one wasn't very interesting, I can't even remember who was performing. Maybe because I'd blocked that from my mind like so many other details of that night, maybe because I just found the show boring and wasn't paying attention. Anyway, I decided to leave early. I was tired from a long day at work and – like I said earlier – I kept thinking about that chocolate marshmallow ice cream waiting for me at home. So I said goodbye to everyone, then began making my way through the park to the 79th Transverse Road that would let me out on Fifth Avenue not far from my apartment.

Standing there now at the place where I'd nearly been killed, I thought about how different everything looked in the daylight. It was all still there. The path where he'd first come at me. The trees where he'd dragged me afterward. The hilly ravine that he'd tossed me down where they found me the next morning.

I remembered reading how in the days afterward – when the entire city was praying for my recovery – that people would leave flowers at this site. There was nothing like that now. Nothing to indicate there was anything special about it at all. Nearby, a young woman was walking her dog. There were some kids on roller blades a few yards away. People rode by on bicycles. Life goes on.

I kneeled down at the spot and tried to remember more about that night. I wasn't sure what I was hoping to find here. Some clue. Some inspiration. Some kind of insight that would suddenly make everything clear. But there was nothing. Just a soft breeze rippling through the trees and the sounds of traffic in the distance.

Twelve years ago, I had testified against the man police arrested for attacking me. I'd done it for a very personal reason. I didn't like being a victim. I'd never been one before in my life, I'd always been someone who was in control of my destiny. And I didn't like the feeling of being helpless. I wanted revenge. I wanted to make someone pay for what they had done. Going to court to testify against Darryl Jackson was the way for me to accomplish that.

That sense of justice – or closure or whatever you want to call it – has sustained me over the years since then. No matter how much pain and emotional torment I've had to endure from that terrible night in the park, I'd put the sonuvabitch who did this to me in jail. And the fact that he died there made it even more satisfying for me.

But there was always still this lingering doubt about it for me – a vague feeling, or maybe even a premonition, that the story wasn't completely over. And all this came rushing back to me when I heard about the Yankee baseball cap in the park on the night Cheryl Lee Barrett died.

A New York Yankees baseball cap like the one I saw my own attacker wearing now in my nightmares. Was it possible, as far-fetched as it seemed, that it was the same person both times?

Except Darryl Jackson was dead.

I never met the Central Park jogger. The Wall Street broker who'd made headlines when she was brutally attacked in Central Park way back in 1989. But I'd read a lot about her and that case as I struggled to deal with my own recovery. I thought many times about reaching out to her, but I never did. I was always afraid, I guess, that reliving her ordeal with her would bring back too many bad memories of my own. I was also bothered by the way her case had turned out. The five men sent to prison for attacking her were eventually exonerated by new evidence, and it wasn't until years later that her real attacker was convicted and sent to prison. I was luckier, I told myself. I knew exactly who attacked me, and I was able to get my revenge by sending him to his death in prison. I always felt sorry for the Central Park jogger that I was able to gain that kind of closure, while her entire world had suddenly been turned upside down again with the revelation that authorities had sent the wrong men to prison for the crime.

Now my entire world had suddenly been turned upside down too.

What if… no, it was an unthinkable possibility.

But I thought about it anyway.

By the time I got home from work that night, I'd managed to pretty much convince myself that my imagination was simply running wild.

I'd even counted the number of people I saw wearing Yankees caps on the street and on the subway for the rest of the day to reassure myself it wasn't that unusual. There were quite a few of them. *See*, I told myself, *this really doesn't mean anything.*

I tried to put it out of my mind and focus on other things. I made myself a nice dinner: a chicken dish with some new sauce I'd found a recipe for recently; a salad with tomatoes, onions and cucumbers that was a favorite of mine; and a glass of wine to drink with it while I ate.

After dinner, I watched an old movie I loved on TV – *Broadcast News* – then an episode of *The Big Bang Theory*, which seemed to be on every channel all day and night; and finally some news just to make sure I hadn't missed anything that day.

As I got ready for bed, I thought again about Logan, wondering idly if one night very soon I might be sharing a bed with him. It was a pleasant thought, though I wasn't quite sure how we'd get there after I'd turned his offer of dinner down.

But, no matter how hard I tried to distract myself, I couldn't escape the thought that the New York Yankees baseball caps worn by both attackers – Cheryl Lee Barrett's and mine (at least in my dreams) – might be more than just an explainable coincidence.

It got worse when I tried to get to sleep. I lay awake for a long time, tossing and turning and trying without success to fend off the nightmares that came every time I did manage to close my eyes and drift off to sleep.

By the time I woke up the next morning, I'd made a decision.

I'd started out investigating the present-day murder of Cheryl Lee Barrett, but that had led me to these new questions about my own attack all those years earlier. Did I keep covering the story about Senator Lansdale and the Barrett woman because that was the most obvious focal point of everything that was happening? Or – if there really was some inexplicable link between the two attacks – should I go back and look at my own case again in the hope that it would somehow also lead me back into the Cheryl Lee Barrett murder?

Even though, for the life of me, I couldn't figure out how Senator Frank Lansdale – who I was convinced must have had something to do with Cheryl Lee Barrett's murder – could possibly had have any involvement in the attack on me.

And did it really even matter which approach I took? If Cheryl Lee Barrett's murder really was somehow related to the attack on me, then continuing to investigate Cheryl Lee's death would logically provide answers to my own case too.

But the Cheryl Lee Barrett murder wasn't the most important thing for me anymore. All I could think about was what happened to me in the park.

I knew what I was going to do. Knew what I *had* to do. I needed to find out the truth about myself.

Sure, all the evidence in my own case was very cold now. And Darryl Jackson, the man who'd gone to prison for the crime, was long dead. But, no matter how difficult it would be, I knew I had to go back.

Back to that night of horror for me in Central Park.

Back down the tangled trail of evidence and memories to find out what really happened on that night that changed my life so irrevocably.

And back to wherever that trail might lead…

CHAPTER 25

The old police files – the solved cases, the long-unsolved cases, all the cases that no one cared about anymore – were kept in a big old warehouse building in Lower Manhattan, across town from Police Headquarters. Some of the newer case files were on computer now. But a lot of the older cases – like mine – were still kept on paper and filed away in boxes there.

I had spent a lot of time at this place a year or so ago when I did a series for the *Tribune* called "New York's Most Wanted: The City's Most Notorious Unsolved Crimes." I'd worked on it with the cooperation of the Police Department, which normally did not allow such open public access to its official files. But the commissioner's office decided that the publicity on these long-buried cases might spark some new leads from the public. And that's exactly what happened. A few days after one of the excerpts ran about a drive-by shooting of a young girl five years earlier, a suspect was arrested – because of a witness who came forward after reading my article. The series later won me an investigative reporting award from the New York City Press Club.

There was a cop there named Billings – a sergeant in the Police Records Division – who I'd worked closely with on the project. I'd mentioned him in my acceptance speech at the Press Club Awards Dinner and also wrote him a long thank-you note after getting the award. I hoped Billings was there now. It would make what I had to do a lot easier.

As it turned out, it didn't really matter. The cop on duty was a young guy in his twenties named Donald McCracken. I didn't remember him from last time. But he knew me.

"Jessie Tucker!" he said with a big smile as soon as I walked up to the front desk. "What brings you back here? Are you working on another one of those big series?"

"Something like that," I said.

"Well, you certainly got us a lot of good publicity with that one you did. You know, a lot of people – even people in the department – don't take what we do seriously down here. I mean, I know it's not as glamorous as busting drug dealers or shooting it out with bank robbers, but record-keeping is an important part of police work too."

I nodded solemnly and tried to look interested as Donald McCracken went on like that for another few minutes. Once or twice, I interrupted to tell him what a great job he seemed to be doing. A little flattery never hurt in these situations. McCracken wanted to be my friend and I needed a friend to help me right now on this story.

"How many files do you want to see?" McCracken finally asked.

"Just one."

"Name?"

"Darryl Jackson," I said, giving the name of the man who attacked me.

"And he's the victim?" McCracken asked, not making the connection to who I was asking about.

"No, that's the perpetrator."

"We generally file everything under the name of the victim," McCracken said. "Do you have that? Or the date of the crime. Or the place?"

"The victim was Jessie Tucker," I said.

McCracken stared at me in surprise.

"I want to see my own file," I told him.

*

Reading my own case file was even more difficult than I had thought it would be.

I had tried to prepare myself for the shock of it beforehand, but nothing I had ever imagined was like seeing the cold, hard facts about the event that had changed my entire life recounted by investigating cops in such an objective, matter-of-fact manner.

The report began by describing how a passerby had found me lying unconscious and badly injured shortly after dawn that morning.

There was a lengthy description of the crime scene and the desperate condition I was in. At first, I read it all in a curiously detached way, as if I was reading about some other crime victim – not myself. I'd covered stories like this hundreds of times in my newspaper career. But this wasn't just another story. This was my own life. No matter how hard I tried, I couldn't put that out of my mind.

The first part of the report dealt with the incident, the clues found at the scene and interviews with the person who found me as well as other people who might have seen anything unusual in the park that night.

The second part dealt with the arrest of the suspect, Darryl Jackson.

There was a report attached by Detective Steve Fredericks, the arresting officer of Jackson, about how he'd apprehended him during the robbery of the store.

The next section dealt with the interrogation of the suspect, who admitted to the crime during a videotaped confession. The suspect's house was also searched where police found the items taken from me in Jackson's room. There was no question at this point that he had done it. File No. 321-87 / Jessie Tucker – was an open and shut case.

Just like Cheryl Lee Barrett had been.

Fredericks had noted in his report:

> Darryl Jackson admitted in his video confession that he had been in Central Park that night looking for a victim. He said he decided he wanted some sex. He spent about an hour searching the park – until he encountered his female victim. He admitted raping her, then fleeing from the park. He admitted to striking the woman as well as raping her, but claimed he never meant to seriously injure her.

I frowned. There was something wrong here.

I kept reading.

The next part was a collection of witnesses they'd talked to in connection with the case. The person who'd found my battered body. The customers in the bodega that Darryl Jackson had been attempting to rob when he was arrested. And people who'd been in Central Park on the night of the attack. A team of cops had scoured the park on subsequent nights to find them – and talk to them about anything unusual they remembered.

One eyewitness remembered seeing someone running through the park wearing a baseball cap. The witness never specifically described it as a Yankees cap. But still…

Fredericks wrote in the report:

> A search of the suspect's home and belongings failed to turn up any sign of such a cap. It is possible it was discarded after the attack. Or, more likely, that the person wearing it had nothing to do with the attack on Jessie Tucker and therefore is of no consequence to this investigation.

The last section of the report was about Fredericks' efforts to get a positive identification of the suspect from the victim of the assault. That victim, of course, was me.

> Victim is still very traumatized by the event. She has trouble remembering the exact details of what happened. Doctors say she may get her memory back as she continues to recover, but that this could conceivably take years. However, the victim did positively identify the suspect from mugshots provided by this office. The information was forwarded to the District Attorney's office for use in the prosecution of Darryl Jackson.

There were three things wrong with this report, I realized.

First, Jackson claimed in his confession that he had raped the victim. But I had not been raped. There was no evidence of that, according to all the medical reports. Just that my clothes had been ripped during the attack. If his motive was rape, why didn't he finish it? And why would Darryl Jackson say he had raped me in his original confession if he didn't?

Second, the eyewitness had seen someone wearing a baseball cap. But no one ever told me that at the time. I didn't know about a cap until I started seeing it in my dreams. The description wasn't very specific and it wasn't even confirmed. But now it seemed very significant.

Third, and perhaps most importantly, there was Fredericks' description of his conversations with me. I had identified the suspect, he said, but it hadn't really happened that way. Fredericks told me that they had positive identifications of the suspect from other witnesses. He said they had an airtight case against the man in custody. That my testimony would just be the icing on the cake. The suspect was a bad guy who already had a criminal record, he had admitted to being in the park that night and he confessed to the crime. That, combined with the fact that I had seen him in the park earlier that evening, meant that by the time I testified at the trial six months later, I was convinced that Darryl Jackson was the one who had attacked me.

I put down the file, walked over to McCracken's desk and asked if he had any coffee. He did, and he gave me some. I sipped on the coffee as I attempted to rationally collect my thoughts – and, even more importantly, my emotions – over what I'd found out from the file on my case.

It wasn't easy to do.

Finally, I went back and read through the file all over again, from start to finish. Trying to figure out what it all meant. And hoping upon hope I could come up with a logical answer that was anything other than the one I feared the most.

I've lived my life for the past twelve years with the comforting belief that the man who did these horrible things to me was gone – first to prison and then he was dead.

Darryl Jackson couldn't hurt me anymore.

I was safe.

Except…

Well, except there were holes in my case and I couldn't remember ever seeing my attacker's face. And somebody spotted a witness running away in a Yankees cap that night…

I didn't want to admit the possibility that I could have been wrong when I identified Darryl Jackson as the man who attacked me.

I didn't want to admit that Fredericks and the District Attorney and the jury could have been wrong when they sent him to jail for the crime.

But no matter how many different ways I looked at it – no matter how many alternative scenarios I played out in my head over what I'd just read in my file – I was left with one inescapable conclusion.

Maybe Darryl Jackson wasn't the one who did it.

CHAPTER 26

Steve Fredericks had come a long way in twelve years.

Back then, he'd been a young, up-and-coming detective with a top-notch educational background and a record that certainly made him seem like someone who was going places in the department. But the Jessie Tucker case had turned him into an overnight star. He was the cop who caught the suspect, who got him to confess to the crime, who helped the victim through her long, painful recovery until she was even able to identify her attacker in the courtroom. It was the career break of a lifetime for him.

Now Fredericks was a captain working at Police Headquarters, and the word was he was soon headed even higher. He was always a smart guy. His specialty was criminal psychology – he'd told me that he majored in psychology in college. He worked on stuff like serial killer profiles, analyses of the criminal mind, etc. – a long way from carrying a gun or working the street anymore. Which made sense, of course. I had never seen Fredericks as the type to become a career street cop. He seemed too nice, too kind, too gentle for that kind of life.

"Jessie!" he boomed when he saw me. "It's so great to see you!"

I told him how happy I was to see him too. Then I sat down in a chair across from his desk. There were pictures of his family on it. Him and his wife Kathy, smiling at the camera in front of a big suburban house. Sarah and Mary, their two daughters. They were teenagers now, growing up so quickly. Sarah was wearing a cheerleaders' outfit. Mary was all dressed up in a formal gown for a big school dance.

"They ask about you all the time," Fredericks said. "Especially Mary. She wants to go to journalism school and be a reporter – just like Jessie, she says. If I were you, I'd be flattered."

"I am. Has she looked into any journalism schools yet?"

"A few. She's still got another year of high school left. But I know she has to start thinking about that stuff pretty soon."

"Maybe I can help. Ask around with a few people I know."

"That would be great. I'll tell Mary. She'll be excited to hear I was talking to you. Hey, better than that – you should come by the house and see them. Kathy too. We can cook out in the backyard – I still make those mouth-watering barbecued ribs, you know. The ones you just can't say no to once you take the first bite…"

"I'd like that." I smiled.

"How about you?" Fredericks said. "I've been reading your stuff in the *Tribune*. It sounds like you're doing really well."

"I can't complain."

"How's your personal life?"

"Personal."

"C'mon, it's me, Jessie. Is there a man in the picture right now?"

I thought about Logan.

"Well, there is someone I met recently."

"Are you in a relationship with him?"

"I'm still working on it."

For the first time in my life, I felt uneasy with Fredericks. I knew now there were holes in the case he'd built against Darryl Jackson as my attacker. But were those just mistakes on his part, or did he do them on purpose to make sure Jackson got convicted? I'd trusted the man implicitly since the first day I'd met him at the hospital, but had I been wrong to?

I decided we'd spent enough time on small talk. So I got to the point of my visit.

"I read the file on my case yesterday," I told Fredericks.

He seemed surprised. "Why?"

"I have some questions."

"What kind of questions?"

"Well, I've been covering the Cheryl Lee Barrett murder."

"Right. Central Park again."

"Is there any possibility at all it could be the same man, Steve?"
He looked confused.

"Jessie, the man who did that to you is dead."

"Is he?"

"What are you talking about?"

"I'm not sure about that anymore."

"Look, Darryl Jackson died in prison years ago. I don't know
what kind of crazy ideas you've gotten into your head about this
or why it's happening now after all this time, but I can assure you
that—"

"How do you know you arrested – and we convicted – the
right guy?"

"Of course he was the right guy. You identified him as the man
who attacked you. In court. Remember?"

"Yeah, I remember. But what I also remember is that I never
really got a good look at my attacker that night. To this day, I
can't tell you exactly what happened. I guess I lost consciousness – whether some of those memories are hidden inside my
head or not, I'm not sure. I really don't know. But it was you who
convinced me that Darryl Jackson was the man who attacked
me, and I believed that because I trusted you. I didn't realize that
until I read the police report again. You say in the report that I
positively ID'd a picture of the suspect to you. Except that's not
what happened. You told me other witnesses had already identified
him, and all I was doing was confirming what you already knew.
So I did. I wanted revenge against the man who did that to me
so badly that I actually convinced myself it must be true. But I've
looked through the file and I can't find any evidence of any other
witnesses. Were there any?"

Fredericks shrugged. "That was a long time ago, Jessie."

"And what about the confession?"

"Jackson confessed. He admitted everything to me. Then he got himself a lawyer who told him to rescind the confession. It didn't matter though. The judge let us enter the confession into evidence during the trial anyway. He left it up to the jury whether to believe the original confession or not. The jury did."

"How long did it take Darryl Jackson to confess?"

"How long?"

"Five minutes? Five hours? A day?"

"I questioned him for a total of thirty hours," Fredericks said quietly.

"After thirty hours, maybe he was willing to admit to anything just to get it over with."

"Look, that's the way it's done. Criminals don't sit down and blurt out the truth. You have to work at getting it out of them. Sometimes it takes a while to do. Sometimes you have to play a few mind games with them along the way. I don't deny that. That's how we close cases. If we didn't, we'd never get any convictions. Christ, you know that, Jessie. You know how the system works."

Fredericks gave me a big smile. His best smile. The smile I remember so well from those days back when he made me feel so much better in the hospital.

"Jackson was the guy who attacked you, not someone else. Even if you hadn't identified him, even if he hadn't confessed – we had him dead to rights. Christ, he had stuff in his possession he'd stolen from you. That's pretty solid evidence."

I told him the rest of it then. About the link I'd discovered between the Cheryl Lee Barrett murder and my own attack years earlier.

"A witness says Cheryl Lee Barrett's killer was wearing a New York Yankees baseball cap. I now remember that the man who attacked me was wearing one too."

"It could be coincidence. Your imagination. Lots of reasons."

"There's something else. You thought at first that I'd been sexually assaulted. My clothes had been ripped off."

"I know all that. I handled the case."

"It was the same with Cheryl Lee Barrett."

"So both times the guy got interrupted—"

"Or someone wanted to make it *look* like a sexual attack both times."

Fredericks looked at me with real concern now. Just the way Norman Isaacs had.

"I've been reading your stuff in the paper," he said softly. "About that murder in the park. I really think the parallels between her case and yours brought back a lot of bad memories for you, Jessie. I'm sorry. But you've got nothing to worry about. What happened to you happened a long time ago. The person who did has since paid the price. He can't hurt you anymore."

"Everyone keeps telling me that."

"It's just your mind playing tricks on you."

"Look, I wish that was all it was, Steve. I really do. I desperately want to believe it was Darryl Jackson who attacked me, and he got what he had coming to him. It's so much easier that way. But I'm not sure that's the way it happened anymore. And that scares the hell out of me."

"What are you going to do, Jessie?"

"Find out the truth, once and for all."

CHAPTER 27

Darryl Jackson's last cellmate was a guy named Ronnie Gutierrez. If Jackson had taken any secrets to the grave with him, Ronnie was the one person he might have confided in before he died. Prisoners tended to open up to other prisoners, I'd discovered in the past. The problem was, would Gutierrez talk to me?

But Gutierrez did agree to meet with me when I contacted Attica State Prison to request an interview.

On my way up there, I texted Danny Knowlton at the office and told him where I was going. I said I'd gotten some more information from Aguirre and the police about the Cheryl Lee Barrett murder and I needed to check out a possible angle at the prison.

I wasn't any more specific than that. I didn't want either him or Isaacs to find out that I was really chasing after answers on my own case. Not yet. I'd wait to see what I found out from Gutierrez.

Danny did try to call me back, but I let it go to voicemail. I figured I could always tell him I'd lost my cell phone signal up here.

I thought about calling Logan too and telling him where I was. Maybe even asking him to come along with me.

I knew Darryl Jackson was long dead, but the idea of going to meet his cellmate still scared me. I wasn't sure who I could trust anymore – and the thought of being a lone woman in a maximum-security prison filled with violent men didn't make me feel any safer.

But, in the end, I didn't reach out to Logan for help. I guess because I was afraid he might think I was crazy doing this, and he sure wasn't going to want to spend time with a crazy woman.

No, I was on my own here, as frightening as that concept was.

But I told myself that I was tough enough to handle it. Hell, I was tough enough to survive Central Park.

I wasn't going to let Ronnie Gutierrez or anyone else scare me away from doing this.

At the prison, they gave me a visitor's pass to wear and then led me into a small room, which was divided by a glass partition. There was a telephone on the partition so that visitors could talk to the prisoners. I sat down in a chair next to the phone and waited for Gutierrez to come out of a door at the back of the room.

I wasn't quite sure what to expect. Gutierrez sounded like a pretty scary guy. He'd been convicted for assault and armed robbery and other violent crimes. But, when he finally did come out to meet me, he didn't look as bad as I expected.

He was about thirty, with short black hair and a goatee that was longer than the hair on top of his head. He was wearing a blue denim inmate suit, with the sleeves of the shirt rolled up to his elbows. There was a tattoo on each of his forearms. The first one said "Ronnie." *Not very original*, I thought. The second one read "Born to Be Bad."

He sat down on the other side of the glass and picked up the phone. So did I.

"Do you know who I am?" I asked.

"Sure, you're a visitor here to see me. It says so right there on the card you're wearing."

"Do you know who I am?" I repeated.

"You're a woman. We don't get too many women in here. Nice to be around a woman again."

"Is that why you agreed to see me?"

"Why not? What else do I have to do in here?"

"My name is Jessie Tucker. I'm a reporter for the *New York Tribune*. I want to ask you some questions about Darryl Jackson. The man who used to be your cellmate. He was convicted for attacking me."

Gutierrez nodded. He knew all that. He was just playing games with me.

"Darryl's dead," he said now.

"I know, that's why I'm talking to you."

He told me then about his relationship with Darryl Jackson. They had been cellmates during the last year Jackson was alive. Locked up in a small cell together, sometimes for as much as twenty-three hours a day, they talked about a lot of things, he told me.

"Did he tell you about the night I was attacked?"

"Sure."

"What did he tell you?"

"He said he was innocent."

"Then why did he confess after he was arrested?"

"Darryl said he was tricked into making that confession – but I'm sure you don't believe that."

"I'm not sure what I believe anymore. That's why I need to know exactly what Darryl Jackson told you about what happened."

Gutierrez shrugged, then started talking. "Darryl admitted to me he wanted some sex that night. So he went looking for a girl in the park. Hell, he'd done it before, he told me. It was no big deal. She doesn't want it, she shouldn't be wandering around the park after dark – that was what he figured. He told me he'd never really hurt a woman before. Just slapped them around a bit to scare them into not resisting. Most of the time they were so frightened or embarrassed by what happened that they never even reported it to the police. They just went home and didn't tell anyone what happened, he said."

There was something particularly terrifying to me in the casual way Gutierrez said all this. Like it was no big deal. Me – and all these other women – were just prey to be hunted down and used in whatever way people like him or Darryl Jackson wanted. It was becoming more and more difficult for me to control my expression as I listened to him.

But I managed to do it. I've always been able to get the best out of interviews with witnesses or criminals because I approached it like an objective reporter. That part of me – the objective reporter – was able to keep the emotional victim inside me from coming out.

Sometimes I even surprised myself by the way I was able to compartmentalize things in my life that way. Despite the feeling of rage and fear and everything else I had toward Gutierrez right then, I just wrote everything down as he talked in my notebook.

"And that's what Darryl did again that night in the park," Gutierrez said. "Found himself a woman to have some sex with."

I looked over at him through the glass partition that separated us.

"I thought you said he told you he was innocent."

"He did."

"That doesn't sound too innocent to me. You said he admitted to attacking a woman in the park. Well, that woman was me."

"No, he said that's not what happened."

"But you just told me—"

"It wasn't you."

I stared at him. "What are you talking about?"

"The woman Darryl found in the park that night. It was somebody else. Another woman. Not you."

"How did he know?"

"Well, for one thing he said he didn't beat the woman up the way someone beat up on you. Hell, they said you were almost dead. The woman he went after was so scared that she let him do anything he wanted to her. He remembered she kept pleading with him not to hurt her. That doesn't sound like what happened with you. And besides, he told me she didn't even look like you. She was about the same age, he said. But she was bigger than you. She had different hair. She—'

"I had longer hair back then. I've lost a few pounds too."

"It wasn't you."

"It was dark that night—"

"It wasn't *that* dark."

"What do you mean?"

"She was black."

I stared at him.

"Darryl said that woman he attacked in the park that night was black," Gutierrez said. "Now, you may have cut your hair and lost some weight, but I don't think you could have ever passed for black. That would be a tough one to pull off." He laughed. "No matter how dark it was."

"Did Darryl say he had sex with the woman he attacked in the park?"

"Yeah," Gutierrez laughed. "That was the idea."

I sat there trying to take it all in. I'd come here looking for answers, but I wasn't really expecting this.

"So how did he wind up with my iPod – and the other stuff of mine they found in his room?"

"He said he saw you lying there that night as he was leaving the park. He thought you were dead. Your stuff was just sitting there for the taking, he told me, so he took it. But he always insisted he wasn't the one who attacked you."

"Did he ever tell anyone about this other woman?"

"He tried to. Claimed it was all a mistake. That you weren't the woman he attacked that night. How he wound up with your iPod and all the rest. But no one wanted to listen. Not even his own lawyer. The lawyer didn't want the jury to know he had raped someone in the park that night and robbed you when he thought you were dead. That kind of would have ruined his innocent victim approach. So he never let Darryl testify about any of that. He promised he could get him off without being charged with anything. Turned out he was wrong. I bet that lawyer was just looking for publicity from the trial, and he got what he wanted, I guess. But all Darryl got was a one-way trip to this place."

"Did you ever tell anyone this story before?" I asked.

"No."

"Why not?"

"Well, I saw what happened to Darryl."

"What are you talking about?"

"Darryl, he got himself stabbed to death in the prison recreation yard. People do get stabbed to death sometimes in prison, I guess. But no one ever found out who did it to him. That's kind of weird, don't you think?"

"Are you saying that you think there's something suspicious about his death?" I asked.

He shrugged again.

"So... why tell me now?"

"I don't know. Maybe I thought you had a right to know Darryl's version of it, not just the official story."

"What if I print this?"

"Just don't tell anyone it came from me. Or else I might end up dead too."

I tried to sort it all out in my head on the drive back to New York City. I worked very hard not to jump to any conclusions. To keep on being objective and thorough and level-headed about this. Just like I was on any story I covered. After all, there were a lot of possible answers to the questions that were now bothering me after the visit with Gutierrez.

Maybe Darryl Jackson had lied to him about what happened.

Maybe Gutierrez was lying to me about what Darryl Jackson had told him.

Maybe Gutierrez was just confused about the story and had mixed up some of the details.

Or maybe, just maybe, there had been a second female victim that night.

She had been the one Darryl Jackson raped.

And I had sent the wrong man to prison for attacking me.

Which meant that my real attacker was still out there. The same person who then attacked – and murdered – Cheryl Lee Barrett in almost the same way twelve years later.

CHAPTER 28

"Why are you doing this?" Ellen asked.

I had stopped by her office on the way back from the prison. We were sharing a bag of potato chips while I filled her in on the case.

"Because I want to know the truth."

"About Cheryl Lee Barrett?"

"About both of us."

"And you think – now tell me if I've got this right, because I truly don't believe what I'm hearing – that the two cases are somehow connected." She grabbed a handful of chips then offered the bag to me. I shook my head.

"Yes. I realize now that I don't really know anymore what actually happened to me in the park that night. And, even though the evidence says Joseph Enrico was the one who killed Cheryl Lee Barrett, I don't think he did. I'm not sure why. But every instinct in my body tells me that something else is going on here. And that it somehow involves me and what happened to me back then."

Ellen shook her head sadly. "Have you thought about the consequences of what you're doing here?"

I knew what she was talking about. It was the same argument that I had been having with myself ever since reading my own police case file.

"You've spent twelve years trying to put what happened to you that night in the park behind you, Jessie," Ellen said. "Everything you've done, every move you've ever made since then – it's all been about getting on with your life in a positive way. This isn't positive, kiddo. It's going to undo a lot of the good things you've accomplished and take you back to something you've tried so hard to forget. Are you prepared for that? This thing could take away the life you've built for yourself here, Jessie. It's a good life. Are you ready to give that all up? To open up the door again to everything that happened back then – and deal with it all over again. The nightmare is over for you now. It was over a long time ago. You don't want the nightmares to start all over again, do you?"

"That's why I have to do this," I said. "To stop the nightmares."

I had the dream again that night.

Like it always happened in the dream, he was chasing me – and I was powerless to stop him or do anything about it. And then he was on top of me. I felt a terrible pain on the back of my head. Then the ground beneath me. Someone was beating me, punching me, kicking me. Unseen hands groped my body and ripped off my clothes. He was going to rape me. I tried to scream, but no sounds came out.

Oh, God, the pain! I can't stand the pain.
Someone please make the pain go away.

Just before I lost consciousness in the dream, I saw it. The baseball cap. I saw the face underneath the hat too for the first time ever in one of my dreams. But it wasn't Darryl Jackson. It was Frank Lansdale. Then it changed into Steve Fredericks. Then it was Ellen. What were they doing here?

Suddenly, I was in a hospital bed, working my way out of a coma as the city prayed for my recovery. When I opened my eyes, my doctor was standing by my hospital bed. The person who'd saved my life. But it wasn't Dr. Spitz. Not in this dream. The person standing by my bed was smiling at me like Dr. Spitz used to do. But it was a man, not a woman. That's when I recognized him. It was Darryl Jackson. Holding out his hand to me as I lay in the hospital bed, trying to fight my way back out of the darkness into the land of the living.

I woke up screaming. I was back in my own bedroom. The TV was still on – I'd been watching a movie when I fell asleep. A book lay open on the nightstand next to me. I was sweating profusely and breathing heavily. I took a few seconds to get my bearings back, then pushed away the covers and sat up on the side of the bed. I did not want to go back to sleep.

I usually didn't put much stock in dreams, but you didn't have to be a professional psychiatrist to figure out the significance of this one.

Everything was the opposite of the way it was supposed to be.

The good guys had become the bad guys. Or at least I wasn't certain about them anymore. And the bad guys – the people like Darryl Jackson who I had hated for more than a decade – were the only ones in the dream who could save me.

It was as confusing as what was happening in my real life. All of my previous ideas and theories and beliefs were being systematically destroyed the more I looked into what actually happened that night.

What could I really believe?

Who could I trust?

And how was I going to find out the truth?

CHAPTER 29

I debated for a while in my mind about whether to go to Knowlton or Isaacs. I trusted Isaacs more, but it wasn't trust I was looking for now. I needed to play on Knowlton's ambition if I was going to pull off my idea. I had to convince him there was still a big story here that could boost his own career if he helped me. Even if I didn't tell him exactly what my idea was.

I went to see Danny as soon as I got to work the next morning.

"I want to write an open letter in the *Tribune*, appealing to a woman who may have been raped in Central Park to come forward and tell her story," I said.

"Is this about the Cheryl Lee Barrett story?"

"No, this is a different attack."

"But you don't know who the woman is?"

"No."

"Or even for sure if she was raped and attacked?"

"I don't."

"Was this around the same time as the Barrett woman's murder? Is that the link you're looking for?"

"No, this happened a long time before that."

"How long ago?"

"Twelve years."

He looked confused. "Twelve years? Wait a minute – isn't that when you were attacked in Central Park?"

"Yes."

"What the hell is going on here, Jessie?"

I explained to him how covering the Cheryl Lee Barrett murder – just like people suggested it would – had brought back a lot of bad memories for me about my own attack. And some new questions. So, I'd gone back and read the police file of my own case all over again and talked to several people about it.

I didn't go into any more detail than that, just made it sound as if I was curious about a few details of my own case.

And I damn sure didn't tell him anything about my suspicion that the two attacks – me and Cheryl Lee Barrett years later – were somehow connected.

I had to be careful here. Yes, I needed Danny to get on board with this idea and run interference for me on it with Isaacs or any of the other *Tribune* bigwigs who might object. Danny was good at pushing stuff through that he wanted. But, in order to get him to do it for me now, I had to convince him the idea was a good one. And, even more importantly, that I was absolutely sane and not having crazy flashbacks or anything to my own case.

"I've come across information that indicates to me that another woman might have been raped in the park on the same night that I was, but she never reported it," I said. "I don't really know much more myself right now. It's all suspicion, theory and hunches. But I think there's something there."

"And you think this was done by the same person who attacked you?"

"Possibly."

"Which means Darryl Jackson attacked two women in the park that night?"

Not really, I thought to myself. But I couldn't tell Danny that. So I stuck to my game plan I'd concocted as a reason for doing this.

"That's what I want to find out. Think about what a great story this could be, Danny. We run an open letter looking for a victim from that night – someone besides myself – that no one else ever knew about. We don't have to even explain that much – we can make it sound mysterious. All the other media will pick up on it. It'll make the news. My story's always been big news. If I start writing about it again, it would get a lot of attention. That would be good for the paper. Good for you. Good for everyone. And it might just turn out to be a good story too."

I knew one of the reasons Danny liked me – why he always wanted to be my editor, instead of Isaacs – was because of my background as a media star from the Central Park attack. I was a big name then, and I was still a big name as a reporter because of that past. This could be perfect for him – Jessie Tucker, the crime victim, and Jessie Tucker, the ace reporter, now going back on her own case for more information.

"What about Cheryl Lee Barrett?" he asked.

"I really want to focus on a story about my own case for now. Go back and visit that again, in the light of the new Central Park crime. This appeal for a mystery woman that night – a possible second victim of a rape attack that was never reported – could be the way to do that. What do you think?"

Danny hesitated before answering. I could see the wheels turning in his head, trying to figure out if backing my idea was really something that would help his career chances to become city editor sooner.

And, even more importantly, if he was willing to take a chance on it backfiring on him.

"Okay, if that's not good enough for you, how about this?" I said. "I've worked for years here at the *Tribune*. I've won awards, I've gotten exclusives, I've given you a lot of front-page stories. In all that time, I've never asked you for a favor. Now I'm asking you for a favor." I took a deep breath. "Please."

"A favor," Danny said.

"Yes, a favor."

"And you're certain that you're telling me absolutely everything you know?"

"Sure," I lied.

He's going to go for it, I thought.

"Okay, but let's just keep this between us for now," he said.

"What about Norman?"

I was concerned about Isaacs. I'd already passed my end of the week deadline from him on the Cheryl Lee Barrett story. This was different, but still linked to Cheryl Lee Barrett. I was afraid he might overrule Danny and kill my idea for a public appeal to an unknown victim that long-ago night.

"Norman is taking a few days off," he said. "A long weekend with his family. I'm in charge of the city desk until then."

Perfect, I thought to myself.

The article ran in the *Tribune* the next day.

APPEAL TO A RAPE VICTIM:
IT'S TIME TO TELL YOUR STORY

By Jessie Tucker

This story is not written for all the readers of the *Tribune*. Just for one. One who has kept a terrible secret hidden for a very long time.

You are a woman. You are an African-American. You are probably in your late 30s or early 40s now.

On the night of June 4, 2007, something terrible happened to you while you were in Central Park.

You have never told anyone else about this since then.

Tell me. I'll understand.

I was there too that night…

CHAPTER 30

I was sitting with Logan Kincaid in a pub on the Upper East Side.

The place was dark, and he had picked out a booth in the corner. It was very small, and we had to sit close together. Technically, I wasn't sure if this was a date or just a social/business dinner since he'd been helping me on the story. But it was the closest I had come to an actual date in a long time.

He'd called me that afternoon. I'd been thinking about calling him if I could think of any reason to do that, so I was excited to hear from him again.

I really liked Logan.

And – for some reason – I felt I could trust him.

I didn't feel that way about many people anymore these days.

I'd debated beforehand how much to tell him about everything I had found out about my own case and the possibility of some kind of connection – absurd as that might sound – to the death of Cheryl Lee Barrett.

In the end, especially after I'd had a few glasses of wine that helped loosen me up, I told him everything I knew from the past few days.

"I realize now that this was something I had needed to do for a long time, even before this happened," I said. "Ever since the attack. Everyone told me it was over. I even believed it. At least I convinced myself I did. But somewhere, deep down inside, I knew it wasn't over at all. I knew that there were still questions that had to be answered. And that I couldn't ever live a normal life until

I found out those answers. Now the death of Cheryl Lee Barrett in the same park where I was attacked – and all that's happened since – has brought this all home to me."

"What will you do next?" he asked after we ordered. Veal parmigiana for me, lasagna for him.

"Keep asking questions."

"What if you don't get any answers?"

"Then I'll ask more questions – until I do."

He smiled.

"You get so excited over a story like this," he said. "I mean, I can see it in your face. It's like adrenaline is running through your entire body. It must be really fun to be a reporter, huh?"

"It's about the only fun I get these days," I joked.

"Aren't you involved with anyone?"

"No, not in a long time."

"Were you ever married?"

"I was engaged once."

"What happened?"

"He decided he didn't want to be married to a cripple."

"But you're not crippled," Logan said.

"Yeah, but he didn't know that then."

I told him about me and Gary Bettig.

"Hey, I thought I had a pretty good life back then. Great job, great guy I was getting married to – and then I lost it all. I have a different life now. Maybe better, not worse. But, well… different. It's not always been easy adjusting to everything I've had to deal with since the attack."

"Your fiancé, he just dumped you while you were in the hospital recovering?"

"He came to see me right at the end of visiting hours one night. I guess he didn't want to have to stay long. He brought me flowers though. I remember the flowers. I remember what I was eating for dinner too – hospital chicken à la king – when he walked into my room. I was so happy to see him, and then, a few minutes later, I wasn't."

"What did he tell you?"

"That he needed to move on with his life – and he couldn't deal with 'babysitting a cripple'. Those were his exact words. I can repeat them by heart even after all these years."

"You must have been furious at him."

"Oh, I was. But I was more heartbroken than anything else. Thinking about how I'd lost the man I was going to marry and screwed up my whole life by doing this stupid thing of walking through that damn park at night alone. I begged Gary Bettig not to leave me. I'm not proud of that, but I did. He left anyway. I still think about him sometimes – wonder how things would have worked out between us if I hadn't become the poster girl crime victim that I did."

"What happened to this Bettig guy?"

"He got married to someone else. Had a couple of kids."

"So you didn't keep in touch after that day in the hospital?"

"Uh, no, we don't exchange Christmas cards or anything."

"You clearly still think about this a lot, Jessie," he said.

"Well, it's not like I fell down and scraped my knee or something like that in the park that night. You don't just wait a couple of days for a scab to form and the bruises to heal. These wounds took a lot longer. And those are just the ones on the outside. The ones inside don't seem to heal at all. Or at least they haven't for me yet. Oh, the nightmares are getting better now. They're down to only maybe two or three a month. Maybe if I live to be hundred—"

I never talked about this with anyone. I always kept my emotions about it all bottled up inside me. But, like I said, I trusted Logan for some reason, even though I hadn't known him for very long. And maybe the wine was really going to my head a bit by that time. I noticed he hadn't been drinking anything at all, but I'd put away a lot.

I stopped myself at that point.

"I'm sorry," I said.

Way to go, Jessie. Terrific way to turn a man on. You think maybe you might want to sleep with this guy, so you start telling him about your nightmares. That's all he needs – some crazy woman waking up screaming next to him in the middle of the night.

Maybe I should tell him about how my father left my mother too before I ever knew him? How my mother had lied about that to me for years. How, after I found out the truth, I blamed her for chasing him away. And how Gary Bettig leaving me in the same way meant I was no better than my mother had been.

Sure, that ought to really make this guy want to spend time with me, huh?

"It's okay," Logan said. "I like getting to know the real you."

The waiter brought our food. Logan took a bite of his lasagna.

"Is it good?" I asked.

He nodded. "Delicious. This place sure beats the restaurant at the hotel where I've been staying."

"Tell me about that," I said. "How do you still afford to travel around the country like this, living in hotels or whatever, while you try to resolve this thing about your sister?"

"Actually, I'm going to have to get a job – and, as for living at a hotel, that's about to end too. I'll be heading back to Santa Barbara soon, I guess."

"Oh," I said softly. "That's a bummer."

"The Barrett woman's murder really has nothing to do with my sister's death. You know that as well as I do. There's nothing more for me here in New York City."

"Nothing? I guess I should be insulted, huh?"

"Well…" he stammered, "I didn't mean—"

"I know what you meant." I laughed.

We sat there for a long time, exchanging more stories and talking about our lives. The kind of things two people do when they're about to begin a relationship or maybe even sleep together for the first time.

It was such a nice feeling being there like that with a man I felt so comfortable being around. Talking. Revealing secrets. Laughing too. And maybe, most of all, feeling a sexual connection.

At one point – when we were talking about our childhoods – he reached over and took my hand. He held onto it for a long time. I didn't pull away like I probably would have with anyone else. I looked at him and smiled. He smiled back.

It really was a terrific evening. And I thought it was going to end up with him asking me back to his hotel. What would my answer be? I'd have to wait to see how it all played out, but I decided right then at that moment – when he held my hand and smiled at me – that I wasn't going to play games. My answer for Logan was going to be "yes".

Except I never got a chance to tell him that, because he never asked the question.

Instead, he looked uncomfortable as we left the restaurant. Not like he was looking forward to whatever happened next, but like he was trying to find a way to avoid it. I didn't understand.

It got even more confusing when we got in a cab. Not knowing what to do, I gave the driver the address to my building. When we got there, Logan didn't even get out of the cab to walk me to my door. He just gave me a quick kiss on the cheek.

I stood in front of my building and watched the cab with him in it pull away.

I kept hoping that he'd tell the driver to turn around and come back. That he'd then take me in his arms, come upstairs with me and we'd have the sort of sex I used to have a long time ago, before everything changed.

But there was no returning cab. No Logan.

Finally, I went inside and up to my apartment.

Alone.

The way I always did.

CHAPTER 31

The next day I went to see Professor Howard Bush, a professor of criminal psychology at John Jay College. A few years ago, Bush had written a book called *Inside the Criminal Mind*. I had done a Sunday feature on it, using the examples Bush cited in the book and comparing them to criminal cases that I'd covered for the *Tribune*. The publicity helped Bush get on several talk shows and even option the book to Hollywood, although a movie was never made. Bush told me afterward that he owed me a big favor if I ever needed one. Now I did. One more favor of mine being called in.

Howard Bush greeted me warmly in his office on the seventh floor of the school's faculty building.

"I'm working on a story," I told him, "and I thought maybe you could help."

"What's the topic?"

"Confessions. I want to know everything about them. There's a whole chapter on the subject in your book, if I recall correctly. Tell me all about people who confess to crimes. Why? How? What makes them admit it? And, most importantly of all, how often are they telling the whole truth? I mean, what if the confession is a lie? How often does that happen?"

"Is this about the dead woman in Central Park? I've seen a couple of articles in the papers about that by you in the past week or two."

"Yes, that's what I'm working on," I said.

"But the man who did it – the ex-con who was shot to death by the cops – he never had a chance to confess, did he?"

"No."

"Then why all the questions about confessions?"

"I'm looking into an old case too. One that happened a long time ago. The suspect confessed to the crime and was sent to prison. I want to find out if there's any possibility his confession wasn't true. And, if it wasn't, why did the suspect confess to the police?"

"And you think this old case is somehow connected to the recent death of this woman in Central Park?"

"Yes."

"How?"

"I'm not sure yet."

Bush spent about forty minutes telling me what he knew about confessions:

"A surprisingly large number of all confessions to the police are not true," he said. "That is, they are not exactly what they seem to be. Some of them are mostly true, but not completely. Others have only a glimmer of truth to them. And some are complete lies from start to finish. But the idea of a confession always being the end of a case is not really accurate. Every time I hear that a suspect has confessed, I'm still skeptical that I'm hearing the whole story. And a lot of the time I'm right.

"Now, of course, there are a lot of different reasons why people give inaccurate – or false – confessions.

"For instance, every time there's a serial killer on the loose, you get kooks coming out of the woodwork to 'confess'. Most of the time these are just people who are lonely and envious of all the attention the real criminal is getting and simply want to be part of the action.

"Then there are the 'conscience-stricken' ones who've never gotten caught for anything, but feel guilty over the things they've done. So sometimes they confess to a crime they didn't do. It's an act of redemption – a cleansing of the soul – sort of like confessing to a priest. We all have consciences. Sometimes it just pops up in different ways.

"And, of course, there's also the true crazies, the people who are so delusional that they actually believe what they're confessing to. They're the hardest to be sure about, because even a lie detector test won't always give them away. In their mind, they're telling the truth.

"But all these only made up a small percentage of the phony confessions that I studied in my research for the book. That's because there's an even more important factor at work here. You see, the most common reason for false confessions doesn't come from the criminal, it comes from the police."

"You mean the police coerce people into making false confessions?" I asked.

"That's right."

"And this happens a lot?"

"All the time."

"Why?"

"Why do the cops do it? To pad their arrest record. To close cases. To get their job done. I think that most of the time cops who do it are pretty sure they've got the right person – and it's good for everyone if he's put away in jail. So, they take a shortcut. They get him to confess. Only they're the ones who are telling him what to confess to, not the other way around."

"I mean, why do the suspects confess at all?" I asked. "And what would prompt a person to admit to something he didn't do? Physical coercion? This isn't some South American dictatorship we're talking about here. It's the American justice system."

"No, of course not," Bush said. "I'm sure some do still use the old brass knuckles and bright light in the eyes technique, but you don't hear about very much of that these days in police stations. Too many lawyers, too many civil lawsuits. But there's still coercion. Only it's mental, not physical. Sometimes that can be even more effective than physical abuse."

"I don't understand…"

"Oh, the technique's been well documented," Bush said. "All the way back to the time of the Korean War when our GIs were brainwashed. An expert – who knows the right psychological techniques – can get a person to admit to almost anything. Maybe he'll even believe he's guilty. After hours of interrogation, repetitive questions, lack of sleep, deprivation of contact with the outside world – these are powerful tools in the hands of an experienced police interrogator. It's not that hard to get a suspect to say what you want him to say."

I nodded.

"Tell me more about this case," Bush said to me.

I told him just enough so he could answer my questions. That a man did confess to a crime. And later he said he didn't do it. I also told him about the discrepancies in the description of the victim and the question of whether or not the victim was raped.

"Well, it seems pretty obvious," he said when I was finished. "He attacked someone that night. Just not the one he was arrested for. So when the police started questioning him about the crime, it was easy to get a confession. He thought they were talking about the other woman, the one he really attacked – not the one he didn't. He got confused. Until someone explained to him later the criminal consequences of the two different cases. One was a sex attack, the other was very nearly murder. That's when he tried to rescind the confession, but it was too late. The cops had him. They had lots of evidence. They also had a positive ID from the victim you said, right?"

"Yes," I said quietly. "Do you really think that's what happened here?"

"It's possible."

"And…"

"And if it was, then a good police investigator might have been able to get a confession. He probably thought he was guilty. He just wanted to put him in jail. That's what the criminal justice system is about sometimes. The ends justify the means. Hell, you know that."

"And you say there's a lot of cops who do this when questioning suspects?"

"More than you think. Of course, it's easier if you've been trained in these types of techniques. If you have something that gives you an advantage – an edge – over the suspect…"

I thought about Steve Fredericks, who had gotten the confession out of Darryl Jackson for attacking me. Fredericks was a college graduate. He'd majored in psychology.

"You mean like a criminal psychology degree?" I asked.

Bush nodded.

"Ms. Tucker, this case we're talking about – the attack and rape of a woman – it sounds a lot like your case. Is that what we're talking about here?"

"Yes."

"I don't understand."

"Neither do I."

On the subway ride back to the *Tribune* offices, I kept going through everything over and over again in my mind – trying to make some sort of sense out of it all.

Everywhere I had looked since the murder of Cheryl Lee Barrett, I kept finding out new things about myself and what happened to me. Steve Fredericks wasn't the hero cop I always thought he was – he was at best not a great cop who took some shortcuts, and at worse he had knowingly coerced a false confession. Darryl Jackson, who I'd hated for twelve long years, might very well not have been the man responsible for my attack. All the details of my attack are confusing for me now too. I wasn't sure about anything anymore.

So what about everything else – and everyone – I remember from back then?

My entire life – the one I'd painstakingly put together ever since that horrible night that changed me forever – was suddenly falling apart around me.

How did any of this relate to the murder of Cheryl Lee Barrett? I didn't know. I was sure about one thing though.

Cheryl Lee Barrett was dead – I could never bring her back to life.

But I sure as hell could try to find out some answers about my own life.

CHAPTER 32

Darryl Jackson's mother had moved from the housing project on the Lower East Side where police had arrested him and found my belongings under his bed.

I tracked her down to a rent-subsidized building in Queens. Her husband had worked as a driver for the board of education, Betsy Jackson explained. When he died of a heart attack ten years ago, she'd used his life insurance money and pension to get herself and her two other children out of the housing project. She said she wished she'd been able to do that in time to save Darryl too. Darryl was a good boy, she insisted, he just got caught up with the wrong crowd while growing up in a bad neighborhood.

"All of his friends, they never were any good," Mrs. Jackson said. "I told Darryl so many times not to hang around with them. He said he knew they were trouble, but not to worry about him. He'd never do anything bad like they did. But he was wrong. I guess they just led him astray…"

I didn't say anything. No one had forced Darryl Jackson to attack women or rob a bodega or any of the other things he was accused of doing. But there was no point in arguing about that with his mother. Betsy Jackson only wanted to remember good things about her son.

Mrs. Jackson knew who I was from the minute I introduced myself. And why not? I was the victim that her son was convicted of brutally attacking. But, if she had any guilt or remorse or even simple sympathy for me, she didn't show it. She seemed more angry than anything else. Angry at the people who had taken her son away from her. Angry at whoever in prison had killed him. And, maybe most of all, angry at me for being the one who caused all of Darryl Jackson's problems.

Yep, she railed on for a long time about all the injustice done to her son – including a lot of victim bashing.

And, of course, I was the victim that she bashed.

"I don't understand the women who put themselves in that situation, who allow things like that to happen to them. Like you in in the park that night. What were you doing out there in the dark at that hour? What kind of a decent woman does that? I mean, if you ask me – I think you were just asking for it."

I bit my lip and let the woman talk for a long time. All I wanted was information. And I was willing to endure whatever she wanted to say in order to get that information from her.

"Tell me about the day the police came to get Darryl," I finally said when she was finished.

"They broke the door down and burst in," she said. "They told me he'd been arrested and charged with attempted murder. That he'd beaten up and left for dead some woman – I guess that was you – in Central Park. Then they searched the house. They found… well, they found some of your belongings underneath his bed. That was the evidence they used to help convict him at the trial."

"Did you ask your son about the stuff of mine they found?"

"Yes. He admitted he'd taken it from you that night in the park. But only after he found you there unconscious. When he thought you were dead. He told me he stole it all, but said he wasn't the one who hurt you."

It was the same story he'd told his cellmate Gutierrez and apparently repeated until his death. It was a pretty absurd story, but that didn't mean it wasn't true.

"Did you believe him?" I asked her.

She shrugged. I think she wasn't sure what to believe.

"I read an old interview with you back when Darryl was arrested, Mrs. Jackson. You claimed then that the police planted the evidence in Darryl's room. That he never had my stuff at all."

"Well, it could have happened that way," she said, crossing her arms.

"But those are two totally different stories," I pointed out. "And, if the police really did plant evidence, where did they get it from? The only person who could have had them was someone who had taken them from in the park. So none of that makes much sense."

"The police lied," Mrs. Jackson said, as if that somehow resolved the matter.

I asked her then about the story from Gutierrez about Darryl attacking another woman in the park that night. A woman who wasn't me.

"Darryl never hurt any women that night. He didn't hurt anyone. It's all lies."

"Then why would he have claimed that's the way it all happened?"

"Darryl was scared because everyone blamed him for what happened to you. I think he just made up that other story because it was the only thing he could think of to get out of that. But I don't believe he hurt you or any other woman. Darryl was a good boy. And you people – the police, the D.A., the media – you killed him!"

This was clearly going nowhere. Darryl's mother had created some kind of memory of her son as a victim, not a predator. Nothing I said would change that.

Betsy Jackson told me about getting the phone call that her son had been stabbed to death in prison. About how she'd been to see him there just a few days before. About his funeral and burial.

"Do you remember anything about your last conversation?"

"We just talked. Like we always did. Nothing special about it. I mean, it wasn't like I knew that was going to be the last time I saw my son or anything."

"Did Darryl ever talk to you about me?"

"Not by name."

"What do you mean?"

"Whenever he talked about you, he just referred to you as 'that bitch who put me in here.'"

Mrs. Jackson smiled at the memory, apparently pleased that she could share it with me. I wasn't going to be able to take much more of this. But that was okay. I was almost out of questions anyway.

"Did he mention me during that last conversation you had at the prison?" I asked.

"As a matter of fact, he did. He said somebody had contacted him recently about you. He said this person wanted to come visit with him there to talk about you."

"Who?"

"Some doctor."

"A prison doctor?"

"No, a doctor from New York City."

"What was his name?"

"It wasn't a he, it was a she. A woman doctor named Jane… or something like that. She worked at one of the big hospitals in Manhattan. Lenox Hill, I think."

"Dr. Janet Spitz?"

"Yes, that's the name."

I sat there stunned.

"Do you know her?" she asked.

"Yes, I did."

Dr. Janet Spitz. The doctor who'd operated on me, worked with me through my rehabilitation and nursed me back to the living. Why would Dr. Spitz go to see the man who had been convicted for brutally attacking me?

"Do you know if the doctor ever met with your son?"

"I'm not sure."

"Or any more about what she wanted?"

"Like I said, that was the last time I talked to Darryl before he died."

"This could be very important, Mrs. Jackson."

"Why don't you go ask the doctor then?" she said.

When I got back to the office, I looked up information on both deaths.

Darryl Jackson had been stabbed to death in the Attica Prison yard on April 27, 2012. A homemade knife was found near the body. No one was ever caught. The story in the *Tribune* gave a few more details about the circumstances of Jackson's death, including the fact that he was the man convicted in the Jessie Tucker attack several years earlier. That was pretty much the only news peg in Darryl Jackson's short but unpleasant time on this planet.

Dr. Janet Spitz's death was big news that landed on Page One for several days. "TOP WOMAN DOC GUNNED DOWN IN FAST FOOD ROBBERY" was the headline on the first story that ran in the *Tribune*. I looked at the date on the article. May 3, 2012.

More coincidences?

It took a while, but I was finally able to confirm through the New York State Prison Board records that Darryl Jackson had met with a visitor identified as Dr. Janet Spitz. The meeting took place on April 19, 2012. Barely a week before Darryl Jackson died in the prison yard stabbing. And two weeks before Dr. Spitz was murdered in the seemingly random Manhattan robbery at the McDonald's.

Damn.

The close timing of the two violent deaths hadn't set off warning alarms with anyone back then, including me – because no one knew of any connection between the two people. But now I did.

What did it all mean?

Well, thus far, nothing about this story had turned out to be what it seemed.

So maybe Dr. Janet Spitz's death wasn't either.

CHAPTER 33

Charles Spitz, Dr. Spitz's husband, was an executive with a big pharmaceutical company. He had remarried since her death. His new wife was a doctor too. An anesthesiologist at New York Hospital, he said. There was a picture of the two of them on the mantel in the living room where he and I sat. There were also pictures of their little baby girl and two older children – a boy and a girl – from his marriage to Janet Spitz. The girl was the spitting image of her dead mom.

The house was a split-level in Ridgefield, New Jersey, a suburb about fifteen miles outside of New York City. He said he'd moved there after she died – and even before he'd met his new wife, whose name was Roberta – because the old house where they'd lived just had too many memories for him and the children. He wanted a fresh start.

"I realize we never met," I explained when we introduced ourselves to each other. "But I feel like I know you very well. Dr. Spitz used to talk about you all the time."

"Well, I have to tell you the same thing."

"She talked about me?"

"Constantly."

"I guess I was a pretty formidable medical challenge for her," I told him. "If she could cure me, she could cure anyone. I was in awfully bad shape when she first saw me. I owe her my life. It's a debt that I'll never be able to repay."

"You were more than just a patient to Janet," she said. "You were special."

"Well, thank you."

"I think Janet would have wanted you to know that."

I took out my notebook then and began asking him questions.

I'd told him I was coming to see him because I was doing a retrospective article about everything that had happened to me – and Dr. Spitz obviously played a large role in that. I said I wanted to find out some more about her. Her background. Her personal life. The time between my medical crisis and her own death a few years later.

It was a pretty good cover story. Who knows – the paper might even want me to write something like that one day. But, in any case, I could always tell him later that some stupid editor had spiked the article.

Of course, I could have just told him the truth. Except I wasn't sure myself what that really was. And what was the point in upsetting him and raising questions about the death of the wife he'd buried a long time ago? No, as had happened a lot of times in my career as a reporter, the lies just seemed to work better.

"I remember Janet would come home every night from the hospital and tell me about you," he said. "She'd say 'Jessie moved her hand today'. Or 'Jessie talked to me'. And one day – I can remember that day just like it was yesterday – she said to me: 'Jessie walked – she got out of her bed and walked across the room!' She was so happy. Of course, there were days too when she said she felt depressed and powerless to help you. When she thought you would never make it. 'This girl needs a miracle from God,' she told me one day when you were in a great deal of pain. 'I can't do anything.' And then a few days later, she was on top of the world. 'She's back!' she said. 'It is a miracle. God must have heard my prayers.'" He shook his head sadly. "That's the kind of doctor – the kind of woman – Janet was."

I wrote all that down, trying to remember I had to be professional and treat this just like any other story.

"Don't get me wrong – I love Roberta. She's a wonderful woman. I guess I've been very lucky. It's just that I lost Janet so quickly that – well, I never really had a chance to say goodbye. One day she was there, and then she was gone. It all seemed so unnecessary, so pointless. I mean Janet was going to get lunch at a McDonald's in the heart of a good neighborhood in New York City. And that's why she died. I have to tell you – the senselessness of it tore me up inside for a long time. It still does, I suppose. I wish I could see Janet one more time. I wish I could I tell her I'm fine and tell her all about my life now. I wish I could tell her I miss her – say goodbye. Do you understand what I mean?"

I nodded.

Then I went through the details of Janet Spitz's murder with him. It was painful, and I was sorry about that. But I needed to know if this man knew anything that hadn't been in the newspaper accounts. As it turned out, he didn't. The version he gave was the same one I already knew. A gunman wearing a ski mask burst in, announced a holdup and took the money from the cash registers. Then, on his way out, he turned and – for no apparent reason – shot Janet Spitz in the chest.

"And the police said that the shooting of your wife appeared to be totally random? There was no motive?"

"Why would anyone have a motive to kill Janet?"

"Oh, I don't know. Maybe he was a disgruntled former patient or something. Did she ever mention anyone like that? Someone who had filed a malpractice suit against her…?"

He shook his head no. "That thought crossed my mind too after the murder. But the police checked and said there was no evidence of anything like that. The gunman never said anything at all to Janet, didn't act as if he knew her. He simply shot her. It was just a holdup gone wrong, that's what the police said."

I had one more question I needed to ask, which I'd been saving until the end of the conversation.

"Shortly before your wife died, she went to visit an inmate in prison. The name of the prisoner she saw was Darryl Jackson. Jackson was the man sent to jail for attacking me in the park that night. Do you have any idea at all why Dr. Spitz wanted to see him?"

"You know, it's funny that you bring that up. Janet did say something about that before she died. And she mentioned your name."

"What did she say?"

"Just that she'd gone to see this man in jail. And that she wanted to talk to you again too. She said she had something to tell you."

"But she never told you what it was?"

"No. She said she'd tell me more as soon as she worked it all out. Except she never did. She died right after that."

CHAPTER 34

Driving back to Manhattan, I tried hard to control the rising wave of paranoia that threatened to engulf me.

There was no question I was having a lot of trouble being objective about all this. I might keep telling myself it was just another story, but I knew the truth. This story was about my life now. The stakes in this story were much higher for me than they'd ever been before.

And, no matter how hard I tried, I couldn't stop thinking about all the questions I'd uncovered:

Did Darryl Jackson really attack another woman in the park that night?

Was his story true about finding my belongings *after* the attack on me when he found me unconscious?

Why did Dr. Spitz go to see Darryl Jackson in prison just before he was murdered himself?

Why did the new witness, Phyllis Lachman, see someone running away from the Cheryl Lee Barrett murder scene wearing a New York Yankee baseball cap – the same kind of baseball cap I'd begun seeing in my dreams on the head of my own attacker.

And – most importantly of all – if someone else, not Darryl Jackson, had really attacked me in the park that night, then he could still be out there. Which meant he might have attacked other victims too.

Maybe Cheryl Lee Barrett, as I now suspected.

But possibly other women in similar crimes over the years that no one had ever linked together.

I went back to the Police Records Division and talked again with McCracken, the friendly young guy who still thought I was working on a feature story. I said I wanted him to run some computer checks for me on every fatal – or near-fatal – seemingly random attack that had occurred on a woman in New York City for the past twelve years.

Of course, that would be a large number, I said, so I asked him to narrow it down into the following: Attacks in which the motive appeared to be sexual, but no physical evidence of rape was ever found – just like with Cheryl Lee Barrett. I also suggested he focus on high-profile crimes in good neighborhoods – not, for example, gang killings. I wasn't sure about that part of it, but both the attacks on Cheryl Lee Barrett now and me in the past had been front-page news. I was assuming that a killer – if there was one killer doing the attack – would have followed that pattern in identifying his targets.

In the end, I came up with a handful of murders that fit the pattern.

All of them had taken place in safe neighborhoods. That is, they weren't the kind of spots where you would normally be concerned about crime. One happened in a garage near Lincoln Center, another on Park Avenue and so on. All of the incidents were at night, between the hours of six p.m. and midnight. Interesting.

There were a lot of other things that didn't seem to match though.

The time frame, for instance. There was no particular order to them. The first one was me. Then there were more over the next couple of years. After that, nothing until Cheryl Lee Barrett was murdered.

The ages of the victims were very different too, ranging from twenty-four to forty-one. They had different kinds of jobs, everything from secretaries to waitresses to female business executives. Some were single while others were married and – from the pictures in the story files anyway – it looked like two of them were brunettes, one a blonde and one a redhead.

For what it was worth, none of the earlier victims looked particularly like any other in the pictures. And Cheryl Lee Barrett and I sure didn't look very much alike either.

But all of the victims, including me, had had their clothes ripped off, but no other evidence was found of a sexual assault. In some, witnesses even reported seeing someone wearing a baseball cap nearby, even though this hadn't seemed significant to anyone at the time. Some of the cases had been quickly closed with the arrest or death of a suspect or suspects. Others had never been solved.

So where did that leave me?

Well, I could go visit the men in prison who'd been found guilty of the crimes. I could ask if there was any possibility they'd been set up by someone who was trying to hide something else about the case. I knew they would all say yes. So that wouldn't be very productive.

Or I could go back and talk to family, friends and co-workers of the dead women from the old cases. But what would that accomplish? And it would reopen a lot of old wounds among the living. These were people who had made peace a long time ago about the loss of their loved ones. Did I really want to tell them that maybe justice wasn't done exactly as they believed it had been? Besides, none of these people probably knew anything that would help anyway. Most of them had happened a long time ago, and the trail of evidence was old and very cold.

The Cheryl Lee Barrett murder, on the other hand, was still fresh.

I was back to where I started. If I could somehow get to the bottom of that, the rest of the pieces of the puzzle might come together.

CHAPTER 35

"Do you have any idea how crazy all of this sounds?" Ellen said to me.

"I do."

"And you still really believe this stuff you just told me could be true?"

"I'm not crazy, Ellen."

"The very definition of crazy is that the person who is crazy has no idea how irrational they are acting."

"Actually, the definition of crazy – or insanity, as the saying usually goes – is someone who does the same thing over and over again expecting different results. Albert Einstein said that. Doesn't apply here. I'm trying to do something different. I'm trying to take a new look at everything. I'm trying to find some new answers. What's wrong with that?"

We were at the gym again. I was on the exercise bike and Ellen was doing the treadmill walk next to me. I'd purposefully come at this time because I knew she might be here and I wanted to see her. I felt like I needed to talk to someone about these ideas racing around in my head. Someone who could understand me. Except it wasn't really working out like that.

"Just to be clear," Ellen said now, "you now believe that the attack on you and the murder of Cheryl Lee Barrett were done by the same person?"

"Yes."

"And the killer just might have murdered other women too."

"That's my theory at the moment."

"You also believe that the prime suspect in all this is Frank Lansdale, who just happens to be a highly regarded U.S. senator as well as an American war hero?"

"Uh-huh."

"How is any of this even remotely possible, Jessie?"

"I'm still working on that part."

Ellen got off the treadmill and began drying herself off with a towel. I knew then she was finished exercising for the day. Not me. I kept pedaling away on the exercise bike. My body needed a lot more work than Ellen's did.

"Did you get any response for that plea for a mysterious woman victim from the park that you wrote about in the paper?" she asked, stretching out her hamstrings.

"Not yet."

"Do you have any solid evidence of a connection between you and the attack on Cheryl Lee Barrett? Or the deaths of any of the other women? Or any of the rest of the stuff you've told me?"

"Ellen, I understand how it sounds." Sweat was pouring off me now and I was breathing hard. "That's why I came to you, instead of my boss at the *Tribune* or the police or anyone else. I really need your advice on what to do next."

"You want my advice? Okay, here it is. Just go out and cover the Cheryl Lee Barrett murder, like you started out doing. Move on from what happened to you. Forget all these other cases you came up with of women who you claim were mysteriously – and similarly – murdered over the years. Why do you even want to go there? That's all in the past, the Cheryl Lee Barrett murder is news that's happening now."

"The person who controls the past controls the future," I said. "And the person who controls the present controls the past."

"Huh?"

"George Orwell said that."

She rolled her eyes. " I can't believe you're quoting Einstein and Orwell to me in the same conversation. When did you become such an intellectual?"

"Well, at least it shows I'm not totally crazy." I smiled.

"All right then, you're not crazy. But you're acting very weird and paranoid. I mean thinking a killer from the past is still out there after you when everyone else knows he's dead? That sure sounds paranoid to me. Even you have to admit that sounds paranoid, right? I'm going to take a shower."

I kept pedaling away on my exercise bike after Ellen left.

It was always difficult for me to get started on the bike. But, after a while, I got into the flow of it. My legs pumping, sweat dripping down my face, my breathing getting quicker. Twenty minutes a day was my absolute minimum on the exercise bike, thirty minutes was the usual and sometimes I kept at it for as long as an hour or even an hour and a half. Especially when I needed to think. I found that the exercise bike was a good way to think about things that were bothering me.

As I pedaled now, I remembered again what it was like when I took my first few steps in the hospital as I began the long road to recovery. Ever since then, I always believed I could do anything I put my mind to. Determination and hard work could solve almost any problem. That's how I lived my life then, and that's how I still lived it now. If determination and hard work was what it took to accomplish something, then I was the woman to do it.

But now I had to make a big decision over what to do next because I was at a crossroads on this story.

Was I just letting my imagination run out of control?

Was I really acting paranoid, like Ellen said?

Maybe I was.

But all the way on my trip to the *Tribune* office after I left the gym, I couldn't help thinking about an old expression I'd once heard someone say:

"I might be paranoid, but that doesn't mean someone isn't out to get me."

CHAPTER 36

Ellen was right about one thing though. I needed to concentrate more on the present, instead of the past. The present was the one thing I could control. And the present meant the Cheryl Lee Barrett murder. Which took me back to Senator Frank Lansdale again.

No matter how confusing this all was, I was certain that Lansdale was the key to Cheryl Lee Barrett's murder. He could be the key to everything else too. I needed to talk to Lansdale. So I decided to try the easy way first. I called up Lansdale's office and requested an interview with him.

"May I ask exactly what it is you want to discuss with him?" Betty Whalen asked. She didn't sound very friendly this time. Must have gotten word about the nosy reporter from the *Tribune* that was asking too many questions.

"Margaret Kincaid."

Whalen put me on hold while she went to consult with someone. Maybe the senator himself. When she came back on the line, she seemed to be trying very hard to keep her emotions under control and sound poised and professional.

"Senator Lansdale says that the death of the woman he knew as Margaret Kincaid was a tragic loss. He is glad the police quickly tracked down the perpetrator of this heinous crime. Although subsequent developments have revealed that she used a false identity, the senator knew her only as a dedicated, conscientious campaign worker who shared his dream of a better America. He was not aware, of course, of the alleged criminal activities in her past."

The words sounded very formal. I knew why.

"That was his prepared statement, wasn't it?" I asked Whalen. "The one he released to the media right after the murder."

"Yes, I suppose so."

"That's not good enough."

"I'm afraid it will have to do."

Well, so much for the easy way.

The senator's New York campaign office was on the twelfth floor of a midtown high-rise. The first time I'd gone there after the murder I'd gotten a warm reception. I didn't figure that was going to happen this time. I sat at a sidewalk café across the street from the building, drank coffee and tried to figure out a clever way to get inside the office to talk to Lansdale. I couldn't think of a damn thing. Even waiting for him on the street and trying to confront him there didn't seem to be a viable option. The building had an underground garage, and Senator Lansdale struck me as the kind of guy who probably had a limousine waiting for him down there. Finally, I decided to just storm the ramparts and see what happened. Sometimes the best plan is no plan.

Betty Whalen looked like she was going to have a heart attack when I walked up to her desk.

"What are you doing here?" she asked.

"I came to see the senator."

"But I told you on the phone that he wasn't available."

"I just thought he was playing hard-to-get."

"He's meeting with some campaign fundraising people."

"I'll wait."

"I'm sorry, but you'll have to leave—"

"The only way I'm leaving without seeing the senator is if you throw me out yourself." I looked at Betty, who was probably no more than five feet tall, about fifty and plump. "I don't know about you, but I lift weights every day in the gym. I figure I can take you, Betty."

Whalen picked up the telephone and dialed a number. I wasn't sure if she was calling the senator or some kind of office security. But it didn't matter. Just then, Senator Lansdale emerged out of one of the offices. He was surrounded by a group of about a half-dozen men. The fundraisers, I assumed. Lansdale looked as stunned as Betty Whalen had when he suddenly saw me standing there.

"Hello, Senator," I said. "This is perfect timing. I need to talk to you."

"You'll have to make an appointment," he said coldly.

"Yeah, well, I really don't have time for that. According to Betty here, you seem to be booked up for the next hundred years or so. So we'll just have to have our little chat now." I looked at the fundraising men who'd just been meeting with the senator. "I think it might be better for you if we did this in private. What I have to say, you don't want these gentlemen to hear."

Lansdale's face flushed with anger. "I have nothing to hide," he insisted.

"Okay, it's your call."

I walked closer to the senator until I was face to face with him.

"I've been doing some investigating into the murder of your campaign aide," I said. "I found out some really interesting stuff."

"I know what you've been doing," he said. "You've been harassing my son. You've been snooping around and asking questions about me and my family. I won't stand for that. I will not allow my reputation to be dragged through the mud over a pack of lies."

"Okay," I said. "Let me tell you what I know. You were having an affair with the dead woman. You met her in hotel rooms where you secretly had sex with her. What you might or might not have known at the time was that her father served with you in Iraq during Desert Storm. Cheryl Lee seemed to hold some kind of grudge against you because of that. I think Joseph Enrico, the man the police say murdered her, did too. He was in your unit in Iraq, just like Cheryl Lee's father was. You must have recognized

Enrico's name – how come you never told anyone about that after he was shot dead by police? Anyway, I don't think Cheryl Lee Barrett and Joseph Enrico thought you were such a big war hero like everyone else. I think she came here with Enrico to New York City to blackmail you. Now Cheryl Lee is dead. So is Enrico. Ergo, I've begun to suspect there might be some connection between all of these things. How am I doing so far, Senator?"

There were more people in the room now. Big men wearing suits and carrying walkie-talkies. Betty Whalen must have called security after all. Two of them grabbed me by the arms and began pushing me toward the door. I kept talking all the way out.

"This isn't going to go away!" I yelled at Lansdale. "You're going to have to answer these questions sooner or later. To me. To the police. To your constituents. No one is bigger or more important than the law, Senator. Not even you."

CHAPTER 37

"What did you think you were going to accomplish by going to Senator Lansdale's office?" Logan Kincaid asked.

"I didn't exactly have a well-thought-out plan."

"Then why do it?"

"I wanted to shake things up. When I'm at a dead end in a story, not sure what to do next, I like to shake up everything – and everyone involved – to see what happens. Sometimes you get answers from doing that. Answers you weren't really expecting."

"But that didn't happen this time?"

"Uh, no."

"Will you get in trouble at work for causing the scene you did with Lansdale?"

"Oh, I'm sure there will be repercussions for me when I get to the office in the morning. Senator Lansdale is a very powerful man. Plus, my boss, the city editor there, isn't exactly a tower of strength when it comes to a messy situation like this."

We were having dinner again, but this time in my apartment. Yep, I'd finally gotten him to come up to my place. Just not quite the way I had hoped for after that first date we had. But I'd decided to try to move past that and try again with him. So, when he'd called me up to ask what was happening with the story, we agreed to meet up for dinner again – and I'd suggested eating at my apartment rather than go to a restaurant.

"A real home-cooked meal?" he asked.

"Well, it would be in my home and it would be cooked so yes… a home-cooked meal."

"I'd love that!"

I figured Ellen would be proud of me.

If at first you don't succeed…

There was a slight problem though. I hadn't had time to go to the store to buy anything. I told Logan that when he got there. He said that was fine, we could just take potluck with whatever was in my refrigerator. Except when we opened the refrigerator, the only things to eat in there were a couple of TV dinners, a half carton of eggs and some kind of lunchmeat that I'd wrapped in tin foil.

"What kind of meat is that?" he asked.

I opened the tin foil and checked it out.

"Either very old salami or very new cheese."

"What do you suggest?"

"That we stay away from the lunchmeat."

So now we were sitting on the floor around my living room coffee table, munching on cheeseburgers, French fries and onion rings from a Burger King around the corner.

"Am I a great cook or what?" I asked.

"This meal is a real gourmet's delight, all right." He laughed.

"I don't really have much time for cooking."

He was impressed by my apartment. He looked out the window of the living room and at the Empire State Building glowing in the distance. He checked the posters and pictures on my walls – and he looked through a lot of the books on my bookshelves.

"This looks like a comfortable place to live," he said.

"Yes, it's my refuge from all the craziness of New York City."

"I didn't think people lived like this in New York. I imagined it would be more of a shoebox one-room place in a not-so-great building. I always heard you couldn't afford an apartment like this in Manhattan unless you were rich. Are you rich?"

I laughed. "I just got lucky."

I told him how I'd been walking down Irving Place one day looking for an apartment, and I talked to the doorman of this building. The doorman said an elderly couple had just moved to Florida after living here for nearly forty years. And that meant the rent – which is regulated by the city in New York – had remained very low. I slipped the doorman fifty dollars to get me an early appointment with the landlord, and I got the apartment.

"I don't get to spend enough time in it though," I said. "I'm always too busy at the *Tribune*. As you might have noticed, being a newspaper reporter is not a nine to five job."

Logan picked up an onion ring and nibbled on it while he talked.

"Is your life always like this, Jessie? Running around after a big story?"

"No, not quite that bad. A lot of it can be boring. Press conferences and stuff like that. But I am on the go a lot. I sure as hell have been on the go with this story."

I told him pretty much everything I'd found out since the last time we talked. The meeting with Darryl Jackson's mother. The questions about Dr. Spitz and what she was doing right before she died. And even about my speculation that there could be more women victims than just me and Cheryl Lee Barrett.

"Do you think I'm crazy like everyone else does?" I asked him, sinking back into the couch.

"No, I don't think you're crazy."

"So you agree with me about all this?"

"I didn't say that." He reached into the bag, pulled out a cheeseburger and handed it to me. I took a big bite.

"And you really think the same person could be responsible for everything?" Logan asked. "The attack on you ? The murder of Cheryl Lee Barrett? And maybe these other women too?"

"Yes."

"Not Darryl Jackson."

"Obviously not, that makes no sense. He couldn't have killed Cheryl Lee Barrett. He's dead."

"Not Enrico either."

"Unlikely. I still don't think Enrico had anything to with Cheryl Lee Barrett's murder, or that he was somehow in the park twelve years ago with me."

"So we're left with Senator Frank Lansdale, huh?"

"He's my number one suspect."

"But why would Lansdale do it?"

"Maybe because he was having affairs with all those other women too? Just like we now know he was with Cheryl Lee Barrett. So, in the end, he had to kill these women to keep them quiet. To avoid a sex scandal that would ruin his marriage and his political career. That could be the answer for all this."

"But what about you? You didn't have an affair with Senator Lansdale, did you?"

"God, no way!"

"Then how do you explain the attack on you?"

"I didn't say I had all the answers." I shrugged, then sighed. "Look, all I know is that Lansdale is the key person in all this. He's behind it somehow. And I'm not going to rest until I get the truth about him and what he's done. I owe that to Cheryl Lee Barrett. To those other women. And to myself. I'll nail that sonuvabitch. One way or another, I'll get the real story and I'll print it in the *Tribune*. No matter how long it takes me."

"I'll bet you will." He grinned. "You're really something, Jessie Tucker."

He reached over and squeezed my hand. I squeezed his hand. We sat there like that, holding each other's hands, for what seemed like an eternity as I waited for him to make the next move. When he didn't, I decided to make the move myself. To be assertive. Just like Ellen always told me I should be with the men in my life.

I moved my hand up and gently stroked his hair. My other hand went around his shoulder. I moved closer. We were looking directly into each other's eyes now.

Then I leaned over and kissed him.

He kissed me back, tentatively at first and then with more passion.

But then he suddenly pulled away from me and stood up.

"I really should be going," he said.

I was completely confused now. "Is there a problem?" I asked.

"No problem."

"I'm sorry. I thought you liked the kiss…"

"The kiss was fine."

"You have a funny way of showing it."

"Look, I can't do this right now with you."

"Why not?"

"Because of my wife."

"The wife you divorced?"

"Yes."

"You're still in love with her?"

"Let's just drop the subject, okay?"

"Wait, is this because I was attacked? Do you not want to kiss me because I was… because I—"

"No! Look, like I said, I've got to be going. Thanks for the dinner. And good luck with your story."

Then he was gone.

"I'm hopeless," I told Ellen over the phone afterward. "This is more than just going through a dating dry spell. Men now actually run away to avoid any kind of physical contact with me."

"Tell me everything that happened."

I did. Ellen always made me feel better at times like this. Sometimes I didn't know what I would do without a best friend like Ellen.

"Maybe he's gay?" Ellen suggested.

"I don't think so – he was married. He mentioned his ex-wife, remember?"

"Oh, so gay men never get married?"

"Pretty sure he's not gay."

"You're sure he's turned on by women?"

"Yes, but apparently not by me."

"By the way," Ellen asked later, after we had thoroughly dissected every aspect of my night with Logan Kincaid. "What are you doing about that video of the senator you showed me?"

"I'm not sure yet."

"It could be very valuable."

"What do you mean?"

"Those videos showing Lansdale and the woman having sex could change the course of the next election. Some people would pay a lot of money for them – we could make a nice profit." I could hear mounting excitement in Ellen's voice.

"I'm not selling the video, Ellen."

A sudden worry crossed my mind. This was a side of Ellen that I rarely saw. Ellen the businesswoman. The one who'd turned my story into big money – putting a book about me on the top of the bestseller list and landing that big TV-movie deal. Now there were dollar signs clicking in Ellen's head again.

"You haven't told anyone about the videos, have you?" I asked then.

"Who would I tell?"

"One of those people you think might pay big money for them."

"Of course not."

"You're sure?"

"Jessie, you can trust me."

"Of course, I know that, Ellen."

Except I was still worried.

Could I really trust anyone anymore?

CHAPTER 38

When I got to work in the morning, Danny Knowlton told me that Norman Isaacs wanted to see us right away in his office.

"How much trouble am I in?" I asked Knowlton.

"Old man Larsen came down here to see Isaacs."

"Jonathan Larsen, the owner of the *Tribune*?"

"The way I hear it Larsen got a call from Frank Lansdale – they belong to the same country club, by the way – and Lansdale really gave him a piece of his mind about you. Then Larsen came down here and gave Isaacs a piece of his mind. Again, about you. Now Isaacs wants to talk to you."

I shook my head. "They belong to the same country club? It just keeps getting better. Are you going to back me on this, Danny?"

"I've always supported you, Jessie. You know that."

"Good, because I have a feeling I'm really going to need someone in my corner in there now."

"I've got your back, Jessie. Don't worry about that."

Isaacs was waiting for us in his office. He shut the door, glared at me and told me to sit down.

"What the hell happened at Senator Lansdale's office yesterday?" he asked.

"The senator and I had a full and frank discussion on some of the developments in the Cheryl Lee Barrett murder."

"The way I hear it the only one being full and frank was you."

"I did do most of the talking, and he did most of the listening. In my defense, I would have been happy to listen to what he had to say except he tried to throw me out first. One minute we're holding a conversation in the middle of his office. The next thing I know two of his goons are hustling me down the elevator and out onto the street. I'm not sure the senator understands the concept of a free press, Norman."

"Cut the crap, Jessie," Isaacs said. "You crossed the line. You violated the rules of ethical behavior for a reporter on this newspaper. *And* you went behind my back and broke your word to me about not pushing too hard on this story – and on the senator."

"I was simply doing my job as a reporter. I kept trying to get answers from the senator, but he wouldn't talk to me. This was the only way I could get to him. I had to break a few rules to do that."

"You should have followed the rules."

"Sometimes the rules just don't work."

"If you don't follow the rules, you can't work here, Jessie. It's as simple as that."

Was he going to fire me? I couldn't let that happen. So I laid it all out for him then. Told him pretty much everything, except for the sex videos I'd stolen – making it sound like I'd just stumbled across the information about his affair. I told him about the things I'd found out about Lansdale. About the conversation with his son. About the Iraq connections between Lansdale, Cheryl Lee Barrett's father and Joseph Enrico. And yes, about the new developments I'd uncovered about my own case.

"You really believe there's a link between what happened to you and the murder of the Barrett woman?" Isaacs asked incredulously.

"I think it's possible."

"Jeez…"

"And maybe other dead women too."

"What dead women?"

I showed him the list of women victim names I'd compiled from the old murder cases.

He just stared at me with a look of disbelief on his face until I was finished.

"You think I'm crazy too, don't you?" I said.

"Crazy is a very strong word."

"Emotionally disturbed?"

"I think you're very confused."

He looked over at Danny Knowlton. Danny had not said a word since we got to Isaacs' office.

"Do you know anything about all this?" Isaacs asked him.

"Nothing, boss. It's all a shock to me too. I can't believe Jessie would do something as crazy as this."

I glared at him. So much for Danny Knowlton having my back. I was on my own.

"Norman, listen to me—"

"No, you listen to me, Jessie. You're off this story. You're off everything for the time being. Go home. Stay out of the newsroom for a while. We'll call it a medical leave for now – an *indefinite* medical leave until you can pull yourself back together emotionally. In the meantime, just forget about this whole damn thing – Cheryl Lee Barrett, you, Senator Lansdale, all of it!"

"Please don't do this to me, Norman. I need to keep working! Not on this story, I understand, but I still want to be in the newsroom."

Isaacs sighed and scratched his head. He looked suddenly very old.

"Okay, Jessie. I guess… well, I owe you that much. But you're off the street. Confined to desk duty until further notice, understand? Go home now, then come back tomorrow morning and we'll figure out how to do some damage control with the people upstairs. The only way I can save you is by telling Larsen you're not writing about Lansdale anymore. Are we clear on that? Now get out of here!"

*

I thought things couldn't get any worse, but I was wrong about that. I left the office only to find a message on my voicemail. It was from Logan. He was at Kennedy Airport getting ready to board a flight home to California.

I listened to the message:

> "Hi Jessie. I'm not very good at goodbyes. So I guess this one will have to do. I'm sorry we're not going to get to spend more time together because you're terrific. But I'm not… um… who you want me to be. You deserve a lot better. Anyway, it's the last call for my flight so I better go. If you ever get to Santa Barbara, maybe you and I… Oh, Christ, I told you I was terrible at goodbyes. Take care, Jessie. And good luck."

So that was that. Logan Kincaid was out of my life. And my story had died on me too. Norman Isaacs had pulled the plug on the whole thing and confined me to desk duty. All in all, I'd had better days.

I needed some help.

I needed a break.

And, just when things were starting to look completely hopeless, I got one.

CHAPTER 39

The woman was waiting for me at the *Tribune* office when I got there in the morning.

"Are you Jessie Tucker?" she asked. "They told me to wait here for you. They said you'd be in soon."

"Well, I'm here now." After what had happened yesterday I had no patience to deal with this woman, whoever she was.

"I think I have a big story for you."

"A big story?" I said casually as I turned on my computer. "Hey, then I'm your girl."

I realized as I said it that I sounded rude, but I didn't care. People were always coming to the *Tribune* with what they thought were big stories. Most of the time they weren't anything at all. I had listened to hundreds of people like this over the years. And I definitely wasn't in the mood for it today.

"I'm here about the story you wrote several days ago?" the woman said.

"I write a lot of stories," I snapped.

"I'm sure you do. But this one was kind of unusual."

"Ms…?"

"Willis. Tamara Willis."

"Ms. Willis, I'm very busy right now. Do you mind getting to the point of why you're here?"

"This isn't easy for me," she said.

"If you'd just tell me what it is you think is such a hot story, then maybe we can wrap this up pretty quickly."

"You said you were looking for a woman. A woman who was in the park the same night that you were attacked? A woman who might have been attacked that same night. A woman who never told anyone about what happened. You asked her to come forward now. You said it was very important. You asked her to trust you. I read the article, Ms. Tucker. I've been thinking about what you said. I believed you. That's why I'm here now."

I stared at the woman with astonishment. She was about thirty-five, and she was African-American.

"You?" I asked. "You were the woman in the park."

Tamara Willis nodded.

It turned out to have happened pretty much the way I figured it did.

"I'd been in the park lots of times," Tamara Willis said, taking a seat next to me, "but always earlier in the day. When there were more people around. Of course, I'd heard all the warnings about being in the park alone at night – especially for a woman. But I'd grown up in New York City, lived in it all my life. I knew how to handle myself. Or so I thought anyway.

"I never saw him until it was too late. At first, I couldn't believe it was happening. I'd just been on this path where there were still some people around me. But now I'd gone too far into the park. I was alone. No one was around to help me. I started to scream, but he put his hand over my mouth. He told me to keep quiet and he wouldn't hurt me." She reached up and wiped a tear from her cheek.

"I'd read somewhere once that the best thing to do was not resist, that you had a better chance of staying alive that way. Later on, I found out that I was wrong. The experts say you should begin screaming for help right away and make as much trouble as you can – a lot of times the attackers will just run away. But, like I said, I was too scared. I let him do the things he wanted to me. I just kept praying that he would let me live when it was over. It was the same man you identified in court and sent away to jail for attacking you. I'll never forget his face. When I saw him on TV the first time – and heard he'd been arrested for the attack on you – I just wanted to cheer.

"It was all like some terrible nightmare. I can still remember every second of it, just like it happened yesterday. But, as it continued to go on, I realized at some point that none of it seemed real. It was like I had shut down all my systems, all my emotions. I felt like an observer, not a victim. It was almost like some kind of out-of-body experience. Maybe that was the only way I could survive it."

"Why didn't you go to the police afterward?" I asked her.

"I was ashamed. I didn't want anyone to know. I was engaged then. My fiancé came from a very strict religious family, he was religious too. We didn't even have pre-marital sex. I was afraid that if he found out he'd think… well, he'd think less of me. That somehow he and his family might think I was at fault. I never did marry him, but that's why I kept quiet back then."

"But didn't you want Darryl Jackson to pay for what he did?"

"I didn't have to. Like I said, I saw his pictures in the papers a few days later. After he was arrested for attacking you. He was going to go to jail anyway. I had my revenge. And I never had to tell anyone my secret. It seemed, at the time anyway, to be the ideal solution."

"So you forgot all about it until you saw my article?"

She shook her head no.

"But you just said—"

"I didn't do anything about it. But I never forgot. I still think about it every day. Every night too. Especially at night. Don't you, Ms. Tucker?"

I took a deep breath. "Yeah, I do."

"Then the other day," Tamara Willis continued, "I picked up the newspaper and read your article. I was surprised, but at the same time I guess I always knew I was waiting for something like this. I knew it wasn't really over. So I thought about it for a little while – even though there was no decision to really make – and then I came here to see you. To tell someone the truth. At last. The only thing I don't understand is why you've opened it all up again after all this time."

"I'm not so sure anymore that the man I put in jail was guilty of what I thought he was."

"But he definitely was the one who attacked me."

"I know that now."

"But you don't think he did it to you?"

"That's right."

I told her about my conversation with Gutierrez in prison. How he'd told me for the first time about the second attack. How I finally admitted to myself I now had doubts about my own testimony in court that sent Darryl Jackson to jail. About the discrepancies in the police case against him.

"Darryl Jackson was a bad guy," I said. "He attacked and raped you. Then he cold-bloodedly stole my belongings when he thought I was lying there dead. He deserved to go to jail. I don't really have any guilt about what happened to him. Especially after hearing what he did to you. But it still leaves me with one very big question."

"If Jackson didn't attack you that night in the park," Tamara Willis said, "then who did?"

"Yes."

I reached out and grasped Tamara Willis's hand. She squeezed my hand back. I felt a unique bond with this woman. We had both been through the same nightmare. And yet we had survived.

Now it was time to fight back.

"Ms. Willis—"

"Tamara."

"Tamara, I want to write a story for the *Tribune* about all of this."

"I understand.'

"I'd like to name you and have you tell your story for the record."

She took a deep breath. "I'll do that."

"Are you sure you're ready for this?"

"I've been ready for this for twelve years," she said.

The article ran on Page One of the *Tribune* under the headline:

MY NIGHT OF TERROR IN CENTRAL PARK

Twelve years later, new facts emerge about the crime that shocked a city.

I told Tamara Willis's story. The things she'd found out about her own attack. And how I now believed that everyone – including me – had been mistaken about what happened to me that same night. Yes, Jackson had attacked and raped a woman in Central Park. But all the facts were now that his victim was not Jessie Tucker, it was Tamara Willis. That meant whoever was responsible for what happened to me must still be out there somewhere.

I didn't mention anything about Cheryl Lee Barrett or any of my other suspicions, of course. Isaacs would never let me do that. He hadn't been happy about me writing the story at all, but I had written the original article, the woman had come forward and now the *Tribune* had an exclusive follow-on on one of the most famous crimes in New York City history.

The Jessie Tucker story was back on Page One.

It was just a matter of time now until the entire investigation into my case would have to be reopened.

Or so I thought anyway.

CHAPTER 40

The next morning I snuck out of the *Tribune* – without telling Isaacs or anyone else where I was going – and went to Police Headquarters to see Vincent Brisco. Brisco was the head of the police department's public information division. I had worked with him on stories for years, and we'd always had a pretty good relationship. But he was not happy with me now.

"I read what you wrote," he said before I even managed to say good morning to him.

"Amazing story, huh?"

"Well, that depends."

"On what?"

"Whether any of it is true."

"Do you really think I'd lie about something like this? Or the other woman would?"

"From what I hear, you've been under a lot of stress. This new Central Park murder has brought back a lot of rough memories for you. Okay, you found this woman who suddenly comes forward after twelve years of saying nothing about being raped that night in the park. Maybe she was, and maybe she wasn't. You don't really have any proof of her rape or any way to get it after all this time. And even if she is telling the truth, Darryl Jackson could have attacked both of you in the park that night. Let's say he rapes her, then can't get it up again for you so he just beats and robs you. Either way Darryl Jackson is still dead. And good riddance for that."

Brisco picked up the *Tribune*, pointed to my story on the front page and shook his head. "By the way," he said, "I would have appreciated a little advance warning on this so I didn't have to nearly choke on my breakfast when I read it this morning."

I had thought about giving some advance warning to the police. But in the end, I hadn't told anyone. I decided to just run the story and see what kind of impact it created. For better or worse, it seemed to have created an awful lot of impact in the police department.

"I've been in meetings all morning about this," Brisco said. "The chief of police asks me what in the world is this Tucker woman doing? I tell him I haven't got the slightest idea. I thought: I used to know her, I thought we were friendly – but now I'm not so sure."

"I'm doing my job," I said.

"And what exactly is that job?"

"I think I've raised enough questions for the investigation into my own case to be reopened by the police." Cheryl Lee might be dead, but I was alive and I was sure our attacker was still out there.

"Christ, Jessie, do you have any idea what you're asking us to do? Throw out all the work and all the evidence we put together to solve your case – and start all over again. The crime scene is long gone, new evidence would be incredibly hard to find, witnesses have moved away or are dead or just aren't going to remember any more about something that happened so long ago. Even if some of what you're saying is true about this new woman and the rest of it – and I'm not saying it is – you're never going to find the answers you're looking for now. Why can't you just leave it alone instead of stirring up this whole big mess like you've done with this damn article?"

Steve Fredericks's office was in the same building. I figured he wouldn't be very happy either. He wasn't there, but I found out pretty quickly that I was right. I checked my voicemail and there was a message from Fredericks. An angry one.

"Jessie, what are you doing? You're putting me in an awfully awkward position. There's no way to read this article without getting an implication that I somehow did something wrong in the investigation of your case. I didn't do anything wrong. I did it all by the book. But now I'm going to have this cloud of suspicion hanging over my head. Your story is going to get people to start poking around into my past. Asking questions, looking for something – anything – that might not be exactly right. It's like being audited by the IRS, for Chrissake. Even if you don't cheat on your taxes, you know they're going to find something. Dammit, Jessie, you've really put me in a bad spot."

The line went dead as the message suddenly ended. It sounded as if Fredericks had slammed the phone down angrily.

I remembered when I was in the hospital and how I used to look forward to hearing the sound of Steve Fredericks's voice. It was so soothing, so reassuring. It had made me feel safe, like nothing bad could ever happen to me again.

But not this time.

This time the anger in his voice had upset me badly.

Scared me a bit too.

Aguirre and Erskine had already read my article too by the time I showed up at the Central Park Precinct. Aguirre rolled his eyes when he saw me.

"Boy, you've been a busy little girl, haven't you?"

I didn't feel in the mood for any of his macho swaggering today.

"I'm not a little girl," I said. "I'm thirty-six years old. I'm a journalist. A professional at what I do, just like you. Don't ever call me a little girl again. It's demeaning and it's sexist."

"What's your problem, Tucker?" Aguirre said disgustedly. "Are you having your period or something?"

"Now that remark definitely crossed the line."

I looked over at Erskine. He seemed to be ignoring everything that was going on. He was bent over a computer keyboard, pecking away at the keys to type out a report. *They certainly were an odd couple*, I thought to myself. Aguirre always wanted to be in the spotlight, Erskine did everything he could to avoid any attention at all. Maybe that's why Aguirre wanted him for a partner.

"What are you doing here anyway?" Aguirre asked. "I heard you've been pulled off this story by your boss."

"I'm trying to get my case reopened."

"How's it going so far?"

"Not too well."

I told Aguirre about my meeting with Brisco. He just shrugged.

"What does all of this have to do with us anyway? You said you talked to them downtown about reopening your case – that's somebody else's headache. But why are you *here*? It's not our case."

"Yeah, but the Cheryl Lee Barrett murder is your case."

"So?"

"I think they're connected."

Aguirre sighed. "Why doesn't that surprise me?" he said.

"I don't think Joseph Enrico killed her. You got the wrong man. I think whoever did it is somehow linked to the attack on me and also possibly to the murders of a series of other women since my attack."

"You're crazy, Tucker," Aguirre said.

"People keep telling me that these days."

"Maybe you should start listening to them. How exactly do you figure that your attack is connected to Cheryl Lee Barrett or the murders of anyone else since then?"

I told him about the baseball cap and some of the other stuff I'd found out. "I don't exactly have all the answers yet, but Enrico—"

"Enrico resisted arrest," Aguirre interrupted. "Why did he do that if he was innocent?"

"That's a good question, Lieutenant. I'd like to find out more about that shooting. Who actually fired first? How many cops were there? I mean, if someone wanted to set up a patsy for a crime what better way to do it? Shoot him before he gets a chance to talk. Then you can say anything you want about him so—"

"I shot him," Aguirre said.

"Okay," I said slowly.

"And I was there too," Erskine added.

"Enrico had a gun," Aguirre said. "He was a murder suspect. It was a clean shooting. The Internal Affairs Division investigated, and we all came out fine. You keep looking for some sort of conspiracy here, Tucker. But there isn't any. Enrico murdered the Barrett girl in the park, then panicked when we showed up at his door to arrest him. End of story. It's really all very simple."

"If there's one thing I'm sure about, Lieutenant," I told him, "it's that nothing about this story is very simple."

After I left Aguirre and Erskine, I went to the District Attorney's office and went through the whole story again with an assistant D.A. named Seth Bracken. I told him that I was requesting the authorities reopen the investigation into my twelve-year-old case based on the new evidence I had uncovered. Bracken told me he would look into it, but I felt as if he was just going through the motions. He didn't seem particularly happy to see me either – just like Brisco, Fredericks and Aguirre. But that was okay. I was getting used to rejection by now.

Besides, I still had one ace in the hole I hadn't played yet.

I knew someone who would listen to me.

He always had in the past, anyway.

I took out my phone and punched in the number for Mayor Jack Hanrahan's office.

CHAPTER 41

Going to Gracie Mansion was always a special thrill. I've never been to the White House or Buckingham Palace or even the Governor's Mansion in Albany. But the big house where the mayor lived on the Upper East Side of Manhattan held plenty of power and grandeur and tradition. There were pictures of all the greatest mayors on the walls – LaGuardia, Wagner, Koch, Giuliani, Bloomberg – and, of course, the current occupant, Jack Hanrahan – who a lot of people thought just might be the best of them all.

Twelve years ago, he'd been an obscure state senator who was just one of a half dozen candidates in the field who were running for mayor. The early polls showed his support was only in single digits. But then there had been the Central Park attack on me, which quickly became a symbol of the crime issue in New York City. Hanrahan jumped on it better than anyone, and political observers say that was the key factor that propelled him into the mayor's chair. *Just one more life dramatically changed because of the events of that long-ago night in Central Park*, I thought to myself now as I showed my ID to the guard at the door. What would happen now that I was opening up the case all over again? I didn't know. It was like throwing a stone into a still pond, then watching the ripples it made.

The first person I met inside was Libby St. John, who was on her way out the door with a bulging briefcase and a big pile of papers under her arm.

"You're not staying for dinner?" I asked her.

"No way. I've been here since six o'clock this morning. I had to write welcoming remarks for the mayor to say to some school spelling bee contest winners that came here for a breakfast awards ceremony. Smart-ass little kids. I wrote up this special proclamation for the mayor to give to each of them. Only, I misspelled proclamation in the title. God, did everyone give me shit over that. And the day just went downhill from there."

"C'mon, stay," I said. "It'll be fun."

"No way. I've got too much to do."

I pointed to the briefcase and papers she was carrying. "Homework?"

"No, I didn't even mean this. This is the everyday stuff. I mean some really important things I have to do. My laundry. Grocery shopping. See if I can still find my way home. I feel as if I haven't been there in years."

I laughed. I'd always liked Libby. Sometimes I wished we were closer friends than we were, but neither of us ever seemed to have much time for socializing. Libby's life was consumed by politics and running the city, and mine by the *Tribune*.

"Maybe some other time then," I said.

"Sure. Hey, I read your piece in the *Tribune* about the second woman in the park. We should talk about this. Call me, OK?"

"Absolutely."

The dinner consisted of just the mayor, his wife Christine and me. I was happy about that. Sometimes in the past I'd wound up at dinner parties with people I really didn't have any interest in talking to. Besides, this way I had more time to talk to the mayor, which was my purpose for being there. This wasn't a social occasion to me, even though Mayor Hanrahan and Christine were treating it like one.

We sat in a dining room with a view of Carl Schurz Park outside. A white-coated waiter moved silently around the room, pouring wine and putting out appetizers. It sure beat microwaving a TV dinner and eating it alone in front of the TV or my laptop – which is what I usually did.

"We don't see enough of you here, Jessie," Christine said.

"I'm sorry about that," I said as I poked my fork into some sort of exotic salad. "But I've been pretty busy. Newspapers are kind of a twenty-four-hour job."

I looked over at the mayor, who was smiling. I suddenly realized how ridiculous that must seem as an excuse.

"I don't have to tell you about that, huh? It's just that I'm not very good at managing my time – when I get involved in a big story, that's all I can think about until it's over. I guess it's a character flaw of mine."

"Newspapers can't be your whole life," Mayor Hanrahan said. "What else do you do?"

"Well, I exercise a lot."

"How much?"

"At least an hour and a half a day. Power bike, sit-ups, pushups, leg curls, rowing – maybe even a bit of weight-lifting when I'm feeling really ambitious."

"I life weights too," Christine Hanrahan said. "In fact, I've got a weight room here. A whole exercise area actually. You should come over sometime. We could work out together. I don't mind the exercise so much as the boredom."

"Tell me about it."

Christine Hanrahan was an attractive woman, probably in her mid-forties and she certainly seemed to be in good shape. She was slim and tanned, but muscular-looking too. She looked good for forty. She looked good for thirty too. Maybe I needed to spend more time lifting weights myself.

Christine had been a TV reporter when she first met her husband. Back then, she'd had that blonde Kewpie doll look that so many women on TV have. She'd lost that now, but she was attractive in a more regal way.

Christine Hanrahan hadn't worked as a TV reporter in a long time, quitting after her husband was elected to devote herself full time to being the first lady of New York City. I asked her if she ever missed being a reporter.

"All the time," she said. "I don't miss the stakeouts and the boring press conferences and all the political backbiting that goes on in a TV newsroom. But I miss the stories – the thrill of working a big story. To bring back that exclusive, to feel the adrenaline… there's nothing like that. God, sometimes I envy you, Jessie."

I grinned. "Being first lady of New York City isn't too bad a job either."

"Sometimes I think I'd trade it all for the excitement of covering one breaking story again," Christine said. "But tell us about you. Your professional life certainly sounds very busy from what I hear… and of course your time at the gym. But how is your personal life?"

"Not so busy."

"Are you seeing anyone?"

I thought about Logan Kincaid. "Umm…"

"Where is he tonight?"

"Well, I've sort of lost him."

"I hope you find him again." Christine Hanrahan winked.

We stuck to small talk until the meal was finished. That's when we finally got around to the real reason I was there. I was prepared to bring up the topic myself, but I didn't have to. Mayor Hanrahan did it first over coffee and dessert.

"You've certainly got a lot of people upset with you these days," he said.

"You're talking about my most recent article."

"Yes, that – and some of your other activities too – haven't exactly been making you a lot of friends from what I hear."

"Who's mad at me?"

"The Police Department, the District Attorney's office, Senator Lansdale—"

"You heard about what happened in his office?"

"News like that travels fast in political circles."

"What does everyone say happened between me and Lansdale?"

"You called him a liar, you accused him of having an affair with his campaign aide – and pretty much implied he had something to do with her murder. Then he had you thrown out by security guards. How does that compare to your version of events?"

"About the same," I admitted. "I don't like that man."

"I don't like him very much either." Hanrahan chuckled. "But then I guess you already knew that."

Christine Hanrahan suddenly pushed her coffee away and stood up. "Excuse me, but I think I'm going to leave the two of you to solve the city's problems on your own. I'm going to bed."

"I'm sorry," I blurted out, checking my watch, "I didn't realize it was so late."

"Nonsense," Christine told me. "You two talk as long as you want. And don't make yourself such a stranger. We have to do this more often, Jessie. It was really nice."

She gave me a hug, then strode out of the room.

"Did I say something wrong?" I asked the mayor after she was gone.

"No, don't worry about it. She's just tired."

"You're sure?"

"Everything's fine," he said.

The waiter poured us both more coffee and brought some after-dinner drinks. A sambuca for me and a B&B for the mayor. He drank a big gulp of it, then took out a cigar and lit it. I normally didn't like men who smoked cigars, but Mayor Hanrahan looked good puffing on one. I remembered seeing old pictures of John F. Kennedy smoking a cigar while he sat in his rocking chair at the White House. That was how the mayor looked now. I thought about how much political charisma he had and wondered what he would do when his tenure as mayor ended in another year.

"This bad blood between you and Lansdale?" I said. "What's it all about? What happened to cause all the bad feeling?"

Hanrahan laughed. "It's just politics."

"What kind of politics?"

"A long time ago I had this bill I wanted to get through the Senate and I made a personal appeal to Lansdale for help. He ignored me. Then he wanted some pet project of his approved by the city, and so I vetoed it. I'm not proud of that, but I was angry. There's always been tension between us – we were always going after the same jobs. It just sort of escalated from there. You know how those things go – sometimes you can't remember how the whole thing started, but it's too late to go back and change things."

"Then why didn't you run against Lansdale for the Senate this year?"

"I already have a job."

"You can't serve a fourth term as mayor. A lot of people – most people – thought you could beat Lansdale. You're a very popular guy and he's made a lot of enemies over the years. But you took yourself out of consideration for the race. Why?"

"I just didn't want to run for office again."

"Ever?"

"Maybe somewhere down the line."

"And that's all that happened between the two of you?"

"Absolutely."

An aide came in and whispered something in the mayor's ear. The two men got into an animated conversation about some City Council bill. When the aide left, Hanrahan refilled both of our glasses.

"So, let's talk about the real reason you came here tonight," he said, stretching out his legs and looking intently at me.

I told him I'd gone to the police and the D.A.'s office in an effort to get my case reopened based on the new evidence of the second attack in the park that night. Without a great deal of success.

"Why won't anyone listen to me?" I asked.

Hanrahan took a long puff on the cigar. "Jessie, you have to understand where these people in the Police Department and the D.A.'s office are coming from. Only a small percentage of the violent crimes in this city are ever solved. That means the majority of violent criminals get away with breaking the law. But then, even worse than that, the conviction rate is probably somewhere around fifty percent, and even less than that in places like the Bronx where a lot of the people picked for juries don't trust the police or prosecutors. So now we're talking about a very low success rate in going after criminals in this city. Not a very satisfying result. Police and District Attorneys get very frustrated at the way the criminal justice system works. Then here you come along – not with evidence that will help them solve a new case, but with stuff that could mess up one they've already solved. A big conviction too. One of the most successful victories in the battle against crime that New York has ever seen. Putting Darryl Jackson away after what he did to you changed the way people looked at life in this city. It showed that the system did work. People felt safer, they felt good, they felt like there was hope after all for New York City. I know this first hand. The voters told me that – they helped put me in office three times because I led this new crackdown on crime. And it all started with you, Jessie. Do you see the dilemma that this new information you've uncovered causes some people?"

"Is that a dilemma for you too?" I asked him.

Hanrahan laughed. "Me? Hell no, I don't care. I'm not running for anything. My term in this job is up soon. I understand that you want to know the truth about what happened to you. And if you're suddenly starting to doubt the story you've been told, why you want to find some new answers. I'm just telling you why what you're doing makes some people very uncomfortable."

"It sure does. People like Lieutenant Aguirre—"

"Is he the cop you went to about reopening your case?"

"No, he's the one I'd been talking to about the Cheryl Lee Barrett murder. But I believe there's some link between her murder and what happened to me. I know that doesn't make a lot of sense."

"No, it doesn't."

"But I know for a fact that Lansdale isn't telling the truth about Cheryl Lee Barrett. And I really believe that if I can find out what really happened to her, that might give me some answers about my own case too. As crazy as that must sound. And yes, even I know it sounds pretty crazy."

Hanrahan looked across the table at me thoughtfully. "What exactly is it that you think happened between the dead woman and Senator Lansdale?" he asked.

"They were having an affair."

"You suspect that?"

"I know it for a fact."

"What else?"

"I don't buy the police scenario that the ex-con, Enrico, killed her. Oh, Enrico was no angel – I'm sure he was guilty of a lot of things, but I just don't think Cheryl Lee Barrett's murder was one of them. I think they were friends. They came here from California together for some reason. I don't exactly know what that reason was, but I think it had something to do with blackmailing Senator Lansdale. Enrico had no reason to kill the girl. I think someone set him up. He was a patsy."

Hanrahan puffed on his cigar for a long time.

"I thought the dead woman was supposed to be dating Lansdale's son," he finally said to me.

"That's the story for official consumption."

"It's a cover?"

"The son is a proponent of an alternative lifestyle."

"He's gay," Hanrahan said.

I nodded.

After a pause, Hanrahan spoke. "I'll tell you what I'll do. I'll talk to the police commissioner about this new evidence in your case. Put a little heat on them over that and the Cheryl Lee Barrett murder too. I'm not saying it'll change anything. But at least we'll get people at the Police Department and the D.A.'s office to sit up and take notice. Who knows – maybe they'll actually find something."

"Thanks, Mayor," I said.

"Hey, what are friends for, Jessie?"

We finished our drinks and Hanrahan walked me out to a waiting cab. Sometimes late at night my legs would bother me – a throwback to the old injuries. I'd feel the same kind of pain I used to have and experience a bit of trouble walking. It would have been easier to use a cane when that happened, except I hated it so much I hardly ever took it with me anywhere. But now my right leg suddenly gave out. It was only for a second, but I stumbled as I walked out the front door.

Mayor Hanrahan grabbed me and held me tight. It had been so long since a man had held me like that – any man – that I found it comforting, even a little sensual.

A long time ago, when I'd first met Jack Hanrahan at a cocktail party I had gone to on behalf of Wiley, Farrior and Mueller, I thought he might even have a thing for me. I'd caught him staring at me several times during the party, and we'd flirted after being introduced. He was already married to Christine then, but I had still felt something between us.

But not this time. This time, as I looked up at his face, it wasn't passion I saw there. It was pity.

"Are you okay?" he asked.

"I'm fine."

"Let me help you to your cab."

"I can do it myself," I snapped.

I got into a waiting taxicab and went home by myself – the way I always did.

Jessie Tucker, everybody's favorite cripple.

CHAPTER 42

I had the dream again that night. But it had changed again.

I was running away from someone just like before. Only this time I wasn't in the park anymore. I was running along a beach. There was white sand crunching under my feet, waves crashing into the shoreline and blue skies above. Everything looked so beautiful. But there was danger right behind me. I tried to run faster, but my legs weren't strong enough. I knew that I couldn't get away. I never could get away, no matter how hard I tried.

I saw the Yankees baseball cap again. I tried to see the face of the person wearing it, but I couldn't. Then I felt a hand reach out, grab me and pull me down to the ground. After that came the pain. And finally the darkness. The welcome darkness – my only escape from the nightmare. But, just before I lost consciousness, I saw something I had never seen in the dream before. A sign. A sign on the beach in front of me. The sign said: "Welcome to Santa Barbara, California."

I was still thinking about Santa Barbara while I did my exercises the next morning. I really worked up a sweat too. I doubled up on everything to try to work off some of the frustration that was eating away at me. Exercise, instead of sex – it took longer and it wasn't as much fun. But, on the other hand, you didn't need anyone else to do it properly.

Santa Barbara.

Why was I dreaming about Santa Barbara now?

Well, Santa Barbara kept popping up everywhere I looked in recent days.

Senator Frank Lansdale had spoken at a Democratic gathering in Santa Barbara in December. A few weeks later, Cheryl Lee Barrett left Santa Barbara for New York City and went to work for him. Had their paths crossed in Santa Barbara during his visit? If not, then something else had happened that set into motion the events that led to her relationship with the senator. Joseph Enrico was from Santa Barbara too. And now Logan Kincaid had gone back there.

All roads sure seemed to lead to Santa Barbara.

I went to see Norman Isaacs in his office when I got to work. I'd thought about going to see Danny Knowlton first. But Danny had made it pretty clear during that last meeting with Isaacs that he wasn't a member of Team Tucker anymore. At least, not until the political winds made it feasible for him to do so. Danny Knowlton was a big disappointment to me. I really didn't want to believe the bad stuff I'd heard about him and the way he used people. I thought I was different. But people like Danny are what they are.

Norman Isaacs was what he was too.

But I had no choice but to deal with him directly at this point.

"I want to go to Santa Barbara, California," I said to Isaacs.

"Why?"

"That's where Cheryl Lee Barrett was living before she came to New York. I'd like to do a long takeout – maybe for the Sunday paper – about her. The life and death of a crime victim. Talk to people who knew her out there. Relatives. Friends. Teachers. Get a real feel of what she was all about. How she lived. And how she wound up dead one night three thousand miles away."

"You're not working on the Cheryl Lee Barrett story anymore – I told you that after the scene you made in Lansdale's office."

"You don't understand. I want to go to Santa Barbara for the *Tribune*," I said. "If I can't, I'll take a vacation or a leave of absence or – if I have to – I'll quit and do it on my own."

Isaacs shook his head. He looked confused.

"What about the new woman in the park – the one you say was attacked the same night as you? The mayor is pushing it with the police brass – he wants them to have another look at that night, see if they can find anything new. Don't you want to stay here and cover that?"

Of course I did, but I had a hunch about Santa Barbara and I couldn't shake the feeling that there were some answers waiting to be found there about my own case too. I couldn't say that to Norman, so I just shook my head.

"I can't just walk away from this story, Norman."

"Yes you can."

"Not this time."

"What part of 'you're off the story' didn't you understand, Jessie? If you get caught snooping around the senator again, we're all going to be in big trouble. No story is worth that. I'm too old for this."

"This won't be about the senator and I promise I'll be on my best professional behavior. I'll just report on the victim, Cheryl Lee Barrett. Not Lansdale. In fact, I'll be on the other side of the country from Frank Lansdale so I can't get into any more trouble with him like I did the other day."

The truth is, I never figured in a million years he'd go for it. I figured I was just going through the motions with him and I was serious when I told him I'd quit and go on my own. Norman Isaacs was what he was – a company man. A scared man. A man who never wanted to rock the boat. That's the way Isaacs had been for his entire newspaper career. So why would he change now?

But every once in a while, people surprise you.

And Norman Isaacs surprised me now.

Maybe he really did figure I'd be less of a problem for him if I was three thousand miles away on the West Coast. Maybe he'd let me go through all of the motions on the Cheryl Lee Barrett story and then just never run it. Or maybe, just maybe, Norman Isaacs decided he wanted to be a real journalist this one time.

"Okay, you can go to California," Isaacs said.

I couldn't believe what I was hearing.

"What?" I asked.

"You should probably go to Ohio too," he told me.

"Ohio?"

"Yeah. Cheryl Lee Barrett was from Kettering, Ohio, according to the stuff you wrote before. She's got a mother there. The mother didn't even come to the funeral. It might be interesting to find out why. And also to find out what she knows about her daughter. If you're going to do the damn story, then do it right!"

Isaacs took out a *Tribune* travel voucher and wrote in both Kettering, Ohio and Santa Barbara, California as the destinations. Then he signed it at the bottom and handed it to me.

"Thanks, Norman," I said.

"Now get the hell out of my sight." He smiled.

CHAPTER 43

I found Cheryl Lee's mother – whose name was now Dorothy Ludlow – working the late afternoon shift at a cocktail lounge in downtown Dayton. It was about four p.m., and the place was nearly deserted. She was the only waitress there. I sat down at a table and waited for her to come over.

"You're Dorothy Ludlow, right?"

"Who wants to know?"

"My name's Jessie Tucker. I'm a reporter with the *New York Tribune*."

Dorothy Ludlow was about fifty, and it looked like it had been a hard half-century. If you studied her face carefully, you could see some resemblance to her daughter and realize that she too must have been a beautiful woman once. But that was a long time ago. I handed her a business card with my name on it. The woman looked at the card casually, then put it back down on top of the table.

"So you're the one who's been calling," she said.

"You haven't been answering."

"I've got nothing to say."

"Your daughter's dead, Mrs. Ludlow."

"She's been dead to me for a long time. I mean, I haven't seen or talked to her in a long time. We weren't exactly close, if you know what I mean. But then I guess you already figured that out, huh?"

"I've traveled all the way from New York City to see you," I said, looking around at the empty bar. "You don't look very busy here.

How about you let me buy you a drink? In return, you give me a few minutes of your time. You owe your daughter at least that."

She thought it over for a second, then nodded. I wasn't sure whether it was the reference to her daughter or the offer of a drink that convinced her.

A few minutes later, Dorothy Ludlow sat at the table, sipping a vodka on the rocks and talking about Cheryl Lee.

"Look, maybe I wasn't much of a mother, but then Cheryl Lee wasn't much of a daughter either. That kid was wild all her life. She was always getting in trouble – first at school, then with men and with the law. I don't know what was wrong with her. She never seemed very happy."

"Maybe she missed having a father?" I said.

"Hell, Cheryl Lee *had* a father. She had lots of fathers."

"You got married again after your husband died in Iraq? Is that where the name Ludlow comes from?"

"I've been married six times, honey. If at first you don't succeed, try, try again." She laughed. "I'm still trying!"

"Did Cheryl Lee get along with the men in your life when she was growing up?"

"Not especially. She never liked them."

"Any special reason why?"

Dorothy Ludlow didn't answer right away. Instead, she stood up, walked over to the bar and poured herself another vodka on the rocks. She asked me if I wanted something. I looked down at the half-empty beer glass in front of me and shook my head no. Ludlow brought her own drink back to the table and took a big gulp.

"Lots of reasons Cheryl Lee didn't like 'em," she said finally. "Lots of men, lots of reasons."

"When did she leave home?" I asked.

"She ran away for good when she was seventeen. She ran away a few times before that too. But she always came back. This time she never came back. Of course, I didn't go looking for her either."

"Why did she run away?"

Ludlow looked down at her drink.

"She said… Well, she said that Harry – the man I was living with at the time – had done things to her. You know, sexual kinds of things. I called her a lying tramp and slapped her a few times. I thought she'd just made it up because she hated me. The bitch of it was that later I found out it was true about Harry. The bastard bragged about it to me one night when he got drunk. But it was too late to change anything. Cheryl Lee was long gone by then."

"When was the last time you saw your daughter?"

"About six months ago."

"She came here?"

"Yeah, I've never been to California or any of the other places where she lived."

"Six months…" I mused. "So we're talking about the beginning of the year. Maybe early January. Does that sound right?"

"Uh-huh. It was right after the holidays. There was Christmas and then there was New Year's and then Cheryl Lee came to see me. I remember that. January."

Just before she moved to New York City to begin her new life as Margaret Kincaid.

"What did you talk about?"

"Old times."

"I don't mean to be rude, Mrs. Ludlow, but from the way you describe your relationship with your daughter that wouldn't have taken very long."

Ludlow shrugged. "She was curious, I guess."

"Curious about what?"

"Her father."

"She asked you questions about your dead husband?"

"Yes, that's right."

"Had she ever done that before?"

"When she was a little girl. She always wanted to know about her father then. What Scott looked like. Things he talked about. How he died in Iraq. She had this image of him as a war hero. She had these pictures of Scott in his uniform on the wall in her room, but that was a long time ago. I figured she'd forgotten all about him by now. Christ, Scott died so many years ago. Anyway, I hadn't talked about him for years. Until she came asking questions again in January. They were the same kind of questions she used to ask when she was a little girl. I did think that was kind of strange at the time."

"Did she mention anything to you about a man named Frank Lansdale?"

"No."

"How about a Joseph Enrico?"

"No."

"You're sure?"

"Enrico is the mugger who murdered my daughter, isn't he?"

"The police believe that's what happened."

"So why would Cheryl Lee know him?"

"Enrico was in your husband's army unit. He also lived in Santa Barbara at the same time as your daughter. I think they may have met there, then both came to New York City together for some reason. It may have had something to do with Frank Lansdale – he's the U.S. senator that your daughter was working for when she died. He also was the commanding officer of your husband's unit in Desert Storm. Does any of this mean anything to you?"

She shook her head sadly.

"My daughter came to see me. I hadn't seen her – or even talked to her – in years. She asked me some questions about Scott, her father. I gave her the same answers I gave her when she was a little girl. Then she left. The next thing I knew I she was a suspect in a murder in California. And then six months later she turns up dead in New York City using a different name.

That's it. When it comes to warm, fuzzy family moments, we didn't have very many."

She finished off her drink and looked across the table at me.

"Ms. Tucker, you've asked me a lot of questions. Do you mind if I ask you a couple?"

"Go ahead."

"How come you care so much about Cheryl Lee?"

"I think she's a good story."

"Why?"

"I'm not sure yet."

"That's not much of an answer."

"When I get a better one, I'll let you know first. That's a promise, Mrs. Ludlow."

She nodded thoughtfully. "My daughter," she asked, "do you think she was a good person?"

"Excuse me?"

"Well, I know I never did very well as a mother to her. But all that stuff I said before about how she was no good and I never missed her… I didn't mean that. I always thought Cheryl Lee was a pretty good daughter. Probably a lot better than I deserved. She was the one good thing I've ever done in my life. That and marry her father. Scott was the only decent man I've been with, but the damn war took him away before I barely knew him. After that, it's been mostly downhill for me. But I hoped Cheryl Lee would straighten herself out and make something of her life. I hate to think that all these terrible things I've heard about her were true. You've found out a lot of things about my daughter, Ms. Tucker. Was Cheryl Lee a good person?"

A good person? Cheryl Lee Barrett was a prostitute. She was wanted for murder. She probably teamed up with an ex-convict to try to blackmail a United States senator.

And yet…

There was something about her that made me believe she was a victim, not a villain.

Cheryl Lee Barrett had never gotten a break in her entire life. Her father died before she ever knew him. Her mother hooked up with a succession of bad men – at least one of whom sexually abused her before she was barely old enough to kiss a boy. Sure, she became a prostitute – I remembered reading once somewhere that a huge percentage of prostitutes were sexually abused as children – and she was wanted for murder and she was certainly up to no good when she went to work for Lansdale as Margaret Kincaid. But at the end, something had happened. She talked about quitting her job with the Lansdale campaign. She got upset with Lansdale for some reason in the print shop. She cut short the phony dinner date she was having with his son at the restaurant. She was trying to do something in those last hours of her life. Maybe something good. Except she got killed first.

"Yes," I said to Dorothy Ludlow, "I think your daughter was a good person."

Ludlow nodded and drained the last of her drink out of the glass.

"Don't you want to know why I didn't go to her funeral in New York?" she asked.

"That's none of my business."

"Sure, it is. You're a reporter. Everything's your business."

"Okay, why didn't you go to your daughter's funeral?"

"I wanted to. I really did. But I just couldn't. You see, I always thought there was still a chance for a happy ending for me and Cheryl Lee. That someday we'd put the past behind us and have all those mother and daughter chats we never had and she'd find a good man and maybe even give me a grandkid. Not very realistic, I guess, but we can all dream. Well, that dream ended when she died. It's too late for me now to ever tell her 'I'm sorry.' That's why I couldn't go to New York City for the funeral. I didn't have the strength to see her lying in that casket. Dying so young like that before she ever knew how I really felt about her. Do you know how I said goodbye to my daughter? I got roaring drunk. I sat right here in this bar the day of her funeral and drank all through the night until I could forget all about it. The only problem with drinking through the night is the next morning. You wake up. And then you remember. I've been remembering Cheryl Lee every day since she died. Of course, maybe if I'd spent a little more time thinking about her before that, she might still be alive today. Hell, who knows? But there's nothing I can do about it now."

"Sure there is."

"What?"

"Tell me something about Cheryl Lee that will help me answer some of the questions I have about her death."

"I've told you everything I know."

"Are you sure there's nothing else she said when she came here to see you in January? Nothing about her life? Her friends? What she was doing? Why she was suddenly so interested again in her dead father?"

Ludlow sighed and thought for a long time. "Well, there is one other thing," she said finally. "But it didn't even happen then. It was later…"

If there was one lesson that I had learned in my years as a reporter, it was to be persistent. Never give up. You can ask a hundred questions and not learn anything you didn't know before. But the 101st question might be the one that breaks the story wide open. That was what happened here. I had thought Dorothy Ludlow was a dead end. I figured the interview with her was a waste of time. But I kept plugging away – asking her every question I could think of – because I couldn't think of anything better to do. "You're a bulldog," an editor at the *Tribune* had once said to me, "once you get hold of a story you never let go." Sometimes it paid off.

"There were these letters," Dorothy Ludlow said. "Cheryl Lee sent me a collection of letters written by her father."

CHAPTER 44

There is no such thing as a perfect story. The pieces of the puzzle don't ever fit together exactly the way a reporter expects them to at the beginning. No matter how hard you try, every story always contains loose ends, unexplained events and questions for which there will never be any answers. But when you were on a roll – when you started finding out some real answers – the rest of the answers sometimes miraculously fell into place too. Even the answers to questions you hadn't asked. That's what happened here.

On the night that she died, only a few hours before her deadly walk through the park, Cheryl Lee Barrett had made a stop at a printing shop. That was when she had the argument with Senator Lansdale that had been captured on video by the store's security camera. I remembered asking the print shop guy what was inside the package she'd picked up there, but he didn't know. Neither did the police. Of course, it didn't really seem important at the time. Just one of those countless little details of a crime that seem to have no significance whatsoever. But that's why a reporter always needed to accumulate every single fact, whether or not it seemed important at the time. Because you never know. *Dammit*, I thought to myself as I looked at the brown manila envelope in front of me now, *you just never know*.

The envelope said Madison Avenue Print Shop. It had been addressed to Dorothy Ludlow at a Kettering address and was postmarked at six p.m. on the night of the killing. That was the last mail pickup of the day. Cheryl Lee Barrett had mailed the

package just before she went to the Park Grille for dinner with
Jonathan Lansdale.

Inside the envelope was a stack of paper – maybe seventy-five
pages or so. Some of the pages were handwritten in ink, others in
pencil and some of the pages were typed. The top page was a note
from Cheryl Lee Barrett to her mother. It said:

> I wanted you to have this. I know that you're sorry about
> everything that has happened. Me too.
>   Love, Cheryl Lee

"Your husband wrote these?" I asked.

"Apparently. They're a series of letters to our baby Cheryl Lee.
Chronicling things that happened to him in Iraq. Scott says at the
beginning that he wanted to keep them for when he came home
and she'd be old enough to read it. He said he wanted her to know
someday what he was doing over there and why he wasn't with
me when she was born."

I paged quickly through the collection of letters.

"This reads almost like a diary," I said.

She nodded. "Yes, Scott had aspirations of being a writer, you know.
That was what he hoped to do when he got out of the army. Go back
to school and take writing courses. He even said he might write a book
about the war he was fighting. I think this was his way of starting to
do that – this series of letters to the baby girl he'd never seen."

We were back at her apartment house in the suburb of Kettering, a few miles from the bar where she worked in Dayton.
The apartment itself wasn't too bad, a one-bedroom place next
to a small shopping complex. But it seemed totally devoid of any
character, any personality, any life at all. There were no pictures
on the walls, no high school diplomas from her daughter, nothing
to indicate it was anything more than a place for her to come
after the bars closed. I wondered what it was like growing up in

places like this for Cheryl Lee. Waiting for her mother to come home after a late shift, having to fight off her sleazy boyfriends. Wondering – always wondering – what life would have been like with the father she never knew.

"I never read most of it," Dorothy Ludlow was saying. "I didn't have the heart to do it. But I saw enough to know what it was. I have no idea how Cheryl got a hold of them, but they must have been very important to her."

It wasn't hard to figure out what probably happened. Joseph Enrico was in Iraq with Scott Barrett, the father. After Barrett died, Enrico found the letters, then held onto them for some reason all these years. Maybe because they reminded him of a different time in his life, before his criminal record and all the rest. Then, six months ago, he'd hooked up somehow with Cheryl Lee Barrett in Santa Barbara. That's when he'd first given her the letters. Soon after that, she started asking questions about her father. She asked her mother, the Defense Department in Washington and God knows who else. Then she and Enrico had likely traveled cross-country to New York City, where Cheryl Lee lured Senator Lansdale into bed while Enrico probably helped her make the secret X-rated video of the action. If that was the scenario, then these letters from Scott Barrett could give me the answer to what set Cheryl Lee off on the journey that resulted in her death.

"You say you never read these?" I said to Dorothy Ludlow.

"Only a few pages. I couldn't go any further. It was just too painful for me."

"But you kept them anyway."

"It's the only thing I have left now."

"Of your daughter?"

"Of my husband."

I was confused. "But you've been married five times since then."

"I was nineteen years old when I married Scott," she said wistfully. "Barely twenty when I had Cheryl Lee. I was a different person back then. I didn't know there was going to be no big houses with white picket fences, no loving families, no happy endings for me. I still had hope then. Reading those few pages made me remember what it was like. What *I* was like back then. What I lost when Scott was killed in that war. I just couldn't handle reading about it all again. I know that if I'd been a better mother, Cheryl Lee wouldn't have wound up with the life that she did. And maybe she'd be alive today."

"We're all responsible for our own lives," I told her. "Cheryl Lee had some bad breaks early on, but she made her own choices. We all make our own choices in the end. You didn't kill your daughter. Someone else did."

"You don't believe it was this man Enrico, do you?"

"No."

"Do you know who did kill her?"

"I think so."

"Why isn't he in jail?"

"He's a very powerful man."

"Put him in jail," she said.

"I'm trying, Mrs. Ludlow. I'm really trying."

CHAPTER 45

I read the letters in two consecutive spurts. The first part that night after I got back to my hotel room, the rest on the four-and-a-half-hour flight the next morning to California. By the time I was finished, I knew a lot more about Scott Barrett. And Frank Lansdale too.

They began with background of how Barrett joined the army, his basic training at Fort Knox, Kentucky, further tank training there and then being assigned to a motor pool unit of the 101st Airborne Division stationed at Fort Campbell. It was a three-year enlistment, and that's all the time he planned to do in the army. His goal was to take advantage of military benefits – especially the GI bill for going to college afterward.

It sure seemed like a good idea at the time. And relatively safe too. The U.S. hadn't really been in a war since pulling out of Vietnam in the early 70s. But then Iraqi leader Saddam Hussein invaded neighboring Kuwait. A UN peacekeeping force – headed by the U.S. – was assembled in the Gulf region to defend Kuwait and stop Hussein's troops. It was called Desert Storm, and Barrett's 101st Airborne unit was sent there to be a part of it.

It turned out to be a pretty brief period of actual combat for the U.S. After weeks of warnings and preparation for war, the U.S. launched Operation Desert Storm in January of 1991. It was over a few weeks later.

Barrett wrote several pages about the mixture of boredom and fear as the troops there waited for word to go into action.

It was on page twenty that I came across the first reference by Barrett to Frank Lansdale.

> My commanding officer is a lieutenant named Lansdale. We don't get along very well. He's the kind of guy who, when you've just come back from an all-night patrol, thinks it's a great time to police up the area for cigarette butts. Or have an inspection. A real asshole. He's a gung-ho, patriotic kind of guy. Talks constantly about how proud America is of what we're doing here, about how proud he is to be with us, how we're going to kick Iraqi ass. Everyone snickers at him behind his back. You learn to recognize bullshit really quick in a place like this. This guy is off the charts on the bullshit meter.

At one point, Barrett writes to Cheryl about finding out that she had been born.

> We named you Cheryl Lee. Dorothy said in the letter that you weighed eight pounds, six ounces, had blue eyes, blonde hair and were cute as a button. I can't wait to see you.
> I spend hours now dreaming about going home. To see you and to see your mom again. To hold you in my arms for the first time. I want to be there when you take your first step. I want to be there to hear the first word you say. I want to be there to send you off to your first day of school. I want to be there every step of the way in your life. I'm your dad. I'm always thinking about you and your mom – and counting the days until I can be with you is the only thing that's getting me through this war.

The last batch of letters described what happened to his unit at Medina Ridge on the night they were ambushed.

It all happened – it all went wrong – so fast.

One minute we were making our way across the desert in a convoy of vehicles. Then suddenly the convoy stopped. Everyone got out to see what was going on. We all mingled around – confused, disorganized, unsure what to do or where to go or what was going on. We needed a leader. Unfortunately, all we had was Frank Lansdale.

I heard a groan of disgust from behind me. "Damn, I can't believe this," my friend Joey said.

I walked back to where he was. The rest of the unit was a few yards behind. They were looking at a map of the area. "What's wrong?" I asked him.

"That damn ass of a lieutenant we have just got us lost," he said. "We're in the middle of nowhere in this damn desert."

"Not nowhere," someone else said. "We're at Medina Ridge."

"Goddamnit!" Joey said. "There are Iraqi Republican Guard units in the Medina Ridge area. We gotta get out of here!"

Lansdale was frantically looking at the map now. "It's not my fault," he whined. "I think there's something wrong with this map. There's going to be hell to pay when I get back to headquarters and report this. Someone's head is going to roll for this—"

"It doesn't matter whose fault it is," I said. "What matters is getting out of here right now."

"I think if we head due west, we should get out of the danger area within thirty minutes or so," Lansdale finally said, still studying the map.

We started out, but only made it about a half mile or so before they spotted us. It must have been a whole Iraqi Republican Guard regiment. The desert was suddenly alive with explosions and gunfire. Before we knew what was happening, they had us surrounded. Soldiers began to fall all around me. Others ran, trying to get to some kind of cover. There was screaming and panic everywhere. More explosions tore apart all the vehicles in our convoy. I looked over at Lansdale, the man who was supposed to be our leader, and saw a look of terror in his eyes – he was immobilized with fear. It was every man for himself out there in the desert that night.

I don't remember everything that happened after that, but I do know that eventually the gunfire and the screams stopped. The enemy was gone.

I emerged from the cover I'd been using along with a few other survivors, including my friend Joey. We moved around grimly inspecting the bodies of all the dead men from our unit lying there in the desert.

That's when I heard the sound. At first, I didn't realize what it was. But then when I did…

Someone was sobbing.

It was Lt. Lansdale, huddled in a fetal position next to one of the burned-out vehicles, sobbing uncontrollably. He was mumbling: "Oh God, oh God."

The others looked at him with disgust. Me, I went over and tried to get him up on his feet.

"Dammit, Lieutenant," I told him. "We've got to get out of here. Get up."

"My career," he said. "My career is ruined."

"You should thank God you're still alive," I replied.

"What if they come back for us?"

"That's why we need to get moving. Pull yourself together, Lieutenant."

But he just kept sobbing, tears coursing down his blotchy wet face.

I picked him up from the ground and began to carry him. The others tried to help too. Our vehicles were knocked out of operation, so our only option was to walk out of that desert. We began making our way through the sand, dragging the crying Lansdale with us as best we could.

And then, just when we thought things couldn't get any worse, they did. We nearly ran into another Iraqi Republican Guard unit, and it was only some quick thinking that meant we weren't seen. We huddled down in the dark and hoped they'd just move on. I had to put my hand over Lt. Lansdale's mouth so they didn't hear him, he was still making that much noise.

But then Lansdale suddenly pulled away from me, stood up and began yelling – pleading with the Iraqis not to hurt us. He said we surrendered. He said he'd do anything – tell them anything – if they just got him out of this desert alive. The Iraqis weren't looking for prisoners though, just bodies. They opened fire on our position as soon as Lansdale gave it away. One of us – a nineteen-year-old from Texas called Billy Watkins – was hit in the head and died.

Somehow me and the others – dragging Lansdale with us – managed to slip away again under the cover of darkness. It was a miracle we weren't killed too.

It took us three days to get back to base camp. All the way, Lansdale kept collapsing and saying he couldn't go on. He didn't seem to be wounded. He wasn't even scratched. It was like he was having some kind of emotional breakdown. Kept saying he couldn't go back. That his career was ruined. That we should leave him there and let him die. I probably should have too, it would have saved me a lot of problems down the line. But I did the right thing. I carried him most of the way, literally on my back part of the time. It really slowed us down. But somehow we finally made it. By then, we were all pretty much half-dead with dehydration and fatigue.

And that's all I remember until the real nightmare began…

That's all there was. That's how the letters ended. There was no explanation of what happened to Barrett and Lansdale and the other men after they got out of the hospital. No indication of the events leading up to Barrett's own death.

The official line was that Frank Lansdale was a war hero. He'd built his political career in part on his war record in Iraq as part of Desert Storm.

This said he wasn't a hero at all. He was a coward.

I looked out the window of the plane. I could see the lights of the city twinkling below as we began our descent into the airport.

Santa Barbara, California.

The letters from Scott Barrett had provided some of the answers I was looking for, but not all of them.

Maybe Santa Barbara could.

CHAPTER 46

The detective in charge of the investigation into the Santa Barbara murder that Cheryl Lee Barrett was accused of committing was a homicide cop named Bobby Delafuente.

It didn't exactly seem like it was keeping him up at night.

"Tell me about the case," I said.

"It's kind of a moot point now, isn't it?"

"You mean because she's dead?"

"Well, yeah."

"That makes it easy for you, huh?"

"Yep, it clears the book on a murder case. I wish they were all this easy."

"What if she didn't do it?"

"Oh, Lord," Delafuente groaned. "Did you come all the way out here from New York City just to bust my balls? What are you looking for anyway?"

"The truth."

"Which is?"

"Look, I don't know much about how you guys operate here. But my guess is that you didn't spend a lot of time on the murder of a pimp by his hooker. I mean, it's not the crime of the century. The girl looked good for it, so you didn't ask a lot of questions. Maybe she did it, maybe she didn't – she was a perfect fit for the collar. And, like you say, at some point it all became moot when she died. Do you have specific evidence linking her to the murder?

Were there any witnesses who saw her at the murder scene? I just need to know for the story I'm doing."

Bobby Delafuente looked a lot different than most of the detectives I knew in New York City. He wore an open-collared pink sports shirt with a bright floral pattern, blue khaki slacks and open-toed sandals. There was a picture of him on his desk standing next to a surfboard. The beachboy cop. The Santa Barbara Police Headquarters was different too. A modern, clean building – Spanish architecture. Not the dirty and grimy kind of squad room that I was used to. But, in the end, Delafuente turned out to be just like most of the police officers I covered in New York. A cop is a cop, whether he's in sunny California or the South Bronx.

"So we're talking off the record here, okay?" Delafuente lowered his voice.

"Absolutely."

"I've got your word on that?"

"The story I'm doing is not about the murder Cheryl Lee Barrett is accused of doing here. It's about the murder of Cheryl Lee herself in New York. I'm hoping that the information you give me on this one could help me on that one. Do you understand what I'm saying?"

Delafuente nodded. "Okay, here's what we have…"

It was pretty much the way I had figured it would be. Victor Gallo – who was Cheryl Lee's pimp and who had a long police record for theft, assault and promoting prostitution – was found shot to death in his apartment. The place had been ransacked and a strongbox pried open – with nothing left inside. The cops, naturally enough, began checking the girls who worked for Gallo. They found out Cheryl Lee had been seen going into Gallo's apartment the night he was murdered. When they went to her place, they discovered she had left town in a hurry. That made her number one on the cops' list of suspects. An all-points-bulletin was put out for her arrest on a charge of suspected murder. Nothing much seems to have happened after that, until she turned up dead six months later in New York City under the name of Margaret Kincaid.

"You didn't really work up a sweat looking for her, did you?" I asked.

Delafuente shrugged.

"What did you do?"

"We checked out all her known associates. Places she might go. We went through her apartment. Checked her bank statements, computer, phone records – that sort of thing – looking for some kind of clue. But we got nothing. She was just gone."

Her phone records.

I suddenly had a thought.

"Who did she call?"

"Nobody."

"There were no calls?"

"Sure, there were calls, but nothing to anyone important."

"So, who not important did she call?"

"Christ, I don't remember—"

"Can you check?"

Delafuente looked up the information in Cheryl Lee Barrett's police file. "Okay, here it is," he said. "There were some long-distance calls to New York City, one to Ohio and another to Iowa. None of them seemed important to us. The rest of it was just local stuff. We ran checks on those too, but turned up nothing exciting. I guess most of her customers called her, not the other way around."

He handed me a sheet of paper with the log of Cheryl Lee's phone calls in the month before she left Santa Barbara. I looked at the numbers on the calls outside the Santa Barbara area code and cross-checked them with my notes. The New York City number was Senator Frank Lansdale's office. So she obviously had him on her mind then. The call to Ohio was to her mother in Kettering, just about the same time as Dorothy Ludlow said she turned up for a rare visit asking questions about her father. The Iowa number turned out to be to a place called Sioux City. It meant nothing to me.

"Who lives in Sioux City, Iowa?" I asked Delafuente.

"Some guy named Fred Sutter. We called him as part of the investigation. Yeah, he said he talked to her, but he was just as mystified about it as we were. Said he'd served in Iraq with her father. Back in the Gulf War. Then one day, right out of the blue, she calls him up and wants to talk about the war. Weird, huh?"

Fred Sutter.

The last survivor, besides Frank Lansdale, of her father's army unit.

Cheryl Lee had tracked him down too.

"Not necessarily," I said.

Delafuente looked surprised. "Are you telling me you think that this had something to do with her murder?"

"Maybe everything," I told him.

Back at my hotel, I called the number for Fred Sutter in Sioux City, Iowa that I'd written down in my notebook while I was with Delafuente.

I'd thought long and hard about some kind of cover story I could use on Sutter to explain why I wanted to ask him questions about his time fighting in Iraq back then. But in the end, I decided to just tell him the truth. Sometimes the truth can set you free. Or at least it can get you some straight answers.

"Yeah, I was pretty surprised to get a call from the police out in California a few months ago," Sutter said. "At first, I couldn't even figure out what they were talking about. This cop said he was searching for a prostitute who they thought killed somebody. But what did that have to do with me? Then, after he told me her name was Cheryl Lee Barrett, I eventually made the connection. I remembered that she had called me up here before that. Of course, that was pretty surprising too. I never even knew the woman – I just knew her father. And that was so many years ago. I mean, this whole damn thing just seems very strange."

"Tell me what Cheryl Lee said."

"She wanted to know about her father. Asked me lots of questions about him, about our time together in Iraq. Jesus, I hadn't thought about Scott Barrett in years. Of course, we were pretty good friends in the army. But then he died."

"So she talked to you about Scott Barrett. What about Frank Lansdale?"

"Yeah, she asked about him too." Sutter sighed. "Old Frank really has done pretty well for himself, hasn't he? A U.S. senator. I read the other day where they were talking about running him for president somewhere down the line. Wouldn't that be something? My old commanding officer winds up as president of the United States."

"Cool," I said. "Maybe you'd get invited to the White House."

"I don't think so."

"You weren't close with him?"

"Hardly."

"How come?"

"Let's just say that Frank Lansdale would never get my vote for anything."

"And why is that?"

"War's a strange business," Sutter said. "It brings out the best in a man, and also the worst. You learn a lot about somebody by seeing them in a combat situation. The kind of stuff you don't find out from political literature or campaign speeches. It's pretty hard to bullshit the guy next to you in a foxhole. You really get to see people up close, warts and all. I got to know Lansdale pretty well. And Cheryl Lee's father, Scott, too. Now one of them is long dead and the other one is being talked about for the White House. Life really is a bitch sometimes, huh?"

Sutter didn't like Lansdale. That was good. I took a deep breath. "Tell me about Medina Ridge," I said.

There was a long silence on the other end of the phone.

"Mr. Sutter?" I finally asked. "Are you still there?"

"I'm here."

"You were one of the survivors of Medina Ridge, weren't you?"

"That's right. I was one of the lucky ones. Me. Lansdale. Scott Barrett. Joey Enrico. And Jack Olsen. Of course, Scott died a few months later. I guess his luck didn't hold out for very long."

"Olsen's didn't either," I said. "He died in a plane crash several years ago."

"Gee, that's too bad. But, like I said, I haven't thought about any of them very much until this all started. I mean the years pile up for all of us. I had a bout with prostate cancer myself awhile back, but it seems like I beat it. I guess I figured that at least one of us must be dead by now."

"Enrico's dead too."

"Really?"

"It just happened a few weeks ago. In New York City."

I told him the details of how he died and about Cheryl Lee Barrett's murder too. Sutter seemed stunned by the news. I could picture him sitting out there in his home somewhere in Iowa, suddenly being inundated by all these names from his past and somehow trying to make sense out of it all.

"I know what really happened at Medina Ridge too," I said.

"Now how would you know anything about Medina Ridge?"

"Someone who was there told me."

"Who? Frank Lansdale? Well, I don't know what Lansdale told you, but it wouldn't be the truth. That's for sure."

"I heard it from Scott Barrett."

"Huh?'

"He left behind a bunch of letters. Joseph Enrico kept them after the war, then gave them to Barrett's daughter a few months ago. I got the letters from her mother. Barrett tells the whole story of Medina Ridge in there. It's a helluva story, Mr. Sutter."

I laid it all out for him, everything that I'd learned from reading Barrett's letters.

"Is all of that the truth?" I asked him when I was finished.

"Yes," he said softly.

"So Frank Lansdale wasn't really a big war hero?"

"No, it's all a lie."

"Why didn't any of the rest of you ever tell the truth?"

Sutter sighed. "Ms. Tucker, do you remember when I said before that I hardly ever thought about Desert Storm or the people I served with in the army back then anymore? Well, that's not true. I still think about them a lot. That ambush at Medina Ridge – what happened to us there – it's a nightmare I've never been able to wake up from. Even now, after all this time, I still sometimes wake up screaming at night. The fear, the terror, the feeling of helplessness – they never seem to go away. Do you have any idea what that feels like?"

"Yes, actually, I do," I said.

"But the worst part – the absolute bummer of all – is that it was all for nothing. No one cares about the truth. The people like Frank Lansdale keep getting richer and more powerful, and the rest of us just try to survive. The war's over, Ms. Tucker. The bullshitters have won. That's what Medina Ridge means to me. So no, I never tried to tell the truth. Scott Barrett did. And he wound up dead."

"Are you saying that Lansdale was responsible for Scott Barrett's death?" I asked.

"Yes."

"Do you mean he shot Barrett?"

"Not exactly. Lansdale wasn't even there when Scott died."

"But then how—"

"When we were first rescued after Medina Ridge," Sutter said, "all five of us wound up in the hospital. We were all suffering from shock, exposure, dehydration, stuff like that. Hell, I don't even remember much about the first forty-eight hours after we got out of that desert. Most of the others didn't either. Except for Frank Lansdale. He was the only one who had the presence of mind to tell people the story right then. His story. So by the time we all came back to the living, we discovered that Lansdale had already set himself up as the hero.

"That wasn't enough for him though. Somebody had to take the blame for taking us into that ambush. Not him, of course. So he picked Barrett. The son of a bitch told everyone that Scott was responsible for the screw-up."

"Didn't Barrett give people his side of the story?" I asked.

"He tried. None of the brass believed him. They thought he was just trying to cover his ass. This was the army, Ms. Tucker. Lansdale was a lieutenant, our commanding officer. Scott was an enlisted man. There was never any question about who they would believe."

"And no one else came forward to back him up?"

"No."

"Why not?"

"In the army, especially in a war zone, you don't make trouble. You just keep your head down and try to get home in one piece. That's the way we all felt over there. You did what you had to do – whatever it was – to stay alive yourself. You didn't think about what was right or what was wrong. None of that mattered. Getting out was the only thing that mattered."

"Do you still believe that?"

"I'm not sure about anything these days," he said. "But if I could go back now and do things all over…" His voice trailed off.

"Tell me about Scott Barrett's death," I said.

"There was an unwritten rule back then," Sutter said, "that if you went through something as traumatic as we did, then they wouldn't send you back out into combat. That's what happened to Enrico, Olsen and me. Lansdale made sure we got cushy jobs at the base camp. We didn't cause any trouble, and we didn't get our asses shot at again. That was the trade-off."

"What happened to Barrett?"

"He was supposed to go to a desk job too. But Lansdale blocked it. Scott wound up going to a hot area near Baghdad where there was still heavy fighting going on. He got hit by friendly fire. A mortar shot fired by one of our own units that missed the enemy target and killed Scott instead. There was a big investigation, and it was ruled an unavoidable accident. Except... well, except I found out later that the lieutenant in charge of the artillery unit that fired the mortar was in the same Officer Training School class as Lansdale. They were friends there."

Sutter sighed, then after a pause continued. "I don't think anyone will ever know for sure what happened that day – it could have all been a coincidence. But Barrett, well... I think Lansdale wanted him out of the way so he couldn't contradict his story."

"So you really think Barrett died because of Frank Lansdale?"

"Some people might look at it like that."

"Someone like his daughter."

CHAPTER 47

My hotel in Santa Barbara was on a road that ran right alongside the coast. There were hotels, restaurants, marinas filled with boats and oceanfront houses up and down the entire stretch of highway. From the window in my room, you could see all of that and the blue waters of the Pacific Ocean. It was very beautiful and very peaceful. But I didn't feel peaceful. I had too many things on my mind.

Exercise always helped me to think. The very mind-numbing quality of pedaling on a bicycle that went nowhere and all the other seemingly endless exercise rituals I did somehow generally seemed to jumpstart my brain. Out of desperation and sheer boredom, I'd worked out lots of problems in the past as I sweated through my daily exercises.

Usually when I was away from home, I found it difficult to keep up my normal exercise regime. I missed my own equipment, my own gym, my own solitary little ritual. But this was a big hotel, and the brochure in my room said it had an extensive gym facility. I called the front desk to find out where to go, put on a pair of sweats and headed to the spa for a complete workout.

It turned out to be just what I needed.

I spent an hour doing leg curls, stomach crunches and working out on the Nautilus Machine. By the time I was finished, I felt exhausted, but also invigorated. I followed that up with a swim in the pool. As I did my laps, I felt the peace and serenity I always did when I was in the water. Someone said it was almost like being in a womb. I didn't know about that, but I could sure feel the tension and stress throughout my body slipping away as I glided smoothly through the water.

Afterward I showered, pulled on a pair of jeans, a T-shirt and sandals and took a walk on the beach I'd seen from my window.

Standing there on the shoreline, I could see long stretches of the Pacific – heading south toward Los Angeles and north all the way up the coast.

I wondered if Cheryl Lee Barrett had ever seen this view while she was living here in Santa Barbara.

Maybe Cheryl Lee had stood at this exact same spot and tried to make sense out of all the confusing facts she'd discovered while opening up the door into her past. Just like I was doing right now.

No one would ever know for sure now exactly what happened. But it must have all begun when she accidentally crossed paths with Joseph Enrico. It's possible Enrico even sought her out because she was a prostitute, but then found out who she was – the daughter of his long-dead army buddy. And he gave her the letters he'd been keeping all those years.

What about the murder of her pimp? Who knows? It could be that he caught her stealing money to finance the trip to New York, and she killed him in self-defense. More likely, she had nothing to do with the murder of Victor Gallo. Cheryl Lee Barrett was a prostitute. She was probably a blackmailer. But I didn't want to believe she was a murderer.

Somewhere along the line, a funny thing had happened. I had begun to identify with Cheryl Lee. More than that, I started to like her.

No one had ever given this woman a break in her whole damn life.

So maybe I could do this one last thing for her: catch her real killer.

And, of course, something happened on that last night of Cheryl Lee Barrett's life. Something that changed everything – derailed the plan she had concocted with Joey Enrico. Why did she suddenly break off her relationship with Senator Lansdale? Why did she seem so upset when she went into the park after leaving the Park Grille Restaurant? Did Lansdale really meet her there to murder her in cold blood?

CHAPTER 48

The apartment building where Cheryl Lee Barrett had lived was in downtown Santa Barbara. This wasn't the rich part of the city, but it wasn't too bad either. There was a Starbucks coffee shop next door and a bookstore across the street. The name on Apartment 2D – the one that used to be Cheryl Lee's – was Kimberly Russell. I pressed the buzzer on the intercom.

"Yes?" a female voice said through the speaker.

"I'm looking to talk to someone about Cheryl Lee Barrett, the woman who used to live in this apartment."

"Who are you?"

"My name is Jessie Tucker. I'm a newspaper reporter."

"From the *News-Telegram*?"

The question stopped me for an instant. Then I remembered that the *News-Telegram* was the Santa Barbara newspaper.

"No, the *New York Tribune*. I'm from New York City."

"Yeah, well I don't know anything about the *New Yawk Tribune*," the woman said, putting on an exaggerated Bronx accent, "but I've got nothing to say to nobody about nothing."

"Did you know Cheryl Lee?"

"She was my friend."

"She was my friend too," I said.

There was a long silence on the other end of the intercom.

"I'm trying to find Cheryl Lee's killer, Kimberly," I told her. "Maybe you can help."

"The police already found her killer."

"I think they got the wrong man."

*

Kimberly Russell turned out to be a real Southern California-looking blonde in her mid-twenties. She was wearing short shorts and a tight tank top and looked ready to answer a casting call at any minute. We sat in the living room of what turned out to be a pretty typical one-bedroom apartment and talked about Cheryl Lee.

"How did you know her?" Kimberly Russell asked.

"I didn't."

"But you said—"

"I lied."

She looked confused.

"I sometimes feel like I knew her though," I said. "I've been investigating her murder ever since it happened. Everyone else thinks it was just a simple mugging. I don't. I think there were a lot of other things that were involved."

I told her about the facts I'd uncovered during the past few days. Not all of the facts, but most of them. Enough to give Kimberly Russell an idea of what I was looking for. Kimberly had been Cheryl Lee's friend – she might have told her something important. I needed to get her to trust me. The truth seemed to be the best way to accomplish that.

It seemed to work. After I was finished talking, Kimberly Russell told me about her own relationship with Cheryl Lee. She said they'd worked together – they'd got to know each other through Victor Gallo – the dead pimp the Santa Barbara police had mentioned. When Kimberly was evicted from her apartment, Cheryl Lee had invited her to move in and share the rent on this place. No, they didn't bring male customers here, she explained. They used hotel rooms for business. Then, after Cheryl Lee disappeared, Kimberly continued to live in the apartment.

"Did she ever talk to you about her father?" I asked.

"You mean her real father?"

"Yes."

Kimberly rolled her eyes. "God, yes. She hardly talked about anything else those last few weeks before she left. I figured she must be going through some kind of therapy or something – one of those self-realization things where you have to go back and deal with people and things out of your past. She really got obsessed about this father thing. Kept talking about how her life might have been totally different if he'd lived and been there for her when she was growing up. I didn't buy it. Me, I couldn't get away from my father fast enough."

"What do you mean?"

Kimberly pulled up her tank top and turned around so I could see her back. She pointed to several ugly-looking scars there.

"Memories of my father," she said.

"He beat you?"

"That's the least of what he did."

Kimberly pulled her tank top back down.

"I told Cheryl Lee once that maybe her own father would have been a son of a bitch too. Just like all the stepfathers she had. Just like my father was. Maybe her real father wasn't so great either. Maybe he wasn't worth all the time and energy she was devoting to him."

"But she didn't agree, huh?"

"She went nuts. Started screaming at me and throwing things around the apartment. She just couldn't handle that. She'd put her father on a pedestal. He was her inspiration for a better life or something. God, the guy had been dead for years and years, but she idolized him." Kimberly shrugged. "I mean, maybe he was a great guy. But we'll never know now, will we?"

I looked down at my notebook. Everything Kimberly Russell had told me supported the other facts I'd accumulated so far. During those last few weeks here in Santa Barbara, Cheryl Lee had become more and more consumed with curiosity about her long-dead father. This finally culminated in her trip to New York City, presumably with Joseph Enrico. Then she'd become Margaret Kincaid and begun the relationship with Senator Frank Lansdale, her father's old commanding officer and the man indirectly responsible for his death. Only that's where the trail ended. I didn't know what happened after that.

"Did you ever talk to Cheryl Lee after she left?" I asked.

"Just once."

"When was that?"

"A couple of weeks ago. I guess it must have been just before she died. She called me one morning."

"What did she say?"

"She said she was thinking about coming back to Santa Barbara. She didn't tell me anything about what she was doing. Wouldn't even tell me where she was. I found that all out later after she died. What she wanted me to do was find some lawyer here to talk to the police and try to get the Victor Gallo business straightened out. She said she could prove she didn't do it. She wanted to clear her name. She said she'd decided that Santa Barbara was a great place to live."

"How was she going to live? Go back to being a prostitute?"

Kimberly shook her head no. "She said she had some money now, and she didn't have to do that anymore."

I thought about Cheryl Lee's nice apartment in New York City with all the fancy clothes in the closets. Yes, she had some money. Frank Lansdale's money, presumably.

"She'd obviously been thinking about this for a long time," Kimberly said. "She had all the details worked out. How she needed to find a bigger apartment than this one – and she went on and on about how she was going to decorate it. She even had the color of the walls picked out. She kept talking about this robin's-egg blue paint she was going to use in one of the bedrooms." She rolled her eyes. "I hadn't talked to her in six months and she's going on about robin's-egg blue paint. It was weird."

"Anything else?"

"We were only on the phone for a little while. Like I said, it was early in the morning and I was still a bit groggy. Then, a few days later, I heard that she was dead. That's really all I know."

I looked back again at the notes I'd been keeping during my conversation with Kimberly Russell. Something was bothering me, but I couldn't put my finger on what it was.

"There's nothing else?"

"Well, she wasn't well."

"Cheryl Lee?"

"Yeah, she said she hadn't been feeling herself – stomach trouble or something. I figured she'd just been partying too much. Cheryl Lee always loved to party."

I suddenly realized what the call could mean. I paged through my notebook one more time. It was all there. I just had to put the pieces together. Cheryl Lee Barrett was in a hurry to move back to Santa Barbara. She was making plans to get a bigger apartment and to paint one of the bedrooms a color called robin's-egg blue.

Cheryl Lee was pregnant.

After I left Kimberly Russell's apartment, I made a call to Lt. Aguirre in New York.

"Was there ever an autopsy done on Cheryl Lee Barrett?" I asked him.

"Sure there was. An autopsy is standard procedure in any murder case, Tucker."

"What did it show?"

"Pretty much what we already knew. The cause of death was a series of blows. From the rock. Probably Enrico's fists too. The first blow with the rock didn't kill the Barrett woman immediately – just stunned her or left her unconscious. But the ones after that did the job."

"Did you know she was pregnant?" I asked.

There was a long silence on the other end of the line.

"Who told you that?" Aguirre asked finally.

"The question is why you didn't tell me or anyone else about it after you got the autopsy report?"

"It didn't seem relevant to the investigation," he said.

Aguirre was right, of course. It wasn't relevant to the investigation. Not if you believed that Joseph Enrico killed her during a random mugging that night in the park. But if you didn't buy the police's Enrico scenario for the murder, then Cheryl Lee's pregnancy did matter. It was relevant to the case. Very relevant.

"Are you going to put this in the paper?" Aguirre asked.

"Why shouldn't I?"

The homicide cop groaned.

"You do that, Tucker, and you're gonna open up a real can of worms."

"Think so?"

"Sure. Everybody's going to start wondering who the father was."

"Yeah, how about that?"

CHAPTER 49

The offices of the *Santa Barbara News-Telegram* were only about five minutes away from Cheryl Lee Barrett's old apartment.

I decided to stop by there and try to meet Andrea Gelman, the reporter who had written the profile of Joseph Enrico I'd read back in New York. Gelman didn't turn out to be anything like I'd expected. I figured her to be an ambitious young reporter angling for a job in New York or Los Angeles or some other bigger market than Santa Barbara. Instead, Gelman was middle-aged – she'd worked at the *News-Telegram* for twenty-eight years, while raising four children at the same time. She was pleasant enough, but she wasn't in awe of meeting a reporter from New York City. She wasn't looking for a big story to put her on the national map. She'd lived and worked in Santa Barbara all her life, and she had no desire to ever do anything else.

"Did you know Joseph Enrico?" I asked her, remembering how her story had talked about him growing up in Santa Barbara too.

"Personally, no."

"But you knew of him?"

"Sure. He was a local boy who didn't make good. That story you read wasn't the first time I wrote it, you know. I'd done a couple of other versions of it over the years after Enrico had been arrested for other crimes. It just seemed appropriate to run it again after he was shot to death as a murder suspect."

"Did you ever figure him for the type of guy who would kill someone?"

"To be totally truthful with you, I was surprised. The guy did a lot of bad things in his life, but they weren't violent kind of bad things. Burglaries, auto theft, drug dealing – that was the sort of stuff that was Joey Enrico's thing. I've been in this business a long time and I've covered a lot of stories. I've found that people generally follow a pattern in their life, and most of the time they don't vary from that very much. What Enrico did – murdering the girl – well, it just didn't fit his pattern. Do you know what I mean?"

"I don't think he killed the girl," I said.

Andrea Gelman shrugged. "The police say he did."

"The police are wrong."

"Says who?"

"Me."

"Their opinion is the only one that counts."

"Aren't reporters supposed to right the wrongs of our law enforcement and government institutions?"

"You've been watching too many old movies." Gelman laughed.

"Did you ever hear of Watergate?"

"Hey, you're no Woodward and Bernstein."

"Neither are you." I smiled. "But we both have our good days every once in a while, don't we, Andrea?"

Gelman showed me the paper's story file on Cheryl Lee Barrett. There wasn't much there. A minor arrest for prostitution a few months after she came to Santa Barbara; then the naming of her as a suspect in the murder of Victor Gallo; and finally the story of her death in New York City and the subsequent shooting by the police of Joseph Enrico. Cheryl Lee hadn't been big news until she died violently.

The stuff about Victor Gallo's violent death pretty much told the same story I'd heard from Delafuente and Kimberly Russell. The *News-Telegram* had covered the case only superficially – burying it in the back pages with the kind of obscurity that newspapers generally give murders of pimps by their prostitutes.

"I think Cheryl Lee was innocent," I said to Gelman.

"You think everyone's innocent."

"Well, there's a lot of injustice in this world. Anyway, how do you know?"

Gelman went through the stories and pulled out a piece from the *New York Tribune*. The one I had written after the murder about how the woman calling herself Margaret Kincaid was really Cheryl Lee Barrett.

"I read your piece, Jessie," she said. "It was good. Really good."

"Thanks."

"Margaret Kincaid's brother just walked into your office and told you all that, huh?"

"That's pretty much how it happened."

"Damn, I wish he'd come to me instead."

"You?"

"Sure. I'm the one who wrote about his sister's death. The real Margaret Kincaid."

"You covered her car accident?"

"Yeah, you don't forget one like that. It was a terrible tragedy. Four people dead. All of them innocent victims. It's hard to understand how something like that can happen. That story bothered me for a long time."

There was something wrong here. "Four people died in the accident?" I asked.

"Yes."

"I thought it was just three of them. Margaret Kincaid and her two children."

"And Stephanie Kincaid."

"Who was she? Another sister?"

"No, Stephanie was Logan Kincaid's wife."

I shook my head. That didn't make sense. Logan had told me that his wife had left him.

"She died in the accident too?" I asked.

"Yeah, can you imagine what that must have been like for him? To lose your sister and her kids and your wife too. No wonder he felt so guilty. I don't know how you ever get over that kind of grief."

I was really confused now. "Why should he feel guilty?"

"Well, he wasn't. The police cleared him."

"Cleared him of what?"

"Drunk driving. Didn't he tell you? Logan Kincaid was driving the car when it happened."

Ever since I had arrived in Santa Barbara, I knew I was going to have to confront my feelings about Logan. It had to happen. I couldn't put the man out of my mind without an explanation about what had gone wrong between us. I needed some kind of closure.

But I'd never expected something like this.

After Gelman dropped her bombshell, I went through the rest of the newspaper stories about the death of the real Margaret Kincaid. I'd never really looked that deeply into the details of Margaret Kincaid's car death. All I cared about was Cheryl Lee Barrett, not the woman whose identity she had assumed. But the Margaret Kincaid car accident happened just the way Gelman had said it did. There were five people in the car. Margaret Kincaid, her two children, Logan and Logan's wife. Logan was driving. It was a Saturday afternoon and he was taking them home. Somewhere along the way, at an intersection where the light was changing, a fast-moving car plowed into the side of their vehicle. The driver of the other car, who witnesses say was weaving all over the road, got away before the police arrived. He was never caught. That was pretty much the way Kincaid had told the story to me. What he hadn't told me was that he was the driver… and that the paramedics tested his blood for alcohol. He'd had a few beers at the barbecue, and he failed the test. They gave him a second test, and he passed this one – but just barely. The last article in the file talked about the search for the other driver.

I looked up Logan's address and wrote the information down in my notebook.

It was time to go see him.

He'd come to me and lied about the details of the accident.

Then he'd lied to me about his wife leaving him.

So what else was he lying about?

CHAPTER 50

"Were you ever going to tell me the truth?"

"I'm not very good at the truth these days," Logan said, his voice low.

We were eating breakfast at a café on the beach near my hotel. He'd returned my phone call that morning, and we decided to meet here. I wasn't really hungry. I just picked at my omelet and drank some orange juice as we talked. From where we were sitting, I could see for several miles down the beach. The water looked very blue in the morning sunlight. Off in the distance, a large white sailboat bobbed up and down on the horizon.

"It was the Fourth of July," he continued, staring down at his coffee cup. "There was always a Kincaid family tradition: a big barbecue on the Fourth of July. Steaks, ribs, hamburgers – and, of course, booze. You couldn't have a barbecue without some drinking. Everybody does it. I never had any kind of an alcohol problem – never even thought about it before that day.

"Anyway, we held the barbecue at my house that year. My sister's car was being repaired, so we'd picked them up that morning and brought them to the house. Me and my wife, that is. Her name was Stephanie. There were five of us in the car. Margaret, her two kids, Stephanie and me. Stephanie was pregnant. That probably wasn't in the story you read. She'd told me just a few days before. We were going to have a baby."

There were tears in his eyes now.

"I never saw the guy who hit us," he said. "I found out later that he just came right through a red light at an intersection and slammed into us. Witnesses said they saw him weaving drunkenly before the collision, but I don't remember any of that. All I remember is waking up on a stretcher in the ambulance. Then the trip to the hospital. And all the pain that I was in. But that was nothing compared to the pain I felt when I found out what had happened to my family. They were dead. All of them. Me, I'd somehow got thrown clear of the car and survived. *Lucky*, they said.

"Then, it got even worse. They did a blood test on me – the one you said you read about in the newspaper article – and it came back that I was legally drunk. Sure, I'd been drinking beers at the barbecue during the afternoon, but I didn't think I was incapacitated. Suddenly though they're talking about arresting me for drunk driving. So there I am lying in my hospital bed – my family's dead – and they're saying that I might be responsible. The driver of the stolen car is long gone. All they've got is me."

I drank some coffee and thought about everything he'd told me.

"But you were cleared," I said. "I read that in one of the follow-up articles about the accident. They'd swabbed alcohol on your arm to give you a shot of a painkiller just before they tested your blood for the alcohol level. They said that could have resulted in a false reading. They gave you a second test, and you passed that one. Maybe because the alcohol had more time to work its way out of your bloodstream, maybe because the first test result was screwed up. In any case, the witnesses at the scene said you weren't at fault. No charges were ever filed. No one blamed you for the accident."

"That's what they all said," he agreed. "The police. Other members of my family. My friends. The people I worked with at the architectural firm. Everyone told me there was nothing I could have done to save them. Everyone was convinced of that.

"But I'll never know for sure if I might have reacted faster – gotten out of the way or seen the drunk driver coming – if I hadn't been drinking myself. Maybe my reflexes would have been just a fraction better than they were. And maybe that fraction of a second would have been enough. Maybe my sister, her two children and my wife and my unborn child would have been alive today if I hadn't had a few beers before I got into the car. Do you understand what I'm saying, Jessie?"

I nodded.

"I kind of just shut myself down for a long time after it happened," he said. "I left my job. I stopped talking to my friends. I've never had a relationship with another woman since my wife died. I was afraid. Afraid to get too close to anyone or I'd lose them too. That's what the shrink I was seeing told me anyway.

"One day I decided there was something I wanted to do. I wanted to catch the person – the drunk driver – who was responsible for ruining my life. That would never bring Stephanie and our unborn baby or Margaret and those children back. But maybe I could save my own life if I did that. Give it all some kind of meaning or closure. So for a long time that's all I did. It was the only thing that mattered to me anymore.

"Until I met you. You were different. I thought that maybe you and I….." His voice trailed off. "But I got scared again. That's why I left."

I reached over and put my hand on top of his. I squeezed it softly.

"I'm scared too, Logan," I said.

"Really?"

"Yeah, I've been living scared for a long time."

I squeezed his hand again. This time he squeezed back.

"Now I don't want to be scared anymore," I told him.

CHAPTER 51

It had been another time and another place – so long ago that it seemed almost in another lifetime – since I had felt like this.

Back in my hotel room, we fell onto the still unmade bed. There was very little talking now. He kissed me, tentatively at first and then passionately. First, on the side of my cheek. Then my lips. And my neck. After that, I lost track as he moved down my body, caressing my breasts and then using his hands to gently explore further. He unbuttoned my blouse and undid the belt on my jeans while I undressed him too.

"I just thought of something," I whispered when we were almost completely naked.

"What?"

"The bed is unmade."

"So you're sloppy." He laughed. "Nobody's perfect. I guess I'll just have to live with that."

"No, the housekeeper," I told him. "She hasn't been to this room yet. What if she comes in while—"

"I hung the 'Do Not Disturb' sign on your door when we came in," he said.

"You think of everything."

"Of course, she could just barge in here anyway."

"Well, then she'll get a real thrill, won't she?"

"I sure hope so." He laughed.

This wasn't the kind of sex I'd seen on the video with Cheryl Lee Barrett and Senator Lansdale. Cheryl Lee on that video seemed impersonal and detached as she did it. No matter how good an act she was putting on for Lansdale and the camera. This was emotional, and intense. It was like Logan and I existed in a vacuum and the rest of the world had simply ceased to exist. Nothing else mattered at that moment. After, I held onto him tightly for a very long time.

"Wow!" I said finally.

"Are you okay?"

"I feel great."

"I wasn't sure because it's been a long time since I've done this, and I wanted to—"

"You were terrific," I said. I kissed him on the lips. Then I lay my head down on his chest and looked up at him with a big smile on my face. "Definitely terrific."

We lay in bed for a long time afterward and talked about a lot of things.

At some point, we even talked about his wife.

"Were you…" I paused, not sure how to exactly put it into the right words, "… well, were you always happy together?"

"No one's always happy, Jessie. We had our problems. We fought about a lot of things. But she was my wife. I loved her, and that was the bottom line. I would have stayed with her forever if the car crash hadn't happened. But she's dead – and so is my sister and the baby I'll never see and all the rest of them. Me, I'm still alive. I have to keep reminding myself of that sometimes."

I liked his answer. It was an honest response. He'd told me – in essence – that he loved his wife, but now he was trying to move on. He'd never met any woman since that time that he had wanted to be with. Until now. I could live with that.

"How about you?" he asked. "Was there someone like that in your life?"

"Just the former fiancé I told you about. Gary."

"I still can't believe what a jerk he was."

I shrugged.

"It's like what you just talked about a few minutes ago," I said, "About how the courses of our lives are determined by the chance everyday decisions we make. If I'd never gone into the park that night, then everything might have turned out different for me. I'd still be working on Madison Avenue instead of being a newspaper reporter. Maybe I'd even be married to Gary Bettig. Everything that's happened to me since then – every significant event in my life – is because of what happened to me in the park."

"That's a tough way to determine the course of your life," he said.

"But I turned it into something positive. I changed my life because of what happened to me. I'm pretty happy with it. Or at least I thought I was. Until…"

"Until what?"

"Now I'm not so sure about anything anymore."

I went through all the new stuff I'd found out with him.

"It doesn't make sense, even to me," I said. "Let's assume that Senator Lansdale did murder Cheryl Lee Barrett because she was blackmailing him. Or because he was afraid she'd reveal he'd gotten her pregnant. Does that mean he attacked me too? And maybe other women? Why? What's the connection?"

"I don't know," he said.

"So what good are you?" I smiled.

He leaned over and kissed me on the chest. I felt a shudder of excitement going through my body again.

"Look, since this worked out so well the first time," he said, moving down my body with his kisses, "what say we maybe do it again?"

And that's what we did.

CHAPTER 52

Suddenly, everything changed for the better.

I filed all the stuff I'd found out back to the *Tribune* news desk in New York. At first, I wasn't sure if Isaacs would print any of my stuff. But he did. I suppose it was because I'd accumulated so many hard facts now on this trip – the pregnancy, the diary – that he really had no choice. And I did find out later that he'd gone to Jonathan Larsen, the *Tribune*'s owner, first for permission to go with my stuff. But I also liked to believe that Isaacs had bought into all this in a big way himself at this point, and he was just acting like a journalist now. Funny how Isaacs had been the one to step up for me in this situation, not Danny Knowlton. You never know about some people. Anyway, the bottom line was I was back on the Cheryl Lee Barrett/Senator Frank Lansdale story.

Isaacs decided to break it up into several stories. The first one was the stunning revelation that Cheryl Lee Barrett had been pregnant when she was murdered. The second article dealt with Cheryl Lee's obsession with finding out more about her father in the weeks and months before her death, and her sudden rise in the campaign organization of Senator Lansdale – who had been her father's commanding officer during the Iraq war. Then I wrote about Joseph Enrico, the supposed killer, also serving under Lansdale in the army with Cheryl Lee's father. After that came a piece raising questions about the accuracy of the senator's war record, based on information from Scott Barrett's diary and the interview I'd done with Fred Sutter.

I still did not come right out and say that Lansdale was having a sexual relationship with his young campaign aide or that he could be a suspect in her murder. Isaacs wouldn't allow me to do that. But the steady procession of stories was bound to create a groundswell of controversy and questions that Lansdale – and eventually even the *Tribune* itself – wouldn't be able to ignore.

It didn't matter how important Frank Lansdale was or how many powerful friends he knew. I had him in my sights now. It was only a matter of time before I brought him down.

The headlines on my stories in the *Tribune* were making big news:

SLAIN CAMPAIGN AIDE WAS PREGNANT
DEAD WOMAN IN PARK'S STRANGE LINKS WITH
SENATOR LANSDALE
SENATOR'S WAR RECORD AS IRAQ HERO
QUESTIONED BY SOME

Another day, another exclusive. Life was good.

I was in no hurry to go home. I had a lot of vacation days that the *Tribune* personnel office had been pressuring me to use anyway, so I told Isaacs I wanted to use some of them now. He didn't ask why I was so eager to take some time off after months of working nonstop without a break. He just seemed happy to say yes.

I was monitoring – and writing some articles – about the investigation into my own case from there too. Mayor Hanrahan had been true to his word – he had gotten the police and D.A.'s office to at least sit up and take notice of the new evidence with Tamara Willis's attack on the same night as mine. An effort was underway to go back and look again at everything that happened all those years ago, to determine if Darryl Jackson had actually been telling the truth when he said he only attacked one woman in the park that night.

It was a slow process. Partly because of all the time that had passed since the original investigation. But also, I believed, because the authorities were dragging their feet and only grudgingly doing whatever they had to do to check it out. That's why I decided I didn't really need to be back in New York for this part of it. Besides, I'd been obsessed with the past for a long time. Right now, I just wanted to enjoy the present.

Logan and I spent our days at the beach in Santa Barbara and exploring other parts of Southern California too. One day we drove up to San Simeon to see the castle built by William Randolph Hearst, the legendary newspaper publisher that the movie *Citizen Kane* was based on. Another time we spent the day in Los Angeles, winding up at the pier in Santa Monica where I got sick riding the Ferris wheel after eating too many hot dogs. We even went to Las Vegas. I won two hundred dollars playing blackjack for four hours, then lost it all in fifteen minutes at the roulette wheel. Logan told me I was a rotten gambler, but a terrific kisser. He was kissing me at the time he said that.

We made love every night, most of the time in my hotel room with the view overlooking the Pacific Ocean. Sometimes, after Logan had fallen asleep, I would lie there and look out at the lights of boats on the ocean and listen to his breathing next to me and wish that I never had to go back to New York City again.

This was perfect.

This was paradise.

This was too good to be true.

Too good to last.

And, of course, it didn't.

The hotel telephone rang late one night, waking me out of a sound sleep. I tried to reach for it without waking up Logan. But he got to it first.

"It's for you," he said. "Someone named Danny Knowlton from your office?"

I took the phone. Danny had been calling me a lot lately ever since I got back onto the front page, trying to mend fences from what happened that day in Isaacs' office. I figured it was just another one of those calls. But I was wrong.

"Jessie, you better get back here right away," Knowlton said.

"What's going on?"

"You haven't heard?"

"No."

"Someone just tried to kill Frank Lansdale."

CHAPTER 53

By the time I landed at Kennedy Airport that afternoon, I had pretty much caught up on everything that had happened.

Some time the night before, as Lansdale was leaving his office at about six p.m., someone fired five shots at his car as he was pulling out of a garage underneath his building. The bullets shattered the windshield and one of the windows of the car. The senator and his son Jonathan, who was also in the car at the time of the shooting, got down on the floor of the vehicle until the gunfire was over. Neither of them was hit.

The police searched the area, but never found the gunman. They did find five shell casings in an alleyway across the street from the garage, where they assumed that the shooter had waited for his target. The garage attendant said he heard the gunfire and ran outside, but never saw anyone. He was the one who called the police. Lansdale and his son returned to the senator's office, where he later met with reporters and held a news conference about the incident. He also delivered a stirring speech on a proposal for a wide-ranging jobs anti-discrimination bill that he was proposing in the Senate, declaring that nothing – not even an assassination attempt – would stop him from fighting for equal rights for all, regardless of race, creed, sex or color.

From the start, it all seemed a little bit too convenient.

One, the gunman was a very bad shot. Based on the placement of the shell casings, he'd fired at the car from about twenty feet away. All of the shots had hit the vehicle, but none of them struck either of the two occupants inside. The shooting occurred at six p.m. when it was still light outside, so the two men in the car should have been plainly visible. And, for that matter, why did the shooter take up a position across the street? Why not wait closer to the exit of the garage where he had a better view? He hadn't hit anything except the windows. Why go to all that trouble for an assassination attempt if you can't hit the broad side of a barn?

Second, from a political standpoint, Lansdale couldn't have asked for a bigger break. The assassination attempt against him was front-page news in every newspaper in town. The kind of sensational stuff that bumped other stories off Page One for a few days. Like stories about his war record and his possible relationship with a dead campaign aide. Those were old news now, the assassination attempt was the story of the day. All in all, it worked out very conveniently for Frank Lansdale.

Third, it fit the pattern I was starting to see – the pattern Lansdale had always used in a crisis. When he was in danger of being blamed for the death of his men in the desert, he'd deflect attention from his own questionable actions by blaming someone else. A patsy. A patsy named Scott Barrett. That use of a patsy – a fall guy, a scapegoat – was a constant element in everything that I had uncovered in my investigations in recent days. The incident in Iraq. The murder of Cheryl Lee Barrett. Even the attack on me twelve years ago, if he really was involved in that. There always had to be a patsy to take the fall.

But who was going to be the patsy this time for the assassination attempt on Lansdale?

Enrico was dead.

Lansdale needed another patsy.

Who?

I found out the answer to that when my plane landed at Kennedy Airport. Detectives Aguirre and Erskine were waiting for me at the arrivals gate.

"You better come with us," Aguirre said.

"I have to pick up my baggage."

"Someone will get it for you."

"Where are we going?"

"To the precinct."

"Why?"

"We want to talk to you about the attempted shooting of Senator Frank Lansdale."

I realized now what was happening – who the patsy was this time.

Jessie Tucker.

CHAPTER 54

I had seen a lot of police interrogations, but always from the outside – never as a participant.

In most New York City precinct houses, there was a one-way viewing window in the interrogation room. The suspect inside the room couldn't see who was behind the window. But anyone could stand outside the room and watch and listen to everything that was going on. There were lots of people who did that. Other cops. Police brass. Assistant District Attorneys who might be asked to prosecute a case based on what they were hearing. Sometimes even reporters. I was never sure if that was legal or not, but on a number of occasions cops had invited me to listen in on the questioning of a suspect who had no idea that his comments were being overheard by an audience.

This knowledge of how a police interrogation worked gave me a distinct advantage in this situation.

"Where were you at six p.m. last night?" Aguirre asked as we sat in one of the interrogation rooms at the Central Park Precinct.

"Who wants to know?" I said.

"I do."

"Who else?"

He looked over at Erskine, who was the only other person in the room. They both seemed confused by my response. "What are you talking about?"

"Look, I don't perform in front of an audience. How about you tell all the people behind that window over there to go away? Then we can get down to business."

Aguirre nodded at Erskine. The old cop stood up, went outside for a minute and then came back into the room.

"Satisfied?" Aguirre asked.

"Do you mind if I check for myself?" I said. "It's not that I don't trust you. It's just that I don't trust you."

"Whatever…"

I walked out the door and looked in the hallway outside. It was empty now. I came back inside.

"Are you happy?" Aguirre asked.

I shrugged.

I knew I had Aguirre off balance. Cops were used to questioning people who were scared and not sure what was happening to them. The problem with me was it was like dealing with another cop. I knew too much about how the system worked – when the person being interrogated knew how to play the game, then the rules all changed.

"The thing is," Aguirre said, "after someone tried to shoot Lansdale, we tried to figure out who didn't like him. We made a list of potential suspects – people who had threatened him in the past, had public confrontations with him, stuff like that. Guess who was at the top of the list?"

"I was just doing my job as a reporter."

"You seem to have some kind of a vendetta against the senator."

"I want to expose him in the press, I don't want to kill him."

"Well, Lansdale wanted us to check you out first – thought you might have had something to do with the gunshots fired at him – so we tracked down your whereabouts. Found out you were on a flight in from California, and that's why we met you at the airport."

"Isn't that a pretty good alibi?" I asked. "I was in California. And you know that because you were there when I got off the plane at Kennedy Airport here." I thought back to the moment Logan and I had parted in the early hours of that morning – I had kissed him goodbye but neither of us had made any promises. With everything that was happening with these cases, I just couldn't.

"It's only a five-and-a-half-hour flight." Aguirre crossed his arms. "You could have come here from the West Coast and then gone back after the shooting."

"You really think I got on a plane, came cross country here to New York City, took five shots at Senator Lansdale – missing all five times, by the way – and then flew back on the red-eye. After doing all this, I got back on the plane and returned to New York just to make sure I could be picked up by you guys. Oh sure, that makes a lot of sense."

"Well, it could have happened that way," Aguirre insisted.

But he didn't seem very confident.

"You realize that we're still going to have to check all this out?"

"I wouldn't have it any other way."

I gave them Logan Kincaid's name and contact information. Plus, the number of the hotel I'd been at which had a record of when I'd checked out after being told about the Lansdale shooting incident on the phone by Danny Knowlton. And Knowlton's number too to confirm that he'd reached me in California right after it happened while I was still three thousand miles away from New York City.

"Well, even if your story checks out about being in California last night, there's still the possibility that you could have hired somebody here to carry out the shooting for you," Aguirre said.

"A hit man?"

"Something like that."

"Are you serious? I don't have the slightest idea how to even start looking for a hit man."

"You could learn."

"Lieutenant, do you have any actual evidence at all or are you just looking to score some brownie points with the senator by telling him how you gave me a hard time? I'm really way too busy for this. Unlike you, I'm actually trying to solve a real crime."

Aguirre looked surprised. He was definitely rattled now.

Erskine leaned over and whispered something to Aguirre. Then the two cops went outside, leaving me alone in the interrogation room. When they came back five minutes later, Aguirre didn't look very happy.

"You're free to go," he said to me.

"That's it?"

"For now."

"Aren't you supposed to tell me to make sure not to leave town or something like that?"

"I said you're free to go," he snapped, then walked out of the interrogation room.

I looked over at Erskine, who was still standing by the door.

"Thanks," I said to the old cop.

"For what?"

"Oh, I've just got a feeling that you played some role in getting him to stop busting my chops."

"Sometimes," Erskine said, "my partner doesn't think things through very clearly. Tommy's a really ambitious guy. Sometimes, that ambition gets in the way of good sense. When that happens, I just try to talk some sense into him. Sometimes he listens, sometimes he doesn't. Today he listened to me a little bit more than he usually does."

"Is he on Lansdale's payroll?" I blurted out, putting two and two together at last.

Erskine looked stunned by the question. "I don't know what you're talking about…"

"Like I said before, dragging me in here looks like he was trying to score some points with Lansdale. Why else would—"

Erskine started for the door. "I think we're done here," he said.

"Lansdale couldn't pull off some of the stuff he does without having some friends in key places," I rattled on excitedly. "Friends like an ambitious young police lieutenant. The question is, what does Lansdale offer him in return? Money? Political clout in the department? I think you probably know the answer to that, don't you?"

Erskine didn't answer, but he didn't have to. I realized that I'd misjudged him. Erskine was a lot smarter than he let on.

I'd have to work on making friends with Sergeant Erskine.

He'd helped me today. Maybe he could help me again.

It was always good to have a cop on your side.

CHAPTER 55

"There's something funny about the Lansdale shooting," I said to Norman Isaacs when I got back to the *Tribune* offices.

"What's funny about someone taking shots at a United States senator?"

"I don't think it happened that way."

"Why not?"

I told him my theory about Lansdale wanting to create a diversion from his own troubles.

"You think he fired those shots at the car himself?" Isaacs asked after I was finished.

"Him – or someone else he got to do it. Maybe he paid off the garage attendant to tell the story the right way. The point is, it's pretty hard to fire five shots into a car and not hit anyone. Neither Lansdale nor his kid got hit by flying glass, even though the windshield and a side window were shattered by the bullets. The whole thing only makes sense if there was no one in the car when the shots were fired."

"So why didn't the cops figure that out?"

"Maybe they're in on it."

"You think the police are part of this conspiracy too?" Isaacs asked.

"Not all of them. Just one or two key people. Aguirre probably. He's involved in this and he was the investigator on the Cheryl Lee Barrett murder too."

"Which you also think the police are covering up the real truth about, right?"

"Absolutely."

"Terrific." He sighed. "Is there a story anywhere in all this that we can print?"

"Here's a story for you," I told Isaacs. "It's a helluva story. With pictures too."

The trick to being a good reporter – just like being a good card player – is knowing how to play the winning hand that you're holding. Getting dealt an ace from the deck is just luck. Deciding what to do with it is where the skill comes in. I had been dealt an ace very early on in this story. Four of them actually. I'd held onto them for a long time. Now it was time to show my hand.

I played him the video of Frank Lansdale and Cheryl Lee Barrett in the hotel room. Isaacs watched it all silently.

"How did you get this?" he asked when it was over.

"You don't want to know how, Norman. Believe me."

"How long have you had it?"

"Not really relevant here."

He didn't push me on either answer.

"There's four of these?" he asked.

"Yes."

"All the same?"

"More or less."

"I don't think we can run any pictures from these in the *Tribune*. Or the video on our website. Not without more information about where they came from and how you obtained them. There're too many legal and ethical issues to publish anything."

"We don't have to, Norman."

Then I told him my idea.

I didn't really expect Isaacs to go for it, but then he'd surprised me more than once recently.

"Okay, let's do it," Isaacs blurted out.

"Are you sure?"

"Fuck it," he said. "I've had this damn job for too long anyway."

It took a while for me to get Senator Lansdale to come to the phone and talk. But I was persistent.

"What do you want?" Lansdale said when he finally got on the line.

"We need to talk about Cheryl Lee Barrett."

"I hardly knew the woman."

"You and Cheryl Lee – who you knew as Margaret Kincaid – had a sexual relationship. Your son was simply a ruse so your wife – and I guess the voters too – didn't find out you were cheating on your marriage vows. Only Cheryl Lee had something on her mind besides sex. She was the daughter of a man who she believed died in Iraq because of you. She wanted to ruin your political career and your marriage. I think you found that out just before she died, and then she wound up murdered in the park. That gives you a helluva motive to kill her."

"You don't have proof of any of that," Lansdale said.

"Actually, I do."

"I don't believe you."

"Maybe this will convince you…"

I handed the phone to Isaacs, who was standing next to me.

"Senator Lansdale, this is Norman Isaacs. I'm the city editor of the *New York Tribune*. I've just seen a copy of a video – there are actually four of them – showing you having sex with the woman who was later murdered in the park. These are more than enough to convince me, and I'm sure our readers too, that Ms. Tucker's accusations about the nature of your relationship with the victim are correct. The *Tribune* is not a scandal sheet. But we believe this information could be relevant to her murder, and so we are working on a story about it now, based on what we saw in these videos. This is very powerful evidence, Senator. We're prepared to print an exclusive story in the *Tribune* about the sex videos, your affair with the dead woman and everything else. If you have any comment you want to make, this is the time to do it—"

Isaacs listened for a few seconds, then smiled at me. "He wants you," he said.

I took the phone back.

"We need to talk," Lansdale said.

"Okay."

"Please listen to what I have to say before you print anything. You've got it wrong. You don't know the whole story. Can we meet somewhere? Just you and me?"

Sure, I knew it could be dangerous. He might be setting me up, trying to lure me someplace by myself so he could get rid of me, just like Cheryl Lee. But I was close now to breaking this story wide open. Tantalizingly close. The adrenaline rush I felt from that outweighed any of the fears.

"The Central Park Boathouse Restaurant," I said. "Just inside the park at 72nd Street, right off Fifth Avenue. In an hour. And we both come alone."

"Central Park?" he asked. He seemed surprised.

"Yes."

"Why Central Park?"

"It feels appropriate."

CHAPTER 56

Lansdale didn't look very much like a U.S. senator this time. He looked tired, drained – maybe even a bit frightened. He wore a windbreaker even though it was a warm day and a baseball cap pulled down over his head so it was difficult to see his face. The cap gave me a start at first, until I realized it wasn't a Yankees cap. It said NASA on the front, the kind of hat the astronauts wear. I remembered reading somewhere in his clips that he was a big advocate for spending money on the space program.

"My editor knows exactly where I am," I said as I pulled up a chair at the table overlooking the lake where the senator was sitting. "If anything happens to me, the police will come looking for you right away. You won't get away with murder again."

"My God," Lansdale said, "you really do think I killed her, don't you?"

"All the evidence points to you."

"The police didn't think so."

"The police had a fall guy. Joseph Enrico. You probably set him up for them. Once they started with the premise that he did it, it was easy to make a case against him. But I started over from the beginning. I looked at all the evidence. And that didn't lead me to Joseph Enrico. It led me straight to you, Senator. When did you find out that the woman you knew as Margaret Kincaid was really Barrett's daughter?"

"The day she died," he said.

"Did she tell you she was pregnant then, too?"

"Yes."

"And so you killed her."

"No, I didn't kill her."

"You're still sticking with that story, huh?"

"I didn't kill her," he repeated. "I loved her."

"Yeah," I said contemptuously, "I've seen on those videos how you loved her."

"You don't understand."

"Tell me."

Before Lansdale started talking, I figured I pretty much knew the whole story. I didn't think he could tell me anything I hadn't already found out.

But it turned out I was wrong.

Dead wrong.

"The thing is, with one or two exceptions, I've always been faithful to my wife," Lansdale said. "No matter what you might think, I'm not the kind of husband who was always cheating with other women. That wasn't how it was. Meg – I feel more comfortable calling her Meg, because it's the name I knew her by – she was different. She was special."

"Those other one or two exceptions," I asked him, "was one of them Alice Woodward?"

He nodded. "I was in love with Alice. Of course, that was a while ago…"

"Your wife found out," I said, repeating what Libby had told me about the relationship.

"That's right."

"And she threatened to destroy your political career?"

"Yes." Lansdale looked out at the water next to the restaurant. There were rowboats drifting by on the lake. A woman and two children had thrown some crusts of bread into the water. A group of ducks was hungrily eating the bread while the kids watched. It was a very tranquil scene. But Lansdale seemed anything but tranquil. I looked down at his hands. He kept balling them up into fists, opening and closing them in a nervous gesture as he talked. He was looking at the lake, but he seemed to be seeing something else besides rowboats and children and ducks. Something that had happened a long time ago, but he had never forgotten. "She threatened to divorce me. She said she would ruin me both politically and financially. It all got very ugly."

"But that never happened, did it?"

He shook his head no. "Alice and I had talked about what it would be like to be together, of course," he said. "Lying in bed sometimes, we'd made all these plans for our future together. I'd divorce my wife and we'd live happily ever after. We knew the scandal might well ruin my political career, but I was prepared to give that up – it was a small price to pay to be with the woman I loved. Or so I said to her anyway.

"But when push came to shove, I couldn't do it. My reputation had come to mean so much to me. So my wife and I made a deal," he said, watching the ducks fly away now that the crusts were gone. "I had to break if off with Alice. And I had to promise my wife there would be no more Alice Woodwards. I kept my end of the bargain too for all these years. Until I met Meg."

"What about the intern?" I asked. "Lisa Eichorn. Wasn't she threatening to bring sexual harassment charges against you?"

Lansdale shrugged. "That was nothing. I had a few drinks at a party. She was young and impressionable – she thought I was flirting with her. Maybe I was, but that's all that happened. She was pretty wacky, I think."

I noticed there was no emotion in his voice when he talked about Lisa Eichorn – certainly nothing like the intensity I felt when he was discussing Alice Woodward.

"Tell me about Cheryl Lee Barrett – or Meg, as you called her."

"Meg came to work for us in the New York campaign office about six months ago," he said. "At first, I didn't pay that much attention to her. Oh, she was attractive – more than attractive, she was stunning – but I've been around a lot of beautiful women. I always resisted temptation. I wasn't crazy enough to try anything like that again – or so I thought."

"But in the end, you did."

"She didn't give me much choice."

"I'm sure you had a choice."

"Christ, I'm only human."

"You mean she came on to you very strong?"

"It was unbelievable."

Of course, I thought to myself, *she seduced him*. That was part of her plan. Come on to him so strong that he couldn't say no – then use that to blackmail and destroy him. Payback time for her father. Only she hadn't done anything with the blackmail videos. At least, not before her death. Why not?

"Okay, so the two of you are into this clandestine sexual relationship. Maybe you start out playing footsie under the desk. Then you steal a few quick kisses by the coffee machine. Finally, you wind up in a hotel room. Then you set her up in her own apartment, buy her lots of fancy clothes, expensive jewelry, etc. Of course, you make it look like your son is really the one having the romance to deflect any scandal."

"I didn't pay for the apartment and all her clothes—" Lansdale started to say.

"But it was really you in the sack with her, not Jonathan."

There was a pained expression on Lansdale's face. I suddenly realized that he seemed to be taking her death very hard. Was that all an act? Was there maybe some remorse on his part now for killing her? Or was there something else going on here that I didn't know about?

I looked down at my notebook. I'd made some notes to myself about the events that occurred just prior to Cheryl Lee's murder.

The fight with Lansdale at the print shop. The scene at the Park Grille Restaurant later with his son.

"What happened on the day she died?" I asked.

Lansdale sighed. "It was like a bad dream. That day she came into my office and told me about her father. The videos she'd made. Her plan to destroy me with them. I was stunned. I couldn't believe it."

Neither could I. Lansdale had just given me the perfect motive for murder. He'd murdered her to shut her up and save his career and his marriage. Was this a confession?

"Why did she tell you all this?"

"Because she said she was wrong."

"Wrong about what?"

"Me. She said she'd hated me for a long time. Ever since she'd found out what happened to her father. The hate had consumed her. It was all that she lived for. It gave her a goal for the first time in her life. But then she met me, got to know me – and decided that I wasn't the devil after all. She said she actually felt sorry for me. And that what happened in Iraq was a long time ago. She wanted to get on with her life now."

He looked out at the lake again.

"She said that life didn't include me. She said she was quitting her job. She said our relationship was over. She told me to go home to my wife. Then she left."

"What did you do?"

"I was supposed to catch a plane to Washington. But I didn't go. Instead, I followed her. Like a dog, I followed her. I don't know why, I guess I just wanted to be near her… to see what she was doing. Finally, at the print shop, I tried to talk to her again. That's when we had the big argument that you saw."

"What happened?"

"She told me something else," he said. "Something she didn't say back in my office."

I realized what that was. "She told you she was pregnant," I said.

Lansdale nodded.

"You couldn't allow that, could you, Senator?" I said softly. "So you told her to meet you in the park that night. Then, when she showed up, you hit her with a rock, and then—"

"You still don't understand, Ms. Tucker."

"What part don't I understand?"

"All my life," he said, "I've always been afraid. When I was in Iraq, I was afraid all the time. You don't know what it was like over there. Every minute, every second I was waiting for the bullet that was going to kill or maim me. And then, when the nightmare finally came true, I panicked. I… let my men down. But I've always been a survivor. And I survived that, even used it to build a political career. I'm not proud of that. But I'm not a killer. You have to believe me about that.'

"Did you have anything to do with Scott Barrett's death in Iraq?"

"That was an accident."

I said it sounded like a pretty big coincidence that the man who could have ruined his career conveniently died from a mortar shell fired by a friend of his.

"No, no!" He was almost shouting now. "I didn't mean to hurt anybody. I didn't want Scott Barrett to be killed there. It was just the way things worked out. I tried to tell her that on that last day."

He sounded sincere, but I wasn't sure I believed anything the man said.

"I never killed anyone," he repeated again. "But I did bad things, I don't deny that. Whenever there was a crisis, I took the easy way out. I did it in Iraq. I did it with Alice Woodward. I did it every time – I've done it all my life."

"And killing Cheryl Lee was the easy way out, wasn't it?"

Lansdale shook his head no. "I loved her," he said again.

"Enough to give up your marriage and maybe your seat in the Senate too?"

"Yes."

"You told her that?"

"I did. I didn't do the right thing with Alice Woodward, but I was going to make up for that now. For the first time in my life, I wanted to do the right thing. Especially after I found out she was pregnant. I told her we'd announce it to the world. I said I'd marry her. I said we could live happily ever after. Just like I once wanted to do with Alice. I really thought it was going to work out between me and Meg."

Senator Lansdale began to cry then. "I'm such a fool," he said.

"Why?"

"She told me the truth."

"Which was?"

"It wasn't my baby."

I stared at him. "You mean… someone else was the father?"

"Yes. She said she was going to tell him that night. She said she was in love with him. She said she was sorry to hurt me, but she was going to be happy for the first time in her life. She said this was the kind of man she wanted to be the father of her baby. Not a man like me. I couldn't believe she was doing this to me. That's when I began yelling and… well, you saw the rest of it on the store video, I guess."

"Did she tell you who the father was?"

"No."

"No clues of any kind?"

He shook his head. "She said I was weak, I wasn't half the man her father had been. She said she wanted somebody like him – and she'd finally found him. She said the man she loved was strong and powerful. 'He's a man of real authority,' she said. I remember that phrase."

"Authority?" I asked.

"That's what she said."

"You mean like a policeman?"

"I don't know."

"And she didn't tell you anything else about the identity of this man – the father of her unborn baby – who she was in love with?"

"Just that it wasn't me," Lansdale said sadly.

CHAPTER 57

On the subway ride back downtown to the *Tribune* office, I realized I had made a big mistake.

The same kind of mistake that I'd accused others – most notably the police – of making in the past.

The cops had targeted Joseph Enrico as Cheryl Lee Barrett's killer at the beginning of the investigation. They then accumulated whatever evidence they could find to support that theory. Any evidence that didn't point to Enrico was discarded or ignored. Usually, I did the opposite: I liked to start a case from the very beginning, break it down piece by piece and then follow all the information I had gathered to a logical conclusion. Or so I told people anyway.

But that wasn't what I had done this time.

Instead, I had done the same things wrong that the police did – even though I came to a different conclusion.

I became convinced very early on that Frank Lansdale was behind the murder of Margaret Kincaid/Cheryl Lee Barrett. I then went out and found a lot of evidence, all of it supporting my theory that Lansdale was the killer. I ignored any other evidence. It was like I was wearing blinders. I refused to consider the possibility that someone else might have done it.

I believed Lansdale's story now though. I'd seen the look of anguish on his face when he talked about the dead woman. I had gone into the conversation convinced that I hated the man. Now instead of hating him, I felt sorry for him. Just like Cheryl Lee Barrett apparently did at the end.

Yes, he'd been a coward, not a hero, in Iraq. He'd done some not so wonderful things as a senator. He'd cheated on his wife a long time ago, promised her it would never happen again and then did it anyway. None of that was good. But it wasn't murder. If he didn't kill Cheryl Lee Barrett, then who did? Maybe someone else who had something to hide. The real father of her baby.

A man of authority. That's what Cheryl Lee had called him.

Was he a cop?

I thought about some of the cops I knew.

There was Lt. Aguirre, an ambitious type who wanted to move up in the department. He was married with a couple of kids, but he had a big ego and I'd seen him flirt with women. Maybe he met Cheryl Lee when she worked for the senator. Their paths could have crossed. Then, if Aguirre really was the father and the one who killed her to keep her quiet, he'd be in the perfect position as head of the investigation to point the finger of guilt at someone else. A loser like Joseph Enrico, for instance.

Or what about my old friend, Captain Steve Fredericks – another man on his way up in the department with a loving wife and family at home? I now believed he'd hidden secrets about the attack on me. What if there were other secrets he was hiding too? What if…

I shook my head. None of this was getting me anywhere. I had no hard facts to tie Aguirre or Fredericks or anyone else to Cheryl Lee's murder. Besides, I was still convinced that somehow Cheryl Lee's death was linked to my attack and possibly the deaths of those other women too. But what was the connection? I thought about this for a long time. I realized I didn't have the slightest idea.

I spent the rest of the day at my desk going over everything. There'd be no shortcuts for me this time. No preconceived ideas. I was determined to start from square one and see where the facts took me. It wasn't an easy job, but I plodded determinedly through story files, notes I'd kept and everything else connected to the case. A couple of times I was almost ready to give up. But then I remembered the way my persistence had helped me crack big stories in the past. I might not be the best reporter in the world, but I damn well could be the most dogged.

In the end, when I finally figured it out, it seemed so easy. I wondered why I hadn't seen it before. Maybe because I didn't want to. I wanted the trail from the murder to lead right to Frank Lansdale. But that wasn't the only place it went. It led right to someone else too.

The clincher was the phone call.

The phone call – two phone calls actually – that Cheryl Lee Barrett/Margaret Kincaid had made on her cell phone the night of her murder had always bothered me. She'd called someone on her way out of the restaurant, but also made a call to someone on her way in, according to the parking attendant. And she'd gotten very emotional and upset during that first call. Even threw the phone to the ground in anger at one point, the attendant said, before picking it up and going into the restaurant. So who was she talking to on that call who upset her so badly?

And who was on the other end of that final call on the way out just before she was murdered?

Her cell phone had never been found – it just disappeared after the murder – so no one had obtained that information. But nothing really disappears in today's world of technology. It's all out there in the Cloud or whatever. All I had to do was figure out some way to access it now.

I remembered how Bobby Delafuente, the Santa Barbara cop, had tracked some of her calls before she left Santa Barbara. Including the ones to Senator Lansdale's office and to Fred Sutter in Omaha. I called Delafuente now.

"Those phone numbers you gave me that Cheryl Lee Barrett called, were they from a landline or a cell phone?" I asked him.

"Both. She had a phone in the apartment she used and a cell phone too. The landline from the apartment was the one she used to call the senator's office and that guy in Omaha I gave you. I think she mostly used the cell phone for her... uh, business. Talking to customers and setting up meetings at hotels or whatever, that sort of thing. Why?"

I told him how I was trying to find out what numbers she might have called on a cell phone right before she was murdered.

"You think she was still using the same cell phone?"

"You tell me. Could you check her phone records again? When did you pull them from the cell phone company?"

"We checked all the phone records when she disappeared right after the Vincent Gallo murder. I told you all that."

"Anything more turn up on her phone since then?"

There was a long silence on the line.

"Detective?"

"No, nothing since then," he said finally.

"No, there were no calls – or no, you never checked again?"

"Jeez, Tucker, what do you want me to say? It was a hooker murdering her pimp. We've got lots of other cases – bigger cases – to chase after here. We made some checks, we didn't find out anything and we moved on."

I understood. What Delafuente and the Santa Barbara department had done was what police do everywhere. They have to prioritize their work. Hell, everyone does that when dealing with crime – cops, prosecutors and even the media like myself. It's sort of like triage in an emergency room. We pick the cases we think we can do the most about, and don't worry too much about all the rest. That didn't make it right, of course. But that's just the way it was.

"Would you go back and check the records again to see if she was still using that cell phone in New York?" I asked.

"She probably got a new cell phone. Maybe used one from the Lansdale office, she was working for him."

"Maybe. But maybe she still kept the old one for more delicate calls – like you said she used it for in Santa Barbara on hooker stuff."

"Why not ask the police there to check?"

"Because they don't care."

"And I should because…?"

"Look, the New York police still think she was a random murder. So they don't care about her missing cell phone and any calls she made beforehand. I don't believe it was random. I think she was murdered by someone she knew. Someone she knew very well. That's why I need to find out who she might have talked to on her cell phone that night. Will you help me?"

He hung up, then called back later with the information.

"Damn, it turns out she did keep this phone active," Delafuente said. "Kept making payments on the bills even after she got to New York. Who would have figured someone on the run for murder would have done that?"

So you could have found her if you'd just kept looking, I thought to myself. But I didn't say that to Delafuente. I needed to keep him on my side.

He went through the recent cell phone records for Cheryl Lee Barret before she died. There were numerous calls she'd made from the phone, but it was the last two calls she'd made that night – going into and then leaving the Park Grille – that I was the most interested in. DelaFuente gave me that information. I thanked him profusely.

"You're not going to make a big deal out of the way we dropped the ball on this, are you?" he asked.

"No reason to."

"Because—"

"It'll just be our little secret."

He breathed a sigh of relief over the line that was audible even from three thousand miles away.

"Thanks, Tucker. And hey, if you're ever out in Santa Barbara again—"

"Yes?"

"Please, don't come see me."

Then he laughed and hung up the phone.

The information I'd gotten from Delafuente was just the numbers she called, of course. No identification of who they belonged to. So I got to work on that. I started by just googling both numbers. The second call – the one she made on her way out of the Park Grille – turned out to be the easiest. It showed up as the number for The Stanton Hotel. That was where Joseph Enrico was staying and had later been shot by police. That made sense. He was her partner, I assumed now. She probably told him where she was going and who she planned to meet. There was no direct evidence of this, but I felt it was a pretty strong hypothesis.

It was the other call – the first one on her way into the restaurant, the one where she seemed so upset – that I was the most interested in. And that one was tougher to track down. There was no hit for that number online. I couldn't find it in any phone listings that I checked. When I called the phone company, I was told that it was an unlisted number and they couldn't tell me any more about who the customer was.

So I finally did what any smart investigative reporter would do when they were at a dead end like this. I picked up the phone and dialed the number. I wasn't sure what I was going to say to whoever answered, but it didn't matter. There was no one there. Just an answering message that played after four rings. But the answering machine message was enough to tell me who the phone belonged to.

I wrote down the name of that person in my notebook.

I underlined the name.

Then I stared at it for a long time, trying to figure out what my next move should be.

I needed some help. I needed some advice.

I needed a friend.

So I went some place where I'd always found a friend before.

CHAPTER 58

As I approached my destination, I thought about how this building where I was going had always filled me with awe. It stood majestically on the southern tip of Manhattan, the center of political power for the most exciting city in the world. City Hall. I looked up at it now from the sidewalk in front.

Then I went inside to see Jack Hanrahan.

My friend.

Libby St. John was surprised to see me.

"Jessie, I don't remember you having an appointment with the mayor today. Did you make the appointment with somebody else besides me? You know that all appointments to see the mayor have to come through me."

"I don't have an appointment, Libby."

"I'm sorry, but the mayor's very busy right now. Maybe if you came back later, I could try—"

"I need to see him now," I said.

"Jessie, he's got a very full schedule today. There's a budget meeting with the City Council, a groundbreaking ceremony for a new subway station, some foreign dignitaries visiting from the UN—"

"Tell him that what I have to say is more important to him. Tell him it's a matter of life and death. Tell him that, Libby."

She looked confused. "What's this all about anyway?"

"Cheryl Lee Barrett."

"What does she have to do with Mayor Hanrahan?"

"I think she was pregnant with his baby when she died."

*

"That's absurd," Jack Hanrahan said.

"Actually, it makes a lot of sense."

We were sitting in the mayor's private office, surrounded by pictures of him meeting with many dignitaries and celebrities over the years. The solutions to a lot of city problems – budget deficits, transit strikes, long hot summers of racial strife – had all been hammered out here in the past. But this was different. This was about a young woman and an unborn baby and their murder.

"How much do you know about DNA testing?" I asked Hanrahan. "I did a series on it for the *Tribune* a couple of months ago. If that really is your baby, they can prove it with a DNA test. Cheryl Lee told Lansdale she was having someone else's baby. She said she was in love with the father. She said he was someone powerful and self-confident – a man of authority. I thought at first she was talking about a cop or some sort of law enforcement agent. But she was talking about you, wasn't she?"

Libby St. John was in the room too. Hanrahan looked over at her now. Like a drowning man, hoping she would toss him a life preserver. She'd always bailed him out of jams before – that's what she'd told me – but she couldn't help him this time.

"Do you think he'll pass the DNA test, Libby?" I asked.

Libby St. John just shook her head and stared down at the floor.

"The mistake I made," I told the two of them, "was focusing all my attention from the start on Senator Lansdale. She worked for him and she was having an affair with him. I knew that. So everything else I found out along the way, I just tried to fit it into my own assumptions. I thought all the evidence pointed to Frank Lansdale. But it points to you too. Even more than Lansdale."

I knew I was right. If I wasn't, Hanrahan would have thrown me out of the office by now. Instead, he just looked over again at Libby St. John. She cleared her throat nervously.

"She was working for us," Libby said.

"She worked for both you and Frank Lansdale?"

"We wanted information about Lansdale, and she needed money. So we hired her to work undercover for us there. Lansdale's been standing in the way of Mayor Hanrahan's political future. We needed some leverage. We wanted to see if we could dig up some dirt on him."

"Or manufacture some dirt, maybe?"

"Maybe."

"The mayor's term of office here is up at the end of the year," Libby said. "He can't run for mayor again. A Senate seat would be the ideal spot for him, a high-visibility post that could even serve as the launching pad for getting him on the national ticket someday. But he couldn't take on Lansdale – for reasons I don't want to go into right now – and the next Senate race won't be for another four years. Unless Lansdale dropped out. Then the field would be wide open. The Barrett woman – I only knew her as Margaret Kincaid too – told us when we hired her that she was already working to bring Lansdale down – even before we approached her. She had this whole plan about seducing him and recording the whole thing on video so he could never deny it. Well, it seemed too good to be true. I loved it."

"You paid for her apartment, her clothes – all the rest?"

"Yes," Libby said.

"Then she turns up dead in Central Park," I said, "and you buy this whole story about it being a random mugging by an ex-con, huh?"

"I had no idea one thing might be related to the other – until you started asking questions," Hanrahan said. "I'm still not sure. It could have been just a mugging that's not connected to any of the rest of it."

"C'mon, Mayor," I said, "even you don't believe that." I shook my head disgustedly. "I was looking for connections to Lansdale," I continued. "Yes, the senator had an affair with Cheryl Lee Barrett, but so did you. And you had an even better motive for killing her than Lansdale did. She could have told the world she was carrying your baby. When did she tell you? When she called you on the night that she died?"

"She never told me. I had no idea she was pregnant."

"Then what did you two talk about on that last phone call the night she died?"

"What phone call?"

I told him how I'd managed to obtain the cell phone records to find out the number Cheryl Lee Barrett had called from the Park Grille that last night.

"There were two calls," I said. "The second one, the one she made on the way out of the restaurant, was to The Stanton Hotel. That's the same hotel where Joseph Enrico had a room. I think she called Enrico to tell him where she was going and who she was going to meet. Maybe he went there too. Maybe that's why his fingerprints were found at the crime scene. Maybe he even took her stuff back to the hotel room with him, although I still feel it's more likely the police planted it there. But he didn't kill her, I'm pretty sure of that. I think she was already dead when he got there.

"It's the first call she made – the one that got her so upset she threw the phone down on her way into the restaurant – that's the really interesting one here. Who was she talking to that time? Well, it was a number in Westchester County, the number of the weekend house you own there.

"That call was made at 6:39 p.m. After that, she went into the restaurant, had dinner with Lansdale's son for the next forty-five minutes or so, left suddenly and walked into the woods – where she waited long enough that she had time to smoke three cigarettes. That leaves plenty of time for you to get back into the city from Westchester and meet her there, Mayor. Is that what happened?"

"No," he said quietly. "I never talked to her at all that night. I wasn't in Westchester County."

"She called your number."

"That doesn't mean I was there."

"Well, according to the cell phone records, the call lasted nine minutes and forty-seven seconds. She talked to somebody at that number."

"It wasn't the mayor," Libby St. John said. "There was a big budget vote coming up in the City Council the next day, and he had a meeting right here with the council leaders. It lasted from seven o'clock until nearly midnight. At least half a dozen councilmen can verify this. There's also an official sign-in log by the security guard downstairs that anyone can check. He never got her phone call."

"The phone records don't lie," I said. "She talked to someone at your Westchester County number for nine minutes and forty-seven seconds. If that wasn't you, then who was it?"

Hanrahan looked over at Libby St. John. She nodded. Then he turned back to me.

"My wife," he said. "It must have been Christine. She was there that night."

CHAPTER 59

"You asked me the last time we talked why Lansdale and I don't get along," Mayor Hanrahan said. "I told you it was just politics. I said it had to do with Lansdale blocking some bills I wanted the Senate to pass. I said that's all there was to it. But I was lying."

There were just the two of us in his office now. The mayor had told Libby that he wanted to speak to me in private, and she seemed happy to have an excuse to leave. After she was gone, Hanrahan asked if he could talk to me as a friend – not a reporter. I said yes. I wasn't sure how long I could keep that promise. This man – who I once trusted – could well be a killer. But I felt I owed him at least that much.

"When I met my wife," he said now, "she was Christine Cochrane, a TV reporter on Channel 10. I didn't know anything about her past for a long time. I didn't think I needed to. She said she was from some little town in Nebraska and she had no family – she was an only child and her parents were dead. Why would I question any of it? But then I found out that none of that was true. It turned out her real name was Susan Gallagher – Christine Cochrane was a name she had used when she first started as a TV reporter because she said it sounded better. She'd never told me that. But that wasn't the only surprise."

There was a picture of him and Christine on his desk. He looked at it now and sighed. The picture was taken at Yankee Stadium. They were both wearing New York Yankees baseball caps. I had been in his office lots of times, but I'd never paid any attention to that before.

"When Susan Gallagher was seven years old," Hanrahan said, "her five-year-old sister died. Drowned when she fell into their backyard swimming pool. Everyone at first thought it was just a tragic accident. But Susan told a counselor that had been brought in to help the family deal with their grief that she was glad her sister was dead. 'Now Mommy and Daddy will only love me,' she said. The counselor concluded that she had pushed her little sister into the pool in a fit of jealousy."

"My God!" I said. "What did they do to her?"

"Not much." He shrugged. "What can you do to a seven-year-old girl who kills someone? You can't put her in jail or give her the electric chair. She underwent intensive therapy for two years at a juvenile facility, then she was returned home to her parents. The doctors said she was cured. She eventually moved to New York, where she became Christine Cochrane the TV reporter. That's the woman that I married."

"How did you find out about all this?"

"I didn't. Lansdale did."

"He uncovered the story in her past and threatened to go public with it?"

"Yes. He sent me a pretty clear-cut message – either I dropped any plans to run against him for the Senate seat or he'd leak the details of my wife's past to the media. I could just see the headlines: "MAYOR'S WIFE IS CHILD MURDERER!" I loved my wife. This happened a long time ago when she was just a little girl. But I knew it would cause a big scandal if it came out. I didn't want to put her through all that. Or, quite frankly, go through it myself either."

"So that's why you never ran against him for the Senate?"

"The funny thing was I had never wanted to try for his Senate seat anyway. I was tired of politics after twelve years here at City Hall. Christine and I had made all these big plans to travel and see the world when I left office. But what he did made me so angry I decided to run against him just to beat him. I wanted to destroy him politically. Except I couldn't because he had the Christine thing hanging over us.

"Then I ran into this woman who called herself Margaret Kincaid at an event one night. She knew from working in Lansdale's office that I was a big political rival of his, and I think she sought me out for that reason. She said she wanted to bring Lansdale down just like I did – that's why she'd gone to work for him – and asked if I'd help her to do that. She had all this hostility against him because of something he'd done to her father, but I didn't really pay much attention to that. I just saw it as an opportunity to get back at that sonuvabitch Lansdale. Libby helped set Meg up in an apartment and bought her clothes and stuff so she could do her thing. We knew it was dirty politics, but I didn't care. I thought if we could catch him on video in this sex scandal the Kincaid woman was plotting, Lansdale and I would be at a standoff. He wouldn't reveal his secret about me, if I didn't reveal mine about him. That's how I figured it was going to be payback time. After that, everything would be even between us.

"What I didn't count on was that I couldn't resist temptation with Meg myself. God, I couldn't keep my hands off her. She was so beautiful. I think at first she got off on seducing both the senator and me. But then… well, she got serious about me and her. She really thought I was going to marry her after I left office and run off with her to California and we'd live happily ever after. I asked her what I was supposed to tell my wife. She said she'd talk to Christine. I didn't think she was serious, but then you just told me that she called my Westchester house the night she died. My wife was there. If she told Christine and then a few hours later she wound up dead in the park…"

His voice trailed off. The conclusion was obvious to both of us. He'd slept with Cheryl Lee, made her pregnant. His wife had found out. Then she did the same thing she did when she was a little girl and she got jealous – she eliminated the competition.

"What did your wife say when you asked about her past?"

"She denied it. She claimed she had no idea what I was talking about. I had my people go back and verify that it was true, then I confronted her again. She got terribly upset and we had a big argument. I'm not sure she was lying to me, at least not intentionally lying. I think maybe she just pushed all those memories so far deep into her subconscious – the Susan Gallagher memories – that she really didn't remember what she did as a little girl. I never brought it up again. I was afraid that might push her over the edge emotionally. But it obviously drove a real wedge into our marriage. You might have picked up on some of that the other night at dinner. Outwardly, we continued to act like the happy married couple – the mayor and the first lady. But we… well, we haven't been intimate since all of this happened."

I took a sheet of paper out of my purse and shoved it across the desk to Hanrahan.

"Do you recognize any of these women?" I asked.

It was the list of women who had died in violent attacks just like those against Cheryl Lee Barrett and me.

"Why?" he asked as he took the list, then began to read the names. He didn't answer the question.

"All of the women on that list are dead," I said. "Murdered during a violent attack – seemingly sexually motivated – over a period of twelve years. Just like Cheryl Lee Barrett."

"Oh, my God!" he yelled out now. "Do you really think that Christine—"

"Did you sleep with these women?"

He had a look of anguish on his face as he looked at the names of the women on my list. Like a man in the middle of a nightmare that just keeps getting worse, no matter had hard he tries to wake up from it.

"Some of them," he said. "I really don't remember for sure. There… um… there have been a lot of women."

I sighed. I felt sick with disappointment at what I was hearing, but I tried my best to stay composed. This was about more than just my friendship with the mayor. "Did you ever tell Christine about your affairs or your interest in any of these women?"

That's when he fell apart completely. He began to cry. Quietly at first, but then soon he was sobbing uncontrollably as he continued to stare at the names of the dead women. I sat there, stunned. Mayor Hanrahan had always seemed so strong, so self-confident, so much in control of every situation – no matter how serious the crisis was. But this was different. He'd suddenly realized that his wife was very likely a multiple murderer, and that it was his secret womanizing that had likely motivated her to carry out these killings. It was all too much for any person to handle, even someone as tough as Mayor Hanrahan.

When he finally pulled himself together a bit, he tried to tell me the story about him and his wife and the other women as best as he could.

"No, I never told her anything, but I think she might have known I wasn't always faithful. Christine asked me about other women sometimes, and I lied to her. I said it was just her imagination. I had needs, you know… and, as I said, Christine and I weren't… but I was afraid to tell her the truth. I didn't want to hurt her. Anyway, I never really saw most of the women again. It was mostly one-night stands. With waitresses I met, or people like that. I never would have known about their deaths or made any connection. I mean they were spread out over a period of years and besides there were many others…"

There was a part of this that still didn't make sense though.

"What about me?" I asked Hanrahan.

"You?"

"I'm on that list too. I believe that the attack on me was part of this same pattern. That what happened to all these women was supposed to happen to me too. But why? I didn't sleep with you. Why would your wife want to hurt me?"

Hanrahan sighed. "Do you remember the first time we met? At that cocktail party at the St. Regis? I was still running for my first term as mayor then. I needed to win support from the business community, which is why you and some of the partners from your advertising firm were there. Christine was there too. She was still on TV then, and I hoped some of her star power would help me win them over.

"Anyway, I think you and I must have talked for at least an hour. We talked about the advertising business, about politics, about music, about movies – about everything. Libby finally had to drag me away from you – she said I needed to mingle with some of the big money people, which was supposed to be the reason I was there. Do you remember that night, Jessie?"

"Yes, I thought you were charming."

"I was attracted to you," he said. "Did you know that? I wanted to sleep with you."

I just stared at him.

"I'd only been married for a year or two then. I'd never cheated on my wife. But that night with you – you were so vibrant, so exciting, so full of life. I wanted you. Christine and I had a big argument afterward. She said I'd abandoned her – left her standing alone at the party – while I flirted with you like some lovesick teenager. I told her she was crazy. But I did want to see you again. I was going to call you, but then the attack in Central Park happened. I never made any connection between the two incidents until today."

He looked ashamed as he told me all this. Like a man who knew his life would never be the same again. My head was spinning too. There was so many things happening at once. Everything I once believed – my own entire life – was being turned upside down again.

"What are you going to do now?" I asked Hanrahan.

"The only thing I can do."

"Have your own wife arrested on suspicion of murder?"

"Yes."

"Do you really think she killed all those women – and nearly killed me too – just because she was jealous?"

Mayor Hanrahan looked at the picture again of him and Christine on his desk. She looked very happy – a hot dog in one hand and a New York Yankees baseball cap on her head.

"On the night after Margaret Kincaid was murdered," Hanrahan said quietly, "Christine and I watched the story on the eleven o'clock news. I was in a state of shock. I couldn't believe it. When the newscast was over, Christine turned to me and said: 'Well, that's at least one of your little bimbos that I won't have to worry about anymore.'"

CHAPTER 60

Christine Hanrahan was missing.

She wasn't at Gracie Mansion when the mayor and a contingent of police went to look for her. Nobody there knew where she was. Neither did her personal trainer, her beautician or any of her friends.

When she hadn't returned home by that evening, I realized there was only one possible answer.

She somehow had found out that the police were after her and now she was on the run.

I broke the story the next day in a front page exclusive for the *Tribune*:

MAYOR'S WIFE SOUGHT IN MULTIPLE MURDER SPREE

CHRISTINE HANRAHAN'S SECRET LIFE IS BARED
By Jessie Tucker
Tribune Crime Reporter

Police last night issued an all-points bulletin for the arrest of Mayor Hanrahan's wife Christine Hanrahan on suspicion of murder charges.

This astounding news came after a series of rapid-fire new developments in the Cheryl Lee Barrett murder case, for which Mrs. Hanrahan is now a suspect.

She is also being investigated for the murders of several other women – and also to a near-fatal attack on this reporter in Central Park twelve years ago.

"If these allegations are true, then a shocking miscarriage of justice has occurred," said a spokesman for the Police Department. "People have been sent to jail or killed by police for crimes they did not commit. A full investigation of all these cases is now being conducted by this department and the District Attorney's office to determine what the appropriate course of action should be."

Sources close to Mayor Hanrahan said he now believed the killings were motivated by Mrs. Hanrahan's jealousy of the female victims.

These sources said that the mayor had revealed that he'd carried on a series of extramarital affairs with several of the victims…

It all seemed to make sense now. Christine Hanrahan was – and always had been – a jealous woman. When she was seven years old, she'd killed her own sister so she could get more attention from her parents. She attacked me in the park because she was jealous Jack Hanrahan seemed interested in me. And she'd killed other women too over the years, including Cheryl Lee Barrett. She was a sick woman, and the fact that this sickness went undiagnosed resulted in the death of at least these women. And that was all we knew about. Jack Hanrahan had an eye for the ladies, that was evident now. There's no telling how many other potential rivals his wife might have targeted.

Meanwhile, Fredericks was currently under investigation for his conduct in my case years earlier, and he'd been suspended from duty without pay until that investigation was completed. I felt badly about that. I think Steve Fredericks truly believed the suspect he arrested, Darryl Jackson, was guilty of the crime against me. I think he thought he was doing the right thing. He simply bent the rules too much in an effort to make sure that justice was done.

As for the other questions I had about the deaths of Darryl Jackson, Dr. Janet Spitz and the police shooting of Joseph Enrico, there was no specific evidence uncovered linking them to a cover-up of Christine Hanrahan's murders. "Sometimes things happen for no logical reason," I wrote in my article. "It's easy to read conspiracy into things that you have no answers for, which is what I did. But I simply don't know the answers at this point."

Ellen called me as soon as my story appeared.

"This has real mega deal possibilities," she said. "'Dogged reporter solves her own twelve-year-old crime' – and more murders too! I love it. I've already talked to some people in Hollywood. I think I can get you a book and TV movie deal in seven figures. That's seven digits, Jessie. Like in a million."

"The story's not over yet," I said.

"For all practical purposes, it is. All that has to happen is for Christine Hanrahan to get arrested or turn herself in. That's got to happen pretty soon. I mean the wife of the mayor of New York City can't just disappear off the face of the earth."

"No thanks," I told her.

"But—"

"The story's not over until it's over," I said.

It ended the next day.

A security guard in front of the Channel 10 News studio, where Christine Hanrahan once worked as a TV reporter, noticed a car double-parked in front of the building in the early hours of the morning. The guard came out to tell the driver to move along. That's when he saw her. Christine Hanrahan. She was slumped over the steering wheel, her face covered with blood. A gun was in her lap. There was one bullet missing. The bullet had gone through her head, killing her instantly.

There was a note taped to the dashboard. It said:

I'm so sorry. I'm so sorry about everything. I just wanted Jack to myself. That's why I kept killing the other women. But I know it's over now. The world will be a better place without me. I used to break big stories at Channel 10 when I was a TV reporter. Here I am again to end it all. My last big story.

CHAPTER 61

I was still trying to sort everything out a few nights later as I did sit-ups in front of the big screen in my living room.

I was doing my sit-ups at night right now because I'd been so busy at the *Tribune* that I didn't have time for my regular morning exercise ritual. And I knew I couldn't cheat on that. So here I was sweating away at 7:30 p.m. while a TV dinner – tuna casserole, a favorite of mine – cooked in my microwave.

I had a news channel on the TV, and many of the media outlets had already moved on from Christine Hanrahan to newer breaking stories.

But not me.

I kept thinking now as I approached my goal of two hundred sit-ups about all the fallout from the Cheryl Lee Barrett story – which turned out to be my story too.

Senator Lansdale was probably the biggest victim of the fallout from the case. Even though it turned out he had nothing to do with Cheryl Lee's murder, the issue of his war record and the cover-up of his romantic involvement with her – including the phony assassination attempt – made him an object of ridicule. Newspaper editorials called for his resignation. Comedians made jokes about him. The Senate launched an investigation into his actions. The *Tribune* ran lengthy excerpts from Scott Barrett's letters and also did another interview with Fred Sutter, who went on the record this time to tell the truth about Lansdale's war stories. It appeared inevitable that he'd have to drop out of the Senate race, and it looked like his political career was over.

Jack Hanrahan fared better. Lying about your war record turned out to be a lot worse than cheating on your wife. I felt a bit conflicted about him. I still liked Jack Hanrahan and was grateful to him for everything he'd done for me in the past – but I couldn't forgive him for his actions that led to the deaths of those women and the near-fatal attack on me by his wife. He was complicit in this too, even if what he did wasn't criminal. The voters didn't seem to mind the mayor's peccadilloes though, in fact his popularity ratings actually went up. There was certainly not much sympathy possible for his wife, who had killed all those people before she took her own life. So the sympathy went to the mayor. There was a lot of speculation that he might even run for Lansdale's Senate seat now. I hoped he didn't.

Darryl Jackson's mother was talking about filing a massive lawsuit against the city as a result of the new evidence that exonerated her son in the attack on me. But it didn't appear she had a chance to get any real money in the suit or a settlement. Tamara Willis's story was public now, and she was on record with the police that Jackson had raped her in the park that same night.

The official story was now that Cheryl Lee Barrett had called the Westchester number – apparently looking for Jack Hanrahan – but got his wife instead. For some reason – maybe bragging, maybe just a slip of the tongue – she told Christine Hanrahan she was pregnant with her husband's baby. They argued and Christine demanded to talk to her face to face. They set up the meeting in the park, where Christine killed her.

Even though it was me who broke the story, I still wasn't completely satisfied with this version of events. For example, why the park rather than a bar or restaurant? The police answer was that Christine probably suggested they meet in the park because she knew she wanted to kill her, and it would be easier to do it there in the dark. Cheryl Lee agreed because she had no idea she was in any danger. That all sort of made sense. Or did it? I was still left with the question of why Cheryl Lee was willing to meet a woman who was furious at her for stealing her husband alone in the woods at night.

I was also still left with the question of how Christine got from Westchester to Central Park. Her driver testified that he never took her anywhere that night. She didn't have her own car with her and the police couldn't find any cab drivers in the area who remembered making the trip.

And it didn't explain how Enrico's fingerprints had ended up at the crime scene either. It's possible he rushed to her aid, saw Cheryl Lee's body, touched the rock for some reason and then fled. He likely didn't want to wait around for the police or get involved in any way that would make him a suspect. That all sort of made sense too. I suppose. But it also seemed awfully convenient for anyone trying to cover up for the real killer.

And how did the police zero in on Enrico so quickly anyway? Who gave them the anonymous tip that Enrico was involved that sent Aguirre and Erskine to the hotel looking for him? What were Cheryl Lee's belongings doing in his room? The police said they didn't know the answer to those questions, and they probably never would. That didn't seem to bother them very much. But, of course, it bothered me.

There were also questions around the timing of Christine Hanrahan's death. The autopsy by the medical examiner's office said she had been dead for several hours when the security guard found her. The authorities explained this by saying that she could have shot herself early in the evening, then the body sat there in the car unnoticed until morning. The TV station was located in a warehouse neighborhood on the West Side, near the Hudson River, that was pretty deserted at night. So the official account was a possibility. But there was another possibility too – that the fatal gunshot wound to Christine happened somewhere else, and she was then brought to the TV station to be found there. That meant another person was involved. Maybe someone who helped her with the attack on me and the other killings too. In the end, this accomplice could have turned on Christine just as she was about to be arrested.

An interesting theory, but I had no proof either way.

There was one other thing though. Something that had been on my mind ever since I heard the news about Christine Hanrahan's suicide. Christine had shot herself in the head, they said. Put a gun in her mouth and blew away most of her face. She was a mess when they found her.

I remembered the last time I'd seen Christine Hanrahan, that night at Gracie Mansion. The way she'd talked about her beauty regime. Her workouts. How proud she had always been of the way she looked. That was the biggest problem I had with the whole suicide scenario.

I found it hard to believe Christine Hanrahan would have shot herself in the face.

She might have taken pills to kill herself.

Or slit her wrists.

Or even jumped off a bridge and drowned.

But shoot herself in the face?

That just didn't seem likely to me.

She was too vain.

Which meant that someone else might have done it.

CHAPTER 62

Maybe I was missing something. It was a slim chance – just a hunch – but maybe there was another player in the game who I still didn't know anything about.

I made a list of who it might be – everyone who had been involved in the case all the way back to the attack on me in Central Park.

Mayor Hanrahan
Frank Lansdale
Jonathan Lansdale
Steve Fredericks
Lt. Thomas Aguirre

The last name practically jumped off the page.

Aguirre had been the lead investigator in the Cheryl Lee Barrett case – the one who led the contingent of cops to Joseph Enrico's hotel room and shot him to death before he could tell anything he knew.

Going through the files on Aguirre, I found out something else interesting about him too. He'd once been part of the City Hall protection detail – serving as Christine Hanrahan's bodyguard before getting a sudden promotion in the ranks into the homicide division.

Aguirre had risen very fast in the department. Maybe too fast. Did he have a powerful ally on his side? Someone like the wife of the mayor? And if so, what did he provide for her in return?

Of course, this was still all speculation. But it made sense. Christine Hanrahan would have needed someone in authority to help her. And he had admitted he was responsible for the shooting of Enrico. Aguirre was ambitious, a man looking for a fast way to get ahead in the city hierarchy. Maybe they'd made a deal. But would Aguirre really stoop to murder to get what he wanted? Well, that all depended on how ambitious he was.

CHAPTER 63

I laid it all out for Erskine.

"I don't think Christine Hanrahan could have done all this on her own," I said. "The attack on me and the deaths of those other women, yes – especially if we assume they were crimes of passion, carried out during periods of uncontrolled jealousy. She was in good physical shape – she could have overpowered me and the other victims, I think. But she would have needed help on the cover-up. The closing of the cases so quickly, the apprehension or deaths of the suspects. That means a second person. A second person who got worried when the cops started closing in on Christine. So he killed her and tried to make it look like a suicide."

We were sitting in a coffee shop on Amsterdam Avenue, which I had suggested because it was far from the Central Park Precinct and there was little chance we'd run into Aguirre or any other cops there.

Erskine sipped his coffee and thought about everything I'd said.

"Do you know who the second person is?" he asked.

"Not for sure."

"But you think it's someone in authority."

"Yes."

"Someone like a cop?"

"That's right."

This was a crucial turning point. I wasn't sure which way it was going to go once we reached this part of the conversation. I thought Erskine might refuse to hear anymore and stalk angrily out of the coffee shop. But he didn't. He just sat there staring down at his coffee cup.

"Look," I said quietly to him, "Aguirre knew Christine Hanrahan – he used to be her favorite bodyguard. And he was the lead cop in the Joseph Enrico shooting. You were there that day. What happened?"

Erskine shrugged. "The suspect – this Enrico guy – pulled a gun. We shot him."

"We?"

"Okay, Tommy shot him."

"He says you were there. He says you saw it – that it was a clean shoot. Was it?"

Erskine looked out the window of the coffee shop onto Amsterdam Avenue. There was a police car sitting at a red light. I was afraid for a second that they were going to come into the coffee shop. That they had been following me. That Aguirre had somehow found out about my meeting with Erskine. But then the light changed to green, and the police car drove away. I breathed a sigh of relief. I had a feeling that Erskine did too.

"He told me to wait downstairs in the hotel lobby," Erskine said. "I thought it was strange at the time, a total violation of departmental police for confronting suspects. But you've gotta remember that we didn't really see this guy Enrico as a serious suspect at the time – all we were doing was checking out an anonymous tip. You get a million false leads in a case like this. He said he'd check him out quickly, and he'd be right back down. So I waited in the lobby. When I heard the gunshot, I ran upstairs. Enrico was dead, there was a gun in his hand and we found the dead woman's belongings in the room. It all seemed so open and shut."

"Why did you lie in the report and say you were in Enrico's room when the shooting took place?"

"A cop shoots somebody, he gets himself caught up in a nightmare of red tape and investigations by the goddamned Internal

Affairs people and citizens' groups and politicians looking to get their name in the headlines. It's always worse if a cop is alone when the shooting happens – then it's only his word. So I just said I was there too. It made things simple. Hell, he would have done the same thing for me."

"And you believed his version of what happened?"

"Sure I did. He's my partner."

I knew that was the biggest barrier that I had to get past here. The partner thing. That was a cardinal rule for any cop. You never ratted on your partner. Partners stood together, no matter what. But it didn't always happen that way. There have been courageous ones – like Serpico in the most famous New York City police corruption case – who had come forward to tell of crimes by fellow officers because they believed that no one was above the law. The problem was I didn't figure Phil Erskine to have that kind of courage. Erskine was no Serpico. He was more like the Norman Isaacs of the police force. Always kept his head down and tried to stay out of trouble.

"Why would Tommy do it?" Erskine asked. "What's in it for him?"

"Fame and fortune. Aguirre's an ambitious guy with a big ego. You know that as well as I do. His best friend in the world is in the mirror. Maybe he stumbled onto what Christine Hanrahan was doing accidentally while he worked as her bodyguard, maybe there was something more sinister than that. But he saw it as a big opportunity. He gets a very powerful ally – the wife of the mayor – on his side. She convinces her husband to give him promotions, awards, all that stuff. At the same time, Aguirre's probably making a lot of money off of Christine Hanrahan too – I'm thinking blackmail here. Did he ever seem like he had a lot of extra money?"

"Well, he wears expensive European suits, Gucci loafers, that sort of thing. He drives a Porsche. And I think he's got some beachfront property in Sag Harbor on Long Island."

"How much is a police lieutenant's pay?"

"… Not much."

"And you didn't think that was all just a little bit unusual?"

Erskine shrugged again. "I figured he was probably doing something a little bit shady, maybe shaking down some drug dealers or something. It happens. But I didn't think it was any of my business."

"Well, it is now," I said.

Erskine shook his head. I knew he was having a lot of trouble dealing with all of this.

"Do you really think he murdered Christine Hanrahan?"

"The cops were closing in on her. If she talked, she'd give him up. Besides, the mayor's term is almost over. She wasn't going to be able to help in the department much longer anyway. The leverage was running out."

"What if you're wrong?" he asked.

"What if I'm right?"

Erskine didn't answer.

"If I'm right," I said, "then Lieutenant Thomas Aguirre is a killer. He's killed before, more than once. And he'll probably kill again. Do you really want that on your conscience? This isn't shaking down some street dope pusher we're talking about here. It's the ultimate bad cop. You took an oath a long time ago to serve and protect the public. If you walk away from this now, then you're no better than Aguirre is. You're going to have blood on your hands for the rest of your life. The blood that's already been spilled, and the blood he's going to spill in the future. You gotta make a choice here, man."

Erskine should have walked away. Everything in his past indicated that's what he'd do. Even I figured that's what he'd do, but sometimes people really do surprise you.

First it was Norman Isaacs. Now Phil Erskine.

"Aguirre's weakness is his ego," Erskine told me. "He likes to brag about himself, especially when he's been drinking. He's told me some stuff before in bars that he shouldn't have done. He can't help himself. He always wants you to know how smart he is.

"So here's my idea. I take him to this cop bar where we both hang out. I confront him with the stuff we're talking about. I'm his partner. I figure he'll admit to at least some of it. He knows I've got no evidence, I can never prove he said any of it. I think he'd like that. Know that I know, but also knowing that I can't do anything about it. He's done this before with me. It's like a game to him.

"Only this time it's different. This time I'm wearing a wire. I get everything he says down on tape. That's what I'll do for you. I won't do anything else. I won't testify against him. I won't be quoted in your story. I won't go on record about anything we said or did here. He's my partner, I owe him that. You can wait outside the bar, if you want. When I'm finished, I'll come give you the tape. Then you can do whatever you want with it. That's my deal. Take it or leave it."

I didn't even have to think about that one.

I had nothing to lose.

"I'll take it," I told Erskine.

CHAPTER 64

The bar was called Finnegan's, and it was on Broadway just north of 72nd Street. I realized when I saw it that I'd been there a couple of times over the years with other cops. I sat in Erskine's car while he went inside that night.

It was the end of the evening shift, and a lot of cops were arriving at the same time. Aguirre showed up about half an hour later. I sat there in the car for another fifteen minutes or so, trying my best to be patient. But finally I decided I couldn't take it anymore.

I needed to be in there – to be part of the action.

I realized it was reckless – and possibly dangerous – on my part to do this.

But I simply couldn't stop myself.

Inside, I saw Aguirre and Erskine huddled together at a table in a quiet corner of the bar, away from everyone else. So far, so good. The rest of the place was big and very crowded. Looking around, I spotted a drug enforcement cop that I knew from a story I once covered. Danny or Donnie or something like that, I was pretty sure his name started with a D. I let him buy me a drink, then listened as he rambled on for a long time about lenient judges, crooked lawyers, drug dealers who drove fancy cars and school kids taking crack in the morning like it was Rice Krispies. I pretended to look interested, while I positioned myself at the bar so I could watch Aguirre and Erskine at their table.

I tried reading their lips and analyzing their body language, but gave up when I realized that I had no idea how to do either one.

The two men talked quietly at first. Just two partners on the force relaxing over drinks after a long day of crime fighting. But then, after about fifteen minutes, Aguirre seemed to become agitated. At least it looked that way.

But I was having a lot of trouble concentrating because the drug enforcement cop kept talking the whole time.

"The other day I arrested this kid for pushing in a schoolyard," he said. "Do you know how old he was?"

"No."

"Take a guess."

"Fifteen?" I said, giving the first answer that popped into my head.

"He was ten years old."

"That was going to be my next guess," I said.

"Ten years old, and he's dealing big-time drugs. I mean, where are his parents, and how can they let something like this happen? Where is the school system? Where are religious leaders? How does a kid like this wind up being my problem? Tell me the answer to that."

I was trying to concentrate on Aguirre and Erskine's conversation at the same time I was talking to this guy, so I didn't really answer him, but it didn't seem to bother him.

"You know it's really great that you're taking the time to listen," he said. "This kind of stuff doesn't get the kind of press coverage it deserves. Maybe you could do a whole piece on our unit – you know, hang out with us for a few days and write about everything we do."

"That's a terrific idea, Dave," I said.

"Don."

"I knew that."

Erskine stood up from the table and headed for the door.

"I gotta go," I told the drug enforcement cop.

"Why?"

"Big story."

"But we're not finished talking here yet—"

"I think we are."

I met Erskine outside at the car. He looked very agitated.

"Where the hell were you?" he asked.

"Inside."

"Are you crazy? What if Aguirre—"

"Don't worry, he didn't see me."

"You were supposed to wait in the car."

"I got bored. Goddamnit, Phil, what happened in there?"

"I got it," he said.

"You got him admitting it on tape?"

"Yeah, it's like I told you. He gets a few drinks in him and he likes to brag. Once he started talking, he couldn't help himself. He thinks he's safe. He thinks I can't do anything about it."

"He's in for a big surprise, huh?"

"Yeah, I guess so." Erskine seemed distracted, like something was bothering him. Maybe it was just the trauma of realizing his partner was capable of such heinous crimes. He didn't like Aguirre. He probably never had during all the years that they worked together. But the realization that Aguirre was capable of helping Christine Hanrahan carry out a series of murders was a lot for him to deal with. I understood that. I wished Erskine would snap out of it though because we had a lot of work to do.

"Let's listen to this tape," I said.

"Not here. He might see us. Let's go back to the precinct. Aguirre won't be going back tonight. We'll be safe.'

"Sounds like a plan to me," I told him.

We got into Erskine's car, and he started driving. I was thinking so much about the tape – eagerly looking forward to hearing exactly what Aguirre had said on it and thinking about what I would do with this evidence now that I had it – that I didn't pay attention at first to where we were going. It wasn't until a few minutes later that I realized we weren't heading in the direction of the precinct. Instead, Erskine was driving directly into Central Park.

"Hey, where are we going?" I asked.

"I've got something to show you."

"I thought we were going to go listen to the tape."

"This is more important than the tape."

Erskine pulled the car into a deserted area of the park. I didn't know exactly where we were, but I thought it was somewhere pretty close to where I'd been attacked.

"Do you want to tell me what we're doing here?" I asked.

He sighed now and looked over at me. "You know," he said, "it really was very clever of you to figure all this out. I mean the whole thing about how Enrico didn't kill the Barrett woman; the affair between her and Lansdale; the connection to your own case; tracking all the victims first back to Mayor Hanrahan and then his wife; figuring out his wife wasn't really a suicide; and deducing from that how someone else had been involved. Probably a cop. A cop like Aguirre. Aguirre was a damn good guess for the bad cop. In fact, the whole thing was brilliant on your part, Tucker. Fuckin' brilliant. You only got one thing wrong."

"What's that?" I asked.

But I already knew the answer before I even asked the question.

"You got the wrong cop," he said.

Erskine had his gun out now and was pointing it at me.

"It was never Aguirre," he said. "It was always me."

Suddenly there was a gunshot. But not from his gun. Instead, Phil Erskine's own head exploded in blood. He slumped over onto the steering wheel. I whirled around and screamed. There was someone in the backseat of the car.

Libby St. John.

She was pointing a gun at me now.

And wearing a New York Yankees baseball cap.

"You got the wrong woman too," Libby St. John said.

CHAPTER 65

Libby St. John had been there all the time, lurking around the edges of this case like a shark silently stalking its prey. The signs were there, and they pointed directly to her, but I had ignored them. I had focused instead on the easy answers – first Frank Lansdale, then Christine Hanrahan – and I'd missed the big picture.

"You killed those women, didn't you?" I said. "It was never Christine Hanrahan."

We were walking through the woods now, a few hundred yards from where Erskine's body lay dead in the car. Libby had the gun pointed at me the whole time. I wasn't sure exactly where we were going, but I knew that it didn't really matter anyway. Libby was going to kill me too. I was the last loose end left in the case.

"So you finally figured it out, huh?" Libby said sarcastically. "Gee, Jessie, you're such a great reporter."

"Why?"

"Because I'm in love with him."

"You love Jack Hanrahan."

"Yes. Does that surprise you? Do you not think he'd like someone like me? Am I not *pretty enough* for him, or something? Okay, I know I don't fit the mold of all those other women he chases after, but we have something deeper. Jack and I are meant to be together. He doesn't understand that yet, but he will one day soon. And then I'll finally be the only woman in his life."

We were at a clearing in the park now. Off in the distance, I could see the lights of the highway. Maybe somebody would come by soon and see the car. Maybe they'd find Erskine's body inside. Maybe the cops would come looking in the park for the killer. It was a long shot, but it was the only chance I had. I needed to buy time. Somehow I had to keep Libby St. John talking.

"And I was your first victim right here in this park?" I said.

"That's right."

"Why me? I didn't have any romance with Jack Hanrahan. I didn't even know him very well until later. Before that night in the park, I'd only met him the one time at a campaign fund raising party."

"I saw you that night," Libby said angrily. "I watched you from across the room. The way he was undressing you with his eyes. The way he flirted with you. The way he kept putting his hands on you. I knew him, and I knew he desired you. I wanted him to desire me like that. It made me crazy. You could get the thing I wanted most in this world but couldn't have – Jack Hanrahan's love. I couldn't think about anything else. I didn't sleep, I didn't eat, I could barely work. I began following you – hating you, envying you, wanting to see you somehow just disappear. That night I trailed you after work – first to the concert, then later into the park. You were so pretty, so sure of yourself, so perfect – little Miss Perfect, that's what you were. Well, I wanted to make sure you weren't so perfect anymore. I hit you when you went by. Then I hit you again. And again. I don't remember everything that happened after that. I didn't exactly plan for it to go as far as it did, but when it did, it felt good. Really good. I liked messing you up. And I got what I wanted. Jack – well, Jack never looked at you the same way again, did he?" She laughed. "You weren't this cute little desirable thing in his mind anymore. You were Jessie the cripple. The cripple that helped get him elected mayor. That was the icing on the cake. I never expected that. But you got us into Gracie Mansion – all those pictures and stories about Jack at your bedside is what did it, you know. God, I loved it. I thought everything was perfect. Until… until those other women began coming along. Jack just couldn't help himself. He was weak. But I was always strong for him. I got rid of all of them. Now there's just him and me. Someday he'll thank me for that."

I shuddered as I realized the enormity of what this woman was telling me.

"Susan Gallagher – the little girl who killed her family – that wasn't really Christine Hanrahan either, was it?" I said. "It was you. It's always been you from the very beginning."

She nodded. "I was the one who told the mayor about Susan Gallagher's violent background. But I just changed one little thing. I said it was Christine, not me. That's one of the advantages of being such a trusted aide. He believes everything I say to him. I was the one who told him never to bring it up again with Christine. I convinced him she was so unstable that we had no idea what she might do if he kept confronting her about her secret past. I got him to promise never to reveal it to anyone else either. For political reasons, I told him. We had to keep it a secret from everyone else at all costs. He did exactly what I told him to do. He always did what I told him to do. Except when it came to women."

"What about Senator Lansdale? Why did he think it was Christine?"

"He didn't."

"I don't understand."

"Lansdale never knew anything. About Christine or Susan or me. I just made that all up along with lying to Hanrahan that Christine was Susan Gallagher."

"Why?"

"I had tried desperately for months to convince the mayor to run against Lansdale for the upcoming Senate seat. But he said he didn't think he could beat Lansdale, that Lansdale was too powerful. He gave me all this crap about how he was going to take a few years off from politics, travel around the world with

Christine and just try to enjoy life for a while with the woman he loved. Christine. Damn, that made me furious! I had all these big plans for our future. The Senate seat. Then something even bigger after that, maybe even a run for the White House. Me and Jack Hanrahan, I knew we could pull it off together. But he just kept saying he was afraid of Lansdale and talked about sitting on a friggin' beach somewhere with Christine.

"I knew I had to take Lansdale out of the political picture somehow. So I made it seem like Lansdale was trying to make sure the mayor never ran by threatening him with this Susan Gallagher information. This way the mayor was furious enough at him that he would go along with anything I said to smear Lansdale back. And then I found out about the sex scandal plot with Margaret Kincaid trying to set him up. I knew, if I could make that work for us too, I could get Lansdale out of the race for good. I knew he would do anything to avoid being exposed in another sexual affair scandal.

"The cherry on top was that all this drove a wedge into the mayor's marriage too. I know he never felt the same way about Christine again after I fed him the Susan Gallagher stuff. He never trusted her again. And their marriage was drifting apart badly before she died. That was all because of me. So, by lying about Susan Gallagher, I accomplished two things – I got him to go after Lansdale with the blackmail scheme and I started to push Christine out of the picture." She laughed. A slightly hysterical laugh. "Two birds with one stone, as the saying goes."

There was something I still didn't understand.

"Why didn't you just kill Christine?" I asked Libby. "Wouldn't that have been easier?"

"I thought about that. Thought about it many times. It would have been easy for me to arrange an 'accident' that would completely eliminate her from the picture. But, as time went on, I began to enjoy watching the dissolution of their marriage. Because

DANA PERRY

the further apart they drifted, the more Jack depended on me. I also liked the fact that Christine knew about his cheating. If I had to suffer through that, I wanted her to feel the same pain from his betrayal too. Oh, I knew Christine had to die at some point. I just needed to find the right time. And I have, she's gone for good. It's all going to work out the way I want it to be now. Don't you see, Jessie? That all makes perfect sense, doesn't it?"

No, it didn't. It didn't make any kind of sense at all. But I was looking for sanity from a woman who clearly had lost hers a long time ago.

My God, I thought to myself. I thought I knew Libby once, but I didn't know her at all. She was a psychotic cold-blooded killer. And I was her next victim. I kept walking with her deeper into the woods because I didn't know what else to do as long as she had that gun pointed at me.

"What about Darryl Jackson?" I asked. "How did you pin my attack on him?"

"That was just dumb luck." She laughed. "Fredericks picks him up and figures he's the one who did it. He's a very ambitious cop. He cuts a few corners, plays mind games to get him to confess and then he plays some more mind games with you to identify him in court. End of story. He's happy, you're happy, I'm happy – everybody's happy. Except the creep in jail, and he would have wound up there sooner or later anyway. That gave me the idea later for the other ones. I needed a cop to help set up some losers for the crime. Erskine was the man. I funneled a lot of money out of City Hall projects to him for cleaning up my little messes. I actually accounted for it in the financial records under the catchall phrase of "city clean-up costs." Funny, huh? Erskine was perfect. He didn't look the part. He looked like a schlep. But the guy has a fortune in payoffs stashed away in offshore accounts. You can't judge a book by its cover, you know. He didn't know the full extent of it – about everything I've done – but he didn't ask many questions as long as I kept funneling money to him. He just pointed the finger at whatever suspect I decided to frame for the murder."

Erskine, I thought. Not Aguirre. Just like with Lansdale and Hanrahan, I'd gone after the obvious choice. There was a lesson to be learned here for the next story I did. The only problem was it didn't look right now as if there were going to be any more stories for me.

"Why did you kill him?" I asked, thinking about Erskine lying dead in his car back on the road.

"The original plan was for me to kill you in the car while you waited outside that bar. Erskine would come out and find you, and Aguirre would be his alibi that he was inside. But you screwed that up by going inside. I waited until Erskine came out, then decided I'd hide in the back seat and we'd go to some secluded place here in the park and finish you off. But the more I thought about it, I realized I didn't need Erskine anymore. My work is done now."

"Done?"

"Yes, thanks to you. Christine's gone. Lansdale's out of the political picture. Jack Hanrahan can run for the Senate now, and I can be right there with him. I'll be at his side, where I've always belonged. Maybe even all the way to the White House. What do you think, Jessie? Would I make a good first lady?"

Another police siren went by, but this one was further away. Maybe because we had walked so far into the park. Of course, even if someone found the car with Erskine's body in it, they still wouldn't know about Libby St. John and me in the woods. Somehow I had to get back to the road. It was my only chance.

"Tell me about Cheryl Lee Barrett," I said.

"That bitch!" she said angrily. I could see the look of hatred on her face. "She was the worst. She was shameless. The way she flirted and threw herself at him."

"But you hired her to work undercover for you in the Lansdale campaign, didn't you? You sent her there to set Lansdale up with a sex scandal."

"It was all going great too until Jack saw her. I guess I should have seen it coming, but I didn't know there was anything going on between them. Until—"

"Until she called you at his Westchester house that last night from the Park Grille?"

"Yes."

"You were one who picked up the phone, not Christine Hanrahan."

"I was there with Christine. The mayor was supposed to come up later that night. When I told Margaret – or Cheryl Lee, whatever you want to call her – that he wasn't there, she got very upset. She said she had to talk to him. She said she had some big news to tell him. That's when she told me she was carrying his baby. She said she knew it was his and she was in love with him.

"She said she was tired of living a lie. She said she was quitting the Lansdale campaign. She said she was finished with our little sex scandal plan too – that she'd told Lansdale she was done with him. That she wanted the world to know about Jack and her and their baby. I told her she couldn't do that. I said Jack didn't feel that way about her. I told her she had to abort the baby right away before anyone found out.

"I guess I got pretty upset – and so did she. We were yelling at each other over the phone. Finally, she demanded to talk to Jack. She told me where she was, and I told her I'd contact Jack and have him meet her near the restaurant in the park. I said we needed to do it that way because the two of them couldn't be seen in public together. She said all she wanted to do was talk to Jack, she didn't care how or where anymore."

Of course, I thought, it all makes sense now. That's why she wasn't afraid to go into the woods alone for the meeting. She thought she was going to meet Jack Hanrahan. The man she loved. Except it was Libby St. John waiting for her that night. Just like she'd been waiting for me twelve years earlier.

"That damn bitch was going to have his baby," Libby said now. "Well, I just couldn't allow that to happen. You can understand that, can't you?"

I tried to act as if what she was saying was the most logical thing in the world.

"What about Enrico?" I asked. "How did you get the police to go after him for the murder?"

She shrugged. "He was the perfect patsy for this one, the obvious choice to take the fall for murder. Only he couldn't be arrested, he knew about Cheryl Lee and the sex blackmail scheme she had with us over Lansdale. So I told Erskine about Enrico and what he needed to do. Erskine was the one that shot him, not Aguirre. Aguirre was downstairs in the hotel lobby. Erskine also planted some of the dead woman's stuff in his hotel room before Aguirre came in."

"Why did Aguirre say he was the one who shot Enrico?"

"I guess he just wanted to take the credit for it. It was a pretty high-profile case, and Aguirre liked being in the headlines. Erskine didn't care about the headlines, he just wanted money. So he was happy to let Aguirre take the glory."

I knew I was running out of time. I had to keep her talking. And she seemed to want to talk. Like she was happy to finally be able to tell someone all she had done in secret over the years to win the love of Jack Hanrahan.

"Why the Yankees' baseball cap?" I asked now, looking at the hat on her head. "That was the thing that got me started investigating all this. Why did you keep wearing it? Why wear it at all?" I mentioned the picture of Hanrahan and his wife wearing Yankees caps I'd seen on his desk. "It was the mayor who was the Yankees fan, right?"

"I used to see that picture of him and Christine in the Yankees hats every time I went into his office. Every goddamn time! It drove me crazy to look at it. That should have been me in that picture, me wearing the Yankees cap with him – not Christine. I asked him to take me with him to a Yankees game a lot of times, but he never did. So I bought my own New York Yankees cap. And I wore it when I…" she smiled maniacally now, "… eliminated the competition."

I swallowed. I was sweating now, and we were so far into the park it was almost completely quiet. "Why did you always make it look like a sex attack was the motivation? The ripping of the clothes and the rest?"

"I wanted to make sure it looked like a man who did it."

"Why are you telling me all this?"

"You worked so hard on this story. I admire that. You got some of the answers too, just not enough of them."

"Is that why you didn't just shoot me in the car with Erskine?"

"I felt I owed this to you," she said.

"If you really feel like you owe me something, how about you let me go now?"

"I'm afraid I can't do that, Jessie."

She gestured with the gun for me to keep walking further into the woods.

"So where are we going now?"

"The place where I attacked you that first night – it's not far from here. We'll be there very soon."

"Why?"

"I just think it will be the proper ending to this story."

"You mean I die there twelve years later?"

"Yeah. They'll find this gun next to you. The same gun used to kill Erskine. They'll assume you shot him, then killed yourself back at the spot of your worst nightmare. Everybody will think that your coverage of the Cheryl Lee Barrett case just proved too much for you. Brought back too many horrible memories. Lots of people said you've seemed obsessed by it. This will be the tragic footnote to the case. You'll be on Page One, one last time, Jessie."

"And you and Jack Hanrahan will live happily ever after?"

"Something like that," she said.

I knew I couldn't go any further with her or I was finished. I had to get back to the highway where maybe I could find help. It was now or never. I started to walk in the direction that she was pointing. Suddenly I grabbed my leg in pain and fell to the ground.

"What are you doing?" Libby yelled.

"My leg. All the excitement. It gets weak when I get too worked up. I can't walk—"

"Get the hell up!"

"I'm trying."

I pretended to struggle to get to my feet. Libby moved closer to see what was going on. The gun in her hand was only a few feet away now. My leg really did bother me sometimes, but it was also strong and very well coordinated from the years of rigorous exercises I'd put my body through. Twelve years ago, Libby St. John had overpowered me in this very park and nearly killed me. But I was different now. I wasn't a victim anymore. If I were going to die, I was determined to go down fighting this time.

I kicked my foot out hard at Libby's hand holding the gun. Libby screamed out in pain. The gun went flying into some deep grass nearby.

I kicked her again, this time in the stomach. I felt the wind go out of her as she fell to the ground.

I scrambled for the gun, but I couldn't see it in the dark.

Libby was on her hands and knees now, looking for the gun too.

I decided to run for it.

It was like something out of one of my dreams. Running through the park again. Danger behind me. Desperately trying to get to safety before the danger caught up with me. But this was no dream. This was really happening. Up ahead I saw the lights from Erskine's car. If I could make it there, maybe I had a chance.

I heard a gunshot go off.

I looked around. I could see the outline of Libby St. John behind me. Libby had found the gun.

A second gunshot went off.

Then a third.

I was out of the woods now. There was maybe a hundred yards of open field between me and the car. I could see the car clearly now. Something else too. A second car. There was someone else there.

A shadowy figure emerged from the second car.

He was holding a gun.

As I got closer, I recognized who it was.

Lieutenant Thomas Aguirre.

"Help!" I screamed. "She's trying to kill me."

"Stop or I'll shoot!" Aguirre yelled out. "I'm a police officer."

"Please—"

"I warned you."

I heard another gunshot, and this time I felt a terrible pain in my side.

Then more gunfire…

The next thing I remember was Aguirre bending down over me on the ground.

"What happened?" I asked.

"She shot you," he said, pointing toward Libby St. John lying on the ground a few yards away. "I shot back then and put her down. You're going to be okay though. It doesn't look serious, and the ambulance is on the way."

"She did it!" I said frantically. "She killed Erskine and Christine Hanrahan and all the others too." There were tears on my cheeks and I was shaking.

"I know that now."

"I thought it was you," I told him.

"Yeah, I figured that too after my meeting with Erskine. Something seemed wrong. That's why I followed him and you into the park."

"I'm sorry," I said.

"Forget it." Aguirre smiled down at me. "Just spell my name right in the story, huh?"

CHAPTER 66

The gunshot fired by Libby St. John had only grazed me. The doctors at the hospital told me it was a superficial wound, and I could go home. That was great news. I'd spent enough time in hospitals to last a lifetime.

Libby St. John wasn't as lucky. Aguirre's shot had hit her in the chest, killing her instantly. The cops who searched her apartment afterward found belongings from some of her victims and what they described as a "shrine" she'd built to Jack Hanrahan. They said it contained newspaper photos of her and Hanrahan together; personal items she'd stolen from him over the years like cufflinks and ties; even a tape recording of his voice that she played over and over again.

It was weird, the cops said, really weird.

You just never know the deep, dark secrets some people are hiding.

Of course, there were some other questions that would probably always go unanswered. Why Dr. Spitz had gone to visit Jackson in prison before both of their deaths. What had she found out, and what did they talk about? And I also wondered if there'd been more women victims of Libby than we were aware of. After all, Hanrahan had admitted he'd slept with "a lot of women".

But, like I always say, there're loose ends to every story. No ending is perfect.

The bottom line was I'd been able to solve a lot of murders – including Cheryl Lee Barrett and Christine Hanrahan – as well as finally getting the truth about the long-ago attack on me.

*

"It's an incredible story," Ellen said to me at the hospital. "I'm telling you… there's big money in this for you, Jessie. Minus my usual fifteen percent, of course."

"You want to be my agent?"

"Why not? Have I ever given you bad advice?"

Actually, she had. When she told me not to worry about the past. *You never know what you're going to find when you start messing around with the past*, Ellen had warned – *it's better to leave well enough alone.*

But sometimes you just can't do that.

Sometimes you have to learn the truth about the past before you can deal with the future.

I had done that.

Now it was time for the future.

Other people showed up to see me before I left the hospital. Danny Knowlton. Norman Isaacs. And even Steve Fredericks.

Ellen asked me about Logan Kincaid.

"He's still in California," I told her.

"Are you going to see him again?"

"I hope so."

"But…"

"Look, Ellen, I don't think Logan and are going to get married and live happily ever after. I think we both needed each other to get through this whole thing together. And maybe something more will happen between us. Logan's a good man, but there's a lot of good men out there and I can do anything I want with my life now. Don't you see? The nightmare is finally over for me."

EPILOGUE

I was standing back where it had happened again.

The same stretch of wooded area in Central Park near the 79th Street Transverse Road where I was found so close to death all those years earlier. I had just finished retracing my steps from that long-ago night to get to this spot. I'd started at the Great Lawn – just like I did back then after the concert I left early – and made my way through the park to the exact location where I was attacked. I'm not exactly sure why I was doing this now. Searching for some kind of closure, I suppose.

It was a beautiful early autumn day in New York City. The sun shone brightly, the temperature was in the 70s and the stifling humidity of the summer was just a memory now. I had seen this spot in the park so many times in my dreams – in my nightmares where it seemed dark and scary and evil. But, looking around now at the grass and the trees and the blue sky above, it looked different. It looked… well, normal.

I thought about the young woman I used to be before everything changed so dramatically for me right here on this very spot that night in the park twelve years ago.

God, I used to feel so indestructible then.

So invincible.

So immortal.

I didn't feel indestructible, invincible or immortal anymore.

But I felt alive again.

That was enough for now.

A LETTER FROM DANA

I hope you enjoyed reading *The Silent Victim* – and that you'll look for the next Jessie Tucker book. If you'd like to keep up to date with all of my latest releases, you can sign up at the following link. Your email address will never be shared, and you can unsubscribe at any time.

www.bookouture.com/dana-perry

I was inspired to write this book because I work in the New York City media, and I've always been fascinated by big, high-profile murder stories like Casey Anthony, Amanda Knox, Jodi Arias and all the rest. But I wanted to approach this from a different point of view – and make it about the victim. What would happen if a crime victim became a big media story by surviving, then turned into a media star all over again by solving the story of her own crime. The result was Jessie Tucker, New York City crime reporter.

If you have time, I'd love it if you were able to write a review of *The Silent Victim*. Reader reviews on Amazon, Goodreads or anywhere else are crucially important to an author and can spread the word about Jessie Tucker to new readers. If you'd like to contact me personally, you can reach me via my website, Facebook page, Twitter or Instagram.

Thank you for reading *The Silent Victim* and spending time with Jessie Tucker. I loved writing this book. So please keep following Jessie's new adventures very soon!

Best wishes,
Dana Perry

🐦 @DanaPerryAuthor
f @DanaPerryAuthor

Printed in Poland
by Amazon Fulfillment
Poland Sp. z o.o., Wrocław

51526592R00204